SIGNS BEFORE SAILING

Durand climbed a greasy stair into a tower some long-dead lord of the Burrstones had cobbled onto the giants' old walls. The best way into the old beacon tower was a half-hidden door near Lamoric's own chamber, far easier to reach from inside than out.

Around one turning, he found a landing and a crumbling door. A glance through the solitary arrow slit showed him the courtyard a dozen fathoms below the rickety tower. Servants darted through the rain, brown as mice.

Durand shoved the crumbling little door wide—

—And got a face full of furious, smothering confusion.

Dark shapes beat his head and warding arms. Hard hooks and needles shot past him and gushed from the arrow loop behind. He pitched on his shoulder, half-falling from the landing—countless birds stormed between the battlements of Burrstone Walls. Starlings.

And he was left, sitting on the stairs as feathers fluttered down around him like snow.

"Hells," he snarled.

D1455469

TOR BOOKS BY DAVID KECK

In the Eye of Heaven
In a Time of Treason

IN A TIME OF
TREASON

David Keck

TOR®
fantasy

A TOM DOHERTY ASSOCIATES BOOK
NEW YORK

This is a work of fiction. All the characters, organizations, and events portrayed in this novel are products of the author's imagination or are used fictitiously.

IN A TIME OF TREASON

Copyright © 2008 by David Keck

Edited by Patrick Nielsen Hayden

Map by David Cain

A Tor Book
Published by Tom Doherty Associates, LLC
175 Fifth Avenue
New York, NY 10010

www.tor-forge.com

Tor® is a registered trademark of Tom Doherty Associates, LLC.

ISBN-13: 978-0-7653-5170-8
ISBN-10: 0-7653-5170-6

First Edition: February 2008
First Mass Market Edition: May 2009

Printed in the United States of America

0 9 8 7 6 5 4 3 2 1

FOR ANNE

Acknowledgments

For their timely insight and encouragement, I am grateful to friends, loved ones, and colleagues, including Chris Friesen, Darren Lodge, Howard Morhaim, and Anne Groell.

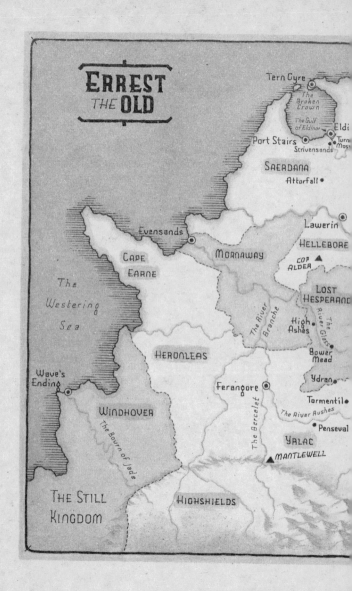

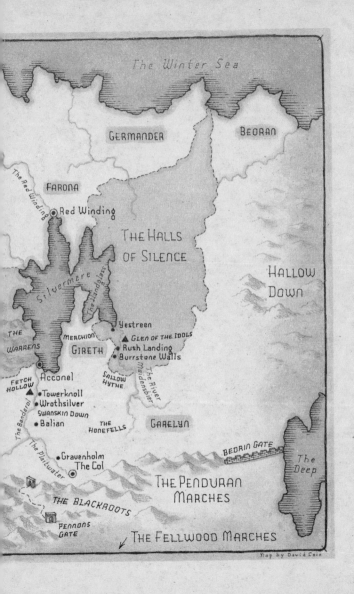

The Winter Sea

GERMANDER

BEORAN

FARONA

Red Winding

The Red Winding

THE HALLS
OF SILENCE

HALLOW
Down

Silvermere

The Handglass

Yestreen

GLEN OF THE IDOLS

MERCHION

GIRETH

Rush Landing
Burrstone Walls

THE
WARRENS

Acconel

FETCH
HOLLOW

SALLOW
HYTHE

The River Maidensbier

Towerknoll
Wrothsilver
Swanskin Down
Balian

The Bandrel

THE
HONEFELLS

GARELYN

BEDRIN GATE

The
Deep

The Platwater

Gravenholm
The Col

THE PENDURAN
MARCHES

THE BLACKROOTS

PENNONS
GATE

THE FELLWOOD MARCHES

Map by David Cain

IN A TIME OF
TREASON

1. A Necklace of Millstones

Durand Col peered up into the vault of Heaven. At long last, the weather had broken, and now was his chance to escape.

His heart jumping, Durand plunged into the gloom of the old stable. His gelding stood with mud to its belly but still looked fit to travel. He would talk to Coensar. He would bid the others goodbye. And he would go. Beyond the narrow yard of Burrstone Walls the roads were drying. With a little luck, he could put Deorwen and Lamoric and the whole mess behind him.

He turned back to the castle yard just as the Heavens opened and the rain thundered down.

"Hells," he said.

Luck and the weather were not on his side, and so this would be another day to avoid Deorwen, and another hour to keep from Lord Lamoric's hall. He had a winter's practice at both.

As he stared into the drenching sky, a voice startled him, close and croaking out, "Durand Col, it is the day and hour of the Accounting. . . ."

It might have been the Voice of Doom, but it was only Father Odwy, the manor priest. The dour old man scowled up at Durand, rain streaming from a beard long enough to tuck in his belt. He was already turning before Durand could make an excuse. The old devil loved his rituals.

"Father, I am sure that one knight more or less will make no—"

A piping whistle escaped the man's nose and he set a pair of prodigious fists on his hips. "You are the one called Durand, yes? You are part of His Lordship's household. A knight, I'm told. And every man of the lord's household must attend before we may begin. It is the Custom. Every man if he must be carted or carried. You're meant to have been at supper. We've already prayed the Sunset. You, sir, are wanted in the bloody hall."

As the fearsome priest spun on his heel, Durand shot a glance toward the castle gates. He could make out a glimpse of light and freedom from beyond the walls—and the guard pacing across it.

Burrstone Walls made a man feel small. The locals said there were giants at the founding of the ancient pile: chill kings who slipped off into the Halls of Silence in the days before the High Kings came east. It certainly had the look of a giant's tomb. Whoever built the place had hollowed a stone hill by the river, and now the gutted heart of the old hill was the castle's long courtyard—more a quarryman's pit than a yard. Where Durand stood at the bottom of it all, he might have been a worm on the floor of a stone coffin, squinting up through a crack in the lid.

He had spent the winter Moons sleeping on damp rushes in the manor buildings that huddled at the bottom of this stone tomb: the seat of Sir Lamoric, debtor Lord of Burrstone Walls.

Shaking his head, Durand followed the priest.

THE FEASTING HALL of Burrstone Walls was a dank cavern of a place. As Durand stepped in, the assembled household turned his way: This is what had become of the glamorous knights of last autumn's Red Knight game. Towering Sir Ouen, built like carthorse, with his gilded leer and haystack beard. Stalwart Guthred the shield-bearer, scowling round the thick knuckle of his prodigious nose. One-eyed Sir Berchard, bald and bearded as an innkeeper, with tales of a hundred battles. Sneering Badan, a balding wolf in knight's breeches. And Coensar, Durand's captain—like a father since Durand left home. These were men who had saved a kingdom and caught a rebel in his own trap. All sitting like owls in this dripping barn of a hall, waiting on Father Odwy's Accounting.

At the head of the hall, Lord Lamoric fidgeted, and Coensar raised an amused eyebrow at Durand's entrance.

At least, Durand thought, Lady Deorwen was not there.

Odwy had hauled tables into a horseshoe with Lamoric trapped in the lord's seat at the top and himself standing in the middle of it all. Durand slid onto the heel of one bench by one-eyed Berchard. "Still here, are you?" said the grizzled knight. "Ain't seen you sit down to supper in a fortnight. You—"

Father Odwy twisted and managed a hard look that clapped the old knight's jaw shut as surely as a good slap. Again the priest's nose was whistling. "It is time," he said, smearing the rain from his face with broad fingers. "The men of the household are gathered. The bailiff and reeves have been feasted, meat and wine." He turned to three squat men at the opposite table. All three grunted a nod.

For a few moments then, there was silence—and dripping. As the silence stretched, the priest raked his sheep-yellow beard and, finally, raised a tufted eyebrow at Lamoric.

"Father, don't wag your bristles at me. I've been pacing this old barn since the Paling Moon, and from the first moment—" But Lamoric stopped himself, taking a breath.

"It's my turn, is it?" he said.

"*Lordship,*" croaked the priest.

Lamoric covered his face. "How does it run? What am I to say?"

"By the Silent King of far Heaven . . ." the priest began.

Lamoric raised his hand, and turned to the three villagers. "By the Silent King of far Heaven, by his Queen, by the Warders at the Bright Gates, by the Champion, by his lance, by the chains of the Chainbreaker, by the Maiden of the Spring this Lambing Moon, reeves and bailiff, you must swear to speak no falsehood on this day of the Accounting."

The priest nodded, turning to the first of the villagers. "Odred the Miller, bailiff to His Lordship's manor of Burrstone Walls?"

"Aye," the man grunted. "I swear."

"Odric, dock master, reeve of Burrstone Landing?"

"Aye, Father. Lordship," said the next. "I swear it."

"Odmund, formerly quarryman, now reeve of Burrstone Pits?"

"As you say," said the last. "I swear."

"*Od*red, *Od*ric, and *Od*mund, Father?" asked Lamoric.

The priest let Lamoric's question pass and pressed on. They kissed a massive *Book of Moons* to seal their oaths, planting their lips on a patch of the heavy cover burnished to a high shine by a thousand Accounting oaths.

And the muttered account began.

It was the Lambing Moon, the eve of First Waning, and so the reeves and the bailiff numbered the spindly additions to Lamoric's flock and enumerated those that had frozen; they announced that a very few calves were expected; they reported that the winter crop in all fields "'twixt Pit and the Burrstone Coppice" had flooded, frozen hard, and would need plowing under for reseeding. It went on.

Durand kneaded his face. All winter, Lamoric had been pacing Burrstone Walls like a dog in a kennel. He was trapped and smothered in the backwater fief. They all were.

The year before, the young lord had planned to show the great ones of the kingdom that he was more than the spoiled second son of the Duke of Gireth. Fighting as the nameless "Red Knight," he'd led his hand-picked band of men from tilt to tilt until they were fighting before the king at the cliffs of Tern Gyre. But, at Tern Gyre, there had been more at stake than one man's reputation. In the end, Lamoric and Durand and the others managed to scotch a rebellion. The king kept his crown, and the rebel duke—Radomor of Yrlac—was left to slink home, looking like a fool.

The whole adventure ought to have made their fortunes, but times were hard for kings in Errest, and Lamoric had only kept the Burrstones through weighty loans from his elder brother in Acconel. And with grim winters like these, a hundred years must pass before Lamoric could repay the debt.

The game was over. A pauper lord could not keep a troop of knights. The men must spring from him like fleas from a dead hound.

"And last night," mumbled Odred Miller, bailiff to Burrstone Walls, "Odwin's lad Gil saw the frogspawn in the quarry at Burrstone Pit."

Lamoric twisted in his chair. "Frogspawn?"

Odred Miller grunted affirmation.

Lamoric turned to the priest. "Why in Heaven's name would this man—Odmund Miller?—report the carnal activities of these creatures to me?" They had ridden to Tern Gyre. They had fought the Duke of Yrlac and saved the Evenstar Crown for the king anointed by the Patriarchs. "Are we keeping a flock of amphibians for—"

"Frogspawn is the customary sign, Lordship. In the pit. Frogspawn being seen, the villagers will make the teams ready for the Plow Chase. The children climb down to look for it. This year the Chase comes later than most, but tomorrow Walls, Pits, and Landing will set their best teams against each other to—"

"I see."

"And this is Miller Od*red*. Miller Od*mund* died in my father's day, buried with his quern and apron in the last years of old King Carondas."

Lamoric mashed his hands over his eyes. "A man to be envied, that Odmund Miller." The reeves and bailiff exchanged glances: a slow matter involving much blinking of dark eyes.

The list went on. "The damp spoiled the seed rye in Burrstone Walls, the great quarry at Burrstone Pits has flooded to one fathom's depth at the place of deepest delving," said one reeve.

"I find that I cannot breathe some days," said Lamoric. "We dined with princes and patriarchs. It is like the bottom of a well."

But the Burrstone men did not hear him. They pressed on with plowshares bought, dung carted, millstones to be cut, iron bought for mallets and chisels, and willows felled.

"And," said Odwy, "there is the matter of the king's writ, just arrived today."

Lamoric shot upright. "You've had a king's writ waiting on bloody frogs?"

Just then something creaked on the landing high over Lamoric's shoulder. Durand glanced and felt his heart stumble, for Deorwen had stepped from her chambers and stood now above the hall: Deorwen with her dark eyes, her petal lips. Pale as an idol above its shrine she stood. All thought of king's writs flew from Durand's mind as he spun in the flicker of her glance.

Her hair—the gleaming red weight of it—was smothered in a married woman's veil. And Durand knew that he was mad, for who but a madman would linger so near his master's wife and hope to be loyal? Every glimpse of her was treason. He could not breathe.

When Durand managed to look away, he found Berchard and Ouen peering at him, gauging his mood for signs of past troubles returning.

"The Writ of the Beacons," the priest was saying. He fumbled among scrolls and catch-pots, finding a scroll. "Here," he said. A red gobbet of sealing wax spun on a bit of ribbon.

Deorwen was about to slip back through the chamber door, vanishing.

"By the Lord of Dooms, man, what are you waiting for?"

Lamoric followed the priest's glance to his wife. "Deorwen!"

She stopped. "I thought I'd—"

"You're better are you?" She must have come up with some excuse to avoid the feast. "Well come and hear! It seems the king knows where we are, after all. The good father is just telling us what orders have come from the palace. And then, Heaven willing, we will learn more about the matter of the frogspawn."

Reluctantly, Deorwen descended into the hall, while Durand kept his eyes from the twitch of her skirts.

"Ladyship," said the priest, bobbing.

"Go on, Father. Let's hear it," said Lamoric.

The priest scratched, and then read, " 'To celebrate the anniversary of his coronation, Ragnal, King of Errest, Bearer of the Evenstar Crown, Heir of the Hazelwood Throne, commands that every beacon from the Blackroot Mountains to the Westering Sea, from the Winter Sea to the Bourne of Jade, be lit so that this good news can march from the Mount of Eagles in Eldinor to every corner of the realm, every prominence crowned with fire, the whole kingdom shining like the stars in the Vault of Heaven.' "

Deorwen took up her place at her husband's side, a red wisp curled against the pale skin of her neck.

And Durand shut his eyes. With better weather, he would have been on the road and gone by now. A stronger man might have dared flooded roads and cold nights long ago.

"Father," said Lamoric, straightening, "what do those in the Mount of Eagles wish from us down here in the damp of Burrstone Walls?"

"Every beacon in the kingdom must be put in order for First Sight of the Sowing Moon."

Lamoric dropped into his seat. "*Beacon*?"

"Should Errest be attacked, a message of fire can stride the high places of the kingdom from the Mount of Eagles to every corner of the realm."

"And so Burrstones is counted among the high places of the kingdom. I confess surprise."

"White Osbald is Watcher of the Beacon Tower," said the priest.

"The pale fellow with the pink eyes?"

"Ten generations have passed since the last invader threatened." The priest scratched his beard with another faint whistle. "It may need seeing to."

Durand opened his eyes—and found Deorwen looking back at him. Her eyes trembled, brown and shadowed. He could stay no longer.

"I'll go," said Durand.

Curious faces turned his direction.

"I'll see how this beacon looks."

As he made to step from the hall, conscious of what a fool he looked, a crash echoed in the courtyard: a sound full of iron rings and the clatter of an axe handle. Down the long yard, he saw the castle's gatekeeper land on his armored shoulders. Someone was coming.

Durand closed a hand on his sword's grip, and—along with every armed man in the hall—braced himself.

"And," conceded the priest, "there is a messenger."

"Lord of Dooms . . ." Lamoric said. A blade in his hand, he looked to tall Coensar, his captain.

The priest said, "We could not delay the Accounting any further just because some errand boy—"

"Are you mad, priest? You've left him out in this rain? Who is it?"

"He has had the gatehouse for shelter. But there was no time to ask his name. The Accounting was already—"

A tall figure stalked toward them down the courtyard.

◉ 2. The Eagle Summons

Lamoric tumbled from his seat while Durand planted himself in the doorway; the stranger could swat village gatekeepers aside, but Durand planned to be a little more stubborn.

The towering man stepped over the threshold, the sopping weight of cloak and hood outlining a broad, straight frame. A big, black gauntlet pulled his hood aside. And the man gave his head an absent scrub that set gray hair standing like a fallow crop.

Over Durand's shoulder, Lamoric gasped. "Geridon?"

Gray eyes glinted like ice above a wry smile. "Lordship." He gave a nod to Lamoric's captain. "Sir Coensar. Beg pardon for any hurt I've caused your man at the gate, but I'd had enough of waiting."

Before them stood Sir Geridon, Champion of Gireth: a man who had laid out some of the best men in the Atthias. Durand had seen him a thousand times in the hall at Acconel. The man had spent a generation keeping drunkards and hotheads in line in the old duke's hall.

Durand stepped aside as Geridon lowered himself to one knee, a grimace flickering.

"What does Father want of me, Sir Geridon?" Lamoric asked.

"Lordship, it's your brother I'm speaking for."

"Landast." Lamoric blinked. "Yes. I suppose that is always more likely. I hope he does not expect repayment of his loans to me." He glanced to Coensar. "If the reports of these Burrstone men are any guide, we shall both be old men before I can free myself of his kindness."

Geridon frowned briefly. "No, Lordship. Your brother's

spoken of none of this in my hearing. Keeping it quiet, is my guess. It's other business I'm on. The king's asked that your father and all the Great Council ride up to Eldinor to feast his anniversary. It's been five years since he was crowned. Did the writ find you here? Burrstone Walls is on the Beacon Roll. . . ." He saw the paper dangling in Odwy's hand. "His Highness asks that in honor of the day these great men come, either in person or through someone who represents their blood, to renew their homage oaths, and 'reaffirm' that our Ragnal is king in Errest and liege lord of them all."

"And my father is not fit to travel to Eldinor?"

"Not no more, really. And your brother's picked up where the old man left off, running this and that. All of these responsibilities? He reckons he cannot leave them unattended."

As the facts took shape in Lamoric's mind, the tendons stood in his neck. "Let me see if I have you, Sir Geridon. Brother says that I must—*must* mind you—leave the Burrstones to travel to Eldinor where I must present myself before King Ragnal and his entire court?"

A crooked grin spread on Lamoric's face.

"He's asking, Lordship," said Geridon.

Father Odwy had both fists in his beard, and looked ready to do himself some injury. "Lordship. The Accounting. We must finish."

"Aye, best get on with it," said Geridon, standing. "I return to Acconel with your answer." He pulled a scroll from his surcoat. "You'll find here some words for the king and council, Your Lordship. From your father."

Lamoric nodded, eyes shining. "We must be quick," he reasoned. "A boat is the only way, so a small party. No horses. I tell you this will make us once more! The heroes of Tern Gyre: Coensar, Ouen, Sir Durand." An involuntary gasp escaped Deorwen's lips. Lamoric caught her arm, giving it a shake. "And His Highness will meet my wife as well. We sail for Eldinor tomorrow after First Twilight!"

Durand found the mirror of his own horror in Deorwen's face. The Burrstones would seem like oceans and continents compared to a tiny boat. They would be side by side for weeks.

As Durand stared up at Deorwen, he found that Geridon

had ducked close by his ear. "Don't think I didn't see you there, boy. I heard what happened last year with that land your father meant for you. Still, maybe this jaunt'll sort something out, eh?" He winked and tugged his sopping hood back in place. "Don't like to be away. It's dark times. Keep your eyes wide, and stick by old Coensar. He's been fighting ages. Knows what he's about."

🌀 3. Signs Before Sailing

D urand climbed a greasy stair into a tower some long-dead lord of the Burrstones had cobbled onto the giants' old walls. The best way into the old beacon tower was a half-hidden door near Lamoric's own chamber.

The old tower was black as a barrel, and Durand could only grope his way upward, climbing like a child while a stream of rainwater made a cataract of the stairs.

Around one turning, he found a landing and a crumbling door. A glance through the solitary arrow slit showed him the courtyard a dozen fathoms below the rickety tower. Servants darted through the rain, brown as mice. If a man stoppered the gatehouse, it looked as though the great courtyard would fill like a horse trough—a good place for drowning.

Durand shook his head. It had been a long winter. Their glamorous brawling under the Blood Moon had left Lamoric a lord of pits and hovels, destitute but for his brother's charity. All winter the young lord had walked the halls of Burrstone Walls unable to sit or sleep, Deorwen looking half-mad. His coffers were empty, his knights must leave him, hope was gone, and the rain and snow had kept the whole lot of them mewed up in a few damp rooms with men like Odwy and the Custom of the manor.

Durand thought back to the night when he first set out on his own, and the promises that had been made to him. He'd heard rapping in the dark, and, in a well in the midst of the castle yard, he'd found one of the Powers of Heaven waiting for him: the Traveler. A giant in rags with silver-penny eyes and a forked staff that shook the world. As Durand left his father's hall, that Power had foreseen love, glory, and a place in the world for him. The winter had got him wondering.

Durand shoved the crumbling little door wide—

—And got a face full of furious, smothering confusion.

Dark shapes beat his head and warding arms. Hard hooks and needles shot past him and gushed from the arrow loop behind. He pitched on his shoulder, half falling from the landing—countless birds stormed between the battlements of Burrstone Walls. Starlings.

And he was left, sitting on the stairs as feathers fluttered down around him like snow.

"Hells," he snarled. It seemed that the tower was a coop for every starling for ten leagues and they'd all been inside to wait out the rain. Durand pushed his way into a white-crusted room whose every crevice was chinked with straw and feathers, and followed a caked ladder to a trapdoor among the ceiling beams.

In the rainy gloom above, dim trees bristled for acres beyond the walls. He had just made out the dark silence of the Maidensbier flowing below when something far too near shrieked to life.

Durand tottered on the edge of the trapdoor, fighting his blade into the darkness. Right by the door, a man of some sort screamed like mad, all white forearms, knees, and elbows. It was all Durand could do to stop himself falling down another set of stairs.

"Host of Hell!" Durand snarled. But it seemed that Durand's words—and the hulking shape of Durand atop the dark tower—were too much for the cowering creature. The pale man scrambled for the battlements, looking as if he meant to throw himself over the brink.

"What are you doing?" said Durand.

"I'm Osbald. I'm Watcher!"

It took him a moment to remember. "Aye. Osbald. Right." He held out a calming hand—in part to catch his balance.

"You aren't to come up here," said White Osbald.

"Too late for that." Durand scrubbed his neck. "How do you get past the bloody birds?"

"Birds?"

"Downstairs."

White Osbald grimaced in extreme discomfort. "I'm Watcher."

"You don't go down?"

"I'm Watcher."

"Right. Daft of me to forget." He spread his hands and sat on the floor while his heart's wild pounding slowed. "You think you could leave me for a while? I'm to check the beacon. Have you got firewood?"

"There."

Beyond the trapdoor, the rooftop was empty except for a massive iron fire basket. The pale man had half-curled himself round one of its iron legs. From the position, the Watcher pointed up at fagots so rotten they looked like rolls of shaggy, gray carpet. This was the firewood.

"Right, Osbald. Why don't you go down and see if you can find us some dry wood? I'll bet that's meant to be a storeroom downstairs. We'll get some dry stuff up here, and it'll be right as rain."

Osbald had uncoiled a degree or two here and there.

"Go on," Durand said. "Firewood. This here's older than the *Cradle*. And we haven't got much of a beacon without a fire. The king says we're to light it."

"The king?"

"And this old stuff won't burn."

White Osbald bobbed his head and, with a last, wary glance at Durand, swarmed down the ladder.

Durand hauled another deep breath, looking out over the Maidensbier. A stick of the firewood in Osbald's fire basket—when examined—turned out to be little more than slime and scabs.

"I should never have set foot in the Burrstone," he muttered. After Tern Gyre, he should have put a hundred leagues between himself and Lord Lamoric's wife. Instead, he filled the dark days riding the hog-wallow tracks around the manor, keeping himself from the temptation of stray glances and chance touches in the narrow passages of Burrstone Walls. A stronger man would have said farewell to Lamoric and Deorwen and the rest back at Tern Gyre and never set foot in the Burrstones. Instead, he would now be trapped in a boat with them all and nowhere to hide.

"Damn me for a fool." He'd thought of talking with Coensar. A man like the captain would have found somewhere to sell his sword as soon as the roads were dry; he'd been fighting in the tourneys of Errest since most knights were boys, and a man felt better riding with a fellow he could trust.

Now, though, it was too late for any of that, and he had to wonder if he'd ever really meant to go, if he'd planned to stay here by Deorwen forever, pining love-struck till the dripping Burrstones rotted him away.

White Osbald appeared in the hatchway, his pasty face twitching with the effort of hauling a bushel basket of firewood through the trapdoor. Durand took the basket. "Here. For Heaven's sake."

The beacon's fire basket would take another five loads. Osbald's hands, wide as baker's paddles, were already shaking.

"We'll get the next ones together, eh? We'll need you in shape to light the thing when the time comes, right?"

When they had finished lugging their baskets to the tower, the hour was late. Durand ordered White Osbald down to warm himself by the fires: he had had some of the kitchen boys start some tallow melting. A little fresh grease would make sure the old wood lit. They would lug it up and get some sleep.

Tonight, he was hauling wood and melting grease. Tomorrow, they were heading for the heart of Errest the Old. He pictured King Ragnal, a caged lion of a man, in robes as heavy with gold and jewels as a Patriarch's *Book of Moons*. He remembered the hop and cackle of the man's train of functionaries. He remembered the Lady of Hesperand appearing like a Power to set the Great Council right. He remembered the fury of Radomor, the Hero of Hallow Down and usurper Duke of Yrlac.

There might still be gratitude in Eldinor if they searched for it. The winter's snows had fallen before Lamoric's men could catch the king and bow before his benevolence. There might be lands and titles waiting. But he wondered: they had handed Radomor a defeat, but he was not dead—and neither were those two black-robed Rooks of his.

Durand eyed the deepening gloom. River, bare trees, and

naked fields crumbled like a landscape of cinders under the drizzle. Somewhere in the wet Heavens, thunder rumbled. He pulled his cloak tighter. He had only small problems: one fool and one heart. Under the Blood Moon, half the king's Great Council had cast their votes for Radomor of Yrlac— the kingdom's troubles might be large.

In the trapdoor, something shuffled. Durand glanced, but White Oswald hadn't poked his head up.

Durand wondered what the king meant to prove with this little party and its hilltop candles. It seemed an empty sort of gesture.

Now, light rose from the starling chamber. Durand would have to get poor Oswald started down there with a broom: a task that might take the Lambing Moon and the Sowing Moon beyond it.

The light moved, and all at once Durand pictured White Oswald—with a candle and a sloshing kettle of running grease with all the clutter in that room. The mooncalf would burn the tower. Durand shoved his head into the trap.

And found himself staring down upon a slender young woman.

The woman had a candle in her hand, but the flame burned in slow tendrils that clung and swirled as she moved. The light it shed was the murky glow of a pond's depths. Shadows lapped. At the touch of it, Durand's nose and mouth were stopped with a stench of stagnant weeds.

And the room around her—in the wavering green light— was not the crusted old storeroom. Neat stacks of wood shivered in alcoves where the green shafts touched. Someone had brought a rumpled pallet: the padded canvas rippled in the undulating shadow. There was a wine pot.

He could not breathe. He might as well have had his head in the river.

He must have made some sound then, for the maiden turned, her hair rippling like a slow streamer in the green light. Her neck was pale as a fish's flesh. He saw the shape of her jaw. But before her eyes could fall upon him, Durand flinched from the trapdoor.

There was no air in the green light of the maiden's candle. And Durand was glad he had not seen her eyes.

It took only instants for him to realize that he was not safe, even on the rooftop. The green shafts of Otherworldly light swelled between the floorboards. Heaven was a black well above him as the light reached higher and higher. In his mind's eye, the strange woman mounted the ladder and rose in the hatchway. But then the light ebbed away, leaving him in the darkness.

For a moment, he breathed in relief, then he remembered where the stairway went: to his master's chamber. To Deorwen's door. There was only one stairway down.

Mastering himself, Durand dropped into what was now, once again, an empty storeroom. Bird shit crunched under his soles, its acid stink in his nostrils. But the greenish light still brimmed in the stairwell. And Deorwen was down below—and Lamoric and others—all a whisper from that tower door. He followed, finding the stairwell air thick with cool reeds and slime.

He chased a long tendril of the woman's hair as it slithered upon the green air and vanished into the passage before Deorwen's door. The woman's tresses coiled before him, alive. And her hand rested on the black face of Deorwen's door. Durand could neither move nor breathe. The pale dome of the maiden's forehead dropped against the wood, her eyes closed and streaming tears.

Durand had no power to change a gesture.

But the maiden seemed to master herself. She turned from the door.

Durand shrank away, gulping air in the clammy dark of the stairs. If she returned to the stairwell, the Hells would have him in a heartbeat.

But it seemed that she pressed on elsewhere, for the light in the chamber passage ebbed away.

Durand followed it onto the landing high above the feasting hall. His mouth opened, and he nearly dropped his blade. The feasting hall of Burrstone Walls brimmed with visions. Long shields and rippling tapestries hung over the bare walls he knew. Familiar men lay on strange floors; wolfhounds curled where cachepots had stood. Spears leaned in bundles, and Durand knew it all for the dreams or memories of the spectral woman who drifted through. Her candle was the only light.

Durand saw her falter at the distant end of the hall, her eerie candle held high at the courtyard door. And he stole after her as she stepped into the courtyard and out through the gates of Burrstone Walls. He had to know where she was going.

Soon, he was following the flickering image down through the slabs and sagging earth of the Burrstones until the river moved in the dark. Durand made out a new light between stones and willows to match the candle in the woman's hand: a slender craft along the bank.

Durand opened his mouth. He knew this scene. He knew the boat: a pale thing that might have been carved by a harpmaker. He had dreamt it under the Blood Moon.

Before him, the maiden caught hold of a willow, a wobble in the candle's flame sending shivers high into the bare tendrils of the willow branches. They might all have been on the floor of the Silvermere.

The woman stepped into the slim craft and sagged back. Her black curls tumbled into the water.

Durand knew the tale. On the Maidensbier—then known by some forgotten name—an ancient duke's young wife, her secret love witnessed by one of the duke's loyal men. The young bride who drank foxglove and set herself adrift upon the river.

She settled, the candle balanced on her chest. One long sleeve dangled in the water. He heard a sigh: the only sound in a mute Creation. He saw her fingers open, and knew, even as the night breezes tugged the craft into the current, that it was finished.

It was just as he had seen it when Radomor or his Rooks had set Lamoric's sister adrift—sending another adulteress to pass her family's city in parody of this night.

Boat and bride drifted downstream, light as a curl of dry leaf. Durand shook his head.

Something moved behind him.

On the stony bank all around, people had gathered: villagers by the dozen wrapped in hairy blankets. Most were women: mothers and daughters. To his astonishment, Deorwen stood closest of all. She wore only a linen shift, the touch of night breezes pressing the pale fabric close.

"What are you doing here?" Durand managed.

"You see her so clearly," said Deorwen. "This was Vigand's hall. Duke Gunderic went off to attend old King Saerdan. He left his bride with one of his men: Baron Vigand. They'd been close. They were meant to have won half of Gireth together. It all happened here. Aralind fell for Vigand. She was seen. Poison was the only way. They say Duke Gunderic's ship pulled into the Handglass in time to see her pass—he among all his men, she laid out as if in a coffin."

Durand looked past Deorwen into the shadowed faces of half a village: squat and stolid women to match men like Odwy and Odmund. Deorwen glowed like a lily among the nettles. The darkness was closing thick around them.

"They see the old duke's bride whenever there is danger for Gireth—and she's come to our door every night since the Wandering Moon in deep winter. There is little to do but watch. Lamoric won't listen, but neither can he sleep." She closed her mouth a moment. "Most do not see what is right before them."

"What was her name?" Durand asked.

"Aralind, she was called," she said, wavering where she stood. The winter had been hard.

Durand nodded. "Aralind." The village women were looking one to another.

"I must get back," Durand managed.

Deorwen looked down.

✣ 4. The *Bittern* and the Bier

When Lamoric tramped from the gates of Burrstone Walls, the sopping earth was frozen. His knot of household knights yawned and stumbled after him, frost crunching under their boots. In Lamoric's haste, poor Odwy had been made to pray First Twilight before he had seen even a trace of light in the mist. Every blade and twig bristled with needles of ice.

"I love a misty morning," said Lamoric in a puff of fog. "It's like Creation's ours: a toy in our hands. We could be on islands with the rest of old Errest fallen away."

Bald Badan bared what teeth he had left, silently snarling from within a hairy twist of blanket. He looked like the wolf who had swallowed the old woman in the bedtime story.

Berchard winced with his good eye. "You'll have to tell us when morning comes so we don't miss it, eh? Did you sleep?"

Lamoric twitched a smile.

"Did you sleep at all?" Berchard pressed. Coensar's glance was like a glimpse of blade. None of them were too pleased about Lamoric's mad rush.

"Lads," said Lamoric, "this summons couldn't have come at a better time. When this moon's waned, the fighting season will be upon us. And you'd have scattered to the four winds, don't deny it. We've got a windfall. It doesn't pay to complain."

Big Ouen reached round himself to scrub at fleabites between his shoulder blades, both hands meeting in the middle of his back. He had arms like an ape. The man's gold teeth glinted. "There's been little enough that pays lately."

"We'll be led before the Hazelwood Throne," said Lamoric. "I'll kneel and place my hands between Ragnal's. There will be a feast. People will remember you. Ouen, Badan, Coensar, Durand. I hope you've all got decent surcoats."

The tottering procession wound its way from the cliff top of Burrstone Walls to the hovels of Burrstone Landing. The livestock was still indoors, but they passed millstones. Of the thousands cut from the old pits, some slender fraction had fetched up along the roads each year, broken. Now, wheels like moldy cheese were heaped by the hundred. Some were cracked, some split, others were lost under carpets of moss and sod. This was Burrstone.

"The blame for delay will not be laid at my feet. We must have a good look at this boat. This *Bittern*. Odric? Odmund? He's told us she's ready. And the river's free of ice."

A few of the men passed an uneasy glance between them. Lamoric seemed more frayed than usual.

Though there were stragglers all the way up the track to Burrstone Walls, Lamoric had reached the pier. A good-sized boat waited there, white and blue on a perfect mirror of still water. Durand guessed it might be forty feet from its high curling stem to the matching stern. The cliffs of Burr-stone Walls cut a smooth backwater from the Maidensbier, though both cliffs and stronghold were little more than a dark suggestion in the clouds as they reached the pier.

Lamoric strode out, rings shivering across the water from the dock pilings.

"You all know how hard we worked last summer. You know what it cost us. We saved a king of the Atthias." The men were nodding warily: everyone from steely Coensar to Badan the wolf. A gangplank bridged the gap to the *Bittern*'s gunnel. Lamoric stepped out. "And now we have a message to put in his own hands."

He made to step into the boat.

And a storm of birds exploded.

An impossible flock of starlings roared from the hollow belly of the *Bittern*, filling the sky with wings and shrill cries. Lamoric lurched on the narrow gangplank, and then he was falling into the frigid water.

Like one man, Durand and Coensar sprang onto the pier, reaching into the spray. Panes of ice clattered and smashed. Durand caught a flailing wrist, and with a few firm jerks, he and the captain had their shuddering lord free.

"She'll be lighter without the passengers," Lamoric splut-tered. He hauled himself up, taking full advantage of hands and shoulders. There was a look in his eye, wary as a wild animal.

"Coen," said Lamoric, "get things started while I sort out this bloody mess. Find the ship's master and make sure he's got oarsmen. The bailiff's meant to have got us provisions, the Host alone knows what he thinks that means. Frogs, maybe." Durand tried to swing his cloak around the man's shoulders. Lamoric scoffed. "Keep it. One of us deserves a dry cloak."

They turned to find ranks of villagers frozen. Scores and scores of men and women stood with their hands in the fist and spread fingers' sign of Heaven's Eye. They had seen omen heaped on omen. Lamoric stalked through them, giv-ing them a showman's wave.

Durand watched him go, wondering what was in their master's mind.

As DURAND AND the others fetched their gear, the village women set to smuggling iron charms aboard and wordlessly painting grease down the long curve of the stempost. Dockhands swung provisions into the belly of the *Bittern*.

A Burrstone man with a cap of sweat-burnished sheepskin knotted under his beard played overseer. This was Odemar the ship's master, and he grumbled as knights looked on. He possessed the same outsized fists and squat frame as all his kin. "It's early to make the passage," he grumbled, "and the Maiden's high."

"What were they doing at the prow there?" said Lamoric. The village women were just bustling from the dock.

Odemar seemed taken aback that his would-be cargo could speak. "It's the grease of nine wrens . . . Lordship." His voice was like the grinding of stones.

Berchard smiled broadly, scratching his grizzled beard. "Never drown, wrens. So they say, but you're never meant to cause one harm, unless—"

"Women's business," grumbled Odemar.

"I suppose," said Berchard. "But you don't normally see them at their b—"

"It's no good thing to rush a sailing."

"Host Below! Is the river free of ice?" Lamoric asked. "Was there silver enough in the purse?"

Odemar's square beard twitched as his lip twisted. "Aye," he allowed.

Before Lamoric could say more, Coensar spoke up. The captain had a thumb on the pommel of Keening, his High Kingdom blade. "Then your *Bittern*'s first load will be men, not millstones, Master Odemar. And we will sail for Eldinor and not Yestreen down the river." He never took his eyes from the boat.

Odemar grunted assent and subsided into silence. And soon four of the men loading baggage abruptly piled into the boat, hunkering down along the gunnels.

"We're ready?" asked Lamoric.

Odemar's beard bobbed once. "Just in time, I think." If

the man hadn't been looking to the sky, Durand would have thought he was talking about Lamoric's mood. Without a further word, Odemar stalked over the gangplank and benches to the stern of his *Bittern*. Durand and the others followed warily, catching stays and sheets to keep upright. They had no horses, no serving men, and only Guthred to play shield-bearer to them all. Durand sat down behind Coensar and felt his world contract. As long as the Lambing Moon remained in the Heavens, the whole company must live in an open boat forty feet long and a dozen feet wide.

Durand snugged his traveling chest against the thwarts to make a place for his heels. Lamoric was still pacing and alternately laughing or cursing.

When Durand looked up, he found Deorwen standing above the cool water, pale and beautiful as the moon. Durand stared, he was sure, like an ox over a fence. She, Father Odwy, and a redheaded sexton had come down from the castle together. Old Guthred put his hands round her waist to lower her into the boat, and she took her place beside Lamoric.

"Just in time, Father," Master Odemar grunted.

Across the blue Maidensbier, the Eye of Heaven cut a seam above the bank.

"When have I not known my time, Master Odemar?" the priest said and thumped the massive *Book of Moons* on the sexton's chest—as though the boy were a lectern—throwing its broad pages wide to find his place.

While the priest started a Dawn Thanksgiving for voyagers under the Lambing Moon, Berchard turned to the ship's master. "Last sailors I knew didn't like priests before journeys."

"*Sea*faring men they must have been. A river's another thing. You'll ask the King of Heaven to keep the river-wights at bay, but there's no power can check the Lord of the Deep at sea, only rile him. Lordship."

The priest climbed aboard, tottering stem to stern as the poor sexton struggled to walk backward and hold the great book where his master could read it. A censor slipped its own sanctuary scent into the mist.

When the priest had finished, he handed the rattling censor

to his sexton. "Come now, the oil, boy," he pressed, and the sexton set to juggling hot brass and holy book to dig a glass vessel from under his tabard.

The oarsmen, even the master, slid the caps from their heads.

"And now?" Berchard asked.

"Oil before water, under the Eye, Lordship," muttered Odemar, and the priest daubed a gleaming Eye of Heaven on each oarsman's forehead.

Lamoric twisted on his bench. "It is not as though we are sailing for the Dreaming Land." But Berchard had untied his cap for a dab of his own before the priest was back ashore.

"Are we off?" Lamoric asked.

The master squinted into the dawn.

"Aye, Lordship." The oarsmen hoisted their sweeps as Master Odemar took hold of the steering oar. "You lot on the pier, cast us off." When the boat was drifting on the cove, and gaffed out to give the sweeps room, Durand saw Odemar nod to his small audience of oarsmen—all facing the stern while their master and his passengers faced the dawn. "All right."

And the oarsmen hauled, driving the boat across the cove, faster and faster, and, as they gathered speed, upstream.

"Master Odemar," said Lamoric, turning, "I thought Eldinor was north. Do you mean to say I've been mistaken? Did old Saerdan Voyager beach his ship in the mountains then?"

The ship's master hardly spared a glance, hauling the tiller in to switch the *Bittern*'s prow into the current as the big river caught the boat.

"One turn sunwise," he grunted, "Lordship, to show respect to him up there." Odemar jutted his chin for Heaven's Eye.

But the boat was caught in the fast-moving Maidensbier. They managed a few strokes upstream, and then the master let the bow fall off. The whole vessel weathervaned around the master's steering oar, and the oarsmen began to pull in the sweeps.

Oars clattered as they slid home along the gunnels. "Now, what is this?" Lamoric demanded.

"We never row downstream, Lordship," said Odemar.

Lamoric glanced to Coensar before pressing on. "Eldinor is not Yestreen, you realize. It's some distance."

"No point rowing downstream, Lordship. Not on Maidensbier." He had shoved the tiller away from himself, picking a course roughly midway between the stone banks.

"You realize that the offense we might cause by arriving too late would be difficult to—"

"Aye, Lordship."

As Lamoric settled back onto his bench, his wife's hand on his arm, Durand took a last glance back: the villagers of the Burrstones looked on like boulders on a hillside. This was the second vessel most had seen leave that day.

WHEN THE EYE of Heaven was high, Guthred passed around the bread and cheese, and the men fished for the wine. Master Odemar led his oarsmen, muttering, through the Noontide Lauds. Durand watched the blue and stony banks from his spot on the bench.

"Puts me in mind of my youth, this does," said Berchard, unwrapping a round, dark loaf. "Up and down the Gray Road we went, just like this—though the Gray Road's a broader, calmer old river than this. This Maidensbier, she runs quick and cold. Puts me in mind of my poor wife, before she passed."

Berchard tore the loaf—tough as a knot of rags—while Badan waited.

As Badan reached, Ouen's long arm slithered the bread from Berchard's fingers.

"It like guarding a merchant's asses?" Ouen wondered, grinning with every gold tooth as he tore a bite of bread.

Berchard produced a leather bottle of claret, but stopped to dig in the puckered flesh of his bad eye. "Yes, aye," he said. "That's all it is really. Easier. Goggling up at the woods. Past that March of Skulls. Fellwood. Some nights, you hear drumming in the hills. Summers you stew in your hauberk."

As Berchard made to open the stopper, Badan twisted the bottle from his fingers. "Teach you to keep your good eye open."

After an hour's silence, Lamoric spoke: "Host Below, you all put me in mind of dinner round my father's table."

Every eye on the *Bittern* turned his direction, some quick, some slow.

Ouen lifted his thatch-straw beard in the air and again the teeth winked. "Genteel, are we?" he ventured.

"No. Not at all, in fact. It's my brother you remind me of. Landast always had a longer arm than I. A good man, but I reached for a lot that he got first."

Durand smiled as the rest chuckled.

"Likely explains more than it should," Lamoric concluded. "You're younger as well, aren't you, Durand?"

Durand nodded. "My brother's got a head start."

Berchard pointed with his bit of bread. "You're both younger brothers then?"

Durand shrugged. "I'd still be in the mountains else."

"What about you?" Berchard asked Ouen. "You cannot tell me you have a big brother."

"I do. Eight foot if he's an inch, the bastard."

Berchard held his hand up, calling for order. "A moment, please. Everyone before the mast. I ask you. Am I the only one here who's eldest? Badan?"

Badan scratched the long fringe at the back of his neck. "Aye. I've an older brother in Andagis."

"Host of Heaven, two of them!" Berchard gasped.

"There's one younger as well."

Half the men in the crew showed Badan the Eye of Heaven.

"And you, Ladyship?" Berchard asked.

Deorwen smiled: a sighing thing. "You've met Moryn. I'm eldest *daughter,* if that discounts me."

"We shall have to take counsel upon the matter, Ladyship," Berchard said before turning to Coensar the Captain. "And you, Captain?"

All eyes turned to Coensar, who stood mum for a moment, then confessed, "My brother's got a fine hall in Lannermoor. He often asks me up there. When I cannot refuse, I sit on a bench by the hearth fire while his wife hides the silver."

"To those afflicted with older brothers, then, poor bastards all," Berchard said, snatching Badan's bottle.

But Lamoric was pointing across the fat, glassy water at the far bank.

"There!" he said. "That's a sanctuary tower. What village do you think?"

There were shrugs, and a few of the others leaned for the gunnel.

Odemar shot them all a stern look as the *Bittern* teetered.

Lamoric was still peering. "Could it be Sallow Hythe?"

"A score more towers, Lordship, and *up*river," Guthred corrected carefully.

The rest threw names around.

"Rush Landing," said Odemar, finally.

There was silence down the length of the boat. "Just down the road?"

"Rush Landing, aye."

"Then we've hardly moved." Lamoric spread his hands over the speeding river. "How can that be?"

"Maidensbier's running quick but she bends . . . Lordship."

"You realize I've no desire to offend the king? That our goal is to do precisely the opposite? A lot of blood went into gaining us the king's favor."

The ship's master was silent.

"Why don't your oarsmen give a pull or two?"

"Where the Maidensbier's carrying us, we'd best not come rushing. The river's as full and fast as I've seen her, Lordship."

Durand heard a strange noise: a moaning over the water. Coensar peered forward.

"They'll have to row when we reach the Silvermere," Lamoric was saying.

"Aye, Lordship. But there is little sense in—"

Deorwen was on her feet in the prow, looking around the high curve of the stempost. Durand heard a peculiar sound: a wild chiming through the belly of the boat.

"What is that sound?" said Lamoric.

The oarsmen were unshipping their oars, all at once and without any signal.

"We should not have come," growled Odemar.

"What?"

"The Sleepers' Cave," Odemar growled.

"I don't—"

The *Bittern* lurched, sliding down a trough. There were high stone walls all around.

"When Maidensbier's high, she swallows the shrine in the rock at Sleepers' Cave."

Now Berchard spoke. "What're you saying? I've seen the Sleepers'. You couldn't flood—" Sweeping past the gunnels went a row of rock-cut steps that might have led to a shrine's riverbank door. You could only see the top few. "Host of Heaven," Berchard said, astonished.

"When the bells ring, the Maid leaves her bed," said Odemar, "and takes another."

"I've seen those bells," said Berchard. "They must be, what? Five fathoms from the floor."

A man at the oars must turn his back on the river and face the ship's master. Only he can see the course ahead. It is an act of faith. There was an oar for every man, and Durand was not alone as he slid his long sweep out over the water and looked into the master's face.

"Pull with the others now," said Odemar. The boat pitched, skidding two fathoms down in a heartbeat. Some of the knights looked round—they flailed with their sweeps—but not one of the oarsmen turned. "Easy," was Odemar's grated rebuke.

Durand tried to reach and haul with the Burrstone men as the boat picked up speed, but half the time Durand's oar beat at spray. The river thundered between high stone banks, faster every heartbeat.

"Hold fast, all," snarled Odemar, fists locked on the tiller as the boat stamped and soared through the rolling explosion of the river.

Then Durand heard a greater roar, and the *Bittern* plunged.

The master heaved upon the tiller. "Together! Hard and together. All you have. More if you're on larboard."

Bittern lurched. Durand's oar struck some immovable stone in the spray, kicking back into Durand's chest like a horse. But before he could take a breath, the master was snarling, "Now, for your lives!" And those still with oars in their hands pulled. Durand hauled with the rest. Their blades clattered and flailed. "Together!" shouted Odemar, then Durand watched the man's face twist. His eyes were fixed on something over Durand's shoulder. "Together!" he screamed.

And the *Bittern* struck.

Timbers snapped with a sound like a thunderclap. Every man was on his knees, howling.

Durand skidded across the plank bottom as the *Bittern* jerked like a fish in a dog's jaws.

"We're caught broadside. We must get her off the rock!" strained Odemar.

Strakes and gunnels flexed like a snapped limb. Durand could see new white wood in long cracks.

Coensar looked straight at him. "Come on!"

Half the men were on their backsides. Water foamed around either side of a stone the size of a mill. Deorwen had been thrown into the bows. In a moment, the boat would fold around the great stone and they'd be finished.

Durand and the captain fought to push the *Bittern* free, struggling bare-handed, sliding on wet boots till Coensar spotted the long oars floating all around them. "Here!" he said, and catching up one of the long poles, he rammed it between the gunwale and the stone. Durand grabbed hold and the two heaved.

And *Bittern* slid—men sprawling—then she stuck fast again. Durand could feel the planks warping as he heaved.

"It must be now," said Odemar.

Coensar turned on the others. "Every man get an oar. If you aren't dead yet, get an oar!" And the men, awkward as foals, scrambled to jam their paddles against the stone. At Durand's hip, Deorwen appeared, stabbing an oar down like a whaler's spear. Durand strained with his jaws locked as white rents opened, and he didn't know whether the *Bittern* would break or go free.

Then she slipped once more.

"Pull!" Coen roared.

And the boat tumbled off. Every fleck of her winter's paint was left on the great stone as the *Bittern* pitched into the current, half-awash and beyond controlling.

Men sprawled into the boat once more, putting the oars to their proper use.

Odemar stood in the stern even still, water sloshing to his thighs.

But the Maidensbier had finished with them. The cliff

walls fell away, and as the channel widened, the river re-
laxed its grip. They rode, freezing among floating provisions
and splinters, until, finally, Durand heard riverbank reeds
brush the *Bittern*'s hull.

Coensar gave Durand a wry grin.

🪢 5. The Glen of Idols

The backwater cove where they arrived was a meadow at
the bottom of a steep glen. Among the pines around the
meadow's edge stood stone figures, neckless and squat as
tombstones: the Powers of Heaven with bulging almond eyes
and sketched limbs.

Under these gray watchers, Durand and the others—
oarsmen and knights both—bailed enough icy water from the
Bittern that the company could drag her up the bank. Lamoric
took Deorwen's elbow, bringing her ashore. And joined the
others, flopping onto the turf and giving thanks to the Host of
Heaven for their deliverance.

But it seemed as though the Powers answered back. Strange
voices hung over the valley.

When Durand levered his head from the sod, he saw a row
of hooded figures, as gray and strange as the stone Powers
beyond them.

It turned out that only nine men lived in the Glen of the
Idols, and they were anchorites: monks who had shut themselves away from the world. Their knot of stone huts at the
valley's head had no rooms where a man could stand upright. There was no dining hall and no sanctuary. But Coensar persuaded the uneasy hermits to allow their party to use
the idols' meadow as a tenting ground and to cut a tree or
two for new planks.

Everyone pitched in, and by dusk they had settled around
a bonfire Deorwen had arranged.

"I reckon our Odemar's still cross," said Berchard.

The ship's master was thumping a makeshift plank in place
with a lump of firewood. The dull report echoed around the
whole valley—as did the oaths he spat when his makeshift

mallet missed. These were nearly enough to make even the stone Powers flinch.

"We've broken his boat, and now he's missing supper," Berchard said. He had a gobbet of wet bread and some slimy cheese. "Say what you like about these horse-loaves. Decent bread wouldn't hold up to a soaking like this."

Lamoric was standing. He swung his damp cloak from his shoulders and opened it before the heat. "I wonder what kind of time we'll make now."

"I wouldn't wonder that too near our friend," Ouen cautioned, waving a bit of sausage.

Lamoric turned the cloak, letting the flames lick steam from the wool. "No. And he's right. Another day or two in Burrstone would have mattered little. Now we'll be spending the time with our stone friends here." The statues looked down with their protruding eyes.

"Husband, you will burn that," said Deorwen, motioning to Lamoric's cloak.

"Where did you say this was, by the way?" Lamoric asked of the company.

One of the oarsmen answered, "A couple of days from Yestreen." He remembered to doff his cap. "Lordship."

"Your cloak, husband," Deorwen repeated.

"Not very far along, then," Lamoric said, giving the cloak a swish over the fire. "Even if the boat would float. I suppose there's little point—"

The cloak caught alight: a moment of brilliance and stink beaten out with curses that threw a scroll from under Lamoric's surcoat. They had last seen the parchment in Sir Geridon's hand.

Lamoric plucked the scroll from the edge of the flames, and then unrolled the page—mottled as a leopard with running ink. He laughed, seemingly on the edge of tears.

"I could say that it is unreadable: very nearly the truth," Lamoric said. "Of course, I had already read it before Geridon was a league down the road."

He looked to the glint of Coensar's gaze.

"Losing the thing in the river, they might have believed. I am not sure about dropping it in a fire. That might have seemed more than accidental."

Coensar had not moved, but Deorwen spoke, "Husband, I've seen you with this letter. It clearly plagues you. Why won't you tell us what it says?"

The men from Burrstone climbed to their feet and went to help their master.

"Yes. This is my father's business with the king. Although I don't suppose he'd see it as secret. He trusted it to me, after all."

"What does he say?" asked Coensar.

"I am asked to present the king with a series of requests. Reasonable things. We are to ask if, after the recent vote at the Great Council, the king might waive any fees or fines due the crown for heirs taking up their birthrights, peers marrying widows under royal care. These fines provoked ill feeling in some quarters before the Great Council vote. To hearten the realm, we are to suggest that he forgive them.

"He asks—on behalf of those who voted to forgive the king's debts—that the king provide relief from certain military obligations. So that they may defend themselves from enemies on their borders."

Lamoric shook the paper in the air. Durand noticed Deorwen putting one small hand over her eyes.

"I am to tell the king, as I read this, that the Great Council dukes who voted to save the king's own crown have a list of things they would like. He should forgive taxes, he should forget duties owed, he should let them keep their soldiers close and send him none.

"My father is a gentle old man: earnest, forthright, and pious. He will see this as a collection of kindly suggestions to prevent trouble: advice from those most loyal to him.

"But how will a man circled by every wolf in the kingdom see this? Will he note that his most loyal are whispering about his business? Will he see a long list of demands, and how they'll empty his coffers, and leave him stripped of an army? You have seen King Ragnal. You have seen how hard-pressed he has been. You have felt his temper. How will he react, do you think?"

Lamoric looked at those around the circle. "Perhaps now you would have me drop this in the fire?"

The flames crackled a hand's span from the parchment scroll.

By the water, Odemar snarled a string of oaths that filled the glen. After a few silent heartbeats, Deorwen straightened.

"That man will need food, the same as the rest of us," she murmured. "I wonder what survives of our stores?"

The *Bittern* gleamed in the glen's last scrap of sunlight. At the boat's flank, Deorwen bent to speak to Odemar. The boat's master tugged his forelock, caught like a crab against his boat's hull by this noblewoman's kindness.

Her hair was free to flash in the amber light. Durand sipped from the wineskin as it passed, then handed the bottle to Lamoric.

"My troubles can all be traced to one day," Lamoric said, taking a quick sip from the skin. "We were in Evensands on the sea. My father had arranged a marriage for me when a rider tracked me down with another of his messages." He smiled. "I remember how I was told about my wedding in the first place! Like a ghost, there was Geridon's stubbled head in my tent as I made to step out of the flap to enter the lists at Beoran. He grins at me and says, 'We get to Evensands while the Weaning Moon's shining, Lordship, and I'll see you at your wedding.' From one sea to another in only a few days.

"I had to ask him who the girl was to be."

Lamoric raised the wineskin in Deorwen's direction. "I was fortunate in his choice. But my father was bent on safeguarding his legacy," Lamoric said. "He's not a young man. My mother's gone. He wanted his kin and his people safe. In the east, he married Landast to Garelyn. In the west, he married Alwen to Yrlac. And I was to marry Mornaway in the north."

This was a tangle of thorns. Durand winced.

"Simple enough," Lamoric said. Gireth would have family on every side. "And so I found myself in Evensands, the heart of Mornaway, on the eve of my wedding. If Father had a duty for a wastrel son like me, I reckoned, I would take it with both hands. I would prove . . . whatever I thought I must prove. But then they brought the news."

By the water, the glen's deep shadow was swallowing the *Bittern* and Deorwen. Odemar, now, was chatting with Deorwen—at ease and munching sausage and cheese.

"Messengers from Ragnal had swept into my father's hall. It hadn't been a week since Geridon told me I was to be married, and the Marches were on fire. Mad Borogyn and his Heithan princes had rebelled and the Host of Errest was to assemble on the border. My father could not send Landast, his heir, off to command the peers of Gireth. But he could send me."

He sneered at himself. "Some news for the eve of a man's wedding! Husband and commander. All of it. All at once. It was only right to mark the event—something of that sort must have been in my head. And a little skittishness on the eve of a great day.

"When Landast hauled me out of whatever alehouse he found me in, the marriage went ahead. I remember a lot of gray faces looking back at me.

"And so my father sent the old Baron of Swanskin Down to lead the riders of Gireth. And, in my stead, my father sent the king a bag of silver to hire a good man. I might have gone from wastrel to great man of the kingdom in a morning. Now, here we are."

Durand imagined Lamoric at peace, a man easy with his responsibilities, a man with time and sense enough to know his new wife. A great deal turned on one night's hard drinking.

Lamoric held the wineskin before his nose for a moment, then tossed it to Badan across the fire. "Perhaps a year has taught me better sense."

He drew himself up. "I should have told you. These are my worries, not yours. Message and monarch must meet, but you are not bound to follow me."

He took Durand's shoulder, a gesture of reassurance, and rose for bed.

"I tell you all: there are villages enough nearby, and you will find better men than me in most of them—brave knights of my father's host. Each of you may take my good word to any of these men. This is *my* errand. I have been coward not to confess. The long winter has me desperate, I think. But you return home, find some better lord, and leave me to my fool's errand. We'll have a laugh about it all when I see you next."

He left with a bow, and the rest soon draggled after him to their own tents and lean-tos.

Durand watched Deorwen trail across the grass to her husband's tent.

UNDER A BUNDLE of damp blankets, Durand lay with the cold mist from the Maidensbier tightening knots in his bones.

He found himself thinking of Alwen, Lamoric's dark-haired sister who'd married for peace with Yrlac. He found himself back in that tower over the gloom of Ferangore where he had caught her by the arm. Where he had stared into her desperate eyes—she might have known him from her father's hall—and then stood guard by her door. He remembered her baby's wails.

The voices of the anchorite monks filled the Glen of the Idols. They did not simply chant the Plea of Sunset or Last Twilight, but wove one prayer into the next from hour to hour.

Even after Durand had confessed his part in Alwen's death, Lamoric had taken him in. Now, he could not get Deorwen from his mind. He should put kingdoms between himself and the man's wife. But he could not abandon Lamoric in the midst of all this. He resolved to see Lamoric safely to Eldinor and then leave—there must be other women in the world for him.

The monks' voices mingled high above the solitary darknesses of their cells.

When Durand opened his eyes, he found Deorwen crouched before him. She was always tinier than he expected.

"Lord of Dooms," he breathed. "You cannot be here."

She crouched with a glance at the darkness. "Last year, in the spring, my mother died. It took a long time. Three years of wasting, hot and pale as candles. I am the eldest daughter. It was my place to care for her while my father paced or snapped at the serving men. I lived with wise women every day. We bathed her with cloths. They spoke of signs and dooms and herbs and dreams. Near the end I would watch her eyes darting like tadpoles under the skin. I dreamt beside her. She slipped back and forth across the border of the Otherworld. It was an open door. I dreamt upon the threshold. You could see her passing.

"Then she slipped a final time. It was the Sowing Moon. Suddenly she was gone. And Father said I was to be married."

"Deorwen," said Durand.

"I had seen Lamoric—at a wedding: his elder sister's, I think. And he was far from ill-favored. I was sick to death of sickrooms and herbs and the wisdom of old women."

Deorwen took a deep breath, staring into the Heavens.

"He was so crushed when his father turned his back. He was a hollow man when his father's host rode off under another captain.

"It's been a year since my mother passed," she said.

She seemed very small as she walked off through the echoes of chanting.

FOR AN HOUR or more, Durand lay still while monks sang and the earth froze under his shoulder. He might have been in the blackness beyond Creation, so dark was the night.

And then the river shimmered.

An Otherworldly light played upon the wavelets, spreading wider, until the prow of a solitary boat appeared, as light as a willow leaf. Here was Lost Lady Aralind once more with her warning for the men of Gireth that trouble was coming to the dukedom.

He looked away before he had seen more. He needed no further reminders. Sometimes the Powers whispered; sometimes they roared. Lying back, he fixed his eyes on the black dome of Heaven and wondered how the old duke's wife had managed to get around the tough bit by the falls.

HE DREAMT THAT he was sleeping on a blanket spread over a thousand heaving others. Their limbs slithered and bulged against his body.

When dawn shone over the far bank, Durand peeled his hair and blankets from the frost and swore. The world was white and glittering.

Beyond it all, the monks were still singing; their chant had not ceased for an instant.

A cord sandal tramped by his fingers.

One of the anchorites wove toward the water, balancing a yoke of buckets—empty by their bobbing. Durand could hear the others singing Dawn Thanksgiving.

He tore a green patch from the frosty turf and lurched after the little man. Others were stirring.

"You should not have slept here," the monk said.

"Your huts are on the only other flat patch of ground, brother."

The monk's path had Durand trailing toward the remains of the bonfire, which suited him fine. The voice of the remaining monks still circled the valley overhead. "Do you never stop, brother?"

"We have found that we can do what we must. The Powers often arrange it so."

If Durand could get a straight answer, he thought he would help the monk with his buckets. Badan—still under a heap of rugs—crouched by the fire, jabbing the embers with a half-burnt stick.

"Do you sleep?" asked Durand.

"Is not Creation dreaming?" The man stopped and turned to Durand at the edge of the fire ring. His eyes were black as beads. Every inch of his face and neck was as yellow as an old bruise. "The Wards of the Ancient Patriarchs are slipping. It is all we can do to keep them bound."

"Durand! Did I see someone by your tent yesternight? Thought I heard a voice . . ." said Badan, too loudly. The man's leer left his eyeteeth standing like a doorjamb round the gap Durand had made for him last year. Nothing had happened, but there were ears to hear him.

The monk looked at the ground.

"I don't know what you heard, Badan."

"Oh, I just wondered. Midnight visitors. And sweet of voice, I thought, but who—Host of Hell!" Badan snarled, throwing himself from the ashes like he'd prodded a nest of adders. The *Bittern*'s folk all around the meadow stared. A few had blades in their hands.

Durand was baffled, but the man's game was done, his eyes fixed on the ashes.

"I think they're alive down there!" he breathed.

Durand stepped past the monk. They had made their fire, without particular thought, in the center of the circling idols. Now, the scorched patch was a scar in the skin of turf, laying bare what had been hidden.

In the hole, he saw gray shapes: a writhing of limbs. He saw fingers and elbows, soft as porridge, stirring. He saw a mass of black hair, turning—and drew back before the face could emerge from the knot of limbs.

Lamoric had charged up at his shoulder, but Durand held him back.

The monk teetered before them. He stood little past Durand's belt's buckle.

"How long have you prayed here?" asked Durand.

"They stepped from the Wards of the Ancient Patriarchs, these folk," said the little man, nodding. "Long before, Gunderic, Saerdan's man, fought wild sorcerers here. Creation was violated: deeply wounded. And so Saerdan's Patriarchs bound that wound, knotting it into the vast wards they stretched across the kingdom, binding it tight—these idols mark the place—and farmers came to the glen. They lived and died here for a dozen generations. Then, after an argument with their priest, they hung that holy man among the idols."

"And those people?" He gestured toward the shapes in the hole.

"Creation is weak at such places. Torn. And with their desecration, these men thrust themselves beyond the protection of the Patriarchs, a perilous thing in such a place. There are a thousand like it in Errest the Old."

"You're bloody madmen!" Badan concluded. He looked ready to launch himself on the monk, but Durand got between them.

Badan subsided, looking up at Durand and the men looking on. "You'd best watch yourself," he snarled. "I know you. I know what you're like." But he backed down, and Durand helped the monk throw earth over the writhing shapes.

The monk touched Durand's arm as he tossed a last shovel on. "The wards are loosening. From the passes of the Blackroots to the Mount of Eagles. Something is on the move in the land."

🔵 6. The Night Leap

Not one man abandoned Lamoric.

Before Master Odemar had finished his porridge, the knights stood by a loaded *Bittern,* long oars in their hands like an honor guard of lancers. This was both a show for Lamoric and something to tell Odemar that they were no longer passengers—an idea of Deorwen's. Every back was ready to row—though Badan had needed a cuff or two from big Ouen.

Lamoric clasped each man's hand; the ship's master simply grunted and got on board.

Despite the men's good intentions, the afternoon's delay stretched to two or three days as they bailed the battered *Bittern* and hauled her out in pastures, by old mills, and among the boats of a fishing village. The forty-foot vessel weighed as much as a yoke of oxen and could be just as stubborn. At the last village, Odemar tramped up among the muddy lanes and appeared with pitch, oakum, and a pair of proper caulking irons. The men decided that he looked pleased.

In the quiet stretches, they drilled, pulling starboard and larboard and "giving way" together. By the end they could even "hold water" from a running start—breaking the boat's drive by jamming the oars deep—or "toss oars," with every oar straight up.

Mostly, they rowed hard.

In the first hour of the fifth day, the cliffs of the Maidensbier opened and the company of the *Bittern* saw the silence of Yestreen and the Handglass still beyond. Seat of the dukes of Gireth so long ago, Yestreen's dark keep now loomed over a fishing village. Durand made out the turtle-back shapes of a few score rowboats upturned below the walls. This was where the Lady of the Maidensbier had ended her journey.

At Gireth's beginning, Yestreen had been the duke's seat and the staging ground for Gunderic and his Sons of Atthi as they carried their banners to the mountains' feet. Now, though generations beyond counting had passed since that time, Yestreen still recalled the days before its duke departed, and the evening when its future closed before it.

The shell of Yestreen stood where the Maidensbier poured into the cool depths of the Handglass. The *Bittern* slid onto the bay, carried by the current. Below the keel, they could see blue pebbles that must be fathoms from the surface. The air was still and cold.

As the river let them go, every eye turned to Odemar. When he nodded, they rowed.

THE LIGHT FAILED as they reached Silvermere itself.

Rowing, every man faced Master Odemar and the high curve of the sternpost. Durand learned to read the knobs and bristles of the master's face. He could see, for example, that Odemar's black-button eyes were searching the shoreline gloom now, looking for a place to put in for the hours of darkness.

He would soon turn the *Bittern* into the wind.

Then the man's eyes were jumping. His beard squirmed. Deorwen passed Durand's elbow. Abandoning her position in the bows, she climbed over thwarts and barrels to the stern where Odemar stood with his well-worn tiller.

"I know little enough about sailing, Master Odemar," she said. "I understand that we must cross the mere to Red Winding and follow the Red Winding to Ragnal's capital. But how is the crossing to be made?"

The man hooked a finger in a tight cord he wore around his neck. "A wise man keeps the shore to windward, 'case the mere blows up. Ladyship."

"And the wind's from the northeast?"

"Last while, aye. Ladyship."

"So, around by the Halls of Silence, then."

The man nodded. "There's coves and bays enough to shelter for the night. So long as no one goes ashore, the old kings don't give no trouble."

Deorwen nodded. "I suppose there are men who live under the eaves of the forest, right now, in Farona. And you've lived across the Maidensbier in the Burrstones."

Odemar didn't smile, though he gave the neck cord a tug under his beard. "I've spent many a night in coves along that shore. Saw one of the old ones once. Tall as this mast here."

"What is that, by the way?" she asked, indicating the twist of leather at his neck.

Odemar scowled. "This? Cauls! They're cauls."

"I don't . . ."

He thrust his beard forward. "A man born in the caul don't drown so long as he keeps it by him."

"Ah. And your wrists?"

"Cauls. Aye, Ladyship."

"You've got three?"

"My brothers, Ladyship. They were ship's masters before me."

"And how did you come by . . ."

"They didn't drown, Ladyship," he explained.

The rowing had ceased.

Coensar leaned on his oar.

"You've heard what we're doing—the message and the oaths?" asked Coensar.

Odemar scratched where beard and caul met. "Aye."

"The way we sail, will we see Eldinor before the moon's out?"

The ship's master stepped out from behind his steering oar—just one hand on the tiller—and squinted straight up into the empty Heavens.

"We might try the night leap," he said.

Some of the oarsmen muttered.

"What is this 'night leap'?" asked Lamoric.

"Lordship. A man sets off by daylight, sighting off the lodestar to keep a straight course."

"Out of sight of land?"

"Aye. You set your course at Last Twilight, then press through. On the sea, you must hope to sight land then, when the Eye rises, or you're lost. It's different on the mere."

"And what of shoals and banks—"

"Best done in deep water. Should be a broad enough channel west."

Durand eyed the others—Lamoric, Coensar, Deorwen— wondering whether this was what they'd had in mind. Sailing alone in the blackness.

As Deorwen nodded and made her way back into the bows,

Durand had a feeling she had known exactly what she was asking—and that there was no one else aboard who could have posed the question.

"Well, gentlemen. It does not sound like the safe course," said Lamoric. "I don't think it would be fair to—"

Berchard stopped him. "Shut up, Your Lordship. We're in the boat already, aren't we?" There was laughter in the gloom.

Odemar merely nodded. "Starboard bank, give way together," he ordered, and the *Bittern* lurched toward Silvermere. Dimly visible, the last quarter of the Lambing Moon already hung in the Heavens. Soon it would the only light in Creation.

"Pick up the stroke, all," Odemar commanded. "Slow and steady. Let's see if we can't get the sail to do some pulling."

THEY ROWED AS the horizon's smudges crumbled into the mere, and stars glittered in the black waves. Before long, they were alone with the sloshing water. Durand could hear, more than see, the breeze playing feebly in the sailcloth.

They dragged up some riverman's chants.

Someone was bailing. Durand could hear the comic-hollow *scoop* of a leather bucket. His back and shoulders ached with the relentless effort of rowing. Behind him, Badan spat and snarled. He swore when Durand's oar crossed his. When Durand's blade skipped a splash back at him, he threatened to stick a knife in Durand's neck.

When songs failed them, Ouen spoke. "I'll tell you about my string of bad luck. The first man I served, I rode five years at his side—until his wedding."

"Wife got a look at you, eh?" sneered Badan.

"He and his brother rode off a cliff the next morning, near as we could figure."

Berchard clucked his tongue. "My wife was a bit like that."

"Fog," said Ouen. "Like you've never seen. That one was a good man. He'd been meaning to have me take over a hall and some river land. I thought I was going to be there for life."

Durand glanced over to see Ouen's teeth wink.

"The next one, I served four years till one day we rode out hunting—too far to get back before nightfall. Rain drove us into a country shrine. And His Lordship didn't like leaving the serving men outside, or the horses outside—or the dogs. The next day, the shrine was heaped with crap and there was His Lordship, blind and full of—what do they call those?—hives! Hives, he had. All over his body."

"You don't make a house of the Powers into a stable."

"Or kennel, aye. We sussed that out right away. I think it might have been a holy day too. His bloody Lordship had been dangling a young widow under my nose, but he didn't need a tournament thug after the blinding. I remember the widow though. Her hair was that red they call strawberry—a sort of roany chestnut, like."

Deorwen laughed.

"Hells, Ouen," said Badan, "you've been an unlucky bastard."

"One killed his own liege lord—accidentally with a hunting arrow—and wound up across the Sea of Thunder somewhere." He paused. "Another choked on a pie of—what was it?—larks, I think. Something like that. Another ordered they build him a ship up in Beoran. I'd managed to fight my way to his right hand. Lost my teeth for him. Called the ship *Otter* and, sure enough, she rolled over the same hour she left the harbor—just like a real damned otter. His wife, his sons, were all on board. You could see them crawling over the *Otter*'s belly, I swear."

Over Durand's shoulder, Badan was cackling. "Careful what you name a ship, eh?"

"The bittern a diving bird?" Berchard wondered, but Ouen kept talking.

"Every time I feel a nice bit of land—a corner of forest, a bit of rolling valley—at my fingertips, no matter how many winters I spend stealing up on it, whisk, something snatches it away."

A cold breeze stirred over the water. The sail flapped, like something fitfully waking, then bellied out—the *Bittern* heeling. In the moonlight, Durand could see Odemar considering. He might ask them to pull the oars out. They might have a break from rowing.

The wind freshened again, pulling creaks of protest from stays and shrouds. The *Bittern* heeled farther.

"Bank oars, all," Odemar said, the sweeps rattling inboard at his command. "Hands to the sheets. Let's brace up. Bring the larboard in." His eyes darted down the boat. "Let's trim her fore-and-aft while we can. By my eye, we're low in the bows. Make fast whatever's loose. I don't know what time we've got."

Any cheer the men felt at hauling the cursed oars out froze in their blood. The men stared from their benches, but the master scratched under the leather at his neck. There was weather coming on. Badan said, "Hells." Durand met Deorwen's glance down the length of the boat. He had seen the mere in a storm, both aboard ship and from unshakable Gunderic's Tower in Acconel. But now, it would be night and in this undecked boat with untrained men. He wanted to lift Deorwen out of it all, to be one of those giants from the Halls of Silence to stride with her across the mere.

"How many, Ouen?" said Durand.

"They called me Ouen of the Nine Masters for a while. Now, I don't count. Coensar's been trying longer than I have—but not much. There's a little poison in hope. You can take that from me."

For an hour, they ran before the spreading wings of the storm, then the *Bittern* rolled through a deep trough and slipped into blackness as the Lambing Moon surrendered the Heavens to darkness.

Another deep trough took the *Bittern*, throwing men on their knees. The wind snapped in the sail, a cold weight.

"Each man, get your oar on a lanyard," said Odemar's voice.

"If I could *see* the bloody oar," griped Badan, "I'd jam it up your—"

The *Bittern* rose and slewed through the blackness, Durand catching an icy wave over chest and breeches. He blinked at the thunderbolt chill. He wondered how the master could keep the boat on course—then he realized. With a twist in his seat, he watched the last stars blotted out. Odemar was as blind as any of them.

The master said, "If you've anything loose, now's the time to—"

Another wave lifted the boat and sent it shuddering down.

Durand heard a clatter from the stern, then Odemar cursing—he was likely climbing back to his feet.

"Who's bailing?" the master demanded.

Deorwen's voice answered, "I will," from somewhere up in the bows. The sound stole Durand's breath.

His oar was alive in his hands, though all but the blade was hauled inboard. It should have been well out of the waves.

Above the creak of the rigging and the splash of water, there came a new sound: a hiss across the darkness, at first far away, and then closer. Finally, a wet-gravel sleet slapped down, drumrolling over the sail.

"That's it! No time to brail up. Mind your heads, I'm bringing the yard down." There was a clatter of parrel bearings as the yard dropped on the forearms of the men in the boat's waist. Tents worth of canvas filled the *Bittern*. "Get it in the boat!" Odemar said. "Lay it down the keel."

The *Bittern* dove; she bounded high.

"Ready at the oars! And watch yourselves when the water catches them."

As Durand braced to shoot the long oar out over the waves, a tower of black water crashed over the boat. In an instant, he was off his bench and tumbling. Voices shouted and bodies collided. Just as he felt the gunnel under his hand, a weight struck him hard against it: a body. In a sick instant, he knew the body was already going over the side.

He heard a voice: a high sound tumbling into the waves. All he could think was "Deorwen!"

Blind, he lashed out, groping into waves and wind. The world was dark and full of storms, but there was no one there. His fingers snagged a trailing line. That was all.

He hung over the gunnel, feeling his heart beating. Then the line jerked taut.

He imagined a cough, snatched by the wind. The line was slithering from his fingers. He caught the hairy rope in both fists. While the others shouted and scrambled around him—all blind, no one seeing—Durand hauled for her life.

Then there were gasps and scrabbling fingers. Durand reached deep beyond the gunnel, catching a fistful of cloth, and then they collapsed into the stern.

"Thank God . . . Deorwen," Durand gasped.

"You've got the wrong girl!" Big Ouen's laugh spluttered. "But, Heaven help me, I'll bloody play along if it keeps me out of the mere."

Now, it was Odemar's turn. The two men had fallen on him. "Get to your oars! I must get the prow in the wind's eye. Do as I say!"

🌀 7. The Winding Road

They wrestled the storm through all the dark hours, rowing by touch while the *Bittern* flexed and twisted. As the boat crashed over the waves, they heaved, racking their oars like a dying man breathes. The wind or waves would catch the prow and throw it left or right, ready to roll the boat and kill them. Oars and gunnels bloodied their noses and blackened their eyes.

Somewhere in the dark, Deorwen cringed under the same coffin-chilled waves, but Durand could not so much as *see* her. Though the *Bittern* might carry them down, he could not say a word. He could only row and hope that she would live.

Then a moment came when Durand realized that he could see the rain that lashed him. Thick, pale ice hung on the gunnels and rolled on mottled waves.

Odemar stood with his fists on the tiller, as he had before the light failed them. He could have been dead. Durand, twisting as he pulled his oar, found that Deorwen still rode in the bow, emptying buckets over the side. Durand shut his eyes in relief.

When he opened his eyes, Ouen smacked a kiss in his direction, his beard rattling with ice. "My hero."

Finally, Odemar's voice croaked out. "Stop. Oars out. Pointless. We could be anyplace." The man's breath floated in the air around his head. The swell had died, and now Creation was a still place bounded by mist.

Boots scraped in the bottom of the boat as the men looked out.

"Some ship's master you are," said Badan. There was a rattle among the man's last teeth. "Whoreson."

"Quiet," said Coensar. "Hold still."

Now that the oars were silent, a faint lapping reached the boat from the fog: a beach or another vessel in the gray distance.

"*That* sounds good," said Lamoric. Frost had stiffened panels of his surcoat. "I think we'd better get these men under shelter while it may still do some good, eh, Master Odemar?"

"But where have we fetched up?" wondered Berchard. "That could be the Fens of Merchion, or the Halls of Silence we hear lapping out there."

"Lost Hesperand, more like," said Odemar, "with all the sternway we were making."

"Oh, Hells," snarled Badan. "Freeze or Hesper-bloody-rand. Burrstone sons of whores."

"That storm'll have blown us leagues, and mostly west," said Odemar.

Deorwen was still bailing. Water sloshed high around Durand's calves, getting higher. The boat was riding low. His feet were numb.

"Thank you, Master Odemar," said Lamoric. "We need to know."

Odemar eyed his boat. "She's worked a seam open—more than one by the look of this flood. Best if we could get her out. Best if it was quick."

The invisible shoreline breathed in the fog, and Durand closed his eyes. Beyond the cold water smells, there was something else: wood smoke, and the sharp trickle of latrine pits. He held up his hand.

"What're you up to?" Badan sneered.

"Men," said Durand. Other smells joined the stronger traces: a baker's ovens, fish in market heaps, rubbish pits, horse dung. Then they heard sanctuary bells.

"The boy's right," said Coensar, and Durand looked back over a boat full of grins.

Every man unlimbered his oar.

AS THEY ROWED in, the town became clear. A jumble of buildings and narrow alleys spread at the bottom of a slope.

There were stone sanctuaries with squat towers. A river's mouth opened. Piers reached toward them, dark across the still water.

And Durand knew the place. With every stroke, he could see farther up the slope above the city. He made out ring-works under the turf. He saw trees. This was the place he first came after the old Duke of Yrlac set him free. It was here he'd come, knowing Alwen must be dead behind him. It was here he joined Lamoric's retainers. It was here he met Deorwen in a stream with thugs looking on from the bushes. This was Red Winding at the mouth of the river of the same name.

Durand shot Deorwen a look.

But Red Winding was also the road to Eldinor and Ragnal's Mount of Eagles. If it weren't for the oars in their fists, every man would have made the Eye of Heaven.

ONCE THEY'D BAILED and beached the *Bittern,* the huddled knot of them kissed the mud. Coensar had already found shelter, and Lamoric was already calling for steaming hippocras before his men could tumble into the low room after him. Horn-paned lanterns glowed as Coensar shook his head and smiled a crooked grin. Badan took a day's worth of the tavern-keeper's charcoal and tipped it into the grate.

Durand sat in the clammy grip of his sopping gear, but the warm prickle of the tumbler between his hands brought him to life. He drew steam deep into his lungs, feeling galingale and cinnamon steam in the stuffy passages of his skull. A hot pie appeared on the table, and he joined the others in shoveling up gobbets of mutton and grease and whatever else with his bare hands.

To the dismay of the gaunt tavern-keeper, the tavern room was soon hung with steaming cloaks and surcoats, hose and tunics—with the men, wearing nothing but their breeches, draped over every bench, groaning and cursing. Lamoric paced. Deorwen sat in the damp clouds at the fireside, shaking her head.

Someone gave Durand an elbow—Ouen. "Here, look."

Guthred stood in the street door.

Lamoric spread his hands. "Good, Guthred. Good. If you

could listen a moment, everyone. I've had Guthred . . . Well, I've had him go round to a proper inn. He's got you all—knight and oarsmen both—warm rooms, tubs of hot bath-water, and food and drink enough to last a week."

There were puzzled expressions around the room, and Durand looked to Coensar. The Sowing Moon would rise before a week was out. The captain raised an eyebrow.

"When you're finished there, you can take the *Bittern* back across to Burrstone Walls or Yestreen or I'll pay Master Odemar to take you to Acconel itself. By morning, I must find a boat to get me headed downriver once more, but I—"

At this, the men finally shouted him down.

"Is this your clever way of telling us we've got to leave tomorrow morning?" said Berchard.

"It's no game. Guthred's put silver in that innkeeper's fist."

"Well," said Berchard. "That's coin wasted. Can you get it back off him, Guthred?"

Coensar was smiling as Guthred rubbed his heavy nose. "No."

Ouen filled his lungs. "Maybe someone else should give it a try, eh? What do you think?"

"Won't do no good. I never gave the innkeeper a clipped penny." Lamoric turned. "Got stopped by an old clothes man in the next lane. He's got it all now. The stuff's mostly patch-work, but there's enough, and it's dry."

There was a great shout, and again Coensar smiled his crooked grin.

🔗 8. To Race the Moon

They followed the Red Winding down among the ruddy manors of the lowland lords. Hedgerows and towers, monasteries and mills passed beyond the gunnels while cottars stared, alien as their beasts. To nearly every soul on the river, Lamoric called, "How far to Eldinor?" and always the distance was a little farther than it must be. They must reach the city by First Sight of the Sowing Moon; they pulled hard.

Collapsed on one more meadow bank as nightfall drove them from the water, Durand heard Berchard and Guthred in anxious conversation. The two were peering at the horizon.

"No," said Guthred. "That's where she would rise."

"But we have another night!" said Berchard.

Durand levered himself onto one elbow. Other bodies around the ring were rising from the grass.

Deorwen spoke for them all. "What is the matter?"

"The Lambing Moon's gone," said Berchard. "It's calends *now*. This is the night with no moon."

A few of the men around the ring swore. You didn't camp between the moons.

"And we're about to lose the last of the light," Guthred added. "And here we are bedded down on a riverbank."

The threat was real. On calends night, after one moon and before the next, the Banished were restless. The Daughters of the Hag poked their noses into cradles. Things lurked under blackthorn bushes. Washers lingered by the river.

"We set watchers through those nights," said Deorwen. "The Burrstones lit hag fires. We will have to get everyone under shelter."

"Wait!" said Lamoric. "If this is calends, the moon will rise tomorrow! We have leagues to travel yet. We cannot go scuttling under cover now. Why not get back on the river?"

Coensar spoke out, soberly. "There was a sanctuary tower up the hill, if there's a sexton still about, we should get in."

"I'm willing to find a way in, with or without a sexton," said Badan.

"They will sight the Sowing Moon tomorrow," Lamoric declared. "We must be in Eldinor at dawn the day after. There's no time. We've no chance at all if we don't reach the Mount of Eagles by then."

The men were eyeing the darkness, imagining it populated with slinking things. "Lordship," said Coensar, "we're losing the light."

"All right," said Lamoric. "All right."

They left the boat behind and darted for the hilltop sanctuary, stumbling through black hedgerows and rutted tracks. The small priest who appeared at the sanctuary door darted back in horror as a company of armed men stepped out of the night. He did, however, allow them inside. With a wary glance, the sexton closed the door on them and the sanctuary, allowing them only one smoky lamp—a dozen men in the wobbling pool of one little flame.

As the men sprawled on flagstones as cold as winter graves, Lamoric paced in and out of the darkness.

"The king will understand," Deorwen tried.

Lamoric did not even glance up. "I ought to have told my brother to take the message himself. It seems I am doomed to be an object lesson to the kingdom. Mothers will point at my tarred skull: see, children, how vanity and pride drew Sir Lamoric from the safety of his millstones to his shameful end."

"We could go no farther," said Deorwen. "The day was done."

"Perhaps there will be a little pageant." Lamoric clawed his hair. "They could work in my 'Knight in Red' business. I think I would like that."

"Sit, Lamoric," she said. "Rest while you have the chance."

"Sorry to have made you wait, Majesty," continued Lamoric. "But I have a few excellent notions about how you should king it here in Errest. I think you'll find it's just a few simple blunders you're making. I've got a list."

"Don't worry, Lordship. We will get you to Eldinor in time, you watch us," said Ouen. "Come dawn we'll really put our backs in. I'm not sure Badan's quite been pulling his weight yet." Badan cursed the big man, showing the black gap of his missing teeth.

Lamoric crouched by the flame. "Birds will pick out my eyes."

"We'll set out again as soon as there is light," said Deorwen, "and we'll row straight through to the docks at Eldinor. That is what these men are saying, husband." She reached for him, but he stood and paced again.

Shaking heads, the rest subsided in the dark, the smoky lamplight picking out the shape of sanctuary idols standing round them: the Maiden, the Mother, the Warders of the Bright Gates where they bracketed the door, the Silent King of Heaven, the Champion with his empty helm. The flicker set shadows quivering in their blank-eyed stares.

Durand watched the others: Coensar gave him a quiet nod; Lamoric was restless; other men eyed the idols—Deorwen watching them all.

Watching him.

Soon the lamp gave out and exhaustion took the men.

Sounds reached Durand's ears from beyond the shutters: feathery rustlings that might only have been night birds, whispers that might only have been willows. He remembered the various fanged and black-eyed things he'd seen. The others breathed invisibly all around him in the utter darkness.

A hand touched his shoulder. But, after a prickling instant, he knew the touch for Deorwen's. And she had curled on the cold flagstones at his back before he could move or speak, knees folded with his knees. She clung, her small arms clutching him, and she breathed sobs of frustration against his shoulder. Anyone might be awake. With so many ears so near, he could not so much as whisper his understanding.

Still, he caught her hands and squeezed as though he could crush the wall between them.

DURAND WOKE ALONE on that stone floor, friends within inches, and Deorwen watching him across the circle of men.

Shaken, he was glad to join the others, as, from dawn, they rowed like the slaves of the Inner Seas, finding within a few strokes an iron rhythm that did a fine job of pounding thought from Durand's skull. One hamlet ran into the next, the berms and hedges of one village knotting with those of its neighbor. They rowed as the Eye of Heaven rose to noontide and rowed as it blazed low among the chalk hills of Saerdana. The black glass of the river slithered with sunset, and soon the moon must rise.

The men stole glances eastward, searching for the first sliver of the Sowing Moon hooking from the hedges. Finally, the *Bittern* and the eastern horizon, the moon's slender crescent, winked over the shoulder of some shore-baron's tower.

"That's it," said Odemar. "Maybe, Captain, you can get your men back to rowing. It's leagues yet to Eldinor, and not so many hours from dawn."

As Coensar nodded to them all, a fire blazed out over the water. A bonfire as big as a hay wagon roared atop the shore tower they had just left behind.

Lamoric rose from his bench, catching the mainstay for balance. Durand flinched, just seeing the man.

"The beacon fires," Lamoric said. "You can see them up and down the river. That Osbald will be lighting Burrstone Walls. What a sight the Powers must have: the whole of Errest the Old crowned with fire."

The light glowed in Lamoric's face, and glittered in Deorwen's eyes as she stared down the boat at him—desperate.

"Row," said Coensar. "Or none of it matters."

Durand squeezed his eyes shut and rowed.

FOR HOURS AFTER nightfall, it seemed as though they rowed through the Heavens, bare stars glittering in the sky above and the black river below. Their wake set the sky shivering to its banks.

Through the haze of exhaustion, great black buildings appeared along the banks. Once in a great while, Durand saw a window glowing. He heard men and animals alive between wooden walls: dogs barked, babies wailed. A door thumped as someone stumbled out to find the latrine trench.

"We must be getting close," Ouen whispered. The sliver moon barely glinted in the man's teeth. "We could be sloshing past the bugger now, for all we know. Mount of Eagles. The King's Walk. The High Patriarch's whatever he has. Maybe that's Ragnal himself, pissing in that ditch back there. We might be rowing right out to sea. Imagine: past Eldinor, past old Tern Gyre, past the Barbican and out on the wide ocean with nothing but the Shattered Isle somewhere there before us, eh?"

"Would we use the sail then?" Durand wondered.

"I've got used to the rowing, me."

"Hells," spat Badan. "Bad enough rowing all bloody night. You don't know how far we've come any more than I do."

From the high stern of the boat, Odemar interrupted,

croaking, "I haven't been up this way as often as some, but I'd say pull harder."

"Do as the man says, gentlemen," said Coensar, and they did.

TOWARD MORNING, FOG boiled over the bows. Durand and the others kept up their rowing, but the long sweeps clunked and rocked, heavier and heavier with each stroke.

Somewhere some monastery bell tolled First Twilight. If the city wasn't near now, they would arrive too late.

"Come on, boys," said Ouen and, with a haul, nearly lifted the *Bittern* from the river. Durand heaved, feeling the collective strength of the crew drive the boat downriver, picking up speed.

And suddenly—as if by sorcery—they were passing under a bridge, Creation alive with watery echoes. Soon buildings pressed close along the banks—warehouses, mills, tanneries—water echoed from stone and hairy plaster.

"This'll be one of the spans between Scrivensands and Turnstone Moss," said Lamoric, again out of his seat. "We're right across the gulf from the Island of Eldinor." They heard people already awake in the wooden buildings over the Red Winding. There was light glowing in the eastern fog.

Soon, they felt the *Bittern* buck in the collision of currents on the broad face of the Gulf of Eldinor. Ships slept in the mist: dromond warships of a hundred oarsmen, merchantman cogs as tall as towers. Wooden walls rose up and vanished.

It was strange backing into a new place, as you must when rowing. Durand imagined the hidden city over his shoulder. For the first fifteen generations of their rule, the Sons of Atthi had governed their High Kingdom from this island, striking bargains with wild chieftains, conquering the powers of the forest wastes, and forging covenants with Stranger kings. In the days of her glory, wealth poured through the treasure houses of Eldinor's openhanded kings and Eldinor stood like a diadem on the brow of Creation. Now, hundreds of hard winters had passed. The Sons of Heshtar had twice raged over Creation, the heart of the Atthias had gone to Parthanor, so-called Jewel of the Winter Sea, and the High Kingdom had broken.

Forty generations lay in the earth, and Eldinor was a widow city of a lost kingdom.

Durand twisted. In the bows, Deorwen peered up among the vast shapes around them. And Durand managed to follow her eye. Towers shimmered into being from the mist like frost knitting in the clouds, city upon city rising into the air. He had never been to Parthanor the Jewel, but he could not imagine a place to surpass dowager Eldinor. Here were crown upon mitered crown, shining on the cusp of dawn.

Something loomed from the fog.

"You'd best wake up, all of you," said Odemar. He was working the tiller. "I've seen men hurt."

Granite wharves seemed to reach for them, each under a blank-eyed idol.

Lamoric climbed to his feet.

"Mind me!" said Odemar, snapping every man's attention back to him. They were coming in very fast and pulling hard. The *Bittern* shuddered into the slick shelter of the ancient quay. "All hands, hold water!" The oarsmen jammed their oars flat against a hundred leagues' momentum. The grip of water wrenched Durand's hard against his ribs, nearly hoisting him from his bench.

"Toss oars!" Odemar snarled, and the men heaved blades from the water, Lamoric already leaping as the boat skidded home.

A trio of tall men stalked up the wharf as men handed Deorwen down. Ouen had the gangplank ready and bowed to Durand. "After you, my rescuer."

Durand smiled and stepped onto the pier as Coensar climbed onto the plank.

"Milord, Milady," said one of three strangers. The speaker was a head taller than Durand—more. But the shoulders under his black cassock were hardly wider than a man's spread fingers. His long skull sported a very few hanks of blond hair. "No. No one ashore. Not now." Each of the armored giants behind him wore a masked and polished helm, and carried both an ornate broadaxe and a long, teardrop shield. Durand had never seen city watchmen like these.

"We've been ordered to attend the king," said Lamoric.

"Yes? Have you? And you are?"

"I am Lord Lamoric, son of Duke Abravanal of Gireth."

Now the strange figure nodded from somewhere between his shoulder blades. "Of Burrstone Walls. Second son of the duke by his late wife Truda. One of three surviving. This would be your wife, Deorwen, daughter of Duke Severin of Mornaway by—"

"It is beginning!" Lamoric said.

"And you must go, by all means." A wan smile flickered. "But we are not having armed retinues in Eldinor. No. Not today."

Durand took a deep breath. There was no time for argument. He would climb back in the boat.

"No no," said the official, now nearly leering into Durand's face. "No, indeed. *You* may come. Yes. Certainly *you* may come. But three is a sufficiency, I think."

Durand glanced, and saw Coensar still poised upon the gangplank, his eyes dark.

"I will give you all a bit of parchment with my seal upon it," said the official. From the man's neck dangled a large ring seal, with an angular hawk or eagle upon it. "I would suggest that you leave your belongings to avoid time-consuming inspections and seals for your goods."

While the dockmaster bowed the gray avenues gaped behind him, half of Lamoric's men were on the point of defying the man.

"The Eye of Heaven will rise in moments, gentlemen," said Lamoric. "I will ask Coensar to get you all to an inn, and leave a message at the docks so that I may find you. If I don't . . ." He stroked his throat, and winced a grin. "Check the pikes around and about. You may see my head grinning down. We're off."

The captain's mouth tightened, but then he nodded and stepped down into the *Bittern*. There was nothing for it.

With an apologetic shrug, Durand set off alone with Deorwen and Lamoric.

9. In the Hall of Eagles

They climbed empty avenues lined with sanctuaries and hollow mansions. Shabby wooden constructions leaned against the ruined glory of their neighbors, and sometimes the rubble walls of meager dwellings sported stolen masonry. Lamoric had Deorwen's hand. She glanced at Durand.

"We will have no time to change our surcoats," Lamoric announced. "Secondhand rags in the Hall of the Voyager King! Though it may do us some good. What will I say to the man? You would think something would come to me. A great deal will depend on the man's mood. Here we are, threadbare and exhausted. Red-eyed and pale with fatigue. His Majesty may assume Gireth's come upon hard times. Perhaps there will be pity!"

Idols grinned down from every corner, watching each twilit crossroads. Banners had been mounted to every house, blue and gold for Errest's king. High above, the sky seemed ready to burst with light.

"We must run," said Lamoric.

But then the bells tolled.

From every sanctuary tower in the aged city, bronze notes jarred the Heavens and mortar trickled from high places. In the streets it was still twilight, but beyond the marble walls and spires, the Eye of Heaven must have returned to Creation.

Lamoric stopped, spinning and staring heavenward, lost for a long moment in the cacophony. There was a good heartbeat of honest despair in Lamoric's features—Durand felt like a murderer—and then Lamoric tried to smile.

"Well," he said, "I suppose that is—"

But at that moment, a sudden change came over the old city. A great wind bowled down the street, lashing heavy banners. Durand caught his cloak before the gust could snatch it from his shoulders. The sky dimmed, and thunder boomed in the north.

"This is no natural storm, husband," said Deorwen. "We should find cover."

"How far can the palace be?" demanded Lamoric, but lightning cracked the Heavens. They could hear dogs barking and asses braying behind the doors of the city.

Durand spread his hands. "Quickly, then."

They jogged up avenues and alleys. Faces peered at the storm from shuttered windows.

Finally, they darted through a gap between mansions, and stumbled into the great courtyard called the King's Walk that stretched between the soaring high sanctuary of Eldinor and the Mount of Eagles. Here, armies had mustered in the High Kingdom days.

Deorwen was looking at the clouds. "Husband, there is something very wrong." Heaven twitched in a thousand shades of bruising. Durand remembered the rings he had seen over Yrlac when the river hag broke free. The ranked towers of Saerdan's Mount of Eagles and the spires of the high sanctuary shuddered in the strange light. "You must hear me. This is no natural storm. There is a warning in it."

Before the gates, three thousand beggars waited for the handouts likely to accompany a royal celebration.

"I *must* press on," said Lamoric. "Every instant compounds my folly. His Majesty will think my father's turned his back on the crown. A simple errand, and I could bring the Host of Errest down on the old man's head. I must get in there."

Durand grimaced. They would have to pass every beggar within fifty leagues. There was only one gate. "We'll have a hard job getting through."

"And worse convincing the gatekeepers to let us in, dressed in these rags. Host of Heaven! We'll be fighting for leftovers when the feasting's finished," Lamoric said. Durand set his teeth. Lamoric did not deserve to be made a fool.

But then a roar arose in the old courtyard.

Durand joined the others, staring in astonishment. It was rain, falling like a battalion of cavalry. It rebounded from the courtyard's white cobbles—bouncing—and in moments the whole city was rattling, full of ice and sliding roof tiles. The crowds scattered.

"Hail," said Deorwen.

"Here's your sign, Deorwen," said Lamoric.

They chased him across the empty square for the gates.

A MAN WITH a face like two jet buttons and a blob of dough led them through the passageways of the rambling Mount of Eagles as the storm clattered above.

"Come. Yes. Things are under way. Under way. We are busy here. It is only the Mount of *Eagles*." The man waddled, his breath steaming. His bare head seemed to roll around the collar of a cassock. Durand noticed inky blotches.

"Can you tell me of His Majesty's mood?" said Lamoric.

The little man flapped his hands. "Late. No help for it. Still. A shame. You will wear these clothes?"

They crossed a courtyard of hog-backed cobbles that ran with ice water. Durand listened for the hubbub of feasting, on edge at the idea of standing up in front of the throne, but was distracted when a flock of black-clad functionaries darted across the other end of the yard. Had he startled them?

Their guide led them deeper.

"What about the king?" pressed Lamoric. "There must have been receptions leading to this one. He will have enjoyed greeting—"

"You might have borrowed a servant's spares but for the time," the man grunted. "A shame. A grand design marred."

Lamoric was about to press further, but Deorwen spoke. "I am sure it is a great effort to plan such an event."

The little man fluttered around, stirring the reek of sour bacon in his black garb. "Master of Tapers, am I."

Lamoric's mouth opened. "They sent the Master of Tapers to greet the emissary of Duke—"

"I suppose it is a very great responsibility," Deorwen said.

The Master of Tapers bobbed his head. "Not one building, the Mount of Eagles. No. Hundreds. Streets. Alleys. The High Kings, they needed halls for herd-feeding; cookhouses, steam and cauldrons; storehouses; barracks for guards and their iron pots; rooms for the shining winking things; dovecotes crammed with pigeons; armories heaped with bladed things; cesspits for a thousand bowels; cellars; and narrow rooms for those who've done wrong. Yes."

"It seems a very great place indeed. Is it very far to the oathtaking then?"

Sometimes a passage opened on the rude flank of some stronghold now smothered in palace corridors, sometimes a grand presence chamber sat under dust.

But at the end of every passage, there seemed to be a flock of the king's black functionaries. The first group they passed were sitting, the next were on their feet, and the next were on the move. Like so many starlings, these black creatures darted off each time Durand caught a glimpse. The castle was thick with them, and something had stirred the creatures up.

And the storm mumbled beyond the old roofs.

"And I must watch that grease is rendered and wicks dipped," said the little man, "and each must find the court where it squats by nightfall. Thousands they need." He grinned. "Hot work."

"But still," said Deorwen, "it must be done, I suspect." She glanced Durand's way. "All of these halls must have light. Is the Hall of Kings near? You must take many candles there."

"A great many. But there are pleasures to be had in the rendering. Cheerful things." He bared a row of yellow teeth, and snuffled noisily at the air. "Though the children hate it. Hot work, poor sweeties."

"How will I approach him?" Lamoric said. "There will be Ragnal on the Hazelwood Throne and kinsmen of every duke in Errest the Old, all kneeling before him. I will give my father's oath." He scratched his neck. "Perhaps I can bring up the rest of it later on. Not before everyone. There will be other chances. A man must ask the king's leave even to depart. Hells. My heart's in my mouth. I'd rather play with lances."

Sandals and whispers rushed along before them like a bow wave of dry leaves. But Lamoric was already before the throne in his mind, imagining the throngs of noblemen and servants.

Durand heard only starlings and thunder.

"Near now," said Tapers. "Very near."

The corridors narrowed, cold as mountains. Now, they were in Saerdan Voyager's footsteps. But Durand heard the rattle of soldiers on the move—shields and axes on armored backs. Thunder growled.

And Tapers led them into an aisle of statues: men made giants; Powers made stone.

"Here!" said the little man as he rounded a last idol's knee. The parade of kings and idols had become the doorposts of a great brass portal. This was Saerdan's ancient fortress, trapped in palaces. "Beyond is the Hall of the Kings," said their guide.

And there, as they turned the corner, huddled Heremund the Skald.

The tiny, rumpled man stood against the gleaming vastness of the doors, slack-jawed and staring. Here was Durand's comrade of the autumn—bowlegs, gap-teeth, saddle nose, shapeless hat and all. He huddled by another of Ragnal's functionaries. Dark reflections of the pair quivered in brass above and marble below.

The skald gaped. "*You* can't be *here*!"

"I assure you—" began a consternated Master of Tapers.

There was a commotion behind the great doors. It sounded more like a riot than a feast. A table scraped on stone.

"No. Not here," Heremund's companion stammered. An epic paunch had this man's cassock short in front and long behind. "Uh. You're what? The chandler?"

Their guide flinched. "Master of—"

"—Ah, Tapers, aye. Uh, no. You'd have had no way of knowing. Who would think to tell you?" After a moment's hesitation, the man smiled. "I'll have to take them now. There's nothing for it."

Someone roared beyond the doors.

"I don't—" began the Master of Tapers.

The new starling shook his jowled head. "No reason you should, friend. They are mine to deal with now."

Heremund got his hand on Lamoric's arm. "We must be off," he whispered. "There's no time." In a moment, they'd put three corners between themselves and the astonished Master of Tapers. The bulky new starling yanked open a door, and they all darted inside. Deorwen stepped in ahead of Durand, and Heremund's friend slammed the door just as Durand realized they'd stepped into some black cupboard or closet.

Deorwen must have turned. Her breath feathered his neck, her chest rose and fell against his tunic. He wished he'd had a chance—any chance—to speak with her. The door shook against his back with the sound of footfalls—full of muscle and armor. He remembered the whetted curve of the guardsmen's broadaxes.

The rumble ebbed away, and the stranger's voice breathed into the narrow space. "Heremund, you've killed me. Host of Heaven. My heart's pounding fit to burst."

Durand could find no air. Deorwen moved. Her hand slipped into his, gripping hard.

"What is all this about?" demanded Lamoric. "I'm meant to be carrying my father's oath to Ragnal."

"Is there a way out of here, Hod?" said Heremund. "Any way these buggers won't be watching?"

"It is too much," the stranger answered. "That pig-boiling goblin back there might have known my face. I'll end my days guttering on a candle-spike."

"You underrate yourself, Hod. They'll make more than one candle from a man your size. Don't—"

There was a furious and invisible struggle that jostled Deorwen hard against Durand. He felt a thigh, the curve of her ribs—

"Heremund," Durand snarled, "on my oath . . ."

"I'm opening the door," said Hod. "Heaven help me, but be careful, all of you."

Deorwen's hand slipped from Durand's, and the door opened.

They stumbled into the passageway and everyone jogged after Hod. Durand took a moment to shake his head. Hod stumped down a rabbit's warren of stairs and passages.

"It's Ragnal," Heremund said, explaining.

"It's not," said Hod.

"He's thrown everyone in bloody prison," Heremund said.

"He hasn't!"

"Heremund!" Lamoric said. "I have a duty back there. What is going on?"

"They're hostages," Heremund explained. "All of them! I suppose he had to do something after the Great Council last year."

Hod shook his head. "They've been nattering at him. 'The only certainty is blood.' Nattering in his ear all the moons of wintertide. Drip, drip, drip the poison goes."

They trotted into a black passageway lit by crabbed fans of light from its arrow loops.

"Oaths weren't enough for him," said Heremund, "so he seized every man and woman the barons sent. Sons. Heirs. The Duke of Garelyn came himself!"

Abruptly Hod shot his arms across the passageway, barring all progress. Heremund made to open his mouth, but was wrapped in smothering hands before he could make a sound.

"We must stop here a moment, and then proceed with care," Hod whispered. "I will go first. You all will follow—after an interval. Move quickly and quietly. Follow too quickly and they will have little doubt what's happening. And try to look as if you know what you're about.

"Certain death." He raised a thick finger to his lips, then disappeared around the next corner.

Heremund turned to the three who remained, whispering, "He's seized them all! There's been no oathtaking. Armed men at the doors, and they the sons of great men. I don't think his knights liked the plan. It was mostly these commoner sergeants. There was Ragnal on the Hazelwood Throne with the planks of Atthi's coffer under his damnable backside. He'll win no friends with this."

"Was everyone there, skald?" said Lamoric.

A scuff from somewhere in the passageway behind them made Durand turn and he stepped to get Deorwen behind him. He heard the rattle of mail and took a stride away from the others, making ready to draw his blade. It would be treason. You could not strike the king's men down.

"Durand," said Lamoric, "I'd back you against half the knights in Errest, but you're no use against fifty. We'll have to follow this Hod, no matter how long it's been."

As the voices closed in, everyone gave their nod—Heremund last—and the party strode around the corner.

And into a crowded room. There were tables and horn lamps. Black-cassocked scribes sat at parchments, penknife and quill in stained fingers. Every face turned their way, cocked like mooncalves' at their arrival. Eyes glittered. Many mouths looked full of ink, blotted black.

Heremund thrust his chin into the air and bandied down the long aisle between the scribs' tables. "I have strummed for many a feast," he chatted. "But we'll need all our players now. The rebec. The viol. The harp and the fipple flute." The others followed on his heels. But many of the scribes got to their feet, baring all their teeth in sly leers. "Is there one of you who plays the tabor pipe, did you say?" By the time the party had crossed the scriptorium, the room was full of rustling parchment and sandals.

The devils were following.

On the far side, Hod met their party in a doorway. Durand reckoned they had moments.

"I did not expect you so soon," Hod said. His voice was still.

"There was naught else to do," Heremund said.

Hod shut his eyes and nodded deeply. "It doesn't matter now. There are bedchambers in this tower. Princes', till they grew up. This way's down." He raised a clay lamp, and spoke to Heremund. "Tell the big brute to shut the door behind you."

Durand closed the door.

Down a low and narrow stair they crept, Durand bent between the walls as he chased the silhouettes of the others down.

"Hod, where've you taken us?" whispered Heremund.

"A bolt-hole, in case the Mount of Eagles was ever taken. A few of the king's retainers could bundle the monarch out while the rest fought from the towers."

"We're nowhere near the walls yet."

"Ah. But that was once-upon-a-time, Heremund. The Mount is riddled with bolt-holes now. Most were swallowed up as the High Kings heaped masonry on the Mount in the days before Parthanor." He brushed a wall, and a blanket of dust detached itself to tumble over him. "Hells. How am I to explain that I am covered in dust?"

"These men, these clerks . . ." Lamoric ventured.

Heremund spoke. "Hod. You might as well give him your speech."

The jowled head turned a moment. "Venal, dangerous men. Flatterers. Most are newcomers since His Highness was crowned; some I've known for years. But it could not matter less. They are changed, and none can be trusted any longer."

"How have you managed to keep clear of it?" asked Lamoric.

"Oh, I've been a wise man. Wise enough to bite my tongue, no matter what I've seen."

Lamoric blinked. "Surely your duty to—"

"Ah, Your Lordship, but that is the first part of my wisdom. Duty, conscience, honor—all of it, I have cast away. I have watched fierce men steeped in wisdom stand before the king only to be grinned at by these toadies—the rage of great men sweetly tolerated like the shrieking of infant children. But, afterward, they are never heard of again.

"To remain myself and alive, I have made myself perfectly ineffectual. A serpent envies my spine for suppleness; I carry worthlessness as my shield. There is no force so weak that I cannot submit to its might."

"What becomes of them, Master Hod?" Deorwen asked.

"I do not know, but soon enough they are grinning along with the others. One turns to an old friend and there he stands, smiling as though at an idiot child."

"Anyone would be fearful," asserted Deorwen.

"You are kind to say it, Milady," Hod replied.

"He's hazarded a great deal, talking to me," said Heremund. "There're strange things going on in the Mount of Eagles, and news must get to them who might talk with our Ragnal. I never thought to see this hostage business, mind. I reckon the rebellion's unhinged him."

"Slanders!" said Hod.

"What will his allies do?" asked Lamoric. "Host of Heaven, there will be blood spilt in the land when the rest hear. My father must have word of this as soon as it can reach him. He must call the host from their manors. Some of the seed grain should be kept in store against wartime."

Lamoric stopped on the stairs. "What will Ragnal do when he has no hostage from Gireth? I will have provoked the king against my father, my brother. My house holds

Gireth from Saerdan himself." His mouth opened and closed. "I must go back."

"That's mad, Lordship," said Heremund.

"Skald, great men of my line have given their bodies to preserve the throne of Errest for two thousand years. Will *I* be the one to dishonor them?"

Hod climbed back to Lamoric, raising his lamp and peering close in the young lord's eye. "*Let* these toadies trap you here. Let your father swallow the humiliation of seeing his own son shackled to keep him honest and stomach the shame of his king's mistrust. *Do* what these creatures wish. *See* what your father does then." The man's face was hard and yellow in the oily light.

Deorwen clasped her shoulders. "Was every duchy represented at this oathtaking?"

"I don't think so," said Hod. "No. There was no one from Yrlac."

"Of course," said Lamoric.

"Gireth was absent. Mornaway," finished Hod.

"I must warn my father," said Lamoric. "He'll need a word with Mornaway. There may be some way they can set this right. The king cannot be at war with his Great Council."

"Let's start by getting you out of this place," said Heremund.

Lamoric allowed himself to be led.

On they walked, following Hod. He opened a door seamed with daylight and they climbed scabbed stairs under the churning storm. They threaded dusty passages hidden in the thickness of a great tower's wall. They crept along minstrels' galleries in the rafters high above a feasting hall where starlings whispered in circles.

As they returned once more to the darkest bowels of the palace, Deorwen spoke. "Master Hod, how can you know so many secret ways? I do not think there has been so much as one wrong turning."

Hod saluted her with a wry wave of his lamp. "My Lady, I was tutor once to the Princes Biedin, Eodan, and Ragnal—and such other young ones as were packed off to court by the great houses of the realm. And so it was my duty, from time to time, to travel these paths searching for my enchanting little charges. I nearly lost my head over Biedin. This is the very lamp with which I searched." He lifted the clay dish and its wavering flame.

"He was the prince who vanished," Deorwen remembered.

"A little adventure that may well be our salvation, My Lady," said Hod. He shook his head. "It is a shame to see the sons of Carlomund at odds. Eodan will not come to court at all; Ragnal sneers at the man, remarking on how their father died in Eodan's lands. And Eodan is too proud to hold his tongue around his brother. Biedin tries to help, I think: he has ridden three times to Windhover since the Blood Moon. But reconciling Eodan and Ragnal is an impossible task. Eodan would not even come to the Tern Gyre council. It is said that a great man's children learn jealousy at their mother's breast.

"Here," said Hod. He bowed, wearing a wistful grin. "Beyond this point, I am as useless to you as I am to my king. Get yourselves free of this place."

There was nothing but a wall of broken stone before them. The ceiling had collapsed, and there was no sign of daylight. "Hod?" said Heremund.

"Unless you are willing to hop from the curtain wall—and I would not permit you to so mistreat a lady—there is no better way to fly from the Mount of Eagles than this little hole. Biedin was always the most restive and after his mother died, he was always moving. We searched everywhere. I even had the Master of Hounds loose in the rafters with his dogs. But this spot I never found."

The group peered at the rubble.

"I believe there is an aperture here." Hod raised his lamp until one black cavity stood out from the stones. "The prince appeared in the high sanctuary three days after he vanished, you see. He never passed the gates." He pointed at the black gap. "By my reckoning, the high sanctuary is five hundred paces in that direction." He spread his hands on his stomach. The gap was hardly more than a foot across. "But I have never tested my theory."

Heremund nodded, scrambling up the rubble. He held his hand out for the lamp, and then peered into the black. "Hod! Did you think you were rescuing weasels?"

"It lets onto some vestige of an antique sewer, or a passage for the Patriarchs to the king. I found black threads among those stones. The boy wore a black tunic after his mother passed. He got through."

Nodding, they climbed the stones, Durand's heart pounding as he saw just how narrow the opening was. It was clear that they must get Lamoric and Deorwen free of this place. The black socket exhaled a steady, cool current of air.

"I will go first," Durand said, mastering himself. It would be like climbing into a pot.

But there was a hesitation behind him. Hod stared up from the floor.

"Come with us," Heremund said. "Try."

Hod did not reply for a time. "I stole a bundle of rushlights." The things were a peasant's candle: skinned rushes dipped in grease. "I hope your Master of Tapers won't miss them." He lit one and passed the rest to Deorwen. "I will be interested to hear if I was correct after all about little Biedin." The tiny flames fluttered. "Soon, those fiends will realize what has happened. They will be combing the streets for you. There will be men at the docks.

"Help my king," he said, and left them.

Heremund grimaced at the others where they clung around the tunnel mouth—the lamplight dwindled and disappeared. "I met him when I sang for the princes' father. All the clerks in the scriptorium, the scene before the Hall of Kings: the starlings would know what Hod did.

"Hod's a lovely man," he said. "They will kill him for this." Hod's lamp vanished from sight, and no one said a word.

❧ 10. The Dust of Princes Lost

The collapsed section was little more than fifty feet long, and Durand writhed the whole way with the brittle, greasy rushlight spitting in his fingertips, cursing the madness of it all. They had rowed across the whole of Errest, and for what? Ragnal had gone mad. The Mount of Eagles was full of whispers, and they were crawling like vermin in the cellars.

Finally free, Durand slithered down a rubble slope and crouched in an empty tunnel. The rushlight's flame lit a dozen paces and left a juddering void before him.

"Wonderful," he said. Somewhere above were the cracked-tooth cobbles of the High King's Walk. He already knew that the ceiling could fall in.

The others slithered down to join him. Deorwen had a streak of dirt across her nose.

"Hells," said Lamoric, "I hope there's another end to this tunnel. If we've got to turn back, you can bury me here."

Durand smiled. "How many rushlights have we got?" he teased gently, lifting his. It was already half-burned.

"You have sworn to be my loyal man, Durand," said Lamoric. "I remember it distinctly. You were kneeling in the muck. Folk were laughing."

Durand nodded.

"I do not like this place," said Deorwen. "We shouldn't waste time."

All but Durand could walk without stooping. On the walls, there was no sign of the crusting you might expect from a sewer.

"I don't see why Ragnal would take hostages from loyal houses," said Lamoric. "Mornaway and Garelyn would never have rebelled."

"Ah," said Heremund. "Equality. Everyone the same."

Lamoric's fist thumped the wall. "He will drive every fence-sitting duchy into Yrlac's camp."

"Such grudging loyalty as they showed? It ain't far from treason. What're their oaths worth in a pinch? You're better off with their kin in your tower. When it's kin against a man's word, blood's more certain than breath. That's the idea."

A door blocked the passage. Durand squinted at long cracks that jagged across the ceiling stones. He winced at the constant spit of the rushlight. The door stood, stuck shut and subtly twisted, under the weight of the stone above. As he moved closer, his little flame fluttered at a gap too narrow for even Deorwen. A glance showed him the ceiling full of cracks—precarious—with the door maybe serving to prop the load.

Durand raised his hand before the others. "Stand back."

"Maybe we should try our luck with the guards. If we find the right man, we could walk out the gates," said Lamoric.

"If there were such a man, Master Hod would have introduced us, I think," Durand concluded. They had cost Hod his life. "We must get as far as we can before they know we've gone." He would kick high where the door was caught against the jamb.

Heremund touched his shoulder. "If you're flattened under fifty cartloads of rock, I hope you won't mind if we try Lamoric's scheme."

Deorwen's eyes were very wide as Durand handed the rushlight to Heremund. He couldn't tell what she was thinking—just that there was desperation. The smudge was still there across her nose.

"A little more room first," Durand said.

The initial kick brought dust sifting down like snow. The second started a rain of sand pouring down Durand's neck.

The door gave way on the third kick, and the ceiling fell in as they ran through.

"Praise Heaven," said Durand as he counted three live people behind him.

THEY MOVED THROUGH a space lined with doorways and alcoves. The warmth of Heaven's Eye had never reached this place.

"I reckon these were cut in after," said Heremund, peering at the masonry. "Cells or cellars. Storerooms maybe."

"A long way to go for a cask of claret," said Lamoric, "though it's cold enough." They were too far under the ground, and the air was thin and dank.

"Durand, here," said Deorwen. On the floor, a collection of litter marked what must have been someone's campsite. "These are candle ends. This is no place to stop."

"Maybe it is only a storeroom after all," ventured Lamoric. "We know nothing else."

But their party was surrounded by cells, Durand was sure—places to put a man away so that he'd never be heard from again. There were no pretty carvings. Some spots had been rudely walled in.

He hoped Ragnal's whisperers would never hear of the place.

"In any case, let's hope the path goes straight on," Heremund grunted. "I wouldn't like to have to root through these holes."

FINALLY, A DOOR appeared: the passage's ending. This was no improvised addition to the tunnel. Sinuous lines adorned its marble surface: the Eye of Heaven blazed above a Creation full of elegant trees. A pair of idols flanked the door: the Warders of the Gates of far Heaven. In the stories, the Warders wore coats they'd improvised of iron nails. The carver had chiseled every one.

"Is there some magic formula we must say?" Lamoric wondered.

Durand raised his rushlight for the others to see, and they all came closer, Deorwen setting a hand on his arm.

"Perhaps there is, but I think there's a handle as well," said Heremund. "Just here." An elbow of copper jutted from a tear of green verdigris.

"Just as well," Lamoric decided.

"A little room again, I think," Durand said and took the handle, feeling big cogs turning under his fist. The door broke free. No light. With the rushlight high, he peered through the widening crack, not knowing what eyes might be on the other side.

And eyes there were: empty skulls stared back at him. Papery corpses. The room beyond was heaped with bones.

"What's wrong with you?" asked Heremund.

Sucking a breath through his nose, Durand said, "There's no one here. I can't see if there's a way through."

With no way around, he pushed straight in, climbing onto the sagging, crackling heap. Swimming, nearly, as dry things slid from their winding sheets and yellow grins rolled against his chin.

A plain bronze door beyond the ossuary opened at Durand's first touch. It might have been another panel in the walls. Durand summoned the rest on, and once free of the ossuary, the group stepped into a chamber of massive pillars where the air hung thick with beeswax and balsam.

Lamoric slapped dust from Deorwen's dress. "Perhaps we were better off to leave the courtly costumes home."

"All of those people. They were priests and rich men," Deorwen said. "I saw amulets." Tangled in neck bones and ribs. "There was a fat sapphire on one hand. I think the priests have been moving bones here from tombs and graves. If it is like most cities, there is no room to bury within the walls unless space is made."

"My skin's alive," said Lamoric. "Like the fleas are marching over me."

"This will be the crypt under the high sanctuary," Heremund said.

Durand saw a score of great sarcophagi within the range of their light, the first traces of a vast arc that must circle the whole of the high sanctuary, below the floor. You could wind a good horse, riding from side to side through the dark. Feet rested on hounds, eagles, and Powers. Royal feet.

Lamoric spun.

"This is where the new kings must keep their vigil, yes?"

"Aye," said Heremund, "I reckon so. 'Three days under stone,' they say before they'll crown 'em. It's here somewhere that a crown prince bides that time in darkness."

"They have all lain here. All the kings of twenty centuries," whispered Lamoric. "We should be struck dead for trespassing in this place. I am surprised that we have breathed this long."

"Ain't too late," said Heremund.

The floor was chased with sweeping symbols, arcs and rays of gold. The intersecting curves circled a shape cut at the chamber's heart: it could have been the shadow of a tall man upon the floor.

"There," Durand said, and all four refugees trailed across the honey-shining marble to find a rough silhouette of a man hacked in the floor: head, shoulders, and the long shape of the body. Durand's fingers tingled. He raised his light. The cist was deep, penetrating a fathom or more into the stone of the island.

Heremund raised an eyebrow. "It's here the Patriarchs lay the young prince down, droning their great thaumaturgies, filling the air with smoke and Powers. And finally leave him to darkness and dreams. Half of the old spell's carved in these stones."

Deorwen shuddered, and Lamoric puffed out his cheeks. "Days in the dark, starving with the kings and Patriarchs rustling in their tombs."

The tombs beyond were nearly invisible.

"There are stories of men consumed," said Heremund. "Men whose hearts couldn't take a long look from the Eye of Heaven."

"Who could? Who could stand it?" Deorwen said.

"A man must know his heart before the Patriarchs lower him down," said Heremund.

"I have heard that, afterward, the king dreams," said Deorwen. "He hears the whispers of his subjects."

"Well. He's knotted into the Ancient Patriarchs' old bindings, that's sure. I wouldn't be surprised if they creak a bit, those knots. They're surely pulled tight some days."

"I don't find myself pitying this king just now," said Durand. There was always a large entrance to an Atthian crypt, for the priests must be free to throw the place open at winter's ending—when Heaven's Eye wins its battle with the long nights of winter. "Here." Durand spotted the first broad steps of a processional stairs, and they moved off, finding a doorway. "What is our plan?"

"Hmm. A point," said Lamoric. "The sanctuary sits at the heart of Eldinor. We'll be free of the tunnel but trapped in the midst of the city. I suppose the Patriarch knows his flock, and there's a shrine on every corner."

The flame spat between them.

"Heremund," asked Deorwen, "did the Patriarch attend this hostage-taking?"

"He did, aye. I didn't see it all; the man was roaring."

"The king would never take the Patriarch hostage!" Lamoric declared.

DURAND EMERGED FROM the crypt right beside a small man in priest's robes. Durand got a glimpse of pale, bulging eyes above a cloud of copper beard before the man collapsed, overcome by the sight of filthy, ragged strangers erupting from the grave.

Deorwen crouched to check on the luckless priest—and, somehow, looking up at Durand, she saw something more.

"Durand, look up," she breathed.

As he looked into the vaults above, Creation spun. A field of gold leaf soared more than thirty fathoms above his head, light as silk banners. Powers gazed down. Pillars ringed the dome, sweeping higher than towers like loops of woven gold thrown to tether the vault to Creation.

They had come up in the golden heart of Eldinor, a pace or two before the high altar itself. They stared into acres of leaded glass and forests of pillars.

"Why does Creation seem larger when you throw a roof under it?" wondered Heremund.

The priest was shaking his head.

Deorwen set a hand on his arm. "I am sorry if we have startled you, but we would very much like to speak to the Patriarch."

The fellow leapt onto his bandy legs.

"You—Madam, who are you?" Eyes jutting, the red-bearded priest thrust the fist and fingers of the Eye of Heaven sign between himself and his sudden visitors. He circled as Deorwen rose.

"There was confusion at the palace this morning," said Lamoric. "I have to get home."

The priest stopped. "The oathtaking."

"It is very important," said Deorwen. "May we see the Patriarch?"

The priest cocked his head. "Madam, he has not yet—"

The sound of determined footfalls drew their attention. A sturdy-looking priest was jogging toward them. "Provost!" the priest called. "Thank the Powers I have found you. He is taken."

Their priest seemed to recover in an instant. "What do you mean 'taken'?"

"Provost, Patriarch Semborin is prisoner in the Mount of Eagles, hostage—against his will—in surety of our faithful conduct."

"By every Power of Hell, it's bloody sacrilege!" The man's voice returned from polished vaults, and the messenger raised his hands.

"Kinsmen of every duke but Mornaway, Yrlac, and Gireth have been locked in the towers. Ragnal was in the blackest rage."

The sinews of the provost's neck stood under his beard. "*Ragnal* was in a rage? By Heaven, we will send word to every king and Patriarch from this spot to the Yawning Gulf! With Semborin in chains, he will hear no more of justice or recovering the marches. He will demand that we carry our treasury to his strong rooms, but I'll see him stripped and begging forgiveness in the streets before he gets a clipped penny!"

"With respect, Provost, they will kill him."

"With respect?" the provost stood, crackling. "I will hear that from Ragnal's own lips," he concluded.

"Father, you are provost of the high sanctuary?" asked Lamoric.

The priest rounded on Lamoric. "Sir, you will explain how you've come to be climbing from the crypt of my sanctuary, and you'll do so before you dare draw another breath!"

"We are sorry to have startled you, Provost," said Deorwen. "This is Lamoric of Gireth, son of—"

"Gireth?" The man's eyes flashed. "And you have avoided Ragnal's hospitality thus far?" Smiling, the provost turned to the messenger. "Canon Gilmar, would King Ragnal free Patriarch Semborin for a duke's son?"

He had hardly said it before Durand had his fist on his blade.

The canon quavered, "Provost, I am not certain that these people are within our power to give."

"Provost," said Deorwen. "My husband is not the heir."

"Landast is the elder brother, yes." The provost nodded to himself. "And so there is no reason to deny His Majesty's wishes except spite."

"The king's men will be watching us, Provost," said Gilmar.

"Every man in cassock or cowl, I expect."

"He has Patriarch Semborin."

"Then you must begin by clearing our new friends from this very public place, I think. I find myself in a very spiteful temper just now."

PRIESTLY HANDS PROPELLED them into a tiny windowless room: the vestry. And the three were left to spend all the hours of daylight crowded under heaps of priests' finery. There was Durand crushed in with Deorwen but unable even to ask her what she had meant by that night in the riverbank sanctuary. All winter, Lamoric had been frantic, and the summer before he'd been playing the Red Knight. But he was not a bad man. He had a good heart. Without Durand playing wedge between them all winter, they might have come together. He stared at the two, wondering what would happen if he let them be. There was no way forward for him with Deorwen, and a wound didn't heal with the blade still in it. He had to go.

It seemed days later—darkness filling the ancient vastness of the high sanctuary—that Canon Gilmar's head appeared in the doorway.

"It is arranged," he said. "Come."

At a small door, the provost awaited them.

"Have you got a bit of meat pie or something?" asked Heremund.

The man scowled for an instant, then pressed on. "In my novice days, I studied at the monastery of the Warder's Gates off Farrier's Street. There was a window in the kitchen-house. The kitchen-house was built in the thickness of the ancient wall. The cooks tipped rubbish to the gulls. There will be a rowing boat waiting to carry you across the gulf to Scrivensands."

"Have the king's men abandoned their search?" asked Lamoric.

Gilmar laughed: a puff of breath. "No," said the provost. "There are watchmen and sergeants of the king's guard in every street."

"We must get out," said Lamoric.

"I have recruited watchmen of my own," said the provost. "You will find the first in a shop door by a burning candle. Each has his eyes on one street. You move when the watchman tells you the way is clear. Thus, you will pass from one watchman—one street—to the next until you reach that kitchen."

They would be the only strangers on the move in Eldinor, they knew no one, and a single broken link in the provost's chain would leave them stranded. This was too precarious to trust. "We should have gone in daylight with the crowds," said Durand.

The provost's lip twitched. "They stopped every soul abroad in the streets today. Everyone was questioned. They stood guards on the grand docks. Nothing bigger than a nut-shell's been allowed to set off since the dawn bells rang."

Deorwen nodded. "We don't know these people as well as you must. How will we be certain that none of your watch-men has been caught?"

The man grunted a laugh. "Or turned, eh? They will make the Eye of Heaven when you sight them, one finger bent. And they've been given a bit of the *Book of Moons* to quote you as you arrive. Each man has a line, and none should re-peat."

"Subtle are the priests of Atthia," said Heremund, quoting something clever, but the provost fixed the skald with a steady eye.

"If the enemies of Heaven delve deep, we must dig still deeper, skald. I will not put another life into the hands of this king's sycophants."

Heremund nodded a contrite bow.

The provost turned to his man, Gilmar, who put his eye to the crack at the sanctuary door.

"I see the candle," Gilmar replied. "He shows the Eye of Heaven."

"It is time," said the provost, and Durand felt his heart flinch.

Lamoric took the provost by his arm. "We will see this through yet. And I am grateful to the Powers that my poor hide was not fit to trade for a Patriarch's."

"The king'll choke on this," said the provost. "Go."

With that, they shot from the door, running toward the first candle and a green-kirtled woman in a shuttered cook-shop, sliding to a halt on her doorstep.

The woman's face was broad as a pan. "'Prince of Heaven am I,'" she began. "'Neverborn. Lord of Roads. Warder at Crossroads. The Longwalker, I am called, quoth he.' Come inside a moment, I can't see what Bacca's holding up. The priest's a fool doing this at curfew. Still, it couldn't be helped." Durand blinked at the fragment the woman quoted. She slipped a hand between Durand and Deorwen, squinting between them. There was a crowd in her doorway, and they were in sight of a broad swath of King's Walk.

"Madam," said Lamoric. "I thank you for your—"

"—There it is," she announced, brushing Lamoric aside. "Do you see him? Bacca? He's there past where there used to be a fountain. He's making the Eye. Poor souls. Not even a stitch of decent clothing."

There was, indeed, a small man twenty paces down Sanctuary Street.

Nodding thanks to the woman, they set off, running down the rutted cobbles. A burly man in a hairy surcoat met them.

"You must be Bacca—" Lamoric began.

"'My King, My Brother, I have watched as old spirits preyed on young. I have spent an age at your side, no help to give, too far to reach.' Lordship, Ladyship. Sir. Anno's at the end of Queen's Pell. That's him there, with the scar he got from the foundry. You can't see it from here, mind."

Lamoric glanced vaguely down a street thick with gloom and peat smoke, but each time these people opened their mouths, Durand heard the words of a dream. All this talk of crossroads.

"Wait, step in for a bit," said the man. "Anno's seeing something." Durand twisted to see the little figure dancing and waving his hands. He heard boots and armor between the walls.

Heremund tugged him inside the smoky darkness of the stranger's front room, giving him a good hard look. Durand's head was still spinning. He found himself gazing at the stranger's silhouette as though he might utter prophecies next. What light there was came from a lidded hearth.

After a long spell in silence, the man, Bacca, put his nose out the door, and they were off again.

"'You need not cast me out,'" proclaimed the next man, "'for I cannot remain so far from their need.'" These words pitched Durand's mind back to a well in his father's mountain stronghold. He remembered a figure as large as giants made from scraps of rope and shoeing nails.

The instant the man freed them, Durand reeled ahead, weaving down a foul and dripping alley under the privies of a row of houses to a mouselike woman who peered around her door. She stood no higher than Durand's belt.

" 'I must walk their long roads. I must wait for them at the crossing places, and offer counsel to the lost.' "

"Madam, we are grateful," said Lamoric.

The woman confessed that she could never turn strangers away, and gestured. Above her house was a shrine cut from a high corner. A ragged wooden figure under a wide-brimmed hat looked over them. Someone had a lamp burning there, and Durand stepped right into the lane. In the idol's hand was a knobbed staff.

The Traveler. He could almost see the pennies glinting in its eyes.

Durand gaped at the omen. A lifetime and two hundred leagues from his father's hall, this provost had chosen the words spoken to him by the Traveler when they stood together at the bottom of the well at Col.

Abruptly Lamoric was at his ear. "By the Heavens." There was exasperation in his voice, and he tugged Durand into motion once more.

They darted and they hid. They ran along one alley and plunged down a troughed staircase called the Hundred Steps. They passed a sanctuary dedicated to the Nine Sleepers, whose facade glowed with alabaster children, polished by the hands of the bereaved.

"I don't remember it taking this long," said Lamoric. "We must be circling the city." Besides a splinter moon, the only lights burned in shrines and the high windows of the palace above. Down they went. Durand could not help but eye the towered Mount of Eagles as they ran around its knees.

Soon, the reek of muck and seaweed mingled with the peat smoke of the heights.

"We cannot be far," said Lamoric.

Finally, they were skidding into the doorway of a tavern

on Farrier's Street. Above the door, a stone king's head hung in rust-weeping chains. Down the street, Durand spotted the great entrance to a monastery: a fan of sculpture carried by doorpost kings or Powers—all lit, sharp and clear, by a huge fire basket. Soldiers stood warming their hands at the blaze; Durand thought he saw one of Ragnal's starlings.

From the tavern door, a long man in black-rabbit robes was speaking. In that instant, his face was two beads and a knife's point. "Do you know how many customers I have lost this evening because—"

Durand yanked his blade from its sheath. The guards were turning, and this was not the sign. Bracing the cold edge across the man's gullet, Durand muscled him backward into the room—host or hostage. They weren't getting Deorwen or her husband easily.

Heremund pinned his eye to the door as it thumped shut. "I don't think the buggers saw anything."

Durand heaved his prisoner round to face the others, the blade flat against his windpipe as the bead eyes goggled.

"What have you to say?" asked Lamoric.

"Oh. Host of Heaven! What was it?" the man spluttered. "Ah, yes! 'Take what thou wilt, I shall clothe myself in the castoffs of the road, and this forked tree shall be my sign.'"

It was more of the Traveler's rant—Durand freed the man into the gloom.

A single clay lamp lit the tavern's hall—no surprise—but what its flame revealed had them all staring for a moment. Where the courses of the back wall should be, broad foreheads bloomed in the dark. Shadows wobbled in the eyes of kings, queens, and heroes from floor to rafters. One bare-chinned brute stood as round as a barrel.

"What do you call this place?" asked Heremund.

"The Marbles," said the tavern-keeper. "I am pleased to be the proprietor."

Heremund stepped to one of the tavern's big shutters. "That's our way out done for. I count two dozen men waiting there."

"They've made it a marshaling point," Durand guessed. "I think I saw one of the clerks. The others will be sergeants and runners."

"Hells," said Lamoric.

The tavern-keeper put long-fingered hands over his face. "I told the priest I was more than willing to be of assistance after all his help during my sister's illness, but I cannot afford to close my business for an entire night. There are tithes and taxes and regular customers. I have a dispensation to operate past curfew to pay for."

He paced to a second set of shutters. "I cannot be faulted in this. The priests gave me no mechanism to communicate that there might be difficulties."

As the tavern-keeper peered out, Deorwen crossed to the table where the lamp flickered. Durand noted a blob of red sealing wax.

Glancing back, the tavern-keeper stalked to the table. "Perhaps you could retrace your steps," he suggested. "There might be another way forward."

He idly collected an object from the tabletop, but Durand was well ahead of him. He closed his fist over the man's bony fingers.

"Master tavern-keeper," said Deorwen, "I think I must ask you to forgive a little curiosity this evening."

"There are secrets to every trade, of course," he explained, but Durand gave the man's fist a good squeeze, catching one shoulder as well.

"Your help has been very valuable," he said.

"We have nothing whatever to do with the authorities," said Deorwen. "Please."

The man's fist opened to reveal a ring seal—molded with an angular eagle that Durand recognized.

Heremund cocked his head. "That's the dockmaster's seal, or a very pretty copy. And I expect, if we popped down your cellars, we'd find the dockmaster's seal on a few barrels that never made his ledgers. Yes?"

The man shrugged, waving his hands. "When cost is high or demand low, the dock taxes can be more than any man could be expected to bear. It pains my heart to deprive—"

Heremund put his hands up. "I understand. But it strikes me that you'd be a man likely to know how to get something as large as a great wine barrel up from the docks without anyone being the wiser."

"The dockmasters do not always pay their underlings as they should. There are ways."

Heremund shook his head, wincing. "We'd have to grease more than a customs lackey or two just now. Hmm?"

"There are other ways, but their value is in their secrecy." Durand still had the man's shoulder. "One—one is not too far. The wall is old. There is a drain under the house of an acquaintance."

"You said that the priest helped your sister," said Deorwen. "I know that all of this has made you uneasy, and I would ask you to risk nothing more, but our need is great."

"Ladyship, there is nothing I would rather do than help. . . ."

"We can't afford a wrong turn, and the city is dark and full of soldiers. There is no other way. Please."

"Uh." The man pawed his hair. "Heaven help me, I will take you." He crossed to the door, daring a quick glance. "All right," he said, "follow close."

With a muttered charm, the tavern-keeper led them from Farrier Street into an alley and off toward the wall. Durand followed hard on the man's heels as he loped and darted, teeth glinting bare. They saw guards, but never close.

Finally, the tavern-keeper skidded to a stop at the mouth of an alley. "Lord of Dooms," he said.

A good pool of torchlight shimmered at the other end; a house glowed in the light and its shadow climbed the city wall above. Heremund grunted at Durand's elbow. "And that's our bolt-hole, is it?" asked the skald.

"It is," said their guide. "Perhaps it is not the secret I thought it to be."

They breathed in the darkness.

Lamoric drew himself up before the stranger. "Friend," he said, "there is good reason why we cannot stray far from the monastery." The provost's boat would be waiting there.

The tavern-keeper threw up his hands. His mouth opened and closed. "There are other breaches, but nothing near and nothing unwatched."

Durand blinked. They needed the boat; Lamoric and Deorwen had to get free.

He drew himself to his full height. He could think of only one chance, and it might be the best thing for all of them.

"Be ready to move," he said.

As the knot of fugitives turned on him, he caught Deorwen's eye and bolted into the torchlight.

⊗ 11. Tide, Time, and Laughter

He met six men: sergeants with axes in their fists and hauberks on their backs. Slithering on his soles for an instant, he ran off down the main street with the big wall rippling over his left shoulder, a vague suggestion against the stars.

He crashed through a stone fountain and pitched into black spaces. He reeled over broken cobbles and saved himself by slapping walls.

The guards barked that he should stop.

With the cold knifing at his lungs, he spotted a stairway jagging up the wall itself. With the men behind him likely blind beyond their torches, Durand took his chance, surging up above the houses on the open stairs.

"There!" someone shouted.

Durand cursed.

In the streets below, blobs of torchlight shuddered over storefronts and alleys. Three or four parties had his scent now.

Finally, he stumbled out onto the battlements themselves. Over the wall he saw nothing: no horizon, no waves. Somewhere, there were likely to be men walking the wall, but, for now, he could still get free.

A few hundred paces down the wall, he skirted one tower and threw his back against the next. Behind him, two separate torch parties struggled after him.

He lurched onward, rounding the tower.

Where another knot of torchlight shivered ahead. In desperation, he looked down. On a city side, there were roofs—far enough to break his back. On the sea side stretched a waveless blackness: low tide, he realized. Wet shapes of mud and stone glinted on the flats.

He resolved to try his luck with the weaker gang of guards, but as he made to move, an accident of torchlight threw a fan of yellow out over the flank of the fortress, right through the wall.

The light wavered out once more, and then there was blackness. But Durand had seen what he must see: the belly of the next tower had slumped into the gulf. A great, arched mouth was all that remained of its seaward wall.

The guards ahead had nearly hit it, and in a moment they would cut him off forever.

He sprinted, charging for a tower he could scarcely see down a path no broader than his shoulders. His cloak lashed behind him. He made out helmets—faces—in the torchlight.

Durand dove through a blackness in the tower's flank and plunged down a stair until the great stink of weeds and muck filled his head and the shattered belly of the tower opened onto the Gulf of Eldinor.

He watched where the torchlight on the battlements draped long shadows down the stone.

He clung to rubble and fought for silence, trying not to breathe.

Overhead, two of the guard parties met, surely wondering how they had missed. He could hear snatches of their talk.

In silence, Durand picked his way down the grassy slope of stones below the tower. He tried not to think of when the next block might drop out of the stone gape high above him.

When the slope pitched away to a sheer drop, he threw himself off the brink—and struck the frigid mud with force enough to spit new stars into his heavens.

SKULKING THROUGH THE stones and muck, Durand found no sign of his friends—or of the provost's boat. Above him, the Heavens were full of stars, and the first sliver of the Sowing Moon glinted like a needle.

Once, a party from the walls raised torches over the flats, sending Durand to hide among the ribs of a wrecked boat. Peering out through its swollen planks, he watched the guardsmen stagger in their pool of torchlight. He saw the long trail of pockmarks he'd left in the slime, and swam a winding rivulet when the guards looked away.

At a safe distance, Durand hunkered out of sight and considered his position. If Lamoric and Deorwen had found the provost's boat, they would be in Scrivensands. If they were caught, they would be locked in the Mount of Eagles.

He resolved to reach the wharfs at Scrivensands and see what he could.

Choosing a likely smudge on the horizon, he struck off across the gulf, leaving his searchers behind. At every step, the muck fought him for his boots. From the northern darkness, he could hear a thousand leagues of black water alive and breathing in its restive sleep. He tore a foot from the mud and planted it again.

After all of this, surely, the spark of greed that had sent him trailing Lamoric to court was thoroughly doused. He could not see Ragnal smiling on him soon.

The chill of mountain ice and the northern deeps clenched in the ooze, close to freezing. Around him, the masts and tall hulls of ships stood black against the black night. Stiff ropes snaked the flats, while the ships dozed like hogs in a cold wallow. He pulled the slimy, dragging weight of his cloak from the mud and knotted the thing around his waist.

Hauling and planting his left foot—now without a boot—he weighed the ties that bound him to Lamoric. There was loyalty: he had sworn oaths to the man. But, more than that, Durand had betrayed his lord—and then been forgiven. Thus were true bonds forged. Durand's service was half restitution—payment in sweat or blood—for a betrayal he could not confess.

A faint sound.

Thinking of king's men, Durand twisted in his tracks, but the torches now flickered three hundred paces back.

The sound whispered again, not from behind—from the north. He searched the flats, cursing the feeble stars and sliver moon. And the sound was larger—as though the whole dark sea was quietly waking out there beyond the Gates of Eldinor. Heartbeat after heartbeat, it swelled. He made out a glint as wide as the gulf, rippling silver in the gloom. The whisper roared from shore to shore. The waves of the Broken Crown had crested some clay shelf out there, bulling through the Gates of Eldinor and spilling wide across the gulf: the tide had turned.

Durand was locked to the bottom as surely as if he'd been shackled there.

Casting about, he spotted the nearest of the ships that waited for the tide. The water slid onward, fast and black and gleaming. The boat seemed ten bowshots away. He wrenched one foot from the mud. He set it down. The rush was almost upon him.

In the mud, he felt the hard curl of an anchor rope hard as a root against his shin.

And the water struck—ice and lightning.

Long arms of weed slapped past him.

But he held on.

He climbed the anchor rope, feeling it twist as the water seized the ship and wrenched it onto the waves. The boat lurched—suddenly upon him—blundering like a mountainous warhorse.

He held on, climbing as the boat floated free. Locking his fists on the big cable, catching with his frozen feet and shins, swinging as the boat heeled in the flood.

Finally, he threw one leg over the rail and, with the boat still swinging like a child's toy, pulled himself onto the deck. For a time, he sprawled there, motionless while the stars bobbed above the mast.

Then he heard a sound—*tock*—hollow and distant above the whisper of the tide.

Tock.

It might have been a chain, loose and knocking against some rolling hull out in the gulf, but it sounded like the heel of a staff. The shudder that seized Durand's bones was only partly about cold mud and water.

T-tock. The waves brought the sound nearer.

In an instant, Durand's mind was back in that Traveler's Night when he rode for his father's hall through the knotted woods above Gravenholm. Once again, he heard the iron-shod staff among naked trees.

Tock.

Levering himself from the deck, Durand searched the merchantman for any sign of a ship's boat, but of course, the crew had rowed the thing to some Eldinor alehouse long ago. There was no leaving, so, with the cold choking him, he contented himself with a box of stiff sailcloth. Once the lock was smashed, the mainsail made a serviceable blanket.

T-tock.

Durand squeezed his eyes shut.

Wrapped in his acre of stiff canvas, he resolved that if the Traveler was walking the waves, a Power of Heaven would come plenty soon enough without a man gawking and running in circles.

He hunkered down and drove his thoughts back to the puzzle of Lamoric. All winter Durand had meant to put Burrstone Walls behind him, but he had never ridden more than a few leagues from the castle door. The weather was bad; there was nowhere to go; but, when the others were leaving him, he did not stay behind. Instead, he had rowed the man halfway across Errest the Old.

Tock.

He winced at the cold and the Traveler's staff beyond the gunnels.

All of his loyalty and greed and penitence were lies. He stayed for Deorwen. Until he let Deorwen go, he was trapped at Lamoric's side, faithful in treason. These were the snares the fiends laid before a man, and they had caught him firm and fast. His fist struck the deck.

"It must end," he said. "Whoever finds me on this blasted ship can have me. It must end."

And there was silence on the waves.

The marching staff—or swinging chain—had stopped. He smiled around chattering teeth, and breathed. He was alone. And perhaps that was best.

"There are a thousand knights sworn to the duke. I am one blade in all that. I must put Deorwen—" He corrected himself. "I must put Lamoric *and his wife* behind me."

As he muttered these words, a dry sound—like the crack of a banner—snapped above the masthead. Half expecting to see the Traveler perched on a yardarm, Durand flinched a glance up, but for a moment, he saw nothing. Then, beyond the mast and rigging, a black shape flickered among the stars. It wheeled—or Durand thought it did.

He stood, squinting into the Heavens, wondering what night birds flew in such darkness.

Then the shape detached itself from the sky and caught hold of the rigging. He saw brittle claws clutching the ship's backstay. A beak croaked: *ha!* A nasal, hag's laugh: a rook.

And then there was another black flutter in the Heavens. Another shape descended, catching a second line.

Two rooks stared down at him, ragged, their beaks black points with naked hilts of bone. These were no natural birds. "Bastards," Durand said. Here were the henchmen and councilors of Radomor of Yrlac stealing away after the king's moment of madness. Now they laughed like crows upon tomorrow's battlefield.

The sailcloth slid from Durand's shoulders. "To the Hells with you!" he said.

Ha! the things answered.

The sailors had left a long gaff in brackets by the rail. While Durand's sword wouldn't reach the rooks, he thought the gaff might. In a single abrupt motion, he snatched the weapon and swept for their reptilian eyes with speed enough to make the iron hook whistle. The birds scattered—but only for a beat or two of their wings.

A feather spun down.

Ha!

And the two rooks turned to each other. As Durand balanced the long gaff in his fists, they lurched into the air. He brandished the pole, but they banked beyond his reach.

The rooks spun round and round and their flight seemed to churn a Hellish whirlpool from the mortal night—as black and cold as a winter midnight and full of whispers.

Before Durand knew what he was seeing, frost had locked in his hair. His breath stung behind his ribs, and needles of ice reached from every plank and spar on the deck.

The rooks shocked the spinning air with their convulsive, one-note laughter. *"Where is friendship?"* said a whisper—the sound scurried round the maelstrom. *"Where is honor?"* said a second whisper.

Durand swung, aimless, but the rooks' whirlpool snatched at his breath, tugging life from his lips. He gaped as steam spun upward from his lips till he could no longer breathe.

His life's breath gushed from him, coiling into the dark, as he lashed with the gaff.

"*Hostages among the highborn, brother. Such a base policy,*" said the first.

"*But not a tool to be discounted.*"

The whispering spiraled round and round, louder than the tide.

"*A man might make enemies of his friends, brother.*"

In an instant, Durand would fall. His heart struggled.

"*While another makes friends of his enemy. . . .*"

But then the churning void collapsed, spinning off into the black Heavens with the rooks. Laughter rang in Durand's skull. He dropped to the deck. The two fiends flickered, black, against the stars.

HE HEARD A sound—*tock*—conducted through the bones of his skull. He was sprawled on the deck.

"Oh, for Heaven's sake," he said. He ached as though he'd slept a hundred winters. There was twilight in the Heavens.

Clunk . . . Clunk.

"Durand?" said a voice.

After another *clunk,* there was a heavier concussion.

Though uncountable needles of frost tacked his cloak to the planks, he tore himself free. The *Bittern* bobbed over the gunnel. Lamoric stood in the prow, craning to see him. Coensar stared down the length of the boat. And there were grins even among Odemar's oarsmen. As Durand blinked, Ouen reached up, and Durand clambered into the boat.

"Host of Heaven," the big man said. "Her Ladyship swore she saw something. I didn't think you could have reached the ship before the tide hit, but His Lordship wouldn't hear about turning back until we'd checked."

Beyond the near circle, Durand saw Lamoric—like a man reprieved—and Deorwen, her chest heaving and lips clamped tight.

Ouen sat Durand down on a spare bench. His gold teeth glinted. "The skald's no oarsman, and we'll have to pull hard if we're to make Acconel before the sky falls."

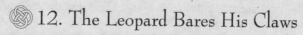

12. The Leopard Bares His Claws

O ver Acconel Harbor, gulls screamed against the sunset. Lamoric's men had rowed and sailed for days, and now the pale city rose like sorcery before the *Bittern*'s prow. The walls of the citadel soared over Silvermere, and the twin mouths of the River Banderol gaped where high kingdom engineers had parted the waters to moat the old city.

In most ways that mattered, this was Durand's home. And it would make as good a place as any to tell Deorwen and Lamoric "farewell" and to get out of the mess he had made.

As their strokes hauled the *Bittern* around the jetty tower, Durand heard the thousand-tongued babble of a crowd. He could think of no reason. At a glance, he saw that a mob had gathered in the quayside shadows, though not a soul among them was turned to see the *Bittern* come. This was no welcome. He wondered what was going on.

"We'll take her straight in, Master Odemar," said Lamoric from his oar. "The whole kingdom's about to capsize. We've no time for signals." They cut a line across the crowded harbor to swing close beyond the pier ends. Durand stole a glimpse through one mountainous city gate and saw inexplicable mobs lining the road. Red-and-white guardsmen topped the walls and managed the crowd. Durand searched his memory for an explanation while Lamoric scowled and consulted his captain.

Odemar sent them past a place in the gatehouse's deep shadow. "Put her in here," said Lamoric. Odemar ordered the oars up, and, as they shot in, Durand got ready with the rope to tie off.

In that tense moment of landing, shouts and horns brayed from the mouth of the gatehouse, roaring with a sound of a market at full cry.

Durand glanced up. Then, quite suddenly, the whole crowd screamed.

At that same instant, the *Bittern* hit the wharf. Durand's hand went to his blade, and—as though the gate were a portal to another Creation—men and beasts exploded from the city.

People ran. They fell. Some were carried straight into the harbor.

As Durand stared, a bull wallowed through bodies. It vaulted up the ramped foot of the city wall, flinging people like rag dolls before its weight heaved it back onto its pursuers. The bull's flanks ran with blood.

"Hells," Durand said. And knew what he saw. Every year it was the same: Driving the Bulls. Even when he lived in the city, he always forgot when it came.

Tumbling through screams and needle horns, half-naked men lashed the bulls into madness. A tide of wide-eyed brutes scrambled and slashed forward with a flood of citizens around it. Bulls leapt like porpoises, crushing and maiming the citizens in their desperation. At the water—at the quay—the river of flesh split, afraid of drowning.

The *Bittern* was shaking already.

For a blink, Durand saw Heremund's face behind him, his mouth a hollow loop. Then Coensar was roaring, "Push off! For your lives, boys!"

Durand took the wharf in both hands, ready to shove, but its timbers came alive in his hands. One monstrous bull was free of the mob with the empty wharf its only channel to liberty. Its muzzle gleamed big as a saddle. Only Coensar's hand on Durand's collar pulled Durand free.

In a hail of spit and blood, the monster roared over their heads, cracking the far gunnel and bowling into the water.

"Heaven's King!" Ouen breathed.

Durand spun.

Beyond the boat, the bull was stiffly erect, swimming for open water. Wherever it had touched the *Bittern,* she had burst like a barrel.

The crowd bayed and whooped, swinging their lashes. They splashed water at the bulls and each other. The animals wallowed and swam, most bound to drown in deep water, but others making their way for the beach beyond the crowd. The frenzy of the mob began to falter, then there came an ordered blast of trumpets from the city walls. Men in the duke's red-and-white had appeared at the parapets.

Durand threw whomever he could get hold of onto the

wharf. Ouen, Coen, and Lamoric got Durand's forearms as the boat sank from under him.

"What in the Hells?" Berchard demanded. His one eye peered up at the walls.

In the midst of the guardsmen was a small figure, stooped under the weight of heavy mail. Even squinting up into the red dusk, Durand knew the opaque blue of his eyes. The Duke of Gireth had come.

Duke Abravanal lifted a too-heavy sword over the mere. On all sides, his guardsmen produced crossbows. And with a downward slash of the sword, bolts leapt from the stuttering clank of a hundred bows. Durand and the others flattened themselves, but the bolts flickered past to bite deep in hock and shoulder of the swimming bulls. A second volley sent every bull to the bottom.

Silence swelled.

A small knight set his hands on the parapet. He wore a mustache like fox's tails, and Durand knew him. "Hear the words of Abravanal, third of that name, Lord of Acconel on Silvermere, Duke of great Gireth, mightiest domain between mere and mountains, bearer of Gunderic's Sword of Judgment!"

Sir Kieren Arbourhall, long Durand's master, paused.

"To the beast of the water, the duke sends his greetings," he said. "All hail Acconel!" And the streets roared once more.

"What was that about?" demanded Berchard.

"The founding of the city," said Heremund. "When our famous Duke Gunderic came from Yestreen, they say some old devil dragged itself from the muck at the bottom of the mere. Rose out of the water like a black bull, running slime and flapping its ears."

Badan grimaced. "This skald of yours talked a lot of ballocks the last time as well, Durand. You shut him up, or *I* shall."

Durand had his eyes on the parapet. The duke was turning. He thought he saw the rest of the old man's family with him: Landast, little Almora, all silhouettes. Sir Kieren lingered an instant to peer out over the quay, fingering the mustache.

"It is the story," Durand affirmed.

"The duke was a good Atthian; he told the thing to go to Hell."

"Ah," said Ouen, "a diplomat, was he?"

The skald shrugged eloquently, allowing all possibilities. "He had his old Isle Kingdom blade—and a bad mood—on him."

The guards were filing off the parapet. On the quay, the battered crowd was thinning.

Lamoric got to his feet, catching a breath. "There's no time. We'll get him in the street."

Coensar nodded, ordering the men to help get Lamoric through the crowd.

As they slipped on the blood and muck before the giant gatehouse, Ouen caught Heremund's shoulder.

"What did the big bugger do about it?" asked Ouen. "When the old duke told him?"

"Not a thing," said Heremund.

"What?" Badan said.

"Gunderic had that old blade. But—see that bull up there?" He pointed at a bull's head thrusting from the keystone of the arch six fathoms above. "Ever since they built the walls, anyone going through this gate—the Fey Gates—alone, especially at dawn and dusk, or at night, they'd meet a big black dog. Or calf. Or a man with bull's shanks. Or a calf-eared giant, hunkered under the gate like a man trying to crawl through a barrel. The buggane."

"This is a good one," said Berchard.

"And those are folk who managed to get away," the skald added.

Badan winced, shoving a finger back toward the water, where the great bodies drifted. "So, is all that tribute, or are they making fun?"

"Depends who's listening," Heremund answered.

For an instant, there was no one under the old gates but Lamoric and his men. Ouen flashed his gold teeth.

LAMORIC WAS ON the march.

People mobbed the streets of Acconel. The bull drive was the real start of the city's year. Townsfolk threw their shutters wide and filled the streets; a fair heaped goods in the markets from leagues around. There was even a good big tournament at the castle.

"There!" said Lamoric.

Beyond the end of Lamoric's finger, the duke's banners swayed between the shop signs and leaning upper floors. Lamoric's men put their shoulders to work, getting their master closer. They jostled jugglers, skalds, and clowns. Puppeteers took their wicker stages in their hands. Badan barked laughter as one man on towering stilts reeled past, grabbing shutters as he flattened himself against the upper stories of a shop.

At their feet, priests collected anyone who'd let a bull toss them. Bodies and blood drew packs of awestruck children.

Heremund elbowed his way to Durand's hip. "You were at Acconel, yes?" There were broken limbs and shattered bodies every dozen paces.

"We did it every year: shield-bearers and some of the older pages," Durand confessed.

They fought just to keep up with Lamoric.

"You're mad," said Badan. "The whole lot of you. Atthians feeding bulls to the lake."

"That's it, likely," declared Heremund, waving at the crowd. "It's not Atthians. These are the same folk who bribed the old bugger before they'd heard of the Atthias. You Sons of Atthi are just skin on a very old stew."

Durand smiled. "There was a lot of drinking."

A broke-nosed face in the crowd sneered at Durand, and Durand put his hand on a shoulder without looking. Suddenly, that hand was upside down and in a twist. He felt like he'd stuck his arm in a mill.

"You're all wet," said a familiar voice. The big knobby face looking down on him was Geridon the Champion's. With a cracked-pearl grin, he let Durand free. "Don't think I didn't see you coming. Not for a heartbeat."

Durand smiled, and Lamoric slid past him, dropping to one knee before the old duke and the other members of his family. Abravanal stooped under his coat of iron and ducal crown. At his shoulder was Landast: an older, more solemn Lamoric with a mane of syrup-blond hair.

"Father, brother," Lamoric said.

Durand and a few others in the front row knelt as well. As

he went down, he spotted old Sir Kieren, looking as he had through all the years Durand served him.

"Lamoric!" old Abravanal gasped. "By the King of Heaven." Wisps of white hair curled from under the chain hood he wore. His eyes were an impossible blue. "Lady Deorwen."

Deorwen's look was stricken.

"We have just returned, Father," Lamoric said.

"You have carried my fealty to our king?"

"Father, Ragnal has—"

A child darted from the front of Abravanal's party, several steps ahead of Landast's wife. The girl's hair was a long brush of ink. This was Almora, youngest of Abravanal's children.

"Lamoric!" She struck Lamoric's shoulder, swinging tiny arms around him. He had to plant a hand in the muck to keep from capsizing.

"Mora," he said, and, after a moment's hesitation: "I think you've grown again."

She tucked her chin. "I have. I have grown. And you never come. I have a horse of my own now. He is brown and he is called Star." She had his hand, and was tugging her much older brother to his feet. "You're soaking. Were you playing at the mere?"

Landast's wife, a fine, tall woman called Lady Adelind of Garelyn, touched Almora's shoulder. "Almora, I think you will find that a duke's daughter does not roll in the street." Adelind, herself a duke's daughter, smiled at Lamoric with an eyebrow cocked. "Lamoric has something to tell your father, I think?"

Duke Abravanal tottered between them under his hauberk and crown. "Up, up!" he said, giving Lamoric his hand. "We will speak during the feast. And poor Deorwen must have dry clothes. What would your father say of me?"

"Yes, Father," was everyone's answer, and they continued their progress toward the white citadel.

Landast stalked alongside Lamoric, his brow clouded. "You have returned in haste, I think," he said. *Or you never made the journey,* he did not add.

"If I never hold an oar again, it will be too soon," Lamoric answered. "But there are—"

Almora walked nearly backward. "Lamoric? Where is your horse?"

Lamoric could not be too frustrated. "I have many horses."

"The knights who have come for the tournament have many horses. All colors. They are camped in the yard. I've only got one," Almora said. "And he is a great responsibility for a girl my age." Adelind touched the girl's shoulder.

"Brother, I was not sure I left you time to reach Eldinor," said Landast.

They had nearly reached the gates of Castle Acconel where the throng of knights and wellborn guests would be waiting to receive the duke.

Lamoric scowled. "My timing couldn't have been better. If I had arrived a moment sooner, I would not be here now."

Now, Abravanal stopped. "I do not understand?"

"The oathtaking was a trap, Father. Sons of duchies, loyal and disloyal. The Patriarch of Eldinor himself. King Ragnal has seized them all."

The old man's mouth hung open.

"We will have to summon the barons," said Landast. His glance took in father, wife, and sister. "Let's get inside."

As the duke's procession took the last turn toward the high white gates of the castle, they saw a great blaze of banners and bunting.

But in the market square before the gates a dark squadron of mounted men blocked their way.

Bared blades caught the sunset, and leopards curled on shields and surcoats. Every sneering man wore green and crimson. At the vanguard sat Radomor of Yrlac, hunkered like some Power of Hell on the back of a monstrous warhorse. Heaven's Eye painted his bare skull red, and the whole of Creation seemed to balance around his black stare. He didn't look like the hero who'd saved the king at Hallow Down.

"Why have we stopped?" asked Almora. From her vantage point at Adelind's skirts, Creation was a place of knees and cobblestones.

Durand touched the grip of his sword. Every man in Lamoric's company had done the same. But if Radomor chose to move, not one of them could stop him.

"Who let them in?" breathed Coensar.

Big Geridon twisted. "Festival time. I'd've had the gates shut tight, me, but who listens to old soldiers?" His grin was quick and crooked.

Tack jingled. Somewhere a sole turned on the cobbles.

Durand remembered the hall of Ferangore. He thought of how he'd stopped this man at Tern Gyre. He sniffed a hard breath through his nostrils.

"My lords and ladies of Gireth," the duke's voice rumbled.

Landast stepped out into the silence, Geridon catching his shoulder before he could go too far.

"What do you wish with us, Radomor?"

Radomor's head tilted a degree or two.

"The tournament," he said.

"Lord Radomor, I would have thought you'd had enough of those. Word of what happened at Tern Gyre has reached us."

The duke made no move, simply staring back with his black eyes.

"Gireth's appearance at Tern Gyre and your kinsman's role on that day stand out in my memory. So I have come. You must allow me to take part."

They had spoiled his tournament, so now he would spoil theirs.

"I will not stop you," said Landast.

"There is one thing more. . . ." Radomor rumbled.

"Name it," said Landast.

"Landast, son of Abravanal, I would face you in the lists. Fight me and learn who is the better man."

Landast's hands opened in the stillness. Durand had some sense that Landast could handle himself, but few could stand against Radomor of Yrlac. Yet a challenge had been made, and there were many eyes on Landast: knights from across the realm, townspeople, family.

"I do not fight in tournaments," he said.

Durand's own mouth opened, and he heard gasps all around. A man does not lightly refuse a challenge.

Horses fussed. Durand heard the creak of his gauntlets, leather caught in Radomor's fists. And the light dimmed—as though the duke's fury could squeeze light from the air. "You refuse me?" he whispered.

"Lord Radomor, you may depart if I have disappointed you beyond bearing. If you choose to remain, there is space enough for you and your men in the outer ward."

Radomor grimaced in disgust.

It was then that Durand noticed the two black Rooks, grinning in the shadows at the roadside. One waved Durand's way, and bobbed his eyebrows.

THEY PASSED THROUGH the pale gates and into the castle's outer courtyard when Radomor stood aside. And the smothering mass of their guests filed silently in behind them. The pavilions littered over the lawn under the walls looked like the aftermath of a ruined celebration.

The duke stumbled along as if tugged on a string. Lamoric's eyes darted, hardly leaving the ground—never settling on his brother. Almora tried to skip: her brother had come, there were knights and dashing ladies, the outer yard was full of horses, but Durand watched as she gave it up.

Radomor followed. As Abravanal's party passed through the inner gates and into the shadow of Gunderic's Tower, a few of Radomor's company peeled off to stake their tents among the others.

The petals of a thousand snowdrops lay heaped in baskets, unthrown. Priests ushered a choir of children from the door to the Great Hall, their songs unsung. Heaven's Eye set beyond the city.

13. Discretion's Cost

Trumpets rang, Abravanal flinched, and the procession filed into the candlelit splendor of the Painted Hall: the feasting hall of Gunderic's Tower. Tabor, shawm, and bagpipe played them in.

"How can you?" whispered Lamoric.

Landast was shepherding his wife and little sister. He ducked close. "I am a lord of this realm, not some vagabond tourney fighter."

"Not *me*, then," said Lamoric.

Landast shut his mouth a moment, helping Almora up the step to the high table. He whispered, "This man's bluster and my pride will not cause me to forget my duty."

Durand could not hear the rest of what passed between them. He and the remainder of Lamoric's soggy band weren't destined for the high table. A bowing, balding serving man led them past the long rows of benches to the lower end of the hall and a few spare places by the service doors.

Heremund and Ouen sat on either side.

"Do you suppose all this is because I said that everything the boy did must come to nothing," said Heremund.

"What?" said Ouen.

"At Radomor's cradle. I should have kept my mouth shut." The little skald rubbed his chin.

"But this move's a puzzle. He'll have heard about the king's trick, I reckon. Most of the Great Council will by now. There might even be riders in the road already. There'll be talk. And here's Radomor in Gireth, playing the clown."

Last of the wellborn, Radomor and his henchmen strode into the Painted Hall, passing the high table before finding their way down the far aisle, Radomor grim and hunched as a bull. His Rooks grinned.

"What's his game, eh?" said Heremund.

Fresh paint slathered every surface in the long hall. Great swags of cloth hung where trophies, shields, and sconces had been fixed to the stone. High in the crossing vaults overhead, bosses and keystones glinted with gold and firelight. The arms of dead lineages and crusading heroes snarled from their old places. Durand had slept under these ceilings many thousand times.

"Rado makes this challenge, what follows?" wondered Heremund.

When the whole company—two hundred knights-at-arms—stood at their benches, serving men with rods laid table linens, and carried ewers and towels for the washing of hands.

"Landast accepts. Radomor thrashes him like an ugly stepchild, maybe. Maybe kills him." Someone planted a slopping ewer on the table. "Thanks, lad," Heremund said, splashing his hands in the water. "Right there, he's knocked the hand off Gireth's tiller. A staunch ally of the king, adrift. Good."

Up the hall, the green of Yrlac's livery blotted the long table. His whole retinue aped their master's arms; the two preening Rooks the only exceptions.

"Landast says 'no,'" Heremund continued, "how's he stand with the peers then, eh? How's he look to those who'd follow him? Not good. Not strong. It's a sharp bit of politics, this challenge."

The music stopped. At the top of the hall, someone was standing. Tall in bright robes of gold and samite, the Patriarch of Acconel swept the room with his sea eagle's gaze. His beard shone like a sheet of silver.

Heremund narrowed one eye. "Let's see what old Father Oredgar has to say to these new guests, eh?"

The Patriarch filled his lungs. "Peers of Errest. Lords, ladies, and serving men. Sons and Daughters of Atthi, hear one who knows the power of Heaven's King.

"At the word of his Creator, Saerdan Voyager ordered ships built in numbers great enough to carry all who would follow him from the shattered Isle Kingdom. His own vessel he named *Cradle,* and he had his Hazelwood Throne set within it. As the Host of Heaven bid him, he set sail and steered for the dawn."

One of Radomor's henchmen cleared his throat. Durand caught sneers around the grim duke.

And the Patriarch turned his piercing gaze on the men of Yrlac. He reached with one long-fingered hand. On the table before the Patriarch glinted the saltcellar *nef* of the House of Gunderic: a castled ship in precious metals to bear the duke's salt.

He snatched the rattling thing from the linen.

"But the Westering Sea is broad, and the *Cradle* sailed for many days. It is said that our Sons of Atthi knew thirst. Some despaired of reaching the far havens, their masters turning back for the sunset. Days became weeks. The last crumbs were eaten and the dregs drunk. Some men felt they had been misled, that Saerdan Voyager had gone mad in the wars behind him. More ships fell away—now long past reaching home. But then, at last, when the fortieth dawn rose before them, the *Cradle*'s watch sighted Wave's Ending."

The model ship gleamed above two hundred knights-at-arms, and at last the old man clanked the thing on the table before Abravanal.

"Saerdan was Heaven's anointed. The king. We are the scions of the faithful. Our blood is their blood. What became of those who heeded their own diverse masters and turned back upon the Westering Sea, lost upon the deep? What became of those who scattered at the first pangs of hunger? They are lost still. They hunger always."

The men bowed their heads, while the Patriarch stared down on them all.

"Praised be the Silent King of Heaven and the dread Powers of His Host," he said.

Though the company murmured their assent; not one looked Radomor's way. Soon, the procession of platters began.

Durand picked bits and pieces from the carvers' knives. Trenchers were set before him and whisked away. Mostly, he watched Radomor; the man sat like some fiend's idol. Knives clinked, but only Radomor's men spoke. Their every sneer and grunt sent ripples through the stillness. At the upper end of the hall, he could make out little Almora. Lady Adelind was helping the girl to cut, counseling her to eat with fingertips, Landast nodding to her questions, more parents than siblings.

The world beyond the castle sank into darkness, and soon the constellation of candles was the only light in the hall.

"What's this now?" demanded Heremund.

Down the lower table, one of Radomor's Rooks raised his head with an absentminded sigh. Over yards of empty table, a reek filled Durand's mouth as though he had bitten into something hot and putrid.

The Rook hopped to his feet in a flutter of candlelight.

"Atthians," said the Rook, cup raised. "Scions of Saerdan Voyager. Knights of Errest." His gaze danced over the silent faces staring back. "We are reaching the end of a fine meal. I wish to propose a toast. There are many brave men among you. His Grace, the Duke of Yrlac, will be pleased to fight beside you when the Eye of Heaven rises above these ancient towers. But some of you have been muttering, sitting in a gossip's judgment on one of your peers." He gestured with his goblet. "Is it not better to ask our questions? To cease our whispering? Landast of Gireth—setting aside base cowardice—could you explain why you will not test yourself against my master?"

Landast fixed his blue stare on Radomor alone. "Where is your toast?"

Radomor's eyes glinted, as did a few teeth. "What is your reason?"

"Prudence."

Radomor spoke without humor, drawing each word as deliberately as a sword. "An old woman's word."

Landast blinked slowly.

At Durand's side, there was a whisper on the tablecloth. Coensar's hands had disappeared.

Durand shifted his weight onto his toes.

The duke continued grimly. "I do not deal in pretty snares of language: you are the heir of a duke who has two sons. I, *myself,* am a duke. A duke with *no* sons. Who risks most?" Landast blinked slowly, unmoving. "Are you a spoiled child who fights only when defeat is impossible?"

Lady Adelind stood, collecting Almora and leading her from the hall. The little girl looked like she wished to stay, but knew enough to submit. Her feet crunched on the reeds.

"You must draw what conclusions you will," Landast said, eyes flat as turquoise.

Durand saw Kieren's hand restrain Lamoric.

Disgust tied knots in Radomor's jaws.

The second Rook hopped right onto his bench, his cup in the air. "To Landast then. Astonishing is the blood of Gireth. It has bred a fantastic creature. Never before has the world seen one who is, at once, both a man and his grandmother. To Landast, who—"

"Stop!" Lamoric was on his feet, slipping Kieren's grasp. "I will accept your challenge."

The Rook atop the bench quirked his head. "But, Milord Lamoric, you have not *been* challenged."

Lamoric fixed his attention on the little man's master. "Radomor, *I* am the man who upset your plans at Tern Gyre. Me and my men. And I saw what you are. I name you faithless. I name you murderer. I name you traitor. Now, it's my blood you threaten. *I* accept your challenge. You will find that I've no chain of duties to keep me from your throat."

Durand watched as Radomor hesitated. There was no advantage in fighting the younger son. A Rook leaned close to his master, pouring a thick whisper into the man's ear. And Radomor sat, eyes on Lamoric, expression slowly hardening.

"A wager then." Radomor's voice rumbled up from the foundations.

"You wish to risk more than your life?" asked Lamoric.

"Best me, I will remain within the bounds of Yrlac for . . . a year and a day."

"And what must *I* hazard, besides my life?"

"If you are bested—and live—then you must do likewise."

"In Yrlac?" said Lamoric.

Radomor nodded, slow.

"I accept."

The duke let one dry puff escape his broad nostrils, and stood. He nodded the shallowest bow over the candlelit table, and then led his company from the room.

Lamoric remained on his feet until the last green cloak snapped out the door, and then he too marched from the candlelight.

Durand found himself staring into Landast's face, far down the hall. The man's eyes fixedly ignored his brother's angry exit and his father's worry.

Big Geridon's eyes never moved from the direction of Yrlac's departure.

WHEN THE TABLES were down and the torches out, Durand and the others found some good, big pallets and circled the embers in the midst of the Painted Hall with the scores of loyal men who guarded the line of Gunderic. Each slept round his sword.

Though Durand was bone-weary, he stared up into the

painted vaults where the smoke curled. With luck and daring, Lamoric had bested Moryn Mornaway, but Radomor was something else. They would be carrying their lord back in a shroud.

"I hate a late feast before a tourney." It was Badan's voice in the gloom. "Now they'll start first thing."

"Better than an early one," said Ouen. "You ride on a full belly, it's all cramps—and Heaven help you if someone catches you in the guts."

"I thought Lamoric had him there," Heremund said. "Trapped him."

Berchard answered, "Took him aback."

"But that man of his. The one with the grins and whispers, he had something. Neither of those creatures seemed to mind. One brother was good as the next to them."

Straw crunched around the circle as men shifted.

"Hells, it doesn't bear thinking about," Badan grumbled.

"What are they planning?" Heremund said.

Badan levered himself up on one elbow, his voice hissing from a faceless silhouette. "I'll tell you why that bald bastard doesn't mind. It's simple: he'll win, and he knows it. You're as stupid as our bumpkin here." He gestured to Durand.

Durand thought about cracking Badan another rap in the teeth. The fool still had a few left.

"Surely," Heremund agreed. "But even given he's likely to win, why pick on younger sons? He gambles his life for nothing."

"It's no gamble if—"

"*Hostages,*" Ouen declared. "He must be jealous of old Ragnal's collection."

Heremund began, "We must watch—"

"Enough. All of you." This last voice was Coensar's. The man's eyes were twin winks of steel—and fixed on the doorway arch.

Lamoric was walking down the hall.

The young lord walked through the sudden quiet, a pallet hung like a corpse over his shoulder. Deorwen trailed after him. He chose a spot on the floor and the two lay curled in the fire's glow.

"I'm due some luck," Lamoric said, finally. "Maybe I'll get the bastard."

No one spoke from then on.

LONG AFTER THE others subsided into the tidal breathing of sleep, Durand watched the embers glitter in the stare of Lamoric's wide eyes—and in Deorwen's.

14. Death and Dreaming

Durand realized he was lost.

He didn't know where he was or how he'd come there.

His chest ached. He was blind. He tasted metal and dead leaves. But he drifted, cold as the Gulf of Eldinor.

And there, in that clouded deep, he heard a strange mutter, muffled. Someone whispered, and the shape of the words churned the frigid murk around him, pulling at the gloom as an oar hauls the water. His lungs ached. He could not breathe.

Durand felt himself gripped in the strange eddy.

The sound was a call: a summoning. He felt something stir in the impossible depths below him. There was moaning: a horrible moaning that shot through him, cold and shivering. The thing heard the pulling words, and the darkness moved with its coming—roiled with the great churnings of its alien bulk.

It came, roaring its despair.

And Durand could not move. He could not breathe.

And when its chaos shuddered past he could have cried for relief—until the wake of its passage seized him, catching hold as surely as any jaws. And he was drawn as the lamenting titan surged for some impossible surface.

WAS THERE A single gulp of air?

IN ANOTHER PLACE . . .

He looked over the circle of sleepers by the hearth's embers: men-at-arms by the score, sleeping light.

But he was not in the Painted Hall—not with them. Again, his lungs ached—pressure bulged.

Had he died?

He hung in space not an arm's length from some arrow loop in the wall of Gunderic's Tower. There was a crust of bird shit. Pavilions spread below him, dark wheels, but he hardly looked—a shape hovered at the neighboring slit: a man of smoke and threads, somehow more real than the whole Creation around it. And caught in the webs of its chest hung a fragment of bone, pierced like a whistle and filigreed with alien marks. The bone was a man's.

Mute and paralyzed, Durand shuddered.

This was the black thing from the deeps, knotted to the world.

The figure's slender arm—wisps, ink, writhing threads—groped through the slit-window and into the warm gloom inside.

Against Durand's will, he followed, drawn in and pulled behind.

He and the billowing thing swarmed the passages of his onetime home without false turnings, deeper and deeper, twitching and flowing. There were regions of blackness. His chest ached as though an ox stood on his ribs. He began to dread their errand, whatever it might be. Passing moonlight or fluttering torches, he tried to glean hints from the drifting horror's limbs. There might have been robes. Passing a whitewashed wall, a vial winked in the writhing curl of one hand. Light glittered through glass and a blood-dark fluid: wine?

The thing lashed and swirled up a spiral stair to pause before a chamber door. Durand tried to call out, but felt his lungs trapped and struggling. He did not know the door. In the shadow's fist, the handle turned. And the spirit flinched inside, like ink spilled in clouds. Just within, the big, square face of Geridon the Champion glowed dimly in a brazier's fading coals. He slept against the doorpost. Durand made out the draped planes of a four-post bed. Again, he tried to call around whatever clamped his lips. An ember winked in the vial as the shadow crossed to the bed.

It parted the curtains on the intimate space above the coverlet. Durand followed, entering that close cell of warmth and human smells.

He burned with shame. He wanted to tear free, but could not even struggle. Then the specter dipped toward the blankets. Durand wanted to shout a warning, but could not. It was so dark. A glass stopper came free like a clucked tongue; a vial's lip clicked against teeth. Durand imagined the foul liquor pouring over lips and tongue.

Then there came a piping whistle: a human shriek.

A face leapt from the bedclothes; a woman's eyes flashed wide.

And he and the assassin were smoke on the wind. A single gust threw them spinning down the spiral stair, through dark passageways and out the arrow loop window. And the shadow man was rent to tatters. The pale, sigil-carven bone tumbled from the window like a misfired arrow. Suddenly freed, Durand spun above the pavilions, and watched as the spinning bone dropped into the waiting hand of a Rook.

Radomor looked on, his eyes fixed on the Rook's narrow shoulders, resigned and brooding.

DURAND WOKE WITH small hands on his shoulders.

"Durand!" A slap cracked against his cheek, and he filled his lungs in a single gusty breath. Deorwen's hair feathered his face.

Then the dark hall boiled with curses.

Lamoric took Durand's shoulder. "She said you weren't breathing! I could see you struggling."

Durand pitched himself onto his hands; the darkness flashed with every blink.

"I saw something. I—"

"Durand, you were moaning," said Deorwen. "I heard it." The hearth's embers glittered in her eyes. Around the circle, he saw Heremund, Ouen, Coensar—all looking on. Nightmare memories spun in Durand's skull, then snapped clear.

He grabbed Lamoric's tunic. "Your brother, Lordship!"

The young lord looked from Durand's face to the top of the hall. He broke into a run and Durand lurched after. Before the door of the bedchamber was a landing.

Stopped in the doorway, Lamoric swayed like a hanged man. He wrenched an unlit torch from a bracket on the wall.

Inside, the room was as dim as it had been in Durand's nightmare: one brazier smoldering. Lamoric stepped over the threshold, hesitating as the stone crackled under his feet. Durand could see that the nearest of the bed curtains was down. Lamoric thrust his torch into the brazier, and the air came alive around him, twinkling. The floor where he stood seemed to be covered in crushed sugar. An impossible hoarfrost bristled from every surface.

By the wall, Geridon's body lay crumpled, his eyes two more stiff wrinkles among the folds of his face.

Durand followed his lord, drawn on. Lamoric halted again at the torn bed curtain. Durand stepped close, almost past him. Landast and his wife were white effigies on the stone folds of a sarcophagus. Landast's eyelids were shut: twin curls of icing. Adelind's stood like fat pearls, still trained on the thing she'd seen alive under the canopy above her.

Durand's tongue felt thick in his mouth. It would have been better if she too had not awakened. She might have seen him as well as the man of shadow in her last moment.

Lamoric was murmuring. "Durand, what did you see?"

Like filings around a lodestone, each needle radiated from Landast's lips: fans and flowers of ice.

"I was dreaming." The rest were making their way up the stairs. He would not hide anything anymore. "I saw it. A summoning, I think. Radomor's man. Lordship, I saw—"

A small voice behind them spoke, bright and muddled: "It sparkles." It was Almora, come from her father's room. "I heard people."

The two men turned, but Deorwen was there first, stepping between the child and the bedchamber. She caught the girl's shoulders, saying something like, "Come away. This isn't a good place anymore."

Standing in that cave of frost as his wife and sister withdrew and the throng on the stair gazed on, Lamoric said, "I am heir to Gireth now."

"There was no way to stop it," Durand breathed.

"This was the whisper in bloody Radomor's ear yesterday. What have I done?"

15. A Mortal Game

Coensar and Durand stood guard on the landing outside the duke's chamber. "Keep those eyes of yours open," Coensar said. "Whatever comes, do what you can."

Inside, Lamoric paced with Heremund Skald while the duke sat on the bed. In the next room, wise women tended to the cold shapes that had been Landast, Adelind, and Geridon. Deorwen had Almora.

Heremund winced and scratched through his rumpled cap. "There's a lot of them down there, all wondering what's to happen. They're bickering about whether there will be a tourney this afternoon."

Lamoric paced to an arrow loop, looking down on tents and tiltyard. He said nothing.

Heremund grimaced. "I reckon someone'll have to speak to the buggers."

A fierce voice echoed on the stairs. It was the Patriarch's. "Kieren Arbourhall, you villain, why are all these people gathered? I'll have your red whiskers if you don't tell me why you've hauled me from the high sanctuary."

Sir Kieren appeared at the top of the stairs. "Be still, Oredgar." The Patriarch drew up as he reached the landing.

"What has happened here?"

"Patriarch," said Lamoric, "we have decisions to make."

"Who has done this?"

"Come inside," said Kieren and led the Patriarch into the duke's chamber. "It seems our Durand here had a dream. He saw an assassin of some sort—a shadow." He explained.

Father Oredgar stood very tall. "Landast, Adelind . . ."

"And Geridon," said Duke Abravanal. "And my Champion, Geridon. What shall I do?"

"The Wards of the Ancient Patriarchs are indeed weak when such a thing can happen in Errest the Old."

"Radomor should hang," said Lamoric.

Kieren grunted. "For treason to begin with."

The Patriarch turned a skewering glance on Durand. "Boy, you saw nothing with your own eyes?"

"It was a nightmare. Others saw that I dreamt."

But the Patriarch's scowl only deepened. "Closed eyes do not a witness make. Neither law nor custom permits it."

Lamoric threw up his hands. "What is the point of law? They wait for answers. All those men in the hall."

"There is the tournament to consider," said Kieren.

"There are the *funeral rites* to consider," countered the Patriarch.

"Host of Heaven," Abravanal gasped.

"I am no great admirer of tournaments either, Patriarch," Kieren said, "but there have been games and bloodshed in Acconel on this day since Gunderic."

"And I have challenged Radomor," said Lamoric. "Would they understand that, those men? My brother's dead, so I must withdraw? This Radomor likely killed him, and I'd like to reconsider? No, I will not ask. This is my doing, and I will see it through. It may be that we will need no hanging. I still have my sword."

The din of murmurs in the Painted Hall was clear.

Heremund winced. "That'll be the buggers downstairs."

Lamoric opened his hands before his father. "What will we do? These men want answering."

"What can I tell them?" whispered Abravanal. "Landast is dead. Adelind was a second mother to my poor little Almora, since my Truda died. The only mother she's known. How can I tell Duke Alret that his daughter is dead—in my home?"

"Alret of Garelyn's locked in Ragnal's Mount of Eagles," said Lamoric. "Hells." He sucked a good lungful of the sick-room air. "Don't worry, Patriarch. There will be funerals aplenty by day's end. Durand? Coen? Let's take the news to that pack of fools downstairs. Radomor will have his little bloodbath. And if the Host of Heaven is with us, we'll drown him in it!"

HERALDS AND CRIERS ran to every street corner of Acconel. There would be a tournament: single combat and a great mêlée to follow. The men in the Painted Hall flooded the outer yard, hunting their war gear. Horses needed saddles. Blades had to be ground sharp. For Lamoric's men, there was a moment's hesitation. Who among them had so much as a donkey to ride on?

As the hall emptied, Lamoric caught Durand by the sur-coat. "My brother had horses. I remember he had a bone gray. Big bruiser. He'll do me, I think. You and the others, take your pick." What would it matter? Their ride into the mêlée would come after Lamoric tangled with the duke.

Coensar ordered the men into motion, setting Guthred in charge of the scavenging. Some shook out rust-clotted hauberks from the armory while the others prowled among old friends and bare acquaintances for serviceable gear. Durand sought out the stables, Heremund bobbing after. "You can feel it in the air," the skald said. "The great ones'll be leaning close now, waiting to see how Radomor's dice land. It's all happening now."

A twist in the passageway led toward the thick smell of horses. Heremund stepped through an outside door. "Keep your eyes wide," said Heremund. "I'll be among the crowds."

Agents would be thick on the roads to and from Acconel, for here was the opening of the great and fatal game that would catch at the oaths of ten thousand men and drag them into carnage. A storm was poised to break.

Durand and the rest of Lamoric's men were like children.

He pushed into the great, dark stables.

"I know you, you know," said a small voice.

As his eyes began to make sense of the shadows, Durand saw a woman's shape by one of the stalls: even in the dark, he knew Deorwen. There was a small face at her hip. He remembered that Almora liked horses. Now, she had a bucket of oats in both hands. This little girl had seen her sister drift under the walls outside; the wise women had laid out the only real parents she knew. Deorwen met his eyes.

"While he was getting ready, I thought we should find something to occupy our attention," said Deorwen. Durand nodded. The girl, at least, would need this.

"You say you know me?" Durand asked the little one.

"You lived in my house. In the castle. You were one of the boys," said Almora.

Among the stalls, a horse shook its head.

"I was, yes. I remember you too." He scratched his neck. "I am very sorry about all that has happened."

The little girl's mouth was a small, straight line. She

wrapped her arms around her bucket. "Yes," she said. "You are going to fight for my brother?"

Deorwen had her hands on the little girl's shoulders.

"Your brother is very brave," said Durand. Lamoric was going to have to fight Radomor alone; Durand could do nothing to stop it. "I'll do what I can for him."

In the nearest stall, there was a black monster. The thing was looking down on him from the warm gloom.

"That one is Pale," Almora offered.

The brute's big dark eyes glistened somewhere under the rafters.

"Lovely," said Durand.

"Sir Geridon said it was funny," Almora offered. "Because he's black. The stripe on his nose, that's a 'pale'—like a fence post. Sir Geridon rides him." She caught her lip between her teeth. "I'm not allowed. Sir Geridon says if Pale's tame enough for little girls, he isn't much of a warhorse, is he?"

The door creaked. Ouen, Berchard, and Badan ducked inside. With a look they plucked tack from the walls and disappeared.

Durand swallowed, and gave her a nod. "You'd better get clear then. I'm going to have to lead him out."

"He's Sir Geridon's," Almora repeated, and Deorwen led her from the stable.

"I'll keep him safe," Durand said.

"I will watch. Father has said. We must all watch. Every year."

As the little girl ran ahead, Durand looked to Deorwen, and she gave him a small nod. The girl should be nowhere near the lists when her brother rode out.

And they had an instant alone.

She kissed him, deep and breathless with her eyes shut, before tearing away to follow the girl.

He walked out with his heart thundering.

"Ha!"—A HARSH voice, mocking.

Durand froze on the threshold of the outer yard. Then he saw. On every side, slate black gallows-birds clotted the battlements, overhanging the courtyard like bloated eaves. Swags of the brutes choked every embrasure above the heads of the uneasy crowd. "Ha!"

Durand led Geridon's "Pale" out.

Under the feathered spectators, every street of Acconel had been poured into the narrow tiltyard and now they watched, gray-faced and cold on the grass bank under the wall. At one end of the lists, Duke Radomor waited. And at the other, Lamoric stood while Guthred tugged at the straps of his harness.

Everyone but the old shield-bearer had his eyes fixed on Radomor. The Duke of Yrlac hulked like some cultish idol. A shadow clung to his face, but nothing could hide the glint of his dark eyes. From the man's shoulders, the Rooks watched, smug and grinning. And there was the Champion: the mailed monster as tall as the stone kings in the Mount of Eagles, his helmed head bent over the bowl of his mailed hands.

"Hey." Berchard handed Durand a scabbed bundle. "Ouen found a hauberk that should fit you and a gambeson with some stuffing left . . . if we get drawn into the mêlée, after."

"Good," said Durand. Rust is too much like old blood. But, in hopes that there was a sound ring or two left under the crusts, he set about hauling the stuff over his head.

Above them, Duke Abravanal gazed across the crowd with a stare like cold water. By his side were Deorwen and little Almora, her dark eyes more somber than a little girl's should be.

"They're pounding the stakes," Berchard murmured. "The heralds are at Rado's end now. I've had a word with them." He pointed down the wall. "The first stake's elder." At the foot of the spectator's bank, a carrot-headed herald peered up at five thousand feathered onlookers before driving the stake that marked the lists' south corner.

Coensar spoke at Lamoric's ear; the man was smothered in mail hood, stuffed arming cap, and leather knots. "Take him from horseback, if you get the chance."

"Excellent idea. How lucky I've brought lances," quipped Lamoric. Guthred threw a shield over his master's shoulder, checking the length of the straps.

Durand glanced back at Berchard. "This elder. It's a nice, cheery tree?"

"They call it 'cursed' elder more often than 'cheery,' as I hear it: there's a smell, and the heartwood's soft, soft. But I hear a man can make whistles from the stuff, it's so easy to hollow. That's cheery enough."

The herald drove the elder stake with two quick taps—a sound that spurred some malicious croaking among the black onlookers.

Berchard scratched his beard. "Cursed elder, driven deep."

"Make the passes pay," said Coensar. "Hit him square and you and your name may live awhile. Unhorse him, and he might just spring a shoulder or snap a leg, and this mess is done before it's started."

Guthred planted a borrowed helm over iron rings and padding, working at the red paint with his thumb. Unhappy, he wrenched the thing off.

Lamoric blinked. "Hells, Guthred. You've done all this six times. I've got to live at least until they can start the joust."

Guthred was already rechecking the man's spurs.

The herald and his helper had reached the eastern corner, right at Radomor's feet. The two Rooks peered on, preening as always. Radomor smoldered in his bit of clinging shadow. The herald drew another stake.

"That there's the boneyard tree," said Berchard. "Yew."

"Lord of Dooms," said Durand.

" 'Fatal' yew, they call it."

The herald gave the thing a good whack with his mallet. It didn't set. At the second blow, the stake split—the crack shooting across the courtyard—but sunk deep. Horses tossed their heads.

"The death tree driven quick," said Berchard. "And cracked."

"What follows from that?" asked Durand.

"I don't want to think."

"You're a lot of old fishwives," said Lamoric. "How long now?"

Coensar wasn't listening. "If it does come to the ground, Radomor's a bigger man than you. He's got guile and power, a long reach, and there's no quit in the whoreson."

"So I should wager on him, then?" asked Lamoric.

Guthred jerked the man off balance with a tug on his harness, grunting, "Your man's hobbled, Lordship."

"Aye . . ." Lamoric said, recalling. "His neck. Yes?"

The heralds had crossed the long tiltyard, and were ready at Lamoric's end. "It's to be oak in the west," Berchard said.

"A good strong tree," said Durand.

"But killed in a tempest, this one."

"A windfall then?" said Durand, thinking it *must* mean good fortune.

"That would be a lucky stroke, but this poor devil was blasted by a bolt from the Heavens."

That stake sank at the first tap, sticking deep. "Radomor's lands are west, aren't they?" said Durand.

"Aye, that they are," Berchard agreed.

Coensar was speaking. "Rado's half-crippled from last summer on Hallow Down, and his neck looks no better than at Tern Gyre. From what I hear, Mad Borogyn's boys broke that neck. Even healed, it'll give him trouble."

"What are you saying? He won't be sleeping nights? He'll have trouble getting a tunic to fit?"

"Use your legs," said Coensar. "Make the whoreson turn. Make him stalk you. Keep moving. Swing a blade for it if you get the chance."

"Hmm. A man's vulnerable at his neck, you say? What else have you been keeping secret, eh, Coen?"

The redhead herald and his man crouched right at their feet. "Hello, boys," said Berchard. The pair winced up.

Lamoric put his mailed hands over his face, hardly able to find skin. "How long must I wait? I've picked my headsman. He'll have measured my neck by now. Let's get it over."

"Almost finished," said the herald.

Lamoric laughed.

Now, Ouen leaned in, asking the herald, "What's that you've got now, eh?"

The stake in the man's hand was a long thing, gray as a taper. "Willow." Tree of grief, of loves lost. He swung the hammer. There was dry chuckling among the birds; some crossed from perch to perch. He swung again. It looked like the rooks had gathered to stare down over their necks. The herald's man reset the stake. He swung again, and again.

Guthred had stopped pulling. Lamoric looked. Every man stopped to watch.

No one counted the blows.

Radomor still sat in his shadows.

Abravanal, Almora, and Deorwen looked on. Durand and she shared a sober glance.

"Host of Heaven," Berchard muttered. Closer to home, something like tears were running down the gray willow stake: water squeezing out of damp wood. There wasn't a sound among the thousand under the wall.

"We do not want for omens, do we lads?" Lamoric took a shaky breath. "Is it too late for me to reconsider? Would everyone be very much disappointed?" The next instant, trumpets rang under the Heavens.

"There's my answer," Lamoric said and heaved himself into the saddle of his brother's bone gray.

A WIND STIRRED under the clouds, jostling the carrion birds and lifting the tails of Lamoric's borrowed panoply as he rode out alone.

Radomor climbed into the saddle of his big black. The animal shied as creaking leathers took the weight of the duke and his mail, and it jittered against the pain of the bit and spurs that forced its obedience.

Above the scene, Abravanal stared out from the ducal box. Trumpets flashed, poised for his command, but the old man hardly seemed to see what was happening before him. In a moment, his only son would ride against a man who had single-handedly turned battles for the king. The duke trembled, but, at a quiet touch from Sir Kieren, he climbed to his feet.

Deorwen led Almora from the box.

The ancient Sword of Judgment rattled from its scabbard, the blade of Abravanal's long lineage shimmering under the clouds. Dead Landast's gray stamped; Lamoric's lance bobbed in his fist. Radomor's head turned within its shadowed helm.

And Abravanal let the broad blade fall.

A lance is a terrible weapon. Its blade splits helms and

shields. Its impact alone can heave a man yards and leave him forever broken. Throw the force of two charging horses behind the blow, and there is nothing to match it. Stout hard-wood splinters. The skin of the lancer tears at the sudden wrench of his own weapon under his arm.

Under the eyes of his city and his father, Lamoric charged away from his comrades. As the distance closed, he swung the lance point down, clamping the ash beam in a vise of ar-mored ribs and mailed arm. Durand felt every step as Rado-mor loomed beyond the sights of the man's helm.

They struck with a thunderclap of splintered lances that stung rooks into the air. And Lamoric's warhorse recoiled onto his haunches. While Lamoric and his brother's gray seemed to cower, Radomor's cloak filled, billowing above his foe—whose horse staggered and lolloped to its feet like a crippled thing. Both men had hit squarely, but both held their seats. And Radomor might have been a dragon with vast wings spread.

The men on the sidelines hissed while a hundred rooks pinwheeled back down into the yard, their black claws catch-ing lines and poles.

"The bugger's a stone tower," whispered Coensar. Lam-oric had hit the man square on the shield with all the force of arm and galloping horse—and the duke simply stormed away, back into his own company.

"Lamoric hung on," countered Guthred.

Now they were shouting encouragement; Lamoric rode back for a new lance. They could see him working his hand.

He made no jokes. Guthred passed a second lance up. They would have three passes with this and then fall to blade work.

Again, the eyes of the crowd turned to Abravanal. He tot-tered above them, then the ancient sword fell, and the trum-pets rang.

Once more, Lamoric allowed his brother's warhorse to gather speed, opening into a rolling gallop. This time the tall gray shied before the duke's onslaught, veering toward the crowd. Still, Lamoric brought the point to bear, and struck.

Once again, Lamoric's aim was good. The point shrieked a flash from the duke's helm: a prize hit. But even as Duke

Radomor rocked, his own point struck. The steel bit through shield to jut three feet beyond. Again, Lamoric's horse recoiled, his haunch knocking one spectator into his fellows. A thousand rooks lifted their wings.

Adrift above the crowd, Lamoric canted in the saddle.

Every man around Durand clenched his fists, every eye pinned on the filed blade. Had it gone under the arm? Had it gone through their man?

Radomor's cloak billowed with the black wings all around as he too watched—the snapped haft of his lance still in his fist.

But Lamoric did not bleed; he did not open like a barrel of claret. Hands from among the citizens of Acconel reached for him as he lolled over their heads. Men and women lent their strength to his, righting their young lord.

And Lamoric managed to face the duke, who cast the broken fragment of his lance into the crowd and made ready for another pass.

Lamoric reached his comrades. They could hear his breath whistling through the mask of his helm.

"Perhaps it wouldn't be so bad to spend a year over in Yrlac, eh?" said big Ouen.

"Am I dead?" asked Lamoric. He held his arms as though both were broken. Durand could see nothing of his face through the helm, but the left side of his surcoat was a ruin. Fragments of his shield hung from an arm still tangled with his enemy's spear.

"When did I ever tell you to hunt a man's head in a pass like this?" asked Coensar. A shield was the larger target.

"I was trying . . . trying for smack in the middle . . . middle of the whoreson's shield. I don't know," gasped Lamoric. "Not used . . . to this horse." His hands shook.

Guthred was tearing and digging at Lamoric's side; the knight hadn't left his saddle. "Looks like it cracked the shield, shot over wrist bone, smacked up against that coat-of-plates you're always carping about, and then out."

"Feels like it's in my ribs."

Guthred scowled. "We'll need a hammer if these plates're to lie right. Never touched you."

"Is this the last pass? Then it's blades?" asked Lamoric.

"Aye," said Coensar.

There was a rush from the sky. The Heavens had filled with rooks, and the men winced at the snap of their feathers and the wheeling shadows of their wings.

"All right," said Lamoric. "Last lance." The rooks swooped low, cawing their derision. Lamoric still had to gasp. "They still up there? Cursed helm. You'd think . . . You'd think these bloody birds could wait for a man to fall down."

Guthred set the final lance into his master's groping hand.

Durand watched as his borrowed helm turned toward the duke's box. His father already stood, the ducal crown on a tangle of floating gray hair. Lamoric's wife was nowhere to be seen; Almora could not be abandoned.

Across the lists were grinning Rooks, green knights, sneers, and carrion birds. On this final pass, Duke Radomor and Lord Lamoric would ride out and fight as long as their wounds allowed.

Abravanal raised the Isle Kingdom sword, then the trumpets rang.

As Lamoric spurred his gray on, Radomor erupted into motion, his cloak another part of the feathered storm above the fortress. Durand wondered how many eyes were on them now. How many spies sat among the burghers on the benches.

Again, the gray shied off. Horse and rider skimmed the reviewing stand, with Radomor roaring over the turf to swing down upon them.

At the last, with all of Radomor's terrible strength wrapped around his lance, the duke spurred his warhorse to leap. For an instant, beast and knight struck as one, jamming the spear's point home.

Lamoric exploded from his seat. Breast band and doubled girths sprang apart. Lamoric crashed into the screams of the crowd with his boots still in the stirrup irons.

Above him, Radomor let his wild-eyed mount kick the air. Lamoric's blade—all that was left of his shivered lance— stood in the duke's green shield. Radomor batted the thing aside and swung right down into the mob to finish things.

People sprawled to get away. Durand couldn't see; none of the men could. He thought Lamoric must be dragging himself.

Radomor hauled out a war sword, stalking him. "Lamoric of Gireth, do you yield?" His voice boomed like the kettle-drums of an army.

Durand thought he heard something snarled back at the duke, then the hollow clang of a helm thrown to the sod.

"He's alive," said Ouen.

"God help him," said Berchard.

Radomor too threw off his helm, his eyes and snarl now visible in the mouth of his chain hood. "If you will not yield, then on your feet." They lost sight of him, then he reap-peared, dragging Lamoric upright by his surcoat. The duke's war sword gleamed in his free hand.

At that moment, someone in the crowd must have disliked what he saw. A clod of earth or dung smacked from the big man's head, and the duke reared up, searching for his at-tacker and seeing only the mob.

Another glob of something whistled from the heaving crowd. And, this time, Radomor lashed out, skipping the flat of his great blade from someone's skull.

The crowd shrieked; there were women and children. Hands reached for the Duke of Yrlac where he stood, poised with Lamoric in one fist and his blade in the other. Lamoric shook himself free.

It was at this moment that Durand saw the Champion: that thing of stinking rags and iron mail had come alive. It bat-tered past the marshals and rode.

"Hells," said Durand. "The devil will—"

The crowd was heaving over itself. There would already be people dying in that mess. Radomor's Champion launched it-self into the mob, its own war sword flashing.

"Let's get him out of there!" said Coensar, and Lamoric's men were in their saddles. Durand spurred Geridon's Pale through the half-sacred bounds of the lists, galloping for his lord.

But Coensar thrust a mailed hand across Durand's path: forty riders stormed into the lists, bristling with spears, Rado-mor's retainers making for their master. The rolling bulwark crashed onto Coensar's party. A hail of blades thundered from shields and forearms. Durand was mobbed. Coensar lashed with a spiked flail. Durand rang his blade from anything near.

And the crowd shrieked like a scalded thing.

They brawled against a welter of slashing blades and tearing spears. They were caught with eight opponents for every man of theirs. Between blows, Durand made out the Champion beyond the riders. Bodies spun from the thing as if from the horns of the festival bulls. And Radomor stalked up the bank. They were only a dozen paces from Lamoric, but they could neither see nor reach him.

Coensar snarled and tore through with a fierce swing that nailed the head of his flail—by its own spikes—to one knight's helmet.

Then Durand lost sight of him. A spear struck him in the mailed jaw, digging—lifting. Iron tore. He hardly saw Ouen before the big man was swinging down with his massive sword of war. The blow hacked the assailant's helm to the eye-slits, both knights flinching from the hot spatter.

When Durand looked again, Coensar had jagged a path to within instants of the duke. Durand's heart swelled as the hero's spiked flail shrilled, but then, abruptly, something ripped the captain from his saddle.

Durand's shout was drowned in the riot.

Ouen stood in his stirrups, high over the throng. "The Champion!"

They threw themselves against the wall of green riders. Badan, in his black and crimson, spat and savaged anyone near him. Berchard turned and turned his mount, tearing spaces from the mob. Ouen spread chaos with his long sword. But they couldn't press forward. Kicking and punching, smashing men's faces with the pommel of his sword, Durand took no time to aim. They were beasts in a pit.

Yrlac's Champion loomed beyond the enemy, hulking like a monstrous spider balled in man's armor.

"Durand?" shouted Ouen. "It's hopeless!"

The eyes of all three turned to Durand. They could never break through this way.

"Follow me! Ride!" Durand tore Pale from the press, and

all three of his comrades swung away with him. He knew that Radomor's gang would be breathing now, the wash of relief spinning through their veins. And they had a heartbeat to sag off their guard.

"Back at 'em!" he roared.

With wild eyes, Lamoric's men tore round, spurring their horses for Radomor's line.

Durand swung his sword high, and raised his shield. There was a leg-breaking tangle of horses between Pale and Yrlac. He would only get one chance to break through. Pale was a thunderbolt fit to shatter trees; the brute's haunches bunched. Durand fixed his eye on the time-frozen turning of Radomor's head as Pale leapt into the sky.

The collision was too quick to dissect. Men sprawled. Almost, Durand's sword was ripped from his fist. Iron rang. Badan's warhorse tumbled, man and horse disappearing. Durand landed, pitching against his saddlebow. Faces and flanks exploded past him. And there he was.

He wheeled Pale before Duke Radomor, three feet of steel in his fist. Lamoric—streaming blood and dazed—was safe beyond him.

Durand extended his hand, and when Lamoric made to protest or stagger, Durand heaved man and iron mail up over his saddlebow.

Radomor snarled.

As Durand made to take flight, Radomor caught Pale's bridle; the huge warhorse might as well have been chained to a stronghold's wall.

Durand swung his blade down: he would sever the devil's arm.

The duke threw up his sword. Durand swung again: sledge-hammer blows to break the bond that held him. But the duke leapt close and suddenly Durand could not keep pace. One-handed, the duke put his war sword to work. The thing flickered like a wasp and cracked down like an anvil. One jab tore Durand's surcoat. Another smashed iron links. Giant Pale could not back away. It would only be moments.

Then Radomor's point crunched home in the folds of Durand's mailed stomach: the duke had reached too far. Doubling over the blade, Durand trapped the sword, and, with a lunge that strained every ligament, he jammed his blade into the man's neck.

The duke's hands leapt to his throat.

Durand swept his blade high and hammered it down on Radomor's mailed head. The duke sagged.

But before the man could fall, a manacle clamped shut on Durand's neck. He twisted to see the Champion, reaching across Pale's back, his fist grinding Durand's neck bones. Light flashed, and he saw the brute's long blade flicker back. Durand would never bring his sword round in time.

Then something struck the monster—nearly hauling Durand down. Ouen had launched himself on the brute. Suddenly, the thing was battered by a sea of knights and horses. Its tomb gray hair burst from its helm in a ragged mane. Durand swung his sword against the arm that chained him.

"I cannot!" the monster's lost voice moaned, enduring the clash of iron.

Ouen hauled at the thing, still behind it. For an instant his eyes were on Durand's: *Go!*

The Champion twisted its head around and seized Ouen. *"Get away!"* the eerie voice sobbed, as, with just one hand, it lifted the massive man bodily. Ouen gaped. The Champion fought to its feet, and when Ouen began to scrabble at the thing's helm, it shrieked and lashed him through the air as though he were a man of straw.

Durand hacked at the monster's arm, now truly slamming the blade down on living bone. Pale screamed and leapt back. Badan, a wild man in black, stepped close and smacked the Champion off balance with a blow across the back of its helm.

And Durand spurred Pale away. The monster's fingers tore loose, and, abruptly, Durand was free in the tiltyard. He gulped air and looked back. Before the great mob, the monster laid about with its fists, flinging men and great warhorses around it. A shriek built, as if the monster were a whirlwind in chains. Badan crashed in a heap of his own armored skirts. Berchard toppled as the brute snapped his mount's foreleg. Rooks wheeled overhead. The Champion straddled Radomor's fallen body, even lashing out at Radomor's own guardsmen in its frenzy.

"Durand! Durand!" a voice shouted.

Coensar wavered among the broken bodies and horrified men of Yrlac. He was alive, though his face was swollen. He reached for Durand, tangling in Durand's surcoat as he got close. *"Durand,"* he gasped. "Give him to me. You've got to get them away from there. Radomor's fallen. That thing'll kill them if we don't get them clear." It was all Coensar could do to keep his feet and utter the words at the same time.

Durand nodded, letting Lamoric slide from Pale's neck.

"Get them clear," said Coensar.

"I will." Durand rode past the mob, screaming: "To me. To me. Withdraw! Get away from the thing!"

Faces turned to him, but, unhorsed in the press, they would never get free. Not only was the Champion chewing up anything near him, but Radomor's staggered conroi was coming back to its senses, flexing like the coils of a serpent to trap their attackers. Before his eyes, a gap opened between Badan and Berchard: a slender, final chance.

"Hells," he said, and charged. As he slipped the gap, he dropped his sword and shield and hooked both startled knights from the ground with a force that nearly threw him from his saddle. Air exploded from between his teeth. Sparks flashed. But Pale slewed through the crowd to freedom.

As he let his friends loose, he wheeled Pale back for Ouen. And the big horse skittered to a halt.

Around the dark bulwark of the Champion, Yrlac's men clutched a bleeding thicket of spears, scrambling over dead men and horses. Each spear was leveled at Pale's chest. Blood stood dark on their green surcoats.

Durand stared into the blades. Pale would do his bidding. He would leap for that hedge of spears, and there would be a moment while the blades held him in the air before they tore.

If Durand had seen only a glimpse of Ouen, Pale would have flown. Durand's gaze flickered through the dripping shafts and faces. The only weapon left to him was his misericorde: a throat-cutting dagger too short for this work. He saw only the black slot of the Champion's stare.

But Ouen had been swallowed up. There was no blond mane. There was no glint of gold teeth.

In the midst of the static frenzy of the green knights,

Radomor's Champion bent to rise again, with his stricken master lifted on his hands, like a sacrifice.

Durand trembled on the edge of jabbing his spurs home.

He heard people move into line around him: Badan, Berchard, Coensar, Lamoric. Someone touched Durand's knee.

"That's all we can do," Berchard said. "That's all there is. We've got to leave the lists."

Durand watched for Ouen. He watched for motion from Radomor. The folds of his empty right hand felt greasy in his fist—full of blood.

"Durand!" Berchard hissed.

Beyond the spears, Radomor finally stirred, a hand pawing his Champion's iron coat. The monster bent its head still farther.

There was no sign of Ouen.

Berchard was safe. And Lamoric, and Coen, and Badan.

"Durand," said Coensar. "It's time to get inside."

🪢 16. Numbering the Dead

Y ou're alive." Deorwen breathed the words, standing in the midst of the Painted Hall, frozen, as Lamoric led his battered men spilling in. Only the Queen of Heaven knew the woman's heart.

Almora had been at play on the rushes. A toy Power winked and shimmered in the gloom of the vaults, riding a shy song on damselfly wings. The little girl seemed as pretty as the song. Lamoric and his limping mob of bloodstained men stank like butchers.

"We heard a great commotion," said Deorwen. Keeping calm for the girl's sake must have cost her. "I didn't know what to think."

Lamoric managed a wavering smile. "A riot, my dear. I am afraid Duke Radomor is most upset."

Durand noted Almora, chin tucked and staring from the hearth as the conroi dropped onto benches. He saw her whispering Power dip toward her hands. They said that she had seen a line of gray men creeping through the dark—her father had been traveling to the marches beyond the mountains— and she had held her tongue until the timid Strangers had slipped into the stones. The last to vanish turned and set the toy in her hand: a gift of gratitude. A little thing like a dove and lion, it woke if a tiny hand turned its key.

The Power settled into the bowl of Almora's hands with a snip of wings and a wink of precious stones.

"Thus am I saved from my own folly. Great is the King of Heaven." Lamoric sprawled on one of the benches. Blood slicked from a cut somewhere on his forehead. "Only with a mob and knot of armed guards am I fit to face bloody Rado-mor."

Berchard croaked around a split lip. "In borrowed gear, on a borrowed mount, you met him. That's not nothing."

Coensar looked gravely from his own blood and bruises.

"A wiser brute than I, that horse," said Lamoric. "But no matter. You all pulled me free. Host of Heaven, that Champion was laying about. Those people with their mud. They'll have paid dearly."

Coensar returned to business. "Now we must see how Radomor reacts."

"Reacts? That son of a whore could die," Badan said. "Our ox here gave his skull a good tap. Maybe he goes deaf."

"A man like Radomor of Yrlac will not go easy," Berchard said.

There were grunts.

"This will have put paid to the tourney," said Lamoric. "There will be bodies enough for burying without further chivalry." He grunted, touching his face. "Father must tell the marshals."

Deorwen had looked over the company. "Where is Ouen?"

"Did you see the grip he took on that monster?" said Lamoric. Lying down, he could not see the others' blank faces. "He could pull up trees by the roots, that man."

Durand's head wasn't good: he could still feel the Champion's iron fingers in the sinews of his throat. And the scabbard at his hip hung empty. His sword was somewhere in the muck under the wall. He took a breath to confess—

But Guthred tramped from the stairs with Heremund in

tow. The shield-bearer lugged a knapsack of bandages, pots, and knives—and wore a murderous scowl. Durand caught a quick exchange between the shield-bearer and the captain: he saw a question in Coensar's look; Guthred shook his head.

"Radomor's men have left the yard," said Heremund. "The duke was up on his own pins. They think he killed a man who tried to lend him a shoulder."

"Damn fools," Guthred said. "All of you." And squatted by Lamoric with a hooked cobbler's needle.

"Ouen might still be all right," Berchard said. "He's . . . he's a big lad."

Lamoric twisted from Guthred's grip. "Aw, no."

If Durand had seen a hair of Ouen in that knot of spears, he would have thrown himself into the heart of it—he wanted to believe that was true—but there had been no trace. Guthred started his needlework once more: click, snip. His stitches crawled Lamoric's brow to bury themselves in clotted hair.

"Where is he?" said Lamoric. "Is the man still out there?"

Durand turned from the others, catching a glimpse of Almora's dark eyes as he left the hall. Plunging down the grand stairs, he breasted servant crowds. Above the yard, only a fraction of the rooks still churned the air. The tide of roaring humanity, now departed, had left only the mud and the stricken behind. Bodies lay everywhere, some writhing. A woman clutched a small shape, rocking and smearing a tiny white face. People wailed. Durand could not remember what Ouen had worn: a russet shirt of borrowed mail?

The castle's priests flapped from despair to despair, too few for too many. A senior man was directing that bodies should be dragged from the muck—or be checked for signs of life. Seeing a priest crouched very close to a long form, Durand knocked the man aside to find a stranger's features: sharp shades of purpled red and silver-gray. The priest tried to take Durand's arm.

Two shield-bearers struggled to corner a limping warhorse that lurched and hopped away from them. They would end its misery.

On the bank by the gatehouse straggled a row of gray

corpses. Priests or sextons had pulled canvas over them. Durand saw only limbs.

He pitched across the yard and began to scramble up the bank, hesitating as he stumbled on a conversation.

A bloated little man stood with hands muddy to the elbows. A bent creature in a saffron tabard squatted by a corner of the canvas sheet, squinting up. "Surely. *Some*'re good, but most're going to need new soles. I could see giving you, say, three pence. What say you?" When the man lifted the corner, Durand had a glimpse of empty boots.

The fat man looked around, his hands muddy from dragging bodies. "Ha. What're the chances you'd be here at this moment, and you a cobbler. Eh?" the fat man spat. "That's what I say. Here is the Lord of Dooms providing for you. If you can't get a penny for each and every pair, you're a dullard and—"

Durand's eyes moved from foot to gray foot beyond the hem of canvas. Some were as creased as the palms of a man's hand. One pair was tiny. Some were bent with bunions. Others were stained red and brown with dyes of their shoes or hose. They faced up and down: heel and toe.

"A man cannot live on nothing," the yellow man said. "If there's no difference between start and finish, then where's a man's life to come from?"

Durand climbed closer, on all fours.

The two men looked down, startled at the creature—muddy as the corpses—crawling the bank toward them. Their eyes scrabbled over him, marking the rust-bleeding mail. Their mouths opened.

A tiny motion of the saffron man dropped the canvas over the boots. Durand's glance caught the movement. "It wasn't my idea, sir, but Ecmon's here." The man made to slip down the bank—the gatehouse was a few paces away.

There were no words in Durand's snarl. His knuckles caught the yellow man. The fat partner sprawled—scrambling—onto the heap of bodies. Durand snatched the misericorde from his belt and, almost, launched himself upon them.

Other men were still hauling bodies: volunteers, sextons, priests. Voices sobbed from the yard below. And Durand checked the fit of temper.

"I have lost a friend," he said. "You will help me find him. Do you understand?"

They stared: the fat man, his face as yellow as his partner's tabard; his partner on his knees, hesitating.

Durand caught the yellow tabard, jerking the man upright. "You will lift the canvas. Your friend, he'll get under there and make sure we can see."

The yellow man balanced between terrors for a moment, then Durand took two fistfuls of the man's tabard and tossed him into the pale tangle.

One by one, they lifted stained heads. Durand watched, blankly noting injuries and indignities. It was hard to judge which had fought for Yrlac and which had been complete outsiders. Finally, the shaking saffron man pulled a long-limbed body free. Before he could grab another, Durand leapt forward, his hand raised. "Wait."

At first, the slit eyes and slack skin bore little resemblance to anyone Durand had known. But he climbed among the slithering shapes, taking that cold face in his hands. A blond beard jutted. He felt the massive bones of his friend's face. His teeth glinted cold between his lips.

"Ouen."

After a moment, Durand stood while the two muddy fools cowered. "If I see you again, I shall leave you as you left him."

The men hesitated, too frightened to move.

Durand skidded down the bank, slapping the white side of the gatehouse for balance.

He heard an order, and a guard touched his shoulder in time that the great portcullis in the gatehouse slammed down without killing him. Rooks—only a hundred now—croaked into the sky below the towers.

Durand stepped into the barred gateway, seeing, through two grilles of oak and iron, green surcoats and red leopards massed outside. Radomor's tourney knights stood in the market before the gate. "Summon old Abravanal! Duke Radomor of Yrlac wishes to parley."

Finding a stairway close at hand, Durand pushed guards aside and climbed to the parapet above the street. Seven fathoms down, Duke Radomor sat on horseback in the midst of his men—and in the midst of a great crowd. His head bobbed like a duck's egg. If there had been a stone loose on the parapet, Durand could have smashed that skull. He judged by the retinue's laden pack animals that Yrlac's liege-men had already struck their tents and quit the castle for good.

At a scuffling on the stair, Durand turned—fist on the misericorde—and found Duke Abravanal clambering up the steps. Abravanal did not so much lead the knights as he was borne along like driftwood on the wave of them. Behind the duke, Lamoric gave Durand a haunted glance. The men nearly pitched Durand over the wall as the press made its way to the gatehouse.

Abravanal leaned over the parapet. "You have left before the Feast of the Bull," he faltered. "It is unlucky."

Radomor's answer was a leopard's rumble. "Yours has been a treacherous hospitality, Abravanal. I will not suffer it again."

Duke Abravanal blinked his wide blue eyes. "This has been a grim time for my family." He tensed. "Why do you summon us from our grief?"

Radomor cocked his head. "Half the kingdom grieves under the yoke of that fool in the Mount of Eagles. The busi-ness of living men cannot wait on a dotard's moaning."

Lamoric lurched forward. "Radomor! This is the house of your wife's people. How have you come to this?" He pointed down on them. "You are the vilest in a menagerie of horrors."

Radomor's tall horse jigged between his heels. "You are quick to speak, child of Abravanal!" He twisted blood from the warhorse's mouth, and the beast shuddered still. "And behind stout walls, you are brave."

The air shivered, hot, from the bald duke's skull but he did not shout. "I will have what is mine. Your brother has learned, and now you all must learn. I will have what is owed me. It might have been a surgeon's cut, but now you have forced my hand."

Radomor jerked his horse around, and with his men bulling the crowd from the way, he spurred for Acconel's Gates of Sunset and the road to Yrlac.

Abravanal turned from the wall, about to say something to the son who had always been at his right hand. When he found Lamoric instead, he faltered. "My barons. We must send riders. They must have warning."

Lamoric stood blankly, shaking, then nodded "yes."

⊛ 17. The Shadow of Black Wings

Two-score desperate messengers galloped over the roads of Gireth, hoping to reach the halls of every baron in the dukedom—and any court in Errest the Old that might send aid to Acconel.

But despite the demands of sanity, there was a feast in the Painted Hall of Castle Acconel that day.

At the high table, only Almora moved—from Deorwen to the duke, the others sat in silence. Durand looked down the empty benches. The great host who had populated the tilt-yard had fled in a thousand directions. While the few dozen who remained stared in the hall, the knights in the outer yard were striking tents and slinging their belongings over their horses. The hollow-eyed men who remained cringed and twitched in the long silences.

Burghers filled some of the empty places; men who brought their wives and elder children. These were guild masters and citizens; they could not flee. The tiny children wondered at the constellations of beeswax candles turning in the huge wheel chandeliers over their heads. The oldest pretended not to notice.

When a deeper hush flowed down the half-empty tables, Duke Abravanal stood before the skeleton crowd, his voice like a leaf's dry flutter.

"On this night we feast the honor of Heaven's King. His Champion. The Warders at the Bright Gates of Heaven . . . Lords of Heaven's Host."

The old man stared out over the hall, his eyes fixed on some faraway point. When his silence had stretched long enough to start eyes shifting down the table, Patriarch Oredgar touched the duke's sleeve. " 'We remember. . . .' "

"We remember," Abravanal said. "Yes. We remember though it was Gunderic who . . . who rebuked the beast of the mere, that it is only with Heaven's strength that we may defy the darkness. His victory was the Creator's victory.

"It is in this knowledge that I repeat the old words: 'You defy Heaven at your peril.'" It should have been a roar. His tongue ran across his lips. "While the Silent King reigns, this land . . . this land is ours."

The faint syllables died in silence.

At the bleat of a tardy fanfare, straining servers wove into the hall, pallbearers for a platter and the hairless, steaming thing it supported. Durand marveled; it was a monstrous, muscular head. Horns curled from a mighty brow—the head of a bull, seared bald. Rashers of bacon curled in semblance of a forelock. Its eyes suppurated with candied fruit.

Abravanal sank into his seat.

As the platter skidded heavily onto the high table and its burden glared over the room, it could not have looked more like Duke Radomor.

As one course followed another, Sir Kieren appeared at Durand's side, swinging his legs over the bench. The man seemed very small.

"Sir Kieren," Durand acknowledged.

"Do you know where I'm from?"

Durand frowned. "We went to Arbourhall more than once when I was your man."

"Arbourhall is my wife's, really. Abravanal arranged it for me when we were both young men. A young widow. *I'm* a Garelyn man. My father had a patch of ground under the mountains." His foxtail mustaches jumped. Both men knew of Durand's own ancestral home hard by the mountains. "And no room for his youngest son.

"We'd go down to see the duke at Bederin. The castle's right on the Deep. There's the gate, like a chain of silver towers. There are mountains before and behind you. It was me talked that old Duke Aymar's son into sending a daughter to our Landast. They say our Adelind raced a water-horse on the dunes by the Deep. Outrode it. And she beat an heir of Beoran in the tiltyard."

And now she'd be entombed in Acconel.

"A good foster-mother for poor Almora, I thought. When the little thing's own mother passed. Now, the girl seems to have attached herself to Deorwen."

Serving men and pages came to take a course away. Durand could not have said what it was.

"I deserted you," Durand said. "I'd sworn an oath to serve you."

With a smile under his mustache, Kieren said, "I would have let you go. You are a young man. What else could a young man do?"

Durand stared at the wreckage of the seared bull, recalling Radomor's great rage.

At the high table, the solemn marshals of the tournament were speaking. Every year, they scattered honors among the men for valor and skill. What would they do for riot and murder?

"Even without you, I made it home," Kieren said. "Lost a good horse getting down from your father's hall. We will have to make certain that whoever holds Gravenholm tends those woods."

Durand sniffed a laugh. Gravenholm, his onetime patrimony, seemed very far from Castle Acconel. Someone on the dais said Durand's name.

"Durand!" Berchard hissed, his good eye darting. *"Durand, you ox. It's you."*

"What?"

Kieren was swiveling. "I was on the point of warning you."

Coensar slipped out and stepped to Durand's side.

Everyone had gotten to their feet.

"You'd best get up," said Coensar. They marched up the hall to the high table where the Patriarch, the old duke, and his surviving family sat: Lamoric, Deorwen, and Almora. Durand felt the eyes of the company squeeze like deep water as he reached the table's edge.

Coensar whispered from behind him. *"They'll expect a bow."*

Durand nodded low, eyes on the duke, while one of the marshals gave the old man a medallion. The thing dangled from the duke's fingers on a bit of ribbon.

"He was in the stable," declared Almora.

Lamoric stepped in for his father. "The voice of the company has spoken. For your actions on the field this day, my father names you the Bull of Acconel, highest honor of this feast day."

Deorwen looked on. Reading a gesture of the young lord's hand, Durand crossed to the duke's side, kneeling for the duke to dangle the medallion high. The face of a bull winked from its loop of silk. This was the sort of thing that champions of Coensar's ilk won after long summer's days in the lists.

Durand shot a look at Lamoric—a ribbon for riot, a medal for murder.

"I had to make a decision," he said. "Who else?" But there was Ouen, now dead. And Lamoric himself. Both had done more.

The duke lowered the medal over Durand's head, and then seemed to master himself. The blue eyes blazed like moons, and he brought Durand to his feet.

As the new Bull of Acconel turned to face the assembled company, every knight raised his blade in a somber salute. He had left one friend to die while he saved a man he betrayed.

Here was a hollow glory.

AFTER SEEING THE feast out, Durand abandoned the Painted Hall, stalked through the inner courtyard, and into the muddy yard beyond it. The shadows had crept from the cracks and filled the field. One last group of knights was checking saddles and preparing to take the road. In a few hours, two hundred men had folded up their shield-bearers, tents, and grooms. Every coward would be leagues away by morning.

He eyed the bank where the crowd had watched. He remembered the spears and the screams. Near the gate where the bodies had lain, a row of tall carts stood under the eyes of murmuring priests. Each cart leaned heavily under sheets of gray canvas that obscured its load.

Durand felt the Bull medallion thump against his chest. He could hear the sounds of men loading horses across the grass. The light that had left the yard would soon abandon the sky as well.

Durand took the bull from his neck and walked to the carts. Eventually, the priests allowed him to search for his comrade. He pulled the medal over tangled hair and knotted beard, then muttered a few words to the Host of Heaven.

Eventually, a voice interrupted: "A man shouldn't stand too long in the night air. Especially here." Durand turned to see Coensar hitching through the gloom toward him. His head was bound. "There's a spot by the gate," he said, indicating a sentry's stone bench in the shadows.

There was a long sigh as he sat down. "How old are you, boy?"

"I've seen twenty-one winters."

"As many as that?" Coensar said. "Twenty-one winters've passed since I won my spurs, I think." He swept his blade, Keening, from its scabbard, and Durand could hear the high, eerie song of its shadowy blade on the night air. "I won Keening the first moon, and fought seven years thereafter to catch the eye of the old Duke of Beoran.

"And the very next moon." He clapped his hands. "It was Cassonel of Damaryn on the stairs at Tern Gyre and down I went. Fourteen years since—fifteen, now."

Durand tried to picture a lifetime of night watches, wild tourneys, and campaigns in the south. He had been a knight less than half a year.

"Ah, watch now," Coensar said, suddenly. Coensar gestured with the singing blade across the dark grass where shadows stirred like ink in the ruts and pockmarks of the yard. They were too thick, stretching with stubborn viscosity, seeming so dark that there must be traces left in the morning.

Durand raised his fingers in the Heaven's Eye.

"Do you see?" And, noting the fist and fingers, he answered his own question: "You must. Death and soldiers. You can't help but see after a time—they are Lost souls," said Coensar. "Jealous for blood. Berchard or your Heremund would tell you more. A conjurer will dangle a bowl of the stuff under their noses."

"Host"—a convulsive ripple passed through the strange

forms as though the word were salt cast over leeches—"of Heaven," Durand finished.

And Coensar chuckled as the the slack shapes knotted, long gaping to break like rings of smoke.

"Will we end up like this?" Durand said. His head swam with the shame and longing of the past days.

"Who am I to say what a man will lose? It's a long road we're on."

Durand jerked the hem of his cloak free from one sniffling spirit. "King of Heaven."

Breathy screams whispered, and Durand realized that they must soon be breathing dead men. Some of the packhorses across the way were nodding now, sensing the Otherworldly crowd.

"They are only the dead, Durand. Few who'd grovel at our feet could do us much harm. The strong take; they don't plead."

What sort of life did these things have, slinking the ditches, starving; trapped in the seams of Creation while whatever made them human wore away?

The knights and their uneasy packhorses were clopping near, ready to pass under the gates.

"I saw what you did with that medal. And I tell you, watch how you tie yourself to the dead," Coensar said. "Hate and grief and guilt're binding things." He narrowed an eye at Durand, ignoring the spirits' coiling. "And don't brood too long in the cold night air." This last was a sigh.

Above them, the party of knights had stopped. One of them was Berchard, leading a pair of saddle horses: a roan and a sturdy blue dun. He had an armory sword over his shoulder.

"Now," said Coensar, "I'd say that while Radomor's ridden off, he's hardly finished with us yet. I've spoken to Sir Kieren. We need a man to scout across the river toward Yrlac while we've still got a chance. You'll cross the bridge with some friends of mine, in case you're watched. Go and come back tonight with news. You must get back how you can."

Berchard nodded.

THEIR BORROWED COMPANY left by the same streets the doomed bulls took the day before, and soon they were through the haunted Fey Gates, half sure the stone bulls were watching them. Durand followed Berchard's lead and mingled among the others with their plain horses and rough gear.

Rather than leaving by the docks, their company swung north for the quayside road, the lower city, and the north channel of the Banderol. The Dukes' Bridge soon loomed under the fading Heavens.

A light on the far bank threw shadows down the span.

Berchard allowed himself to duck close. "You see them?" He nodded toward the far end of the bridge. A bowshot away, three statues towered over the road, tall as sanctuary towers. These were the Dukes, and this was where three roads—and three lands—met below the granite wasteland of the Warrens. Among the stone folds at the giants' ankles, however, were bonfires and a cadre of armed men. "If the bugger's got forty men down here, what'll he have on Fuller's Bridge upriver?"

"Just as well we didn't risk it," said Durand. Only two spans could take a man to the Ferangore Road: the Dukes' crossed down by Silvermere, but upstream, the Fuller's Bridge led nearly straight to Yrlac. Anyone heading to Yrlac by either bridge must pass it.

Berchard glanced at Durand. "Hunch over and try not thinking so hard. We might still slip past them going north and then cut back for the Ferangore Road beyond the Fuller's Bridge." Berchard grinned and touched the patch over his eye. "Maybe I'll tuck this patch under my collar. Best if we're not the festival bull and his mate just now, I reckon."

The water gleamed heavily under the Dukes' Bridge, the men muttered, and, slowly, the Warrens bank hove near. Durand made out crossbows and saddled horses—forty men in mail. Three great ways of ancient times diverged at the statues' feet: the Acconel road lay behind the party, the road to Lost Hesperand to the right, and the road west into Yrlac on their left hand. Above them all towered the founding lords of Gireth, Hesperand, and Yrlac. They were comrades of Saerdan the Voyager. Durand knew Gunderic by the great bull device charged on his shield. Eldred of Hesperand wore the Peregrine Crown borne by his successors, and Thrasimund of Yrlac carried a curved axe long as a ship's mast. Their hands met at a great fire basket above the road. It was three fathoms to their knees.

Down below, Radomor's men were sneering over two dozen crossbows. A twitch on any tiller would stamp a bolt through an armored chest. The fact that Durand had served Duke Radomor less than a year past had likely slipped Coensar's mind.

As Durand's blue dun raised its hoof over the far bank, Coensar's friend was already speaking with the captain of Radomor's watchmen. They got a late start, he said. Someone had stolen a horse. They were traveling north to his brother's land, a patch between Silvermere and the Warrens—a fishing village: Herons. They were taking the Hesperand Road before things cut loose.

Durand reached the bank and felt Creation shudder. The patch of torchlit stones was a dungeon cell between the giants. The ground was ash, and the Warrens, walls of cinders. A lean man in Radomor's leopards jammed a torch into Durand's face, peering with yellow eyes and a thin-lipped grin.

"I know you from somewhere?"

Durand swallowed hard. His head filled with Ferangore towers and barracks halls, but he blinked and forced himself to give the soldier a bored shrug.

And the man moved on.

And soon, the man's captain let them ride away.

Durand gripped the saddlebow like a drunken man, feeling eyes on him from every side.

The watch fires must have been well behind them when Berchard dropped through the ranks.

"All right?" he said. "We'd best do this." He nodded their farewells to the rest while they stopped between broad Silvermere and black Warrens. A wind shoved Durand's hair.

"You think they knew us?" he asked.

"I think I'm going to be sick." Berchard pulled the patch out of his collar and cinched it round the bad eye. "I'm too old for that kind of game so soon after supper. Coensar and I are going to have words."

Durand hauled in a deep breath, eyeing the dark and knotted hills. "You reckon they'd see us if we steal round through the hills?"

The land mounted against the sky as jumbled as heaped boulders. Berchard grimaced at the great bales of juniper and thorn on the high stones by the track. They could never get through on horseback. "We're not carrying the horses," he chided, "so put that out of your head."

Durand managed a grin. "We won't get far scouting on foot. We'll have to see if we can't lead them through." He hopped from the saddle.

Berchard swung his leg over and grunted to the ground in a jingle of mail. "They say there are a thousand paces between West and Dukes' Bridges—though they'll be counting by road. Come on." With that, he took the reins and suddenly took the lead.

With a headshake, Durand followed.

The two men pitched and scrabbled through the granite hills, finding deadfalls or cliffs up every blind ravine. Berchard grunted curses, but sometimes a laugh or oath would shoot over the hills to freeze them both. Durand kept his eyes on the trees and hilltops. He flinched at the passage of an owl. Berchard's every slip clattered like a tinker's cart.

Durand considered his spot with Deorwen and her husband. He wondered if it might still be possible to get out from between them. If not now, then after Radomor's fury was spent. Gireth's allies would sit the man down—dukes did not wage war alone and Abravanal had friends. He could see that, with one thing and another, Lamoric and Deorwen had hardly had a chance. There was plenty in each of them that was good. They needed time and peace to find it without some fool crowding in.

Yet his heart would not be ruled; he wanted to get her out.

They had walked an hour or more of bramble and briar. Durand shot a whisper over Berchard's roan. "Should we cut back?" He was not sure how far they'd come. "That might still be firelight up there, but I can't be sure." Something glimmered in the highest branches down where the road must lay. "There could be two hundred soldiers right over the hill."

"If we feel the bolts raining down, I suppose, we'll know— *Uh, Host of Heaven!*"

"Berchard?" Durand spun, searching the trees, sword in hand.

The old man's breeches and leggings came down as he squatted. Struggling with flaps of armor, Berchard forced a wet flatulence into the bushes. "Oh, such relief, despite the timing."

"Hells, Berchard."

While his comrade strained, Durand put his eyes on the hills off toward the road. The river was out there, and he could still see light among the branches.

He weighed the rusted armory sword in his fist. But as long as Berchard strained, the shadows held their places. No one came.

Berchard stood, tying his waist cord. "Ah, I'm all crossed up," he whispered. "Thirty years, this gear always goes on the same way." He squinted up at Durand. "Leggings first . . ."

Durand loomed in the dark, teeth clenched.

"It'd be tempting fate," Berchard tried.

"If I have to watch you taking all that gear off," Durand said, "you'll ride the rest of the way in your breeches."

"Ah . . . If there's no help for it. I must simply hope for the best."

He stuck his foot in a stirrup, and hauled himself into the saddle. "This ravine's wide enough to ride, I think. These two brutes have eyes like foxes. Little, whatsit, Almora? She pointed them out."

Durand grunted surprise. "And the crossbows?"

"We must be a league past them, and those boys'll be looking for us on the bridge." With a wet *tsk tsk,* the man rode off.

And with hardly another step, they dropped into the road—not a league past Radomor's guards, but scarcely twenty paces from sixty armed men in Yrlat Green. Here was the great span of the Fuller's Bridge with a mighty inn presiding. A caravan yard called Tenter's Field stretched where daylight traders would wait to pay their tolls. Every inch was alive with bonfires and voices.

"Hells," gasped Berchard, and they froze in the lucky few shadows that held them concealed. Dice clicked while the fires crackled. Men debated which whore was best in Feran-

gore. Durand fought an impulse to jam the spurs in and ride for it.

He waited another heartbeat.

"Quietly, I think, eh?" Berchard concluded. A breath.

With the least nudge, Durand started the dun walking westward. With every heartbeat, he waited for a clatter of crossbows.

Slowly, the darkness stretched behind them. They heard less, and, finally, Durand let himself exhale. He made to jam his sword back down his scabbard's throat, but a kink caught it.

"Hells." He felt very shaky. It had been a long day; there had been many long days.

Berchard slipped his roan alongside Durand, smiling. "You shouldn't throw a good sword away."

Durand gave the blade a twist and the thing shot home. "When I plucked you from Radomor's men, I can't remember if I hooked you with the shield or the sword hand."

"Don't mock your elders. It remains wise practice to hang on to a sword. You never know."

"You never know?"

"Well, you might not think it, but this blade of mine's enchanted."

Durand laughed.

"Look here." Berchard swished the wide blade into the moonlight where it shone like a weave of gray syrup. "It's welded. Old, old, old. Those old smiths used to knit a blade from bits of stock, tasted and chosen for bite or bend. It's all lost now."

"Proper steel likely helps."

"I won this one from the last scion of a noble house. One of them families what have every dusty ancestor since old Saerdan a-moldering in the family vault."

Not so very unlike the Barons of the Col.

"The way I reckon, this sword's kept me alive since I won it from the last man who owned it."

"What happened to this onetime master, then?"

"I've given the matter a thought or two over the years, and I'll tell you: I think the blade has a taste for blood. The last owner wasn't worth much in a fight, and before him it'd been hanging on the wall since before the Crusade. Generations, waiting. Think of it. My only worry is that, just maybe, it's the reason that I can never quite get out of fighting. It's been thirty years since it came to me."

He held up the blade once more, letting the moonlight curl in the liquid weave of the steel. "They tell me they used to name these . . ." He pointed at the stitched metal. "These patterns. This one was the 'ladder'—helps a man up to the Bright Gates."

Durand laughed.

For a league, they traveled the narrow way between Banderol and the looming Warrens, their road cut below the roots of bushes.

Cautiously, they entered a crossroads where their track met a similarly deep channel. Something foul hung on the air. Above them, a shape dangled over the road. As they plodded near, Durand tried to make sense of what he saw. Ropes creaked. There was a long form in strap-iron. At the bottom jutted what seemed to be the root-ball of a fallen tree. He was very near before he saw fingers and the white ring of a hollow eye.

He grimaced. The reek stirred in the passages of his lungs, and dead limbs seemed to sway toward living horses and riders: reeds in some invisible current.

"Wise to hang a man at the crossroads," pronounced Berchard.

Durand looked from the reaching hands and let the crossroads fall behind.

"'Specially if he died innocent. The Lost can't find their way to your throat. But a man's got to be careful. Crossroads 're in-between places. You hang a man at a crossroads, he's neither here nor there. Not one road or the next. Seams like that will let things in."

Durand threw his cloak around himself. "Wonder what brought them to this."

Berchard turned in his saddle, smiling archly. "Spies, likely. Sneaked past the sentries at the Fuller's Bridge. No mercy on spies!"

The Warrens drew back from the Ferangore Road, and

Durand guessed that they had left the no-man's-land: this was Yrlac rolling under the vault of Heaven. Silent cots and hamlets lay in the distance.

Soon, they saw a black copse of trees squatting like an island in the fields to the south. A track forked from the road, offering a route.

Durand kneaded his shoulder. "Know anything about the wood?"

"Just a thicket, I suppose. But I tell you, I've had enough riding for one night. There's something . . . I don't know— What say we go that far and then head back?"

They'd spent an hour beyond the Fuller's Bridge and seen nothing but hanged men. "Coensar should know about the men back on those bridges, but aye. That far."

Slowly, they closed the distance to the bristling gloom. On its threshold, elms billowed overhead like a storm. Within, thornbush stood taller than a mounted man, but the track led straight in.

Berchard looked up at the trees. "We said we'd come this far, yes?"

"Aye." There was something about the dark.

"Bugger it," said Berchard and nudged his mount under the trees.

As Durand's dun stepped under the first bough, Creation heaved once more. Even with the branches bare, the forest was black as a well. The air sopped with mold and last year's leaves. Durand clenched his teeth against the urge to haul Berchard out. The pale backs of his hands were nearly invisible on the reins.

"Blast." Berchard cursed from somewhere ahead. "Let's hope the horses know the way back home."

Durand nodded. He put his hand on the hilt of his sword— the borrowed sword's pommel had petals like a blunt iron flower.

"You remember that madman at that village?" said Berchard. "What was it? Ydran? Where they'd all gone off and left him."

"The Steward." He remembered a man with long mustaches in a village where no one lived but a few pigs.

"And the whole village'd gone off into Hesperand. They'd

had a look at what was coming." Durand heard the man sniff. "I wonder how the village fares."

He felt uncertain distances opening up around them. They rode into wood smoke.

"Berchard!" Durand whispered.

"Shh."

Durand listened. The smell of a recent fire was strong and mingled with soft horse dung. He heard nothing.

"Berchard? What?"

For a moment there was nothing, then Berchard's voice said, "Never mind. I thought I heard something shift. Scream if something drags you off."

Durand eyed the blackness, hoping that anything lurking would be as blind as they were.

"When we come back, let's see if we can find a few more midnight woods to traipse through. Yes? At my age, I need a little excitement after dark."

"As you please."

He heard Berchard's *tsk tsk,* and the man's stolid roan clomping away. He followed.

They plodded through the disorienting blackness, smelling horses, green timber, and even excrement. Finally though, they had a bit of clear heaven overhead. Durand could see Berchard's silhouette hunched in its saddle.

"That's better," Durand sighed.

"Aye . . ." Berchard sounded distracted. He dropped into the track with a jingle of armor, squatting low over the road.

"Hells," he said. "Hells!" And he turned his wide, good eye to the wood.

"What've you seen?" said Durand.

"Here. Tracks." The trail under Berchard's hand was churned and rutted. He scrambled up a low bank into the glade. "Everywhere."

Durand swung down. In the slanting moonlight, he could see dozens of tracks. Hundreds. A multitude had trampled the mud.

"It's all fresh," Berchard breathed.

"Travelers to the festival?"

"There were never this many people at that festival, Durand." His eye was on the wood, and he hardly breathed the words. "If I were hiding my army near my neighbor's city, I'd keep a cold camp: no fires."

"Word would get out." He heard sounds around them as if the trees were drawing breath. *"It would have to."*

"It's not a secret that would keep long."

But nothing had passed them. Nothing had left the wood, Durand thought.

"And you'd have to shed an awful lot of blood," Berchard murmured.

"—Oceans," said a voice—a slithering voice, like a tongue darting in Durand's ear.

A figure had stepped into the clearing: a man in short, black robes. His face was the pale round of a skull; sleeves dangled to his ankles.

His twin bobbed into view, a long finger over his lips: *shh!*

And now a soldier—a sword flickering. The darkness throbbed with deep-throated laughter—hundreds of voices. Thousands. Here was Radomor's fist and fury, curled in the darkness, and they had blundered right inside. They had ridden into an armed camp.

Durand pulled his sword, but the two Rooks only grinned. At a tilt of their heads, a hundred soldiers stepped into the glade. Durand heard the idiot laughter of carrion birds.

"Ride!" Durand spat. In a moment, he had thrown himself back into the saddle.

Berchard followed, swearing.

With spurs and a madman's lashing, Durand stung the poor dun into full flight.

He heard the stuttered snap of crossbows.

Manic hooves pounded.

Someone screamed, but he punched through blades and reaching arms into the thick dark again, shooting like an arrow for the Fuller's Bridge.

At first, he heard only shouts and Berchard's hoofbeats behind him, but then a rumble swelled and the whole wood shook under the thunder of hooves. It was *so* black. He felt as if he and his horse were careering down a swinging wire. A stumble would throw him blind under an avalanche of horseflesh and steel.

But they tore into the fields.

As the rolling swell of open land stretched behind him, Durand twisted to catch Berchard bursting free—and the whole of the black wood rising in a multitude of carrion birds: the smothering leaves of a forest's empty branches. Under their laughing cloud, a battalion of horsemen exploded into the field. Durand fought for balance and cursed his mount onward.

They must reach Acconel; the city was not ready. Abravanal's vassals must ride the leagues from their countless halls to answer his summons. Just the horsemen in the track behind him would outnumber the guards on the walls this night.

In heartbeats, Durand hit the Ferangore Road—hanging low as the dun's hooves bit the bank on the corner.

Somewhere ahead, the crossroad gibbets swung. A league yawned between Durand and the bridge. He glanced back through and saw the horsemen closing around Berchard and the sky full of rooks. The gibbet cage loomed close, and Durand took the only chance he saw: with all the force of arms and back and speeding horse, he swung his blade against the chain or rope that hung the cage.

Blade, cage, and lashing corpse exploded with the shock in Durand's arm. The blade was broken. The cage was free. Berchard was through. Then hooves and screaming horses met rolling bars of strap iron, and a few hundred paces of darkness opened behind the Acconel men.

A feathered storm swarmed past them.

Durand shot under the shadow of the Warrens, riding hard and praying his horse could see. He marveled at the brute. The animal he'd taken for a plain workhorse stretched out like a racer, its great lungs heaving between Durand's knees. Almora had chosen well.

As the road wove between the Warrens and the river, Durand saw the Fuller's Bridge fires wink across half a league's darkness. Black wings lashed at him. Every rise took them closer.

"Hells!" shouted Berchard.

Durand remembered crossbows and blades and Tenter's Field full of soldiers. At the last, he swung the dun onto the verge, hoping to dull the sound of its hooves. The black-feathered torrent burst over the yard ahead.

There were no clever tricks. Radomor's men were climbing to their feet under black wings, while Durand cursed the poor dun on to greater speed. Behind him, he heard snatches of prayer from Berchard.

And then they were among the villains. Durand shot through firelight, slewing across the yard, eyes on the bridge. Men flew to every side. Crossbows clattered, sending hissing bolts to join the storming wings. Durand's mount gathered itself underneath him and he shot for the ancient bridge, leaping bonfires and sprawling soldiers.

Into the madness of this moment, Radomor's battalion exploded. Sentries screamed and fouled the legs of flying coursers. Crossbows snapped at the dark. Durand landed on the deck of the Fuller's Bridge with Berchard howling after.

They had half-crossed the Banderol before Radomor's soldiers could muster another shot.

"DURAND!"

On the far side of the Fuller's Bridge, Coensar reached as if to catch the dun's bridle. The town of Fuller's Bridge huddled where a patch of Acconel's lower city clung to this westernmost entrance of Acconel Island. On the bridge, a score of Acconel's guards warded off anyone who would continue the chase. "Captain!" said Berchard.

"What have you done?" Coensar demanded.

Durand caught his breath. "We must get men into the Ferangore Road. It may not be too late."

"What are you talking about?"

"We drive them from the bridge. We make a stand between the river and the Warrens," said Durand. "Buy time. We might summon help. Mornaway, Garelyn would come."

Coensar's mouth opened. "Berchard, how many?"

"God knows, Captain. I'd guess thousands or more."

Durand's dun skittered under him. "Only a league or two. We dig in on the road, hold him there. We fall back to the bridges when he's too much."

Just then, a bolt clanged from the bridgehead.

Coensar looked over Durand's shoulder, hauling Keening into the air. "It's too late," he said, already spurring toward the clash of steel. "We'll stand here to delay him, but Radomor will have the bridge before the hour is out! Berchard, ride for the castle. We'll need every man they can spare. Come, Durand!"

As Berchard spurred east for the citadel, Durand wheeled his dun rouncy and hastened back toward the bridge.

While a score of Acconel's guardsmen teetered on the near end, horses flashed in the torchlight beyond. Men shouted. Squads of crossbowmen snapped bolts through fire and darkness. Horsemen jounced into the fight. Someone in the chaos had taken charge. Now, this stranger would wrest victory from the madness, unless they could turn the tide.

Durand did not have so much as a dagger.

Into the line of defenders, Coensar rode, his blade singing on the wind. "Keep low! Lap shields!" Coensar roared. A small band could hold a bridge, but this bridge was broad, the only fortification a stone tollhouse lost on the far bank. Peering round, Durand thought that if they could get Acconel bowmen on the banks and warehouses around, they might make the bridge an open grave for their attackers.

A bolt zipped through the space between Durand's wrist and his horse's neck. He saw two men fall with bloody arrows in their throats.

"Coensar, we must do something about the crossbows!" Neither of them was armored. No one was ready for an assault.

The captain snarled, lashing with the singing blade. But the line of shields was buckling around them. Yrlaci knights roared out of the night, crashing home amid shields and torn defenders. Bolts chopped down in volleys. Dread was like sickness. And Durand found himself caught with the dun spinning like a dory in a flood. He ripped an Yrlaci spear from someone's hands.

"For the gates!" Coensar roared. "For the Gates of Sunset! The bridge is lost!"

And the defenders broke around him. But Coensar caught Durand's shoulder. "Not us, Durand! You'd best not go yet! We'll give them something to think about, you and I, before they go running our comrades down. Stick close, and don't let them guess you're shitting yourself." Durand beamed as the captain's sudden blade sent hair and a gleaming bowl of helmet sailing. Durand jammed his spear into a lancer's teeth. The dun was nearly wild with terror. And Durand and Coensar lived only because the press had grown too thick for archery. Finally, the captain shouted, "All right! Enough!"

And they flew from the bridge and its knot of warehouses and inns, pelting past wide-eyed townspeople, roaring, "For the city! For the walls!"

Ahead, where the road broke into farmland between bridge and city, the defenders had already thrown the stock pens wide. Cattle bawled in the dark. Durand and his captain sped through moments before the brutes flooded across the road.

Lamoric and a few dozen more from the castle guard met them as they reached the lower city. "Radomor's revenge is swift," said Coensar. "Already he has taken the Fuller's Bridge."

Bells rolled above the dark streets of Acconel.

THROUGH THE NIGHT, they regrouped three times, fighting by the light of blazing shops and warehouses. Knights and blinking volunteers fought in the stinging dark undaunted, but Radomor's men were too many and too well led.

Soot-smeared and bloody, Durand followed a gang of knights shambling under the gate to Castle Acconel's inner courtyard. Somewhere, Kieren, Lamoric, and Coensar wrangled over wild and hopeless tactics, but Durand was done for a time. Soon, they would fall back. The outer yard behind him was a makeshift infirmary, and, somewhere in the old city, the priests were murmuring their First Twilight.

Something rushed past Durand from the shadowy precincts of Gunderic's Tower, dim as moths, nearly skipping him from the walls. Hooves clattered.

Durand had an axe now. One of the other knights, Badan, whipped a chained flail from his belt.

"Almora!" It was Deorwen shouting from the yard end of the gatehouse tunnel. The girl stopped, jittering bareback on a black pony.

The knights opened their hands, embarrassed. Badan

wheeled. "What do you mean riding us down, you daft girl? It's the middle of the bloody night!" He made to move toward her, the chain rattling, but Durand caught him, heaving the man—mail coat and all—against the wall.

"Enough," Durand breathed. "Leave them alone."

Badan's eyes glinted near, very wide for an instant. "'Alone with you.' Is that what you mean?" Durand twisted his fists in the man's surcoat; there were three knights looking on. But Badan only sneered. "I'm watching." He wrenched himself free and stumbled away.

Their small audience bowed to Lady Deorwen and left Durand standing under the gate. He could not read their faces.

"You promised to be careful, child," Deorwen said.

"I am. I am." There was a wet catch in her voice. "The cook, he said, he's boiling water as fast as he can boil it and there's no sense hounding him. And he says a lad will be along."

Durand wanted to get his hands on Badan.

Deorwen's voice was soft. "That's fine, Almora. That's fine."

The black-haired little thing peered past her, trying for a good look at the straggling infirmary or the smoke drifting from the pyre of Fuller's Bridge. The bells still tolled above the streets.

"Good," said Deorwen. "Good. Now, see if you can get the house steward to hurry with the blankets."

Now, Almora's head bobbed sharply. "Hurry with the blankets!"

The wheeling pony nearly bashed Durand into the wall once more.

"And carefully!" Deorwen rubbed a hand over her face. "She cannot sleep. It's been a trial inventing errands. She prefers that they involve her pony."

Durand laughed—a cough of a thing that nearly started the whole weight of the day and night crashing down on him. He put a hand on the wall. "What was its name?"

"Star, she's named it." The animal could not have been blacker. Deorwen's fingers touched her brow. "He's got a white mark on his forehead," she explained. Just like Geridon's "Pale."

Durand panted another soundless laugh.

"I'd like to keep her away from the worst of it," Deorwen said.

Durand nodded. She was very close, and, for a moment, they were alone. "I would like to get us all away from here. Somewhere far away. I can't think—"

She kissed him in that archway, her arms snaking round his waist, under his cloak. He caught her up in his arms. He felt her tears on his face. "What is happening between us?" he managed.

"I don't know." She smeared at her eyes. "We are ridiculous."

There were voices close, and Durand remembered Badan's warning. He swallowed. "I want to take you away from all this. I want—"

"It can't be like this." She looked back to the makeshift infirmary. "We must think. What good thing can rise from betrayal?"

There was an army near and fighting on the island itself. "Be careful," he said. He could not think.

DAWN PROPELLED SERVING men into motion, prising their heads from the straw in the cold corridors and storerooms of Gunderic's Tower. Heaven's Eye sent great sheets and blades of light to probe the Painted Hall where the knights lay, sprawled like dead men.

A priest would be making the tower's shrine ready for morning prayers. The kitchens would be sawing at bread and cold pork. He saw Deorwen coming with a bit of bread, but slipped from the hall before she could reach him and searched out a place to get a look west from the city walls.

He stalked through a citadel hushed and strange in the chill. He nodded past the guards on the wall, and climbed into bright dawn on the battlements—as far from the Painted Hall as he could travel. His shadow sprawled a hundred paces over the crooked rooftops of the lower city where he could see men hauling strongboxes and bed frames from their houses. Carts stood under towering loads. Pigs ran in the streets. He heard geese and crying.

There were worries aplenty in the city without his. Men

had already died. Friends. And Lamoric had shouldered his brother's burdens, rallying the citizens. Durand could not trust his heart with Deorwen near, but neither could he abandon the city and his friends—not now. He would just have to keep clear of her. The family would be trapped in the castle, lucky to step from Gunderic's Tower with Radomor's thugs so near. Durand resolved not to set foot inside.

A bent shadow joined his among the rooftops. Heremund Skald grimaced, puffing a little steam. "You walking the walls as well, O knight of the mountain hall?"

"There's an army on the doorstep, friend skald."

"Look at them down there!" His stubby hand darted over the refugees, out of his cloak only a moment. "They're betting on these old walls. Would the buggers be safer in the hills?"

"I've never seen a city under siege," was all Durand could answer. The ancients had girded Acconel with high walls and strong towers, but there were precious few soldiers to man them.

Heremund hauled his cloak tight, puffing. "You remember us two riding double on that poor bay of yours? You remember the woman who blocked that road? Villagers shying stones? That's what they'll meet out there when they run. There'll be some battles when the villagers try to turn them back."

"It'll be wild inside or out." In the distance, Fuller's Bridge town was a smudge of smoke and charred timber. Radomor's men had gouged a line of earthworks around their beachhead. Any who hoped their assault was just a raid knew better now.

The skald clawed the back of his neck. "I've been at this a long time. Traveling. Better part of forty years sleeping by other men's fires." A finger darted out of his cloak to tap his broken nose. "Always curious."

Durand looked at the little man. "Forty years is a long time, I think."

"You're not wrong."

Along the Ferangore Road, mists and snatches of smoke rippled, perhaps veiling the march of an army.

"You'd think I'd know how to watch out for myself," said the skald. "Staying when a siege is closing round. There's enough sorrow in any man's life without such follies. Maelgrin Skald wrote about the fall of Perantur. Said 'The Writhin Men tell us that hunger is a fire. We, the citizens of Perantur, have seen this. In its stalking, hollow flames, all things are devoured—faith, love, hope. Before hunger, Creation is a thing of husks and dry grasses.' Doesn't seem wise to stick by when a man can step aside."

A skald was a traveler, not bound by vows and a knight's foolishness. "Will you leave?" Durand asked. Was that what had the little man nervous?

He flinched a smile. "I find that I can't."

"Ah." Durand tapped his own nose as the skald had done.

"Aye. Bloody Radomor, Duke of Yrlac—if he's killed his father—has been in my head since first I clapped eyes on him in that Ferangore cradle: a naked thing with his mother dying. Was it I who set him on this path all those years ago? 'Everything he does will come to nothing.' I can't guess what fiends flattered me into spitting out that one." Again, he flinched his quick smile, lips folding into the gap of his missing teeth.

"I knew the lot of them in Yrlac," said Heremund, "though you don't tell a man his son will come to nothing, and then beg a roof for the night." He knuckled his oft-broken nose. "And poor Alwen. Such a lovely girl. And I knew Aldoin Warrendel. I remember an old skald chuckling about the town house Aldoin bought by the citadel. The Maiden and the Mother either side of the front door, proud as whatever—had been a bawdy house in times gone by: convenient for the baron with an itch of an evening." As it turned out, Aldoin needed the house so he could be near Radomor's young wife, waiting for her to whistle from her tower window. Durand had stood by while the man drowned in Radomor's well. He had stood by while Alwen and her child starved in her chamber.

"And now I'm tied to Lamoric's misfit band. Here's you: a stray come to my door. You lead me to kings and princes, wars and sorcerers. The Red Knight will be Duke of Gireth

someday. And you? You've bulled your way to the head of
the line. There are men who've fought twenty years but here
you are, hero and festival bull."

"For all the good it's done anyone."

"Well, think on it. You've drawn their eyes now. Geridon
held his spot a long time."

Durand looked back westward. "None of that was on my
mind." He was certain now: something wavered between the
Banderol and the Warrens, as though the boughs had come
alive.

Heremund joined him, taking a long look. "That'll be our
Radomor riding to overturn the kingdom." He sucked a deep
breath. "It's a marvel what one man's folly can do."

From the towers of the citadel, great horns moaned over
the lower city: they'd sighted Radomor's army.

Heremund scrabbled at his cap. "What a teacher is the
world; what lessons there are in a man's life. You be careful."

Durand saw the glint of helmets on the Fuller's Bridge.
They had to hold the walls.

When he looked down, the skald had gone.

🪢 18. The Red Hour

As a ragged squall tumbled in from the mere, Radomor's
host crossed the River Banderol. Durand moved to the
mighty Gates of Sunset, scrounging a meal among the towers. Thousands crowded the arch below, struggling to carry
their lives to safety. Radomor's soldiers shouldered past the
Fuller's Bridge like a rug hauled through a knothole. Their
numbers brimmed the Fuller's Bridge camp and flooded the
fields toward the lower city. They made no pause. Durand
saw knights beyond counting and ranks of spearmen glinting
like the sea. Engines of war arose like outlandish battleships,
rocking in the wake of oxen.

Durand looked back. Dominating the square beyond the
Gates of Sunset was a white idol of the King of Heaven himself. Masses heaved around the feet of the solemn giant.

"Hells, now it's raining," Berchard griped. The old campaigner climbed to the parapet, a crossbow on his shoulder. "Rain plays merry hell with these things." He nodded to Durand. "We're all up on the walls, now. Coensar has the conroi scattered in twos." He managed a crooked grin. "He's got Lamoric, and he had me looking for you. Guthred'll be sitting on Badan somewhere. I think I'll be in charge of our division, eh?"

Durand flashed a few teeth, but nodded his chin toward the advancing host.

"Hells." Berchard grimaced after a good look, his face curling like a fist around the patched eye. "Now why did I want to see that, eh?"

"I've been watching it since dawn."

"That's not just his own boys and sellswords that Radomor's using. I'd wager there's a lot in plain green surcoats who've left their Beoran gear at home."

Durand nodded. A man would need half the knights in Errest for an army that size. The advancing host looked like a city come adrift—carrying its towers and derricks along for company.

Under the patter of rain, Acconel changed color: silver thatch and pale walls darkened, the citadel's courses shining like slabs of clay.

"God." Berchard shook his head, whispering, "She's rootbound, Acconel. Once, I'd wager you couldn't force the Banderol with all the Sons of Heshtar. Now, there are strong stone bridges on every side. This lower city? From what I hear, it was a bald killing ground for generations. They dug ditches to keep you off the walls and packed the towers and the battlements with espringals and ballistae. If some poor devil got over the river, he'd come up to the wall and hell would pour down on him. Now, those engines are dust and houses crowd the walls." Berchard managed a quick grin. "That's peace."

While the two knights watched, the Yrlaci columns slid into the tangled roots of the lower city. Engines of war stole among the rooftops. Nearer at hand, sullen crowds of townspeople struggled to pass the Gates of Sunset, filling the streets before the wall a hundred deep.

"How long can they keep the gates open?" Durand asked. "Yrlac is in the streets."

"They should have had time to spare," said Berchard, peering toward the hidden battalions. "This is mad. Your Radomor's got half the blades in Errest and we never heard a whisper. He must have had an army of carpenters just to build those engines. Even if the barons said nothing, think on how many throats they had to cut. Every fool who gaped at a crossroads. Every shepherd on a hill. Imagine the blood."

The clamor under the gates swelled louder, the crowd surging. Someone had likely spotted Radomor's towers or heard a war horn out among the shops and hovels.

" 'Oceans,' " Durand recalled.

"Lady Deorwen was asking after you. You've been up here all day, then?"

"Little chance of any of us spending much time dining in the Painted Hall now."

"I expect we'll be busy, at that. I got the sense she wanted to tell you something." The man looked at Durand very carefully.

Just then, a group of the guards drew the two men's attention. Some of the guards had moved to the battlements, peering down at the surging masses. With a grunt, Durand got up to join them. Down below was a knot of carts, with something thrashing among them—a hopeless tangle.

"Come on," said Durand. "There's no time for this now." And the two knights descended into the chaos. A mob pressed on every side, and, in the midst of the tumult, they heard something screaming. Durand waded into the throng, Berchard close after him. The pressure of fear and desperation had jammed poles and cart shafts into a knot like a wicker fence—and each cart was stacked higher than a man could reach. Under the heap, one snapped pole had speared a bay carthorse through the neck.

Durand heaved with the rest. Voices rang under the deep arch; they were like people trying to get out of a storm. But soon there were enough hands in the right places. Guards and townspeople jockeyed carts free. A hundred arms

whisked bundles and strongboxes from the street. Someone
gave the carthorse mercy, and it was soon hauled into the
square below the King of Heaven.

Durand sweated and puffed, but found such stern joy in
the work that he stayed on, helping townsmen onto carts,
guiding beasts by their bridles, keeping children near their
mothers—working like spokes and gears to get them through.

"Durand, what's that over there?" Berchard squinted past.

Someone was calling from the low city end of the great
vault: a tall man with cracked green eyes and a shock of
white hair, waving vaguely. "Hello? Can anyone spare a moment? Hello?" The man wore a tabard of undyed wool—and
stood near the head of a long line of men in the same plain
garb.

Durand nodded to Berchard and fought the current to the
tall man's side. They found him with one hand on the shoulder of an adolescent monk.

The little monk winced up at Durand in dismay.

"Hello?" said the tall man. "Is someone there?" His green
eyes were wide and empty. "Novice Gamel, someone here's
breathing like an ox."

"I am Durand, sir. A knight in Lord Lamoric's retinue.
There's little time for talk."

"Novice Gamel, hadn't you better ask him?"

The young man blinked up at Durand, gaping. There had
to be twenty men behind him—all in the same gray tabards,
all with the same vague gazes.

"I see," said the tall man. "Our pilot Gamel here is a good
boy, but we seem to have run aground at the very mouth of
the haven. He has led us from the hospital, but I—"

With an army nearly in bowshot, Durand caught the man's
hand. "All right. Take hold of me, and I'll see you through."
He slapped the man's hand on his shoulder and bulled his
way into the crowd.

People shouted, "Let them through. They're up from the
Sleepers Mercy." And the crowd made way, Durand leading
the line in the wake of a heaped cart.

As they emerged from the gatehouse tunnel, Durand found
himself face-to-face with Deorwen. Almora was riding above

the crowd on her pony, Star. Deorwen had the animal's bridle, and an anxious guard trailed behind.

"What are you doing in this mob, Ladyship?" Durand asked.

"Almora and I were talking, and Almora was concerned that her brother had not been seen in some time."

"He hasn't," the girl declared.

"I thought there wasn't much harm in taking a look. Seeing that he was all right. And how brave he is," said Deorwen. The little girl was scowling at the mob from under her bangs.

"You shouldn't be here," Durand said. "Neither of you." It was already ugly.

"I think it's better to deal with these things rather than to run off and pretend nothing's happening."

"They are seeing Radomor's men in the streets outside these gates. People aren't always themselves when—"

The tall man touched Durand's elbow. "Milord, we're very grateful."

"I'm sorry," Durand said. He had nearly forgotten about the stranger.

The tall man nodded to Deorwen and Almora. "There was no one but young Gamel here to lead us. Father Abbot finally found a cart. They needed every able hand to clear the infirmary."

At this, Durand discovered that the sturdy, redheaded woman who'd been driving the heaped cart was peering down. "Here," she said. "Do you mean to say there are folk still in the Nine Sleepers? There must be a hundred men in the infirmary."

"I imagine," the blind man began, "that everyone thought someone else had—"

"They ought to be ashamed. How many carts did you say?"

"The abbot's man was grateful to have found the one he did—"

"One cart?" the woman said.

Durand glanced west. The army was too close. "Where's the hospital?"

The blind man opened his mouth, but the outraged woman

beat him to the answer. "The Sleepers Mercy backs on farm-land. Yrlac will stumble on it anytime."

"How many men did you say are loading this one cart?" Durand demanded.

"There are five orderlies."

"Five will not be nearly enough for such a place," said De-orwen. "Many won't have left that hospital in years."

There wasn't time enough. Durand imagined Radomor's wolves coming upon a hospital. "They will have one more anyway!" he said. A few others had been looking on, and many gave fierce nods along with him. Berchard blanched. "Right."

The woman on the cart shouted, "Come on, you lot." She looked back at a cart piled with cupboards and benches and linen. "Help me drop all of this in the square."

As many hands seized the accumulated possessions of the woman's life, the blind man got Durand by the arm, his green eyes flashing. "I've got a strong back still, I know where you're going, and, I think, a blind man has as much chance against an army as anyone."

"Come then," said Durand.

He turned to Deorwen. "I am sorry to leave you so soon, but there's no time."

Deorwen slapped Star's reins into the guard's hand. "Almora will return to Gunderic's Tower. Sir Durand, you will need more hands, and I have two."

The woman on the cart shouted, "The dogs will be on them anytime!"

THEIR COMPANY—MOST in the empty cart—juddered into the deep stillness of the lower city. Doors and shutters hung open in the rain. Belongings—those too heavy to carry—stood heaped at doorways. Here and there geese or pigs wandered. Durand winced at the grating echoes of the cart's axle, shooting looks at Deorwen. She was mad to be here. He wanted her locked in the farthest tower of Castle Ac-conel. This was such a risk. And so he walked while the others rode. He couldn't have sat still.

Berchard, bouncing on the back of the cart, peered up

among the empty rooms, whispering, "Lady Deorwen, it's not that I don't enjoy your company, but I'm not sure what I think about your choice of outing. If Radomor knew you were with us, I think he'd take an interest."

"The city is surrounded and caught without provisions or defenses. My husband is ranging the walls within sight of Radomor's archers. Abravanal is mad with grief. And, I am told that I am to sleep in the chamber of my late brother-in-law tonight."

"So you're safer out here?"

"I would prefer not to be useless."

Berchard scratched his beard. "I can see that."

Durand waited for a troop of green knights to storm into the street.

"Now, Durand," Berchard said. "I was meaning to hand this over to you." He fumbled under his cloak, revealing a sword. "I told Coen that I'd cost you another blade. He said you should have this. Some carrion crow tried to sell it to Guthred."

Scowling, Durand took the sword and pulled it from its scabbard. The blade was a hand's span longer than any of Durand's lost swords had been. Rainwater tumbled off the edge. "This was Ouen's."

"We reckoned you should have it, and I thought, if we're all riding out under Radomor's nose again, I'd rather you had it now."

"*Quiet!*—Your Lordships," said the redheaded woman from her bench. The rumble of the army's march poured from a hundred alley mouths.

"What's your name, madam, by the way?" asked Berchard, never looking from the streets.

"Bercta. And I'm no damsel for you to sweep off her feet."

Berchard risked a glance. "I wouldn't have a damsel, ma'am. Not at my age."

"I'm Hagon," said the blind man perched beside her.

Now Bercta turned. "Hagon *Leech*? You're not Hagmund Cobble's brother?"

Hagon raised his finger. "That's a name Hagmund doesn't like."

"It'll be that wife of his put you away in the Sleepers Mercy, I'd wager. Wasn't it?"

The blind man shrugged loose shoulders. "The inmates needed a man with some—"

A slam in a passing street shut all their mouths: whether it was wind or dogs or God knows, they all stood silent for a dozen galloping heartbeats. Durand pulled Ouen's sword, thinking Deorwen shouldn't be there.

"Hagon," Berchard whispered. "He lays cobbles, does he, your brother?"

Bercta put a hand on the blind man. "It's the way he lets that wife of his walk over him makes them call him Cobble. You can see why the soft bugger don't like it—his wife likes it even less."

In Durand's hand, Ouen's long blade beaded and gleamed. If their party met outriders, he would send Deorwen and the rest down an alley, and see how long he could bottle the end of it behind them. He watched for movement down every road.

"And she'd make sure you knew it!" said Bercta.

They hesitated on the threshold of a broad street: Greensmith. It allowed them a long look through the veils of rain toward the army on the Fuller's Bridge Road. They'd be in plain sight. "The hospital's that way," said Bercta.

"Hells," breathed Berchard.

They could do nothing but hope that no one happened to look. Durand set his teeth.

Bercta twitched the reins of her old gray carthorse.

Berchard squinted from the back of the cart. "Madam, I don't suppose this fine animal has a gallop in him."

"Maybe if you pulled and he rode?"

"Ah. A point." Berchard, Deorwen, and everyone else who'd been catching a ride splashed into the roadway. "That'll give the old fellow a fighting chance."

Overhead, a black bird tumbled between the storefronts.

None too quickly, they ducked from Greensmith into a narrow lane under the outsized facade of a stone sanctuary; there was no room for the place in the alley.

"This is it," said Bercta. "The Sleepers Mercy." At the foot of the entry steps was a tall cart and stolid carthorse. The great tympanum above the door carried the alabaster likenesses of the Nine Sleepers and the Queen of Heaven. They looked real as bodies in winter.

On the sanctuary doorstep, they met the orderlies and the abbot: monks and lay brothers gleaming from the effort of shifting bodies. The abbot was short and round-shouldered as a mole, but he was working hard.

"We're here to help, Father," Deorwen said. "We've one more cart and a half-dozen able bodies. There's little time left now."

Past the sanctuary was a plastered hall with beams as twisted and dark as something dried in a smokehouse: the infirmary. Carved screens kept the inmates' privacy.

Hagon grinned at Durand. "It ain't such a bad place really. The brothers treat a man well. There's prayers and decent food and clean clothes. I get to play at my old leechcraft when an inmate's afflicted. And it's convenient for the boneyard when a man's finished—unlike something in the walls where they're packed in and buried standing." There was a war horn sounding beyond the shutters.

"You're thinking we'd best get at it," declared Hagon.

"You're right," said Durand, and they set to lugging inmates into the drizzle. Most weren't so much ill as ancient or infirm. The peace of the Nine Sleepers wasn't for the screaming wounded.

Deorwen directed their efforts outside while blind Hagon was good as his word, taking front or back end of any litter, moving with certainty, and never missing a stair.

Deorwen followed the pair into the sanctuary. "There are birds again. Like yesterday. But the first cart is loaded already, and I've sent them off." Hagon could not see the pleading look she gave Durand.

"Good," said Hagon. "We'll have the second filled in no time." He shook the handles of the litter, smiling.

They were about to part company when a mad yowling came down the range. One of the orderlies called, "Master Hagon? Could you talk old Giseler round? He doesn't know us, he says. But you helped him with his oppressed liver, didn't you?"

"For all he thanked me," Hagon said, stalking off with one hand thrust before him, already calling, "Giseler, what do you mean you don't know these fine fellows, eh? They've only been changing your bedding these past dozen years since your son stopped sending that woman round."

Deorwen pulled Durand back among the idols of the little sanctuary: blank-eyed children, all.

"You're making decisions for me, Durand."

"We've no time."

"When else? I've had enough of people taking charge of my troubles. I want *my* reins in *my* hands. You must speak with me."

A pair of orderlies tramped through with yet another inmate.

"And what can we do?" said Durand. "What decisions are there for us to make? It's mad what's happening between us. What *can* we do?"

"A man doesn't just leave a woman without a proper word spoken. You don't leave me standing alone."

Another stretcher team passed by, and Durand pulled Deorwen into the deepest shadows the place could offer, but even that brusque touch was too much for them. He caught her. Her hands played over his back and face and neck, conjuring walls of lust around him. They kissed like drowning.

"Durand? That's old Giseler settled, I think. We'd better get on. Durand?" Hagon stood in the sanctuary, turning in place.

Durand took a step from Deorwen, trying to breathe. His hands were shaking. "Here I am," he faltered. "Right." There was an army. "Let's get to it." Soon, they had crowded the alley below the stone children with litters and crutches, and were lugging a last man over the rear of the cart as the abbot nodded.

Durand looked from Deorwen to the mouth of Nine Sleepers Lane, thinking that there would be half a thousand soldiers there in no time. The birds were sleeting past. "That it, Father?" he prompted. "They all out?"

The abbot blinked. "One left."

"All right," Durand said. "We'll get him out, and then we can get out of this madness." With Hagon in tow, Durand marched back through the sanctuary.

For a moment, they were alone with the empty eyes of the child idols populating the sanctuary. Beyond the windows, black shapes laughed. Durand stalked through into the infirmary.

"It's only birds," Hagon said.

"Aye," searching the alcoves.

Hagon cocked his head. "They say a blind man can see more than others. Which is right—and wrong. What's between you and that girl, eh? It's that kind of thing gets me wondering. You couldn't tell her no. And you can't stand her here."

A black shape rattled against shutters; Durand flinched.

"There's more than birds on your mind."

Durand stalked past murky alcove after murky alcove, reaching the last screen.

"I see it often," said Hagon. "Haunted men. The worst here—Well. You'll meet—"

Durand rounded the last black screen.

"Get away!" spluttered a voice.

"You see what I mean," Hagon finished.

Durand could make out little more than a shin and a pale hand. "I've suffered enough!" said the voice, wet-edged. "I saw one man, his foot. Another his eyes. Throats cut. Bones like branches. Blades at hands, mouths. I fought at Hallow Down. It was enough."

"Friend, we're getting everyone to safety," said Durand.

The stranger leaned into the light. Someone had struck him a fierce and rising cut to the jaw—axe or falchion. For an instant, his eyes were clear. "You are a fighting man," he said.

"The army of Yrlac has crossed the Fuller's Bridge. They're in the streets. We're leaving now."

"Too much!" Once again he was ranting. The man threw himself from his bed, hauling his body along the floor, short an arm and a leg.

Thinking of Deorwen and Berchard and the armies on the doorstep, Durand ducked close and swung the madman over his shoulder. They were soon stalking down the range.

"I saw things on Hallow Down I knew I could not see and

live!" the man wailed. For a moment, he clutched Durand
like a spider. "They threw me in the wrong tent: a common
man with lords and masters of physic. On Hallow Down. My
face!" He twisted, spitting a hot whisper into Durand's cheek.
"I'd be dead now if the savages had spared it; I'd stolen some
lord's mail coat. I could have been him. How could the bearers know with me all blood?"

"They're going to drop the gates on all of us," said Durand. "I can't lift you if you're twisting."

Durand saw a flash of the man's wild eye. "They carried
a great lord in," the man confided. "Full of mud, he was. The
surgeons, they had their knives. But they were clucking their
tongues. The great man doomed. A hero, his back broke. His
eyes rolling."

Durand ducked into the sanctuary.

"But two men: clerks by their black gear. They wheedled
at him as he lay. There were things that might be done. Bargains made. They said that dreams had drawn them north
to Hallow Down. Whispers. Black as ravens."

Durand clapped onto a sculpted head, tottering. Could the
man be talking of the Rooks? But wings flapped at the high
windows, and there would be riders in the street any moment. There wasn't time.

"I heard him through the night, catching breath and catching breath. A hero, dying. A great lord. And sometime in the
dark, them wheedlers came back."

Durand made to step into the lane, but the stranger caught
the door frame. "I did not mean to hear!" he spluttered. "The
next day's fighting, Mad Borogyn has the king cornered. But
our man comes with his vanguard and nothing but a cricked
neck."

Durand pulled at the man's hand. "Let go!"

"It was them two, I tell you!"

Durand lurched onto the sanctuary step and into wheeling
birds. People were batting them off, afraid for their eyes.
Durand saw Deorwen cover one of the sick men, but the soldier caught Durand's neck.

"What did they do? None of his men came back! How
many shining comrades did His Grace send to—"

Now, one of the wheeling shapes struck the man full in the face. Durand flinched. Another swooped close. People were screaming.

Durand swung at the things, torn between the maimed soldier and breaking for Deorwen. The stranger wrenched his arm, fighting. "They've come! I didn't mean to witness. It was my face!" Wings beat the shrieking air. Beaks whistled past like knives and hatchets, throwing everyone to their knees but Durand. He could not hold the man as the stranger lashed at the storm. Durand reached, blood stinging his eyes between the wings. And just as it seemed the man must drop, the crows caught hold—

In a moment of impossible horror, a hundred beating pinions lifted. The maimed soldier struggled, his limbs twitching in crooked angles, but the gallows-birds tore him from the street, swinging him beyond the roof peaks.

A sandal slapped from the rooftop into the lane.

Bercta stung her carthorse. "Run!"

THEY PELTED FOR the Gates of Sunset. Those who could walk, ran. Every able man had the poles of a litter. The cart carried a dozen men more, heads rolling between ankles.

Durand's head was full of dark bargains and sorcerers. He had dragged Deorwen into the Hells.

Now, more than the dull roll of an army's heels on pavement, they heard voices. As they rounded one corner, the street burst with clattering hooves: a green-cloaked outrider swung onto the scene. Berchard wrenched his crossbow from his shoulder—and snapped a bolt into the face of the man's horse.

"Bloody eye!" Berchard snarled, disgusted at himself. They swarmed the downed rider before the horse could fall.

"He'll be missed," said Berchard, and so they rushed onward, taking the smallest lanes their company could manage—ducking upper rooms, throwing debris aside, both hubs grating over shop doors. Durand breathed through his teeth, jogging ahead—blade in hand—ready to launch himself at whatever he found around each corner. This was not what he meant when he thought of taking Deorwen away from the fighting.

But, finally, the Gates of Sunset stood before him. The mob heaved, knowing death was behind them. Still, someone saw the gray hospital tabards of the men from the Sleepers Mercy and people made way so that soon they were inside and the army had not caught them.

As Durand saw Deorwen walk into safety, he nearly fell to his knees.

THEY HAD HARDLY pitched through the gates when Lamoric rode into the square. Coensar, Kieren, and a conroi of knights followed, all armed. Badan hunkered over his saddlebow, cocking his eyebrow at Durand with Deorwen at his side.

Lamoric was the knight-commander. Without a glance, he called to the captain of the gate, ten fathoms above the crowd. "It is the order of the duke that the great gates of Acconel must stand open! All who wish to flee the traitor Radomor must have their chance as long as it is in our power to grant it. You, the garrison of His Grace's Gates of Sunset, are commanded to hold the portal wide until Yrlac's ladders touch the walls, or his host is massed in the streets before you."

High under the clouded Heavens, the captain of the gates bowed low. "As His Grace commands, Lordship!"

A cheer arose among the mobs, and Lamoric saluted them all.

He had seen the hospital cart, and approached, still waving. "They wouldn't cheer so loud if they knew how little time that's bought them. The siege is on us. Radomor has outriders within bowshot. He's seized the bridges on both sides of Acconel. But old Sir Kieren tells me these gates drop in a heartbeat."

"More will get in if they don't panic and crowd the way," Deorwen said.

"It's what Kieren said. You have been lending a hand?"

Deorwen looked up. "I could not stand by."

"Good, good. I suppose with Durand watching over you, you're safe enough."

Durand set his teeth, he couldn't meet the man's eyes. When he glanced up, he met Badan's stare.

"I never dreamed Radomor could bring so many, or so fast," said Lamoric. "Our men have seen trebuchets. They're throwing the things up in half a day. It's taking us longer to hand the townsfolk weapons than he requires to ring the city. He'll launch the first assault in—"

A great bell tolled.

Knights twisted, and a hundred other bells joined the first: a slow, heavy tolling that trembled in the air.

Lamoric pawed rain from his face. "That will be the high sanctuary. My father calls us." For a moment, the others avoided his face. There was family to bury.

AN URGENT TAP summoned Durand into the darkness of Gunderic's Tower. The bodies lay, shrouded, in the Painted Hall. Men and boys shuffled and stared. And a serving man led Durand to his place: he was to shoulder one of the long poles of Lady Adelind's bier. He glanced over the woman's draped profile, thinking of that dreaming moment above her bed when he had seen her wake—and seen her die.

Deorwen shot him a glance over Almora's shoulder.

With a rattle of censers and relics, the crowd in the Painted Hall drew itself into a solemn file. Priests walked before the draped bodies, chanting under golden standards. The family followed behind.

Durand's hands trembled. He'd had little sleep.

In the castle courtyards, mobs of knights huddled in the rain waiting to join the march and play honor guard. On every side were unshaven men who'd been dragged from the walls—all in armor, all searching for glimpses of their posts. They'd emptied the battlements with Radomor in the streets.

The solemn procession unwound from the castle yards.

They passed files of townsmen in the market beyond the gate—bakers, weavers, stable hands—lined up in the drizzle to get what blades and bows the armory could give them. Most of these men smeared their hats from their heads as the cortege passed. Many fell to their knees. All wore the same look of horror: who was left on the walls? Radomor had five thousand swords.

In a single glance back, Durand saw Abravanal's numb eyes. Tiny Almora seeing her mother. Lamoric gaping at the size of the honor guard. In the rear of the train, pages and shield-bearers carried the warlike relics of House Gunderic: shields plundered by crusading dukes, banners of forgotten houses, the alien charges of lake and mountain peoples lost to time. Some had hung in the Painted Hall two thousand winters; now solemn boys carried these things in the rain.

Soon, the pinnacles of Acconel's high sanctuary appeared over the rooftops. In the streets, people hung from their windows to watch them pass. Even as serving men scattered alms among the silent onlookers, the people counted the knights in the procession.

Finally, the cortege drew up before the great doors of the sanctuary, ranks of haloed icons waiting above gilded priests below. Oredgar the Patriarch spread his arms at the threshold. But before the fearsome old man could offer his greetings, the Heavens opened.

The weight of rain drove man, woman, and priest through the sanctuary doors.

As the ruptured procession splashed into candle smoke and incense, Durand peered around Adelind's pall. He had pictured an empty sanctuary. But now, hundreds—thousands—of hollow-eyed faces looked on from among the sinuous pillars of the ancient place: refugees driven by the storm.

Priests summoned order and the throng parted, leaving an avenue of wet stone to the high altar. Durand swung into step.

Beyond the staring crowd, priests prayed, nose to the wall, punctuating their whispers with rapid nods and genuflections. At the ground and high in the clerestory, their mutterings puffed clouds of steam up the polished stone.

"Let the fallen be laid at the heart of the sanctuary," said the Patriarch.

Durand and the other pallbearers set their burdens before the altar, then joined grieving family, honor guard, and brandished heirlooms as they followed the course of Heaven's Eye, walking solemn rings around the dead, one ring within the other, turning like the chambers of a lock.

As Durand's empty hands dropped, he felt the sanctuary

come to life. The great mass of priests and townspeople beyond the funeral party took up the march, and so many moved that the great sanctuary seemed to come unmoored above them all: a polished Heaven turning over the chanting sea of the masses. So many stricken people, so many afraid—they grieved with their duke, whom they could hardly know. They grieved for the lives that had been torn from them. They sang for the losses they knew must come. Thousands marched. Thousands sang.

In the midst of it all, the Patriarch stood, bright as a flame in his shining robe. With a solemn nod, he summoned the family from the churning multitude.

Lamoric, still in stained and soaking war gear, looked to his father, his wife, his sister. He stepped into that dizzy heart of stillness and, after a moment's blinking hesitation, set his hand on his brother's shoulder.

In that heartbeat, Almora slipped her minders and darted between the long shapes, joining her brother. Someone had found her a bunch of daffodils and she stood with them, frozen like an animal. Lamoric touched her shoulder while Deorwen crouched at the little girl's side. With profound self-possession, the tiny thing got on tiptoe to peck her brother and her surrogate mother on the cheek. Daffodils shivered as she reached high to set a flower by each. Lamoric lifted her from the scene, clutching her to his chest.

Next, Abravanal stepped between the two bodies, hands clasped. He looked to Almora, as if astonished that he hadn't helped her. "My son . . . His wife . . ." The words creaked from his heart audible only to the very nearest ears. "He was the support of my old age. I had seen the future in them. It still hangs before my mind's eye."

He glanced at Almora. At Lamoric. "I do not know what doom will—"

The stones rocked. The air shuddered. A thousand candles swayed. Every foot stopped.

North. *"The Fey Gates,"* Lamoric said. The crowd was looking now.

There was another great boom: south. "Harper's." Lamoric passed his sister into Deorwen's hands. "That was the Harper's Gate coming down." A final boom slammed: west toward Yrlac and Ferangore. "And Sunset. The Gates of Sunset are down. Any who come for shelter now come too late. Radomor is at the walls."

Carrion birds stormed past the tall windows over their heads.

🌀 19. The Night's Messengers

With Lamoric and the duke's guard, Durand sprinted up the lofty Gates of Sunset. The gatehouse parapet hung like the prow of a vast warship above deep ranks of Yrlaci soldiers. They filled the streets, brimming in each channel like the city was in flood.

Kieren shook his head, muttering, "They've used all the green dye between here and the Dreaming Land." The old duke blinked, a robe like a great rug around his shoulders.

In the vanguard of Yrlac's battalions stood a tight squadron of knights. They rode under a new banner: Yrlac's red leopard under a jagged crown. In their midst, Durand saw the hulking Champion, the two grinning Rooks, and—most monstrous of all—Radomor, bald and bearded in his green war gear. All the carrion crows for a hundred leagues were heaped upon the rooftops, greedy for the coming battle.

As Abravanal set his hands on the battlements, Radomor rode out, clattering into bowshot. His charger was nearly wild under the wings of his mantle.

"Duke of Gireth! Your time has come. Submit to the rightful king, or perish a traitor and a fool."

"You are the fool, Radomor!" Abravanal shouted. He stuttered. "What do you gain with this madness?"

"I gain the realm in strength. The people in safety. The crown must be wrested from this, the most stunted branch of an ancient lineage."

"You are mad! Gireth has *allies*. The king will ride with his host. He will teach you your folly."

"My poor cousin has much to teach of folly, but you will not soon see him here. Not for you who denied him his hostage. And your allies? I grant you Garelyn, but Ragnal keeps him penned in the Mount of Eagles. The rest will watch us play our game. They will watch, but you are alone."

Abravanal's fingers clamped the stone. "I will not bow!" Crows shifted their wings.

"Squander time and blood in defiance of your rightful king and I will put the city of your ancestors to the torch!"

The sinews of Abravanal's neck stood like a web of bow cords. "I will not bow! Not to you. Not to your minion fiends! You will not have Gireth from me!" Kieren caught the old man's shoulders before he could fling himself from the gates.

Radomor drew a great blade from his scabbard. To Durand's eye, wings of shadow pressed about the man; almost, he could make out shapes shuddering close as the blade flashed cold above. Durand wondered if anyone else could see it.

"On your head, Gireth," rumbled Radomor. "The blood of Gunderic is at its end. His house is fallen. How many will pay for this last folly of a dead line?"

A final sweep of his blade sent an infinity of black wings to choke the Heavens, and the men of Gireth dragged their lord from his battlements.

BEYOND THE GATES of Sunset, Radomor drew his battalions behind the screen of buildings. Durand thought of a cocked fist or crossbow. Dark eyes glittered from tenement windows of the lower city. Engines moved in the narrow places. Rain fell, and still Durand watched.

He watched as the light bled from the clouds, and dusk settled obscurely. Peering from the battlements, he thought of Sir Agryn and his sundial. The man's prayers were often thwarted by a clouded Heaven.

With a grunted greeting, Berchard joined Durand atop the gatehouse, spying through an embrasure into the lower city. "Host of Heaven, I hate waiting. What is he—*Hells.*" He ducked back as soon as his eyes could focus. Monstrous espringal-crossbows sat like adders in the streets, trained on the battlements, their crews watching for the glint of helmets. "They picked anyone off yet?"

"Not that I've heard. They haven't loosed a bolt. Rado-mor's poised out there like a headsman."

"Waiting for the rain to break. I saw a crew shoot an es-pringal once that had got itself soaked. It leapt up like a scorpion. Whipped ten men blind. Took a dozen arms." He laughed. "Tacked a friendly sergeant to the neck of his horse."

Durand tried a smile, but he could see Radomor's men moving, squads jockeying through the rain.

Berchard shrugged. "Radomor's had a good look at this place; there's a reason no one's taken it. It's still a stout old fortress. Nobody's daft enough to try."

"Except without warning."

Berchard dug a knuckle under his eye patch. "Or with en-gines of war."

Now Durand laughed. "I watched them drag one up this way." He pointed into a long street where a machine stood like a fiend's windmill. Its throwing arm was a cedar as tall as the citadel. "It was a near thing." The streets were narrow and twisting.

Berchard pulled his sodden cloak around him. "Trebuchet. I've seen one of the buggers throw stones it took an ox team to haul."

"Radomor's got more than the one." Rough wooden tow-ers poked through the lines of rooftops. "I've lost count."

Berchard shook his head, blowing out his cheeks. The sight made the old campaigner pale. "Hells. Let's hope he doesn't choose this spot to start."

But several of the big engines were aimed their way, and Durand had watched battalions jockeying through the alleys, massing out of sight. The siege engines would pound the Gates of Sunset and the army would bolt over the rubble. This was where the blow would fall, and this was where they must throw Radomor back.

"What is it?" said Berchard. "Durand . . . ? What are you—"

Some dark humor tweaked Durand's lip, and Berchard clapped both hands over his face.

"And this is where you chose to stand?" The grizzled knight shook his head and shot a glance back through the embrasure. A group of Radomor's men scurried. "Hells, you are green."

"A man has to stand somewhere," said Durand.

Berchard grunted at this. "Green as grass. I wonder if there's time to get an extra mail coat. Maybe another helmet or two. I'll need to be wrapped up like a turtle just to stand near you." He shook his head. "I had a message for you—seems a waste of time now. Coen says we're to get rest while we can. I'm not sure how much sleep a man would need to start catching the stones from trebuchets, but it's your turn. With this sky, the buggers will likely hold out until dawn."

Durand made to protest.

"When Radomor comes knocking, I think you'll know," Berchard said. "Don't worry. You can come fight him then."

Durand looked at Berchard awhile, then nodded. He went to find a dry spot under the walls.

IN A TOWER storeroom nearby, sleep came suddenly.

Durand sank deep—into that place between and below men where the deepest dreams sometimes take them. He sank—with hardly a tremor of recognition—into a midnight sea that stank of clay.

Strange words moved in the dark. The cut and pull of the strange syllables stirred the leviathans of those frigid depths. Not one. Not two. Vast shapes churned toward a gray surface.

And Durand followed in their wake, remembering only a dread of what might follow. He rose from that well through a complicated darkness of roots and soil to emerge suspended above a strange clearing. Some distance away, the watch fires of a citadel rose from ramshackle tenements. This was some grassy wasteland between a river and the outermost streets. Here and there were broken bits of wood, stones, and smashed crockery: middens. The grass stood in tussocks. As he looked over these, his gaze fell on the black sockets of new graves. Heaps of fresh earth were mounded nearby.

More unnerving than these open graves, twitching shadows swung above this wasteland graveyard. Dozens of shapes circled a steaming fire, stirred by strange words.

As he looked on, Durand felt as though he were truly hanged. He could neither breathe nor move and could almost feel the hangman's knot pounding at his throat.

Through this dream of shadows, living beings moved. A huddled pair squatted among the graves, bent over close dirty work. Durand thought of tubers and paring knives. Firelight gleamed on bare scalps and blotted hands. They wore black robes—pendulous sleeves.

A dozen paces away, two figures watched: a mighty warrior, twisted and glowering in cloaks and mail. A step behind him, a giant in a battle helm, the gray-silk threads of his beard flowing in the same current that stirred the shadows.

Durand struggled to draw a breath.

"This is a terrible thing," growled the warrior.

And the smeared men glanced up: twins—Durand knew them though he could not remember how or where. Each had a fistful of smeared white twigs in his hands. "Yet it is necessary," said one. "You have told us so, yourself, or we would never risk it."

The other smiled, his face spattered. "No, never."

"They did not deserve this," said the warrior.

Each twin smiled—spasmodic expressions.

But the shadows surged near, slavering over the dark flecks that dotted the men's skin and clothing. The lashing shapes tugged at the bundles in each man's hands. Durand saw their pale skin flatten under the pressure of lapping tongues.

"Back!" spat one of the smeared ghouls. The twin shook his head, rocked. "Back, by the Eye, by the Lance, by the Coat of Nails. Back, by the Calends Hag and the dark of moons." Each word shot a twitch through the crowding shadows.

Durand could not even struggle; even a hanged man could lash against the rope.

And the two ghouls leered.

The twigs might have been birch rods or candlesticks, splattered with tar—but understanding dawned: they were bones and midnight blood. One had been pried from each opened grave.

The smeared twins found slim knives, and set to work on the bones like scribes. "You have told us that your army must take the city before the garrison is relieved." A pale, glutinous blob splattered one face. Both smiled.

"Even against so few," growled the bent warrior, "hundreds would fall before we could make a breach."

One of the twins spread his hands. "And who has chosen this but the old duke? What are we but instruments in his hands?"

"But these men you exhume were not felons hung at crossroads."

"But murderers all they must be, Lord. Or they could not be bound to do murder again." The ghoul's grin might have been conciliatory had it not been quite so splattered; he raised a fan of fretted bones. "It is done already." He bowed toward his brother.

The twin lifted an ewer from the turf, and raised it high. Upturned, the vessel disgorged its contents over the blade of his jaw, his lips, the dark cloth of his tunic, and down his gullet. Durand could not blink; he could not turn. It was far too thick for dark wine. Wiping his chin, the ghoul set the vessel down and grinned.

To the night, he said, *"Come."* His back straightened as he breathed deep.

The hanging souls swayed while the sorcerer-ghoul's bloody lips twitched through the words of an inverted incantation—every word a *drawn* breath. And, one at a time, the fiend dragged the dead into his swelling chest.

When it was over, his face twisted with the simple effort of containing all he had consumed.

His brother licked his lips, lifting one of the greasy bones. With a grin like a market-day conjurer, he twisted the thing in his fingertips, saying, "Now, each soul to its house of bone once more: murderers for murder."

He held the bone to his brother's lips, and the twin breathed once more, the bottled soul blooming round the bone like a dark flame blossoming round a pale wick.

Soul after soul, the two repopulated the waste with spirits.

As he strangled on the periphery of this mad ritual, Durand became aware that he was not the only anonymous bystander in the wasteland. Shadows flickered among the tussocks, and behind the legs of the standing men. Was he like them? Was he dead? He felt the bands tight around his chest, and gagged on a tongue he could not move.

"Go now," the ghoul was purring. "Go where sleeps the family of the duke. And we shall see how long the limbs struggle when the head tumbles." He raised his crabbed hands, and the tenuous black things turned for the fire-lit city, swinging into the clouded Heavens.

It could not be.

Durand's lungs ached as though the hunger for air would wrench him in two. They were leaving him behind. He tried to master his thoughts. He heard grumbles from Radomor and soothing words from the Rooks. He could not let the things run from him.

Spurred by this one solid thought, he moved over the tussocks and over the grisly work site. Bodies had been tumbled from their shrouds, each bearing the signs of mortal violence. Worse, each body had been torn again. Purple wounds gaped in white flesh. He saw the marks of axes, knives, and pliers, and broken ends of bone.

Then he saw a face lolling above a ruin of meat and splintered bone. The hairs of the beard stood pale as ivory around a wink of gold teeth. A bull medallion gleamed.

"No."

And Durand felt the cold air round him—through him.

"No."

He was a thousand yards away, breathing the word into a space of darkness.

He was a living man.

This was a dream.

And he woke.

For a moment, all he could think and feel and see was blackness. But then the dream was upon him—the faces, the rushing specters—and he pitched himself to his feet. The Rooks! Were their sendings passing the wall? Were they flowing down into the streets of the citadel? He must reach the Gunderic's Tower first.

He scrambled through darkness. Hard corners battered him, but he soon tore free of the tower and ran into the streets.

The city guard had set watch fires against the night. Durand ran blindly between these islands of light, flying past sentries. He stopped for no one, and gave no explanation. One guard tried to block his way, but Durand laid him out with a mailed shoulder. One sounded a horn.

He could almost hear guards at a hundred crossroads shaking themselves into vigilance and readying crossbows or rusting blades. With clenched teeth, he pelted for the next confluence of alleys.

And stumbled into a guardsman leading a horse. Durand skidded to a halt, and the guardsman rounded on him.

"Your horse," Durand said, already yanking the reins from the man's fist.

"What in the name of—"

Durand rammed his knee into the man's groin, and vaulted into the saddle, riding a trail of sparks. A crossbow clanked, but steel and feathers hissed past in the dark.

Durand looked up between the rooftops. Inky shapes flickered against the vault of Heaven—not crows now but ragged grasping shadows. He leaned over the horse's neck.

The castle gates pitched into sight. But the marketplace before the gates was suddenly crowded: heaped with sacks and packs and mounds of cloth. The horse screamed, and Durand flew into the air.

He crashed hard enough to ram flashes behind his eyelids. Watchmen on the walls lifted torches, darting and raising bows. Horns sounded. Then the market bundles all around him came to life—they were refugees.

Durand scrabbled to his feet, spinning. His head was full of the unburied dead and racing spirits.

He stumbled into a woman: a creature of flesh and blood, shaking with cold.

"What are you doing, boy?"

Durand stumbled back. Here were a thousand mortal refugees of the lower city. With a blink, he was off again, ducking past the curious and the sleepy.

Beyond the great gate, he saw gatekeepers.

"I must get in."

"There's some kind of trouble in the city," said one man. A small man, he wore a mustache like the tails of two foxes.

"Hells, Kieren! It's me," said Durand.

"What?"

"They're after the duke."

The moment the gate's long teeth left their sockets in the roadbed, Durand was under and running.

He sprinted the passages of Gunderic's Tower, blind except where light slipped through cracks and windows. He passed shadows colder than the wells in Hesperand. The Painted Hall came to life in his wake.

Finally, he vaulted the stairs to the duke's landing, skidding in front of Coensar and a guard—two crossbows trained on his heart.

But a ragged shadow loomed.

Behind Coensar, the duke took half a bleary step from his door. And the shadow darted. Durand ripped his dagger free of its sheath—a crossbow snapped—but he was throwing.

The sending wailed, its mouth wrenched wide—and froze. Silent, the thing hung like a still image in smoke, already lifeless and drifting. The dagger clattered to the floor, transfixing a white fragment of bone.

By Durand's ear, a bolt had splintered against the wall. Coensar's hand was on the guardsman's bow.

Lamoric was downstairs.

As Durand bounded into the Painted Hall, he found the room motionless. Already, a living shadow stood over a place of sprawled knights like a dark blaze reaching nearly to the ceiling. At Durand's blundering arrival, the thing twitched toward him. Lamoric lay prone at its mercy. He saw, high in the figure, what looked like a wild hillman's beard floating about a dark face.

The black flames of the sending's hands swung toward Lamoric.

"Ouen," Durand said.

And the sending froze.

The rushes crackled on the floor—vermin pouring from their hiding places. The thing reared to the painted vaults. Its hands hovered at Lamoric's throat, a ring of black fire not quite closing.

"Ouen, no!" Durand slid Ouen's sword of war free of its scabbard. The hearth fire sputtered green against the stones.

Ouen's bound soul shivered above them, lashing from its grip like a bonfire in a gale as mortal will fought sorcerous compulsion. Lamoric's life was poised between them.

Then the shadow surged.

Durand shot the tip of the dead man's sword through the bone at the shadow's heart. He felt the contact, ice and lightning leaping his arm. Ouen's howl rent Creation, a shriek that loosened the teeth in Durand's jaws. But it was already an echo. The shadow had frozen. Tied by the long blade, Durand watched the shadow come apart, rags and ribbons of it slipping into the thousand crevices of stone vaults and stars.

"What have I done?" Durand said.

For a heartbeat he saw the wide eyes of Acconel's knights staring up at him, then he collapsed into darkness.

DURAND OPENED HIS eyes to see a pair of dark orbs glistening a few inches from his nose.

He reared up. Almora looked down on him, all alone. He saw the criss-crossed vaults of the castle's shrine. And people were turning.

"The King of Heaven smiles upon us," said a quavering voice.

Coensar's voice said: "The boy's lucky we didn't shoot him."

"That knife! Right at my door."

Coensar stepped close, as did the Duke of Gireth, draped in his coverlet. Durand subsided onto whatever bench they had laid him on.

"Lamoric? The others?"

"Lamoric's just come round," said Coensar. "We rushed everyone into the sanctuary after we understood what was happening. The sendings carry the grave's own chill with them, but they aren't much interested in anyone but those they've been sent against."

Coensar looked around as if the threat was not long gone. There was a railing between the shrine and the Painted Hall. Rows of armored men watched.

Abravanal leaned in with his flat blue eyes, faltering. "They are of an old line in the Col. They had that land of my many-times great-grandfather when the forests rang with the shouts of the Banished and wild men." The duke fumbled at Durand's shoulder, then turned without another word to be at his son's side.

"Kieren asked after you. Bolted into the hall on your heels. You'd better try that arm."

It took Durand a moment to realize that he was meant to perform. The arm was stiff, as though he had spent a long day in sword practice. He held his hand before his eyes and watched it tremble.

"The thing was blue-white when you dropped that sword," said Coensar. "Most of the guards fell at a passing touch from the thing. No one managed to bring a blade to bear." He sniffed a quick laugh. "You'd be little use with just one arm."

"No," Durand agreed.

Coensar leaned close. "Durand, how did you know they were coming?"

Durand frowned. "Another dream."

Now Coensar nodded. He had Durand's good shoulder. "Like the Lost in the courtyard. There's something about being so close to death so often. It opens a man's eyes to—"

Coensar let go. "Durand!" Beyond the wall of people around Lamoric's sickbed, the young lord was on his feet, hands restraining and supporting him. Through a rent in the crowd, Durand saw Deorwen—and met her eyes. "It was Ouen," declared Lamoric. "It was Ouen, but you stopped him, Durand. I could see him, fighting." He waved a hand. "I—He is free now, in any case."

Durand thought of the dead man's howl and the rags of shadow after the blade struck home, but said only, "Yes, Lordship."

Lamoric was pale, his lips bloodless.

Deorwen looked on. Durand saw clenched teeth and tears. He wondered what it must be like for the girl, her husband and her lover right there.

Lamoric took spasmodic hold of Durand's surcoat. "It doesn't matter what abomination Rado throws at us. He hasn't got us yet! He and his—"

A great boom shook dust into the candlelight. It could have been thunder. Durand felt the shock conducted through the bones of old Gunderic's Tower: a great weight of stone dropping from the Heavens onto high walls and cobbled streets. There were screams from the marketplace beyond the castle gates.

Coensar grunted from the back of the chamber, his eyes glinting like steel. "He comes," the captain said.

20. Sunset Falling

Through the night and all the next day, the army of Yrlac surged against the walls. Arrows hissed and sprang from the battlements. Five hundred hooked ladders flew up in the west, only to be followed by five hundred more in the north and south. Defenders swung gaffs and garden bills. Battering rams and siege towers rolled. The espringals with their twisted skeins of maidens' hair flashed their "tongue"-spears at the heads of guardsmen. And all the while great trebuchets cartwheeled boulders against the walls, carrying ancient halls into their cellars under the weight of stone.

All day, Durand ran. There were no ditches to foul the approaches and few bows to hold the storming parties at bay. Each fresh assault triggered sudden, hideous battle on the parapets. Tottering high above the streets, men savaged each other rather than fall, cutting throats and clawing under the lash of Radomor's crossbows from the rooftops. Bolts hammered mail to bone.

When the horizon bled and blazed, the roaring battle knotted round the Gates of Sunset. Durand and the others fought atop the walls, hurling broken masonry onto shields and howling faces to the beat of an Yrlaci ram swinging in the belly of the tower under their feet. Espringals and mangonels dashed men from the heights while the trebuchets beat the walls—each projectile swatting parapets over the streets of the citadel.

Durand and the Acconel men fought and scrabbled on the high rubble while the foundations shuddered below. They threw everything. Men flashed and burst from Creation all around him. There was blood in his teeth.

He heard his name.

Coensar wove across the pitching tower, cringing low. "Come!" he said. "Lamoric wants you to run an errand."

Like a pit dog lifted from the fight, Durand swayed a moment. Stones bounded between them, but he followed Coensar down to the crowded yard under the gates.

Lamoric, not daring to look from the fighting beyond the gate, seized Durand's shoulder. "Durand, we're done for here. We won't hold the gate more than another hour, and the citadel falls with this gate.

"But we can't give in! If we cling to the walls, Radomor will shred us before help can reach the city. If we're to have any force remaining, we must abandon the walls now and save as many as we can before the bugger knows we've run."

There were stones clattering across shields and cobblestones.

"Acconel will fall," said Durand. "He will destroy everything."

"Durand! You must think. We'll need an army if we're to survive! Radomor's thrown his three battalions at this one gate. Everything he has. It's here he'll breach the walls and come pouring through. Tell my father—or Kieren—whoever will hear you. Tell them to order everyone back to Castle Acconel. Throw the Fey and Harper's Gates wide for all I care. Let the townspeople out. But I'll hold the bugger's eye on the Gate of Sunset. He'll see my bull banner till the walls are bare and the castle full and laughing. And I'll make him pay to win through.

"Go!" Lamoric shouted, and Durand ran through the pitching streets of the city to Gunderic's Tower.

As Durand lurched toward the Painted Hall, someone caught his sleeve—Deorwen stood in a dark passage. "You're alive!" she said.

He could hardly believe it was the same world. The nails on his left hand had been torn away. A narrow wall was all that divided peace and madness. "We're holding them, but it can't last. I've a message for His Grace."

A crowd surged by, shoving Durand close, and he found himself mashing a kiss against her lips, shutting his eyes.

She curled her fists in his bloody surcoat, her breath hot against his face. But there was iron mail between them.

"Deorwen! I've been sent with orders," Durand said, pulling free. "I cannot stop. Hells, be careful."

He tumbled into the Painted Hall, blood and desperation winning the argument for him—with one exception.

ORDERS WERE SENT, archers filled the buildings on the road from Sunset, and from every corner of the citadel, soldiers pelted back to the high towers of Castle Acconel.

With his message, Durand wove between pitching buildings, blade and shield in his fists, ready for squads of Radomor's men to have broken through while his back was turned. Arrows clattered down around him, scattering like straw over the street. A squadron of soldiers ran past, gathering basketsfull.

The memory of Deorwen was still in his hands. Still pounding in his heart.

A great block dropped out of the Heavens, carved with finials and proverbs in High Atthian. It bounded through a wall and a crowd of running soldiers. A second great stone landed in an explosion of white marble, and leapt straight for Durand: a idol's severed head grinning. As he tumbled, the thing leapt high, slamming the wall of a house behind him. In one jolt, the building shed five hundred years of plaster.

Durand choked. It would serve him right if something smashed him flat.

There *were* pinned men all around. Men levering stones. Men transfixed by the "tongues" of espringals. He rounded the corner on the Gates of Sunset as a great stone burst the top of one tower. Men fell under the hail of masonry. In the midst of it all sat the Silent King of Heaven, staring westward from his throne. Hundreds of soldiers fanned across the square at his feet, every eye fixed on the great gates.

With each thunderous boom of Radomor's ram, blades of sunset flashed from the huge gates. It seemed as if the doors held the Eye of Heaven itself.

Durand swept the crowd for some sign of Lamoric, and heard the man's voice cry out: "Archers nock. Loose the moment you see a green shirt under that gate." Durand spotted the black bull of Gireth flapping over the mob at the gate.

He shouldered his way into the press. Coensar had a long shield. "Lads," Lamoric was saying, "the walls of Acconel have stood since . . . since Gunderic crossed the mere. We have never been taken." People cleared their hair from their eyes. "The duke asks us to hold this gate with our lives, so our comrades may live through and help reach our loved ones." The ram boomed, and Lamoric sneered. "Radomor tries to take our homeland—our heritage. He can come and come and come again! But knights of five hundred halls are riding to our rescue. We will throw this upstart back till the hooves of our comrades thunder on every bridge, then we will ride through Ferangore. And Radomor will bleed for every drop of Atthian blood he's spilled in our city!"

His sneer glinted in hundreds of hard bright eyes. Yellow teeth gleamed.

"Heap them up between those gates, boys!"

The crowd shouted.

The gate boomed.

Durand wrestled close to Lamoric, and the man glanced up. "He has mangled the outer portcullis with that bloody ram. Now he works on the leaves of some carved door . . . an ornament. He'll be under the gate and at the inner portcullis in no time."

A stone swatted broken masonry across the square: a scythe to cut men screaming.

Durand blinked. "I have word from His Grace."

"Is everyone all right? Almora? Deorwen?"

Durand swallowed; he had the excuse of catching his breath. "Yes, Lordship. And Kieren's done as you asked. There'll be no one left on the walls in no time, and they're throwing the Harper's and Fey Gates wide open."

Lamoric nodded, sighing. "We'll stand him off here as long as we're able, and half the army will be safe and dry behind us."

"No, Lordship." Durand touched the man's shoulder. "You're to flee for Gunderic's Tower at once."

Lamoric batted Durand's hand away. "I cannot abandon the field before the men who—"

At this instant, the Eye of Heaven flashed over the faces of Lamoric's men. Timber crashed—the outer portal wrecked—and Radomor's vanguard roared through. Lamoric turned to his mob—"Shoot! Shoot!"—sending a hundred arrows to dim the sunset.

But Radomor's vanguard struggled on. They braced oxhide shields against the murder holes' torrent of glowing sand and scalding water. As screams seared the air, the hard men of that vanguard snapped arrows back through the portcullis grille, to lash Lamoric's defenders.

One arrowhead flashed in the shadow of Lamoric's shield.

"Lamoric, the gate will not hold," snarled Coensar. "We must get you out!"

"We must hold them!"

Another bow hammered a nail through Lamoric's shield.

"We must get you free of this before it's too late," said Coensar.

"Horseshit," Lamoric said.

"Lordship," Durand pressed. "I'm charged to tell you, *and to bring you back.*"

"No!" He panted. "Not after the tournament! Not after what happened. This time I stay." He looked at both of them, his eyes dark and frantic. "Where did you swear your oaths? To me or my father? My father's concern for his children will not keep me from doing what must be done." He waved at the archers and foot soldiers under shields. "These men will die here. Under my command. Do you understand? On my honor, I will be the last man of Gireth alive in the square before I leave it."

Coensar bared his teeth. "King of far Heaven. We have heard." He looked Durand square in the face. "And we'll hold you at your word, Lordship. Durand and me."

As Coensar spoke his oath, there was a great rush from the gateway arch. Radomor's men wrestled their ram into the choked archway. Scalding water poured down. Flaming straw. But the hide-shrouded ram still swung in its chains, shrugging off steam as its iron beak crashed against the cage of the portcullis. Eighty men clutched its sides.

"Anytime . . ." said Coensar.

Durand and the captain put Lamoric at their backs as smoke and screams snatched the air away. Arrows flickered up the murder holes, and the gate fell.

Through the narrow rent, a battalion shrieked. Durand saw men screaming against the grille as the mob's weight drove the giant dragon through.

A footman in green sprinted up and raised a woodsman's axe, but Durand shot his blade through the fool's coat. He and the captain fell back tight against Lamoric. And as the pressure settled on them, some part of Durand thought: *Here is Deorwen's husband and I'm fighting to keep him alive.* But the mob pressed, and Durand and his comrades hacked and stabbed whomever got near. Coensar was savage, the Champion's blade flickering like a needle to ruin faces, shins, and groins. There was no chivalry, but there were still soldiers running home behind them.

"That's it!" Coensar shouted.

The men of Gireth could hold no longer. The press pitched the defenders against the white statue of the Creator. Durand killed untrained men, shearing through padded canvas and bone with fury. He had trained a lifetime, but he could not be quick enough. Blades hammered down. When a mounted axeman wallowed toward them, Durand threw his masters against the ankles of the Creator. The stone folds of the giant's leggings jammed against his back while the weight of the whole mob balanced on his chest.

Then they were reeling through the crowd. Durand thought of some children's game: three girls arm in arm across a market. He gulped for air. He chopped a man down. He felt the press of green shields. A blow rang from his skullcap, but he stabbed into the flow with fury and speed, pulling the blade, jabbing it home.

Lamoric roared. The man's face was stiff, anchored by will alone against the roaring tide of men and fear. There were still living men of Gireth in the square. He would not leave.

Coensar fought and stumbled, bleeding a red slick over his face. He shouted into Lamoric's ear. "Sound the retreat! Order them out!" Coensar snarled. "We need every man."

Lamoric tried another glance over the heads of the mob.

Coensar grabbed him. "By the Hells, we will *follow* them out if that's what it takes to move you."

Gulping, Lamoric stood. "Retreat, lads! There's no more for us here! Back! Back!"

Coensar counted heads at a glance while Durand fought on. They would run the instant the last man left the square. Durand gutted a spearman who had never learned to parry. He chopped down axe-wielding villagers and laborers with spent crossbows in their fists. Between gulps of air, he killed and killed the men Radomor drove into the square.

A hand caught his surcoat.

Coensar was turning away. "Now!" he snarled—and they were running.

Between the walls of the narrow streets, thousands screamed. Soldiers ran past on all sides while archers bounded along the rooftops like apes. Doors broke. Women shrieked. Coensar shoved at the backs of soldiers and refugees, reeling. Durand caught Coensar and, in another few strides, took up the lead. Coensar bore a great number of wounds, and Lamoric was distracted. Durand threw friend and foe aside as he fought to get Lamoric back to Gunderic's Tower. Men skipped from storefront shutters. He felt bones break over his elbow. Lamoric and Coensar ran in the gap behind him.

They surged at the castle gate, the marketplace crushed with men and women, standing without room to lift their arms. Their wailing was louder than the cry of the armies.

But, in the lofty stone gatehouse, Durand saw the end of everything: the gate was down. Durand felt Lamoric and Coensar stumble into his back as he came to a halt. He was just another head in the crush. There was nothing he could do.

Coensar was suddenly an old man. His face was yellow and bloody, and Lamoric's shoulder was all that kept him from the cobbles.

Durand's head shook in frantic disbelief. He tried to think. "Lamoric, do you know a way into the castle? Is there some secret way?"

Lamoric's face was blank. "Secret way?"

Seeing only incomprehension, Durand swore.

Sergeants and guardsmen pleaded for the crowd to run for

the far gates before it was too late. If they winched up the portcullis, the mob would flood the castle. And with throngs inside, Radomor would starve them out in days. Durand couldn't believe they'd got through the attack at the gates only to die at the castle wall.

He cast around—and saw a narrow chance: the soldiers still outside might be able to hold the crowd off long enough to get Lamoric and Coensar inside.

"We've still got a few men," Durand said. "Lordship, you must order your men to hold the gates," Durand panted. "To the gate! Soldiers of Gireth, to the gate!" He seized shoulders and slapped faces, hammering the men into a wall that might hold the mobs off.

As he muscled close, the guardsmen beyond the oak grille stood, horrified. The crowd crushed Durand against the bars and he shouted, "I'm Lamoric's man!"

And it was Kieren who looked up, hollow-eyed. "It doesn't matter, Durand!" he said.

"Lamoric's here!"

Kieren's mouth opened. He was shaking. "It's too late." Kieren would be picturing Almora and Deorwen on pikes. The old duke cut to pieces. Every hall across Gireth hung with corpses if he let that throng inside. Maybe he *should* leave the gate.

"He's the duke's son. He's the heir!" But he knew there was no hope.

Durand shoved himself a space in the crowd. He glanced up at the grid of oak and iron. He would make a way. "We're coming in!"

The dozen survivors of the Gates of Sunset snatched incredulous looks at him. "Take hold of the bloody gate!" he said, and, at a second roar, they did, catching hold of old oak and iron. Now, Durand was face-to-face with Kieren through the bars. "Draw the bolts," he said. "All I ask is draw the bolts, and we'll hoist the damn thing faster than your windlass can. It'll be up and down before anyone else can get under."

"It's too late," said Kieren.

Durand felt the weight of the crowd against his back. It was all that kept Coensar on his feet. Lamoric was shaking his head. "Do as you must, Sir Kieren." They heard trumpets in the streets. Arrows from the castle.

Kieren pulled the long bolts that held the portcullis.

And Durand grinned a wolf's grin. He turned to Lamoric's mangled rearguard. "Everything!" he said. "Everything you have. We are dead men if you can't haul this from the ground. Take hold!" Lamoric took a place at his side. "Now!"

How much did such a thing weigh? A ton? Two? Durand heaved. His bones locked. Hardwood corners dug. He pushed, instantly sure that a man could squeeze himself fully out of Creation, the weight of muscle and bone jamming him down into the blackness under the world. Monstrous sounds escaped his throat.

But the portcullis moved. Iron and oak rocked. The thing's teeth sucked from their cavities in the roadbed. Durand's soles slid, but he bulled forward. He pushed. Rung by rung then, he and Lamoric's dozen men pushed the portcullis up into its own rattling chains.

Though he heard shouts and prayers, Durand couldn't look. Something battered his knees—desperate people— nearly upsetting his balance. He fought to hold on.

Coensar said, *"Durand."* His voice was calm.

Durand found that he couldn't open his eyes.

"We're through, Durand," said Coensar. "The others have the gate. You'll have to come under, and you must do it now."

The force balanced on each of his joints would crumple him if he shifted. But, with an effort of will and a gulp of air, Durand tore himself free and he tumbled under the sagging gate.

In an instant, he'd joined the men on the other side, and took his share of the weight once more.

Lamoric was shouting at the scrambling river of bodies. "Get clear! The gate must fall!" But the flood of people would not stop—they would never stop.

"God, I must shoot the bolts," said Kieren. "If they all come, we won't save a soul."

The mobs battered Durand's legs as he held the gate, straining men on either side. Radomor was behind the crowd. Coensar or Lamoric must give the order: *Drop it.* Each of them was ready to shoulder the blame.

Before he heard the words, Durand opened his hands and the boom shook the market. Blood sprang from the pavement.

"Again," Lamoric's whisper said. "Again you have saved my life. I would be gone now ten times over."

CARRIED ALONG WITH the mob, Durand fetched up in the back of the tiny sanctuary where he crouched among the duke's inner circle, breathing and staring through a cordon of bloodied soldiers at the throng in the Painted Hall. A silent multitude crowded out there between the walls: porters, prostitutes, beggars, shopkeepers, and a thousand more gaped without a word. In the vaults over their heads, the howl of the city rang like a living thing—no man could speak in the presence of such despair.

The duke's sanctuary was as black as a family crypt. Spattered with blood from the gate's hard fall, Durand could hardly think, and his gaze settled on a pair of large dark eyes in the gloom with him. He realized he was sitting inches from Deorwen, packed in with loyal men and family. Her cheek was smooth as white petals; her breath stirred against his jaw.

"How long can this castle stand when the city has fallen, Sir Kieren?" gasped Abravanal.

Several men flinched at the sound of the duke's voice, including Kieren. "It has never fallen, Your Grace."

"No one has ever taken the citadel until today!" snapped Abravanal. "But now this man is in the streets. This man who slew my daughter. Who slew my son! Now he has my city. His fiends stalk the passages of my castle. He comes for us." There were glances from among the men as the duke clawed his chest, but he subsided.

Deorwen's hand gripped Durand's knee, and he remembered things he wished he had forgotten: her skin under his sliding fingers. Other things.

Lamoric was right there, pressing Kieren. "How many men do we have?"

"Fighting men?" The aging knight shook his head, distracted. "Two hundred sixty. Three hundred. That must be all."

"How many has Radomor got left?"

You could still hear the city's echo. "Eh?" said the Fox.

"How many has Radomor got? The citadel will have cost him a thousand."

A baby was crying somewhere in the throng beyond the cordon of soldiers.

"Thousands," said Kieren. "As many as four or five." Kieren was staring at the mob. He had allowed them in—he and Durand: too many to feed or house.

"Sir Kieren," Lamoric pressed, "how many can we raise? If we buy them time to reach us? And with the Duke of Mornaway's men?"

"Two, Lordship. It might be more."

"And how long?"

Kieren looked to Heaven.

"How long?"

"The roads are a mire. There are distances. If the Duke of Mornaway is on the sea at Evensands, he won't learn of this. Not for days. Our own men will be quicker." If they came at all when the city was lost.

Deorwen was looking up into Durand's eyes, ignoring anyone else who might see. A thousand lungs breathed the stale air. Her fingers dug into his knee.

A ripple passed over the crowd in the Painted Hall, drawing eyes.

"Maybe there's a way we can strike back. Something at night before he's settled in. I can't believe this is possible. What is—"

The duke climbed to his feet and forced himself through the ring of guards. Had the howl of the city vanished?

"Father?" said Lamoric, but the old man continued into the throng. Lamoric darted after his father, and Durand wrenched himself to his feet. He had to move, and so he followed. Every head they passed was turned toward the outer gate: two hundred people in the entry stair, five hundred in the narrow inner court, a thousand more in the tiltyard muck, a few hundred who could fight. He even spotted blind Hagon Leech, listening. Tatters of smoke flew over the walls.

In the high tunnel of the castle gate, Durand caught up with Abravanal and his son. The bright exit hung in the gloom before the old man, twilight caught in the portcullis grille.

Durand could see little more of Abravanal than his scarecrow silhouette. The duke and his son had both stopped where a line of guardsmen and refugees stared out through the bars. Durand stepped onto the blood-slick cobbles.

In the market square beyond the gate, a giant figure stood like a shipwreck. Arrows jutted from the thing's hulking shoulders, and a patriarch's beard tumbled from its battered helm, black with blood. A sword touched the cobbles, its point dragging and clinking with the wind and distant screams. There were a thousand soldiers on the other side of the square.

Abravanal smeared wisps of hair from his face. "This is what comes to speak with us? This is how he parleys, the man who married my little daughter?"

Across the cobbled square, shadowy men clambered on roofs and upper windows, their hands busy.

Lamoric strode toward the portcullis—ready to snarl. But as the young lord moved, the Champion wrenched its dread blade into the sky. The motion triggered a sudden inferno across the square.

The heat—the light—knocked every man a step. But something was visible in the blaze: obscene letters scrawled across the captured buildings. "Surrender the duke and his blood," they said, "and live."

Abravanal pivoted, looking into the firelit faces of guards and beggars and townsmen as the whisper of what they'd seen shivered over the back of the shadowed mob: thousands trapped in smoke and stone. Beyond the tiny duke, the army of Yrlac unfurled leopard banners to lash in the firestorm, the great Champion moaned, and a howl arose in the Tower of Gunderic. Each letter of Radomor's offer was smeared in broad strokes of blood.

THEY RETURNED THROUGH dark courtyards and passages populated with staring eyes. But Durand couldn't face the little sanctuary again. For space and air, he clambered up through the tower, pitching past shield-bearers, pages, and lady's maids all whispering in the stairwells.

The wailing howl swelled as he climbed. He breathed it. It trembled in the stones under his hands.

A last step took him from stony darkness to blazing battlements. Beyond the castle walls, Acconel was aflame. Torch parties rode the darkness, throwing torches through open windows, and the inferno bloomed in street after street as throngs pressed for the gates. Any townsman who thought to hide himself would soon be sucked from his cellar by the fire.

Durand blinked into the smoke. If Radomor had beaten Lamoric or carried him back to Ferangore, the streets of the old city might have been asleep now. If the king had shut Lamoric up in his Mount of Eagles, or if Lamoric had died before the gates, Radomor would not have bothered with the city.

Durand wondered how much of this disaster could be laid at his feet. He had done his share of rescuing, and he now wondered at the cost. It didn't bear thinking about.

The howl swelled, drawing Durand's eye. Crowds poured through the Fey Gates to race the blaze to the harbor. But in the space of a breath, the flame was leaping the harbor road and—before Durand's horrified gaze—swallowing the gates entire. "Host Below," Durand gasped as a gust of smoke snatched the scene away.

When the wind gave him another glimpse, he could see only a strange ripple down the mere wall—like laundry flapping over the battlements. As this "laundry" dropped into the water, Durand understood: he was watching men, women, and children. They dropped from the high walls. They lowered each other as far as arms could reach—but the fall was ten fathoms or more, and who knew whether there was water or a stone quay waiting below?

Durand remembered Radomor's grim offer. How many lives could they save simply throwing Abravanal and his kin over the wall? That was another idea that didn't bear thinking about.

Durand heard a door slap shut, and, when he turned, he found Deorwen looking out over the billowing sky.

"How is Almora?" asked Durand.

There was a half smile. "She is very concerned about babies and horses just now. And who's looking after them."

"I don't think horses will fare well."

"I have maneuvered the Patriarch of Acconel into explaining."

"Oredgar? That old priest could turn a man's hair white with that stare of his."

"Almora has latched on to him. I think she believes he has answers."

"That old man just might."

Deorwen was walking toward the parapet. "The fires spread so quickly."

"Don't look."

She stopped when the firelight touched her face.

From the shadows, Durand said, "I remember when I first came to Acconel. I'd only seen seven winters—every one in the mountains at my mother's skirts. I came down with one of my father's knights. It would have been spring, like this. I was bundled up on the back of this half-stranger's horse. I remember the Banderol—so wide in that green valley. I remember Wrothsilver like a snowcap on its hill. And finally Acconel on Silvermere. High walls and sails beyond it." All of it was dark and fire now.

"My mother and father told me I would be serving the duke, and I had skald's songs in my mind. But my father's man dropped me in old Gunderic's Tower among fifty scrapping boys—mostly older and all from shining lowland halls. I think I was very lonely for a while—plenty of black eyes and bruised knuckles.

"But the city! Everything had been standing a thousand winters: the hall, the bridges, the walls, the gates, the high sanctuary. There was someone who could tell you when every well was dug, who dug it, and why some Lost maiden could be seen sometimes on windy evenings." A gust blew stinging smoke across the rooftop.

Staring out, Deorwen tucked a stray lock under her veil. Firelight glittered in her eyes. "Radomor will turn his might against the castle. When the fires have cooled, he will bring up his engines. There is little food to ration. And, with the city lost around us, the people's will is fragile."

This seemed like a very pretty way to describe oceans of dread and terror. "Abravanal's barons may come soon."

She kept her eyes on the distant fires. Embers spun into a black Heaven. "It's easy to turn inward," she said. And then, after a space of ages: "Hard to see over one's own small troubles." Durand could hear the howling from the streets.

"Lamoric has stepped into the heart of the city's defense," said Deorwen.

"He has been the great commander."

"It's everything he's struggled for, landed in his lap unlooked-for."

She kept her wide eyes on the flames, the light glowing on her skin. "When we were fleeing through Eldinor, your skald said there was no one from Mornaway at the Mount of Eagles," she said. "Just in passing. It is strange how such a brief mention can occupy one's thoughts. Where was my brother? My father would have sent Moryn, I think. Was there an accident upon the road? Did he simply row up to the island an hour after we did? Did he catch wind of Ragnal's trap and save himself? Has he died on the road? He is my brother and I don't know."

Durand blinked. "Abravanal's sent riders to Mornaway."

She nodded without glancing. "Moryn seems so stiff, but when I was a girl, he would appear at my father's hall—where I was chasing the dogs or playing at needlework. There he would be with his riding gloves and his great blue mantle and I would know that he had come for *me*. He hardly spoke, but we would ride, the diamond banners of blue and gold flying behind us. Rain or fair weather. He clutched me tight and we tore away from the walls and serving men and ladies waiting. We would fly for the forests without a word, riding until there was no air left in me or the poor horse. Somehow there would always be a stream. And he would have a knob of cheese or sack of apples. He hardly spoke. But he listened. It was magic to me. Alone with my brother."

In a brief flash of Deorwen's eyes, the spear-straight Moryn Mornaway was transformed for Durand. "You'll soon be able to ask the man himself," he said.

"I'm sure. But it has disturbed my dreams these last weeks. I cannot believe he is safe. But I am so often with Almora, and there are few women at court. I see him in darkness. It has been a job just to keep the poor girl occupied. When can a woman speak of such a thing?"

Weeks, she had said: weeks without a chance to talk over the loss of her own brother. She gave Durand a long look, then lifted her chin. "I came here to get free of the crowd. To breathe. But this is no place for any of that." She looked up into the clouds. "Many have joined the Lost tonight. They are in the air all about us, storming with the smoke and embers. I can feel them pressing in. More and more all the time."

"Deorwen." Durand tried to take her by the shoulders, but she twisted away from him, vanishing into the tower. He could hardly chase his lord's wife through the crowds.

"Hells," said Durand.

He stood in the fiery dark, listening to his heart thunder, and he punched a good stone wall.

THAT NIGHT THEY knelt in the belly of the deepest Hell, the murmur of prayers thick in the air. Deorwen sat by Almora once more, the little girl more sober than any of them though the old castle moaned like the dead were at the arrow loops. Abravanal stared and panted: somewhere else in his head. Durand eyed the throng in the Painted Hall— hundreds looked back, no doubt weighing life against little girls and loyalty as dread sank in.

Deorwen reached to set her hand on Lamoric's, but Lamoric was already rising to his feet. "It'd be just Radomor's sort of trick to storm the walls tonight when we think we're safe behind these fires of his," and he was off to check the sentries. Deorwen watched him slip from the sanctuary. He had only just got back from some similar nervous errand: checking how arrows had been divided among the bowmen.

Someone in the Painted Hall was crying.

The metal Power in Almora's hands clicked while she sucked her upper lip.

At one window, the Patriarch stood. "Thirty thousand souls chased from their city into the fields. Four thousand dead already." His long silver beard shivered with the motion of his lips. "In the black water below the walls or brittle in their cellars." He stopped himself.

His high sanctuary, built in the days of the High Kingdom, now stood beyond the castle walls, the delicate panes of its windows falling in tears of running lead.

Almora spoke. "We will have the city back. Uncle Radomor will be punished."

The tower whistled like a pot in a kiln.

His expression lost in shadows, the Patriarch said, "Ah, Almora. Radomor has only one soul to balance all he's taken."

Almora cocked her head. "They go to Heaven. You told me."

The room stared up at the holy man. "Yes. So I did. But it is hard to be as wise as you. There was a man: a wise man. Marcellin they called him. He warned that we should trade pity for hatred and forgiveness for vengeance, or we might find ourselves in the same Hell as our enemy. But it is hard." The old man turned toward the dark glass of the eastern windows and knelt there. Little Almora stepped to his side, and they were nearly eye to eye.

"Marcellin was born in the Dreaming Lands," he said to her. "I have seen his crabbed writing with my own eyes. Tiny letters he used. An old man showed me when I visited the Library of Vuranna." Almora blinked into his gleaming face. "They all have black hair in Vuranna—like yours—and even the plowmen drink wine."

The girl knelt at the old man's side. Her Power fluttered its damselfly wings.

LAMORIC DID NOT return. Durand watched Deorwen staring over Almora's shoulder as the little girl dozed and then slept. For one hour and another, she stared. Deorwen waited, but Lamoric never came. Her eyes never closed.

Finally, in the near total gloom, Durand got to his feet. He stepped between sleeping forms, invisible as a spirit, and crossed to the woman. "*We'll* talk," he said. "I think there's one place left in this old keep."

And he led her through the blind multitude, past sleeping friends and strangers to an old room he thought no one would have claimed: a storeroom above the keep's door where a windlass used to be. They sat among old hangings and broken tables; an arrow loop overlooked the fires of the city.

And she leaned against him. He felt her shoulder and her forehead, half-nestled, half-collapsed. He felt her hand touch his thigh, hanging on more than anything. And so he held her.

It was like teetering at the peak of some high hill. He tried to imagine sitting through the whole yawning night, so close and never touching. But, more tired and alone than he could understand, he did not turn from her. His hands slid over her body and they kissed until, together, they hung on with the firelight flashing in Deorwen's eyes and the smoke of the city in their mouths as they gasped and grappled through the night.

ONLY THE GREATEST exhaustion could have brought sleep to Durand in that storeroom.

He awoke sure that there were knights on the stair or Radomor at the door. He was still with Deorwen—she struggled: fighting, dreaming. It took a moment to find his balance. She was caught in some sort of fit.

"Deorwen," he said. "Deorwen!"

Now his head was full of his own past premonitions. He lifted her, trying for a look into her face when a great gush of foul, icy water vomited from her mouth.

Durand recoiled. Deorwen's eyes rolled big and glassy as those of some ancient pike from the bottom of the mere. He would have to carry her downstairs, screaming for help.

"Deorwen!" he whispered, now shaking her. "Come on!"

Then she woke, retching and gasping in the narrow space. He had her shoulders.

"Gods," she spluttered. "Gods!"

"What's happened?" Durand asked. How loud could their voices be?

"I'd only closed my eyes. I was somewhere else. Someone else. Cooking. A great stew pot on an open hearth. I could see out the door and the air was cold."

Durand thought of his own visions.

"I was about to fetch a few bits out with a holed spoon," Deorwen said. "My feet were bare. We were talking, I think. Then there was some commotion down in the road. Hooves beating—we don't often hear that on our lane. There were soldiers. Men on big horses." She hardly sounded like herself. "Then they were coming in, down and ducking through our front door. I tried to get others behind my skirts. Children! I was telling them 'the window!' out the back. Then the men caught at my shawl. But I got clear, tumbled out the window. There is a ditch. It's where we throw what we want rid of—it runs to the river. And I think they won't follow. But they're coming round. There's water in the bottom and I slide. I hear screaming."

Durand gave her a sharp shake. "That wasn't you!"

"I remember splashing—falling into water."

"You're safe!"

"She's dead, Durand."

Durand searched his mind, glancing over the city beyond the arrow loop. "It all sounds like the lower city. Something there."

"The air is too full of ghosts," Deorwen breathed, and Durand could nearly see them: mad souls who'd lost too much too quickly, unburied or unknown. There'd been thousands pitched from Creation that day, and few had seen wise women and priests to ease their passing. Many must be Lost now, and one of these had surely found Deorwen between death and sleep.

"I'd hardly closed my eyes," she faltered.

Durand lifted her—half-sopping with ditchwater. "The sanctuary." It had stopped Radomor's sendings. "We'll get you snug by the altar and see if any of these spirits tries to pass Father Oredgar. I wouldn't if I came haunting."

She managed a nod.

He might have stayed by her side until the duke's men came to prise him loose and throw him over the wall, but now he helped the shaking woman to her feet and led her through the black passages of the keep.

21. A Shell of Stone

The Eye of Heaven returned to a black hall. Soot caked every surface in Gunderic's Tower. Every face was black, except for the flash of eyes.

Almora was playing. Deorwen threw Durand strange glances—they couldn't speak. Was she all right? And right beside her was Lamoric. Durand swallowed and clenched his eyes shut, wondering what he was doing.

Meanwhile, the knights in the sanctuary weighed their chances while tearing at bits of breakfast bread. When would the barons ride? How long must the castle hold out? They spun out their arguments until old Coensar spoke into the silence, cold and certain: "It's from Radomor we'll learn the truth. If he comes on with a mad charge and throws his ladders at the walls before the embers are cool, he has seen your men and they're near."

Even the duke's wide blue eyes were on Lamoric's hired captain.

"But," said Coensar, "if Radomor comes on slow and bides his time, then we know there's no help nearby."

Durand joined the others as they climbed the battlements of wall and tower, watching. As the first day wore on, the only sign of Radomor's army was the collapse of tall and distant buildings in clouds of soot. Sappers and soldiers worked on the wide roads, clearing rubble for the passage of Radomor's engines. And the advance continued that way for seven days. Soon, each cautious step was another point in an argument long settled. There was no help on the horizon.

Durand suffocated between Lamoric and the man's wife.

When night's chill gripped the hall, the refugees squabbled over blankets—and even the old hangings in the winch room. In the hall, they argued over bare patches of floor. They were soon hungry, and Durand was among the men who distracted young Almora while other men butchered those horses not fit for war.

Deorwen fought to keep up with Almora. The little thing circled her, like a little black hawk on its jesses: never far, reporting everything in a bright earnest voice.

Each day, Durand resolved to make an end of it. Once, he came down the stairs to find the Patriarch awake: his bearded face as grim and silver as some king on an old coin. The old man had little Almora sleeping against his knee.

Swallowing unease, Durand whispered, "You are good with her, Your Grace. All she's been through at her age."

The old man smiled for an instant. "*She* is good for *me*, I think. It is hard for a man to watch his city burn and still cling to the truths he's rattled off in fat days of peace. 'Where is the Host of Heaven in all this?' I will think, and she will answer."

But Deorwen grew pale, and so, each night, Durand stood, spiriting Deorwen from the silence of their strange prison, and they held each other like the last man and woman alive. The dead were with her when she closed her eyes: men and women dying by sword or fire or flood. He heard story after story, but soon she wouldn't say a word.

All the while, Radomor tightened the knot around the castle, each night renewing his fatal offer: the Champion in the market square, the fires, the bloody scrawl. The duke's men were watchful as the last barrels were emptied and filth steamed in the corners.

ON THE SEVENTH day, Radomor's mighty engines ringed the old castle in a great crescent and commenced to rain stones down on the walls. Castle Acconel was strong, but each blow shook the blackened fortress to its cellars. And there were many hard eyes staring back from the crowd as the duke's men continued their scheming.

Toward dusk, Almora tottered around the sanctuary asking men questions and getting nervous answers. When the little thing heard children crying in the hall, she took a notion that they might be thirsty. She and Deorwen were soon walking among them doling out water.

Durand watched Deorwen, knowing how tired she was, watching her indulge the little girl. He thought he should get up and help with the bucket.

But, among the old gang, Berchard gripped his sleeve. "I don't like seeing the girl out there. It's like watching her skip through a pack of dogs. I mean, there's loyal and there's hungry. With the duke knocking outside, this is no game anymore, and these folk aren't belted knights bred to bloodshed."

"This is my father's city," said Lamoric, "and remember it's heroes and belted knights who've turned traitor out there. They're the ones riding against the king."

Durand didn't like to hear words like "traitor."

Heremund Skald was rubbing his mouth. "There are many siege stories. Hunger does strange things. Sickness comes. You hear of debauchery—and piety. Madness among the desperate. Some folk stand firm beyond reason and others turn on each other like wild cats."

Coensar was nodding. "Radomor's shrewd. We might be wise to look for a room with a strong door, Lordship. One of the mural towers, if we could—"

Lamoric shot to his feet. "Enough!" he said, drawing the attention of half the old hall. He swung his hand to the west. "Our enemy is out there! It's Radomor who's put the knife to our throats. It's *he* who's burned and slain our friends and countrymen. Who could put his faith in such a man? A kinslayer! An oathbreaker! We've seen these things he's conjured into his service. This squabbling is what *he* wants! He's planted this poisoned hope in our hearts. But what mercy can a man hope for at the hands of such a fiend?

"If I cannot trust my people, what is my life worth?" He got Durand's shoulder and gave it a shake. "I am leaving this nest of whispers to look my real enemy in the eye!"

Lamoric pushed past their guards and into the Painted Hall, ready to keep his word. And Kieren caught Durand's sleeve. "A couple of you'd better go with him; he's likely to hurdle the walls and go meet the old bugger!"

Durand nodded, slipping through the huddled crowds to mount the stairs to the outer battlements—and wondering all along whether he should be trusted. He was surprised to find Badan on his heels. "I've sworn the same oaths you have," the man snarled—and he might have done a better job keeping them.

A wind slapped grit into Durand's eyes as he topped the battlements and spotted Lamoric. Durand wished he hated the man. They passed guardsmen crouched as the stones of small engines cracked against the battlements. Even in this mood, Lamoric kept his head low.

He smiled at Durand. "'Look him in the eye.' I'd be bloody lucky to see him at all, this enemy of mine. He'll be in some great tent with a cask of wine and those creatures of his crouched on either hand like some chieftain's dogs. This is no way to fight. There is nothing but fear and squalor."

"And the crowds are a pig," Badan said. "They'll be washing that stink out of this old fort for a hundred years, whoever wins."

"You've got a gentle heart, Sir Badan. No one could say otherwise."

Beyond Badan's grunted reply, Durand heard a groan and swish as one of Radomor's monstrous engines lobbed some great block of masonry into the heavens.

Lamoric turned to the yard: a heaving morass under black walls. "It's more crowded now than the festival day . . . with no hawkers to come peddling pies and—"

A great stone smacked the inner wall, rebounding into the tiltyard. Between two men, it bit deep into the muck, narrowly missing both. Dead shapes sprawled under many others.

"These bastards will hammer your castle to dust," said Badan, swiping a lank ribbon of red hair from his face.

Another trebuchet groaned.

"It's like wrestling in some backstreet gutter—all blood and twisting bones," said Lamoric. "He is killing Sons of Atthi!"

"Lordship, he is—" Durand began, when the battlements exploded between them. The walkway was dropping from under their feet. For an instant, as Lamoric skipped clear, his head crested the battlements. Durand saw whole units of Radomor's bowmen rise in the streets. "Lordship!" Durand leapt for his master while a storm of shafts dashed itself against the battlements. Durand's drive knocked Badan sprawling—but tackled a living Lamoric to the walkway.

Durand closed his eyes, saying, "I'd wager there's a fat reward for the first man who puts an arrow through a man like you."

They levered themselves apart, Lamoric dusting the big

Gireth bull's head emblazoned on his surcoat. "Shooting for the bull's-eye."

Durand sat back against the wall, laughing as stones sailed by.

Badan's spittle struck his cheek.

"You son of a whore!" Badan's fist was on his blade. "I nearly ended up with a broken neck, then." The sound could have been coughing. "You touch me again and I'll gut you. You're not such a riddle as you think. I've had my eyes open, and I don't sleep as sound as some, eh?"

Durand flashed cold, blood like ice.

Badan punctuated his threat with a shove to Durand's chest as he stood up and left bodyguarding behind. Durand could only stare. He'd killed a man over this in Tern Gyre.

But Lamoric was shaking his head and still chuckling— Durand couldn't remember why. "A charmer. You watch your back."

"Aye," Durand managed.

But Lamoric merely glanced out an embrasure. "These whoresons see me stand for a moment: *whack*. Watching for weakness. Very eager to jump on it. I'll have to think about that—maybe we'll get a last chance."

Durand glanced out the same gap and saw men heaving at the spokes of a great windlass under one of the towering siege engines, hauling a load of stones to swing above the street. Once they had the weapon's big arm cocked, the thing would whip another boulder into the castle.

When Durand glanced back, he found Lamoric smearing tears from his face. The man panted a quick laugh. "I shouldn't have been so hard on Berchard and the rest. The hour's coming when the crowd will have to turn. This isn't some holy war. Radomor's a thug. And Ragnal? He's a kidnapper. But we're caught between. I've given my word to Ragnal. Five winters back, I put my hands in his hands, and swore with all the lords of Errest that I was his man." Durand remembered kneeling in the mud before Lamoric, knighted and bound, all by the bank of the River Glass: Lamoric's sworn man.

"The Patriarchs crowned him," said Lamoric. "I vowed to defend him—my father and brother beside me." He managed a twitchy grin. "I stood clear-eyed before him. Who'd trust the man who betrays such a vow?"

Durand kept his mouth shut. He would tell Lamoric—not that the man was a cuckold, but that his wife was alone. He would mention Deorwen's nightmares.

A crow fluttered over the wall, its wings snapping close. A raven followed.

"Already, we're starving," said Lamoric. "I don't think my lady wife has slept since we shut these gates. People are ill. I've had men dropping bodies over the mere wall."

Another carrion bird flashed past, swinging toward the top of Gunderic's Tower.

Lamoric winced. "I won't force them to hold on beyond."

"My Lord!" cried a voice.

In the tiltyard where the stones were landing stood Deorwen. "Your father's gone to the rooftop."

Both men looked heavenward. Gunderic's Tower loomed twenty fathoms above the yard. Durand could see the tiny form of Abravanal of Gireth picked out against the sky, black shapes spinning around him. He had something—someone—in his arms.

Lamoric stared, but Durand got the man's shoulder. "Come on!"

They charged from the walls, ducking through gates and vaulting the crowded stairs of the fortress until they stumbled out upon the rooftop among the silent crowd of the duke's men.

Hanging half above the long fall, Abravanal teetered in the embrasure between two stone merlons. Ravens and jackdaws and rooks and crows churned in a ragged whirlwind around the battlements. The old man clutched Almora to his bony chest as if she were an infant child. The crows were laughing.

Kieren met Lamoric as they stepped from the stairs. "Thank Heaven. We have told him that there's no reason. What Radomor's done cannot stand."

Lamoric grimaced.

He opened his arms and stepped out toward the old man. "Father," he said, "it is too soon."

"They are dying down there," said Abravanal. "Dying because of me. My house. My line. I must defend my people."

Lamoric was stepping closer. "They chose this, Father."

"I will not cling until my own men must bundle me through the gates of my father's hall, and roll me at the feet of the man who slew my daughter—and my son." His blue eyes bulged. "What sort of coward would I be if I forced them to that choice? I must choose my own time."

"And Álmora?" said Lamoric.

The duke strained his neck, peering up where the black birds flew. "How can I deliver her into that monster's hands?"

"And your son?"

The old man's fingers twitched like a crab's limbs in his daughter's black hair. "You will do what you must do."

"Yes . . ." said Lamoric. He had cried upon the wall, marking the despair coming to the multitude. Now, he walked beyond the reach of his comrades, hands falling empty to his sides—drawn on by the brink.

Durand was too slow. No one moved.

"I am so sorry," Abravanal was saying. "This was never a doom I saw before us."

Lamoric was very close. "No . . ."

"There has been so much death."

And with terrible suddenness, Lamoric smashed his father in the mouth.

The old man tottered, high above the yard. But Lamoric was savage, catching hold of his sister's hair and heaving.

"You bastard!" he snarled. The old man crashed back onto the rooftop, falling in a tangle sure to snap bones in a man his age.

Deorwen bolted forward as Lamoric tore a screaming Almora from his father's arms. He bent over the old man like he meant to keep up the beating. The crows were storming, shrieking.

"You didn't think of me at all, did you? You were going to give it all up. Throw my sister to the stones—and you'd forgotten I was alive! There are a thousand people downstairs who would swear that the girl died if Radomor came asking. Before we threw her down! You'd have killed us all! All our sworn men—what do you think Rado would do with them when the gates opened?"

Lamoric's shoulders heaved with the working of his lungs. "You've been asleep too long, Father."

He stood, looking to the spent faces of friends and family all around him.

LAMORIC'S EYES WERE mad and flashing as he tramped back into the tower stair, marching past Deorwen and Almora without a glance. Ashamed, was Durand's guess. The little girl looked after him as he vanished.

Durand joined the others in the crowded stone spiral, wondering what would become of Deorwen. He imagined tomorrows where they were all free of the tower. Durand would ride for the farthest corner of Creation. Deorwen would have peace from her spirits. Lamoric would stand still long enough to learn just whom he'd married.

Durand stepped off the bottom stair to find the whole of the Painted Hall looking back at him: every man, woman, and child up and watching.

Lamoric stood before them, alone.

To Durand's astonishment it was blind Hagon who stepped to the fore, scratching at the white shock of his hair. "Ah," said the man. "You have returned?"

"What is this?" asked Lamoric. His hand moved toward his blade.

The blind man grimaced. "Well. I have been asked to speak for the rest here. We have come to a decision."

"Have you . . ."

Durand watched Hagon, wondering how long a few knights could hold a thousand men, even in the well of a winding stair.

"Lord Lamoric, Duke Abravanal. We are hungry. Some of our number are sick. And there is great fear. A deliberation has been forced upon us."

"I am here," said Lamoric. His father said nothing.

Hagon hauled a good breath through his nostrils. "I know, Lordship. By the King and Host of Heaven, these are hard days. But the men and women of Acconel trapped here have talked it out. And we've sworn to stand by you and yours against whatever comes, no matter what it costs. And that's an end."

A real grin was spreading on Lamoric's face.

"By the Lord of Dooms," he breathed.

"Just so," said Hagon. He turned to the crowd and they stared on, fierce and grim. There were nods and scattered smiles.

Eyes flashing, Lamoric stepped forward, clasping a surprised Hagon's hand. "Here is loyalty that the lords of this realm cannot match, and courage that its knighted warriors might envy."

Durand stared on. This was where he'd meant to be knighted, to swear his oath in new linen so many leagues ago. He spoke: "We have lords and Patriarchs enough for the taking of an oath, My Lord."

"Yes!" said Lamoric, and then to the crowd: "You are the equal of any belted knight in the Atthias, and I will not stand by until you have been granted your due. Gather about Father's throne! Today, I'll see you all made knights of Errest. And before we're done, you'll each have fine halls in the domain of Duke Radomor!"

WHEN THEY HAD finished swearing in the men and women and boys—knights giving each their slap or tap—Duke Abravanal took his son by the arm. The old man had Gunderic's Isle Kingdom blade: the Sword of Judgment. And, in a shaking moment, he pressed the heirloom into Lamoric's hands.

"I will not wear it," said Abravanal. "I will throw it in the mere if you won't take it. It has been the sword of our fathers since Gunderic."

There were tears around the hall.

BUOYED UP BY their fresh oaths, the starving Knights of the Painted Hall—men, women, and children—swayed into motion. They picked the yards for spent missiles, they broke down a bakehouse and sheds to gird the inner walls with hoardings and erect a set of light engines to pitch stones back at Radomor's lines. Inside, men and women shoveled sliding mountains of filth from castle corners and pitched the reeking stuff into the bay. Almora chased whatever passing crowd caught her eye, lending her heart, while Lamoric darted and climbed from battlement to basement, holding the castle together as Radomor's engines beat upon the walls.

All the while, Durand felt Deorwen losing her hold. He wanted to grab Lamoric and make him see that his wife was slipping under, drowning. Each night, he told her, "When we are free of this place, these spirits will leave you." He held her in the secret moments of darkness, but she faded, farther away and farther away. The distance grew in her eyes, until he knew that he could no more cut her off than he could cut her throat. He swallowed honor and shame and betrayal, saying that it would be murder to set her aside. Murder to give up the scent and touch and wonder of her. It was a devil's argument, and the shame blazed of it on his face whenever Lamoric grinned his way.

IN DAYLIGHT, HE stood in the archway where the hall met the family's sanctuary, standing in neither one place nor the other. Deorwen and Almora were back among the listless crowds with their pail of water. Durand's fingers curled in the fluted arch. He resolved to do what he must. He swore to catch Lamoric and *make* him understand: she was so alone—she had the dreams. He would step back to let her husband in. He had to stop himself. He would tell Deorwen.

Just as he stepped into the hall, the world shifted. He nearly stumbled.

No one else seemed to notice.

Across the hall, Almora was asking, "Why can't I see him?" while Durand stood, hands spread and frozen lest his next step bring the tower down.

"You wanted to help with the water," Deorwen answered.

"After, then, Aunty. Star is my horse. He will want water too."

"Star. He is busy."

Durand blinked; he felt as though Creation's heartbeat had caught a hitch, but he'd be damned if he could say why.

Then another stone struck beyond the hall—and he understood: after countless ringing blows, the old walls spoke a different note. Somewhere, the stone shell that saved them was broken. He looked at Almora and Deorwen—and the whole trapped multitude—then bolted down the stairs and for the flawed sound.

He pitched into the crowded tiltyard between the inner and outer walls, landing up at Lamoric's side. Every hollow eye in the yard was fixed on the same spot: a great crack that hung like dry lightning in the high outer wall over all their heads. Then a new missile struck, and the courses bulged. Fathoms above the yard, the men on the outer wall ran from twisting battlements. And another stone fell. Durand imagined Radomor's engineers heaving their engines. The whole siege would bear down on that one flaw. Throughout the city, Radomor's captains would be lashing their battalions into motion, every man charging for this spot.

Another massive block fell from the Heavens and the crack jagged deeper.

Durand caught his master's sleeve. "We must throw some props against this. Get the men down."

"Down? No, Durand! That's the last thing we want." He flashed a savage smile and turned to the crowd. "Quick as you can! Listen sharp and no questions!"

Then they were running.

IN A FURY of roaring and running, Durand and Lamoric's captains packed the outer walls and towers all around the breaking wall—even as Radomor's stones hammered down. Every soul pushed himself on with sheer will, but they were all spent. As Durand drove men up one open stair, he stole a heartbeat to wonder whether anyone had the wits left to play the game Lamoric had in mind.

Scarcely had Durand formed the thought when Creation filled with stone and thunder. For a moment, it was all he could do to hang on, then a thousand hardened soldiers roared from Radomor's lines. Everything would be lost if Lamoric's forces didn't answer. Durand leapt into the yard and sprinted into the thunder.

Though the battlements were still crashing into the cleft, the men of both armies howled in.

"He'll be like a man with his fist round a wolf's tongue!" Lamoric had said. Now, Durand and the fiercest men in

Acconel crammed the gap as blades flashed from the dust. Green shirts crowded through the howling din. Then they were lashing at each other. The weight of two armies met in a space no broader than a doorway. Durand felt his boots slide and his ribs creak as he gulped—and gouged with Ouen's great blade. In moments, dead men lolled, caught and standing among the living.

In snatches, Durand saw hundreds of Radomor's men heaving in the market yard beyond the breech. Durand and a couple of dozen other fools couldn't hold back a mob like that. Soon, they would push through. And so, somewhere behind—high on the inner walls—Lamoric was watching for the moment.

The longer Durand and his comrades held, the worse it was for Radomor. While the bear-pit struggle knotted in the breech, hundreds would be dying as Lamoric's archers lashed the back of the battalions under their wall. Far from retreating, every man looked down on the fight, flinging whatever death he could find on his enemy's heads. Here was vengeance for every soul in Gunderic's Tower.

But they could not hold. Durand saw a man swatted down. And another. The mob outside was pushing hard. It might already be too late.

With flashes bursting in his eyes, Durand nearly missed the call to retreat. Trumpets rang from Gunderic's Tower. Lamoric would be shouting his order, and Durand caught threads of it: "Back! Back!"

Above and on all sides, the garrisons of the mural towers and outer walls abandoned the fight. "Radomor can have his wall," had been the order, "but he won't get a man of our garrison." And so, with Durand's force faltering in the breech, the defenders fled the outer walls.

In front of Durand, the green soldiers were gaining ground. A defender flew from a razor uppercut. Another Acconel man crashed through his fellows with a blade in his throat.

They must hold until the walls were cleared. The garrison couldn't stand to lose a single man, and, as Durand was pushed back, he could still hear the boots of defenders slapping down the stairs behind him. Hundreds could still be caught.

Desperate, he set his boot on a belt, swinging Ouen's big sword high. He warred with two hundred men.

Then a howl struck from behind.

Familiar men battered past him, swamping the broken rearguard: knights meant to be at the inner gates charging forward. A hand grabbed his shoulder, and there was Berchard spluttering, "We've got archers! Let the first wave catch it! Run!"

And so, with a last wild chop, Durand tumbled free, into the space between the walls. Above the old tiltyard, the garrison was thundering through the hoardings atop the inner walls. Every man from the outer walls had pelted up those stairs, and now their arrows flickered down as Durand reeled into the gatehouse, and—when the rearguard was free—the big portcullis fell behind them.

Beyond the crowded inner yard, Creation boiled with Radomor's screaming killers—thwarted, trapped, and under a new hail of missiles.

Durand smeared blood from his face, staggering into the clammy shadow of Gunderic's Tower. They'd pulled a score of horses into the yard. Hundreds of people stared back.

After days of grinding resistance, the garrison had surrendered the outer walls and tiltyard in the space of heartbeats. Creation had locked around them like a fist, but they were still alive and making Radomor bleed. Everywhere he looked, people smiled like savages. They would hold the next wall, and the next if they could.

The keep would be packed now—without a single empty corner for a man and his friend's wife. No matter what Durand's honor or his heart demanded, Deorwen would be alone with her dreams.

IN THE AFTERMATH of the retreat, Abravanal's inner circle made plans. With the throng from the tiltyard now squeezed into Gunderic's Tower and the narrow courtyard at its foot, people could hardly sit or breathe. Radomor's engineers shifted their aim, and soon it was the inner walls and Gunderic's Tower itself shaking with the thunderclap of great stones.

Radomor's Champion appeared once more, standing on

the market cobbles. Abravanal's household climbed Gunderic's Tower to stare down upon him. Carrion birds settled all around the battlements in leering heaps too deep to scatter.

Standing guard among the lords of Abravanal's dwindling domain, Durand expected the brute to roar or unveil another bloody scrawl.

Instead, the sound came from all around the castle, arising among black feathers like the whisper of wind in forest's leaves. "*So alone . . .*"

Durand and the men of Abravanal's household drew blades, Durand, at least, wondering what he could do with one sword.

Abravanal leaned from the battlements like a captain at the prow of his ship. "To the Hells with you!" he shouted, but the whisper pressed on.

"Where is your precious king, do you suppose, in all of this? We have heard there is rebellion in the north. His noble brother, we have heard. There are riders calling loyal men to the banner of Ragnal the fool. They remind Ragnal's lords of their poor sons, hostage in his Mount of Eagles. Brother tears at brother. The realm collapses. The people—"

A door swung wide at the stairway door, and wild-eyed Patriarch Oredgar stood under Heaven with his arms flung wide. "Begone, fiends of the Hells!" And the birds were rising, shrieking into the wind. "The Eye of Heaven has not left us yet. It is not yet time to mock in daylight!"

And the things stormed and tumbled all around, battering every man before they swung off over the city, leaving the Patriarch slashed bloody by beak and talon.

THEY DID NOT die in the first hours.

Deorwen played riddling games with Almora. Plaster fell in great white shards, and the Knights of the Painted Hall slipped their dead into the cold water of the mere.

Lamoric moved among the crowd. "Remember," he said, touching a shoulder, smiling into a gray face, "this is *our* plan, not Radomor's. While that madman struggles to beat us down, we are biding our time. The barons of Gireth are on the roads. They are riding. Radomor does not want us to stand. He does not want an armed battalion behind him when the knights of my father's barons come pouring over the bridges. The traitor has an adder by the throat and wolves at his door."

But his speech could hardly open their eyes. People nodded. They leaned against each other. "Just wait," said Lamoric.

There were too many people, and their strength ebbed with every hour that the great stones clubbed the tower.

Duke Abravanal sat near Deorwen and Almora, watching his son—the only moving being in the hall—understanding something of the man now and fearing the knowledge had come too late.

Lamoric returned to the little sanctuary, gray and wavering though he smiled. He found an arrow loop and peered off in the direction of Radomor's army. As Kieren and Coensar both looked on, Heremund joined the young lord at the window.

"I remember a time up in Highshields," he said. "I'd carried my mandora to some baron's hall. One of those forts on a crag. Nothing but goats." He made a dry sound. "I was teasing the old man's young wife, and she smiled too much, I guess. Then the old man's kicking me down a passage to a guardroom, and I see this ugly grate in the floor, and these grinning thugs. And down I went. A prison pit: an oubliette. For a blink, I was sure it was a well, it was that narrow. I couldn't sit or lie down. Couldn't reach the grate, couldn't climb. A couple of days in, I've got my knees on one wall with my face above them, crumpled and cold and sore as I've ever been. And then they swing the grate open." He shook his head, remembering relief.

"I tell you," he said, "strong or weak, brave or craven, it doesn't matter when you're in a spot like that." Kieren and Coensar were still watching.

"Did *they* send you?" Lamoric asked. "Radomor's boys? If you meant to take our minds from our sufferings, I'm afraid your tale has not hit the mark."

Coensar's eyes glinted in the gloom. "Sickness moves among us," he said. "The people are weak. There is hardly water. We must think."

"No," said Lamoric. "There can be no bargains."

A stone struck the ancient tower; a great crack flickered across the vault above their heads.

Kieren scrubbed plaster from his hair. "What will Rado-mor do? He'll want everyone dead, no matter what he's writ-ten on the walls."

"Weakness would stiffen his opponent's necks," said Coensar.

Kieren glanced Almora's way, and spoke softly. "He might accept our surrender. It would show his nobility."

"I will not hear you speak of this," said Lamoric.

An odd sound drew Durand's eye to one glazed arrow loop in the dark: the debris of some fallen battlement raining past.

"If anyone's to leave this place alive," said Coensar, "they'll have to hand us over." The captain's steely glance found De-orwen and Almora, playing.

Kieren leaned closer. "We must get them out of here somehow."

Deorwen pushed herself up. "No."

Kieren spread his small hands. "It will be all right. The girl will need—"

"You cannot send me off. I don't deserve—" She stopped for a moment, a grim calm passing over her face.

"Radomor will never believe it," she said.

No one said a word.

"Tell them, Durand," she said.

Durand wanted to believe that they could spirit her from the place. But this was Radomor, a man who'd listened to his best friend drown, who'd slain his own father. He could only stare back at her.

A stone struck the upper stories of the fortress, jarring an-other rain of soot and plaster from the ceiling.

Almora was looking up at them all. Durand wished they could all slip over the back wall and swim out across the Bay of Acconel, leaving it all behind.

"Don't worry about that," Kieren said. "There's always a way."

"He won't break us," said Lamoric. "Our allies must have time. Our people will hold out as long as they must."

But what if there was no one riding? They had seen the

city burning. The smoke would have traveled a hundred leagues. Who would ride to a ruin and throw his life away? Many would bend their knees to Radomor if it meant they could keep their lands.

Abravanal was staring at his son, shaking his head. Durand thought he saw pride and regret and despair in the man's face.

Durand looked away, back to the arrow loop—as its leaded casement exploded into the room. Picturing fiends on the wind, Durand charged to the narrow window, sword drawn, glancing down over black and gleaming stones of the harbor wall. He peered out into the night breeze, ten fathoms to the twitching obsidian of the mere.

A white hand waved from the water.

You couldn't haul a man through an arrow slit, but they found a larger window and many hands soon had the casement out and a dripping stranger shuddering in their midst. Patches of copper beard jutted from skin like snow. Every eye in the Painted Hall peered in.

Coensar put Keening at the stranger's neck. "Who are you?"

The man opened his eyes with effort, shaking. "I've come from the b-barons of Honefells. Sallow Hythe. Mereness. Swanskin Down. His Grace's vassals. They're g-gathering."

The duke had come near, his head tilted and his eyes nearly glowing.

The man blinked up. "A raft," he added, by way of explanation. "Had to wait f-for dark. The bastards are watching the water."

"Where are they?" Lamoric demanded. Durand imagined this army gathered just over the fields, south.

"Near the f-fens."

But there were no fens—not within leagues of the city. The messenger coughed.

"What fens?" Coensar pressed.

Lamoric crouched, raised a calming hand. "You mean across the bay: Merchion." It was leagues across the bay.

"Aye," the man gasped. People around the great hall were passing their blankets forward, and the messenger shivered in a hairy cocoon of the things.

Like a man trying to kindle a fire, Lamoric bent near. "What tidings do they send?"

"His G-Grace. His host. It's no match for Radomor's n-numbers. But the ranks grow. Knights riding from the mountains . . . Swanskin and Honefells command. No Gare-lyn, no Mornaway, no king. But I am to tell you that they will ride five days hence."

Lamoric looked back into Durand's face. "We cannot hold five days. . . ." It was almost a confession.

"It will take two days to round the bay," said Coensar. It was time to concede.

"Then," whispered Durand, "they must come now!"

"Lordships," said the messenger. "Radomor's host, it's twice our size."

Lamoric's mouth opened without a sound. For an instant, he was the image of his father. "After so much, is there noth-ing we may do?"

"Lordship," said Durand. "This is why you've salted all these men away." He lifted his hand toward the multitude of smeared faces looking on. "There's half an army in this tower."

"We are sick. Radomor is strong. What chance do we have?"

Durand gestured to the eggshell cracking of the vaults over their heads. Deorwen and Almora were looking on. "A better chance than we do of holding seven days more."

"Yes." Lamoric covered his face. "It cannot be seven days. We must take our chance. They must ride for Acconel at once." A wry smile was starting as he looked up at Du-rand. "And there is only one way to reach them in time." The sodden wretch who'd just paddled the bay shuddered be-tween them. His eyes rolled back in his head.

"Yes, Lordship. . . ." said Durand.

22. The Banished and the Lost

Durand slithered down, barking knees and shoulders against the mere wall as he spun like a fisherman's weight. They were looking down on him: Lamoric, Kieren, the Duke. In another window, he saw Deorwen, her eyes alive with dread.

And then the rope ended, slipping through his knees to drop him into the frigid grip of the mere.

He clamped his jaw against the urge to hiss at the sudden cold. There were archers on the nearest pier; the splash was enough without cursing.

Casting round, he spotted the raft—little more than wreckage—and, with the thing firmly under his ribs, he kicked himself slowly out of bowshot. Never a great swimmer, now he was hampered by Lamoric's parting gift: a token no man of Gireth could ever mistake: the Sword of Judgment, now slung like an anchor around his neck.

For the better part of an hour, he kicked. Muscles locked in wandering spasms as he aimed for the black horizon. The yellow loops of the castle's mere wall dwindled over his shoulder, though he was still nearby when the last refugees in the old fortress sank into sleep and left him alone in the dark.

Soon the waves were his horizon. He could see no more than a few yards in any direction.

Overhead, mists of thin light drifted among the hard points of the stars. With difficulty he found his way among the Lords of Heaven with their shields and spears until he came upon the lodestar around which all the others turned. With the lodestar on his left hand, he kicked his way eastward.

He thought of Deorwen behind him. He wondered how long she had watched.

Rhythm closed around him. He beat his feet. He scarcely felt the blind squeeze of the mere around his legs or the drag of his long linen undershirt billowing. He fought an urge to climb up on his few planks to see how far he could see: they'd never hold him. He might have been alone under the Heavens.

Then something splashed.

Durand froze.

Two broad leagues from any land, something stamped water into spray: hooves. He had expected to drown, for the cold and dark to beat him, the rivers were still whispered full of ice. The Banished had always stalked the wastelands between man's firelit circles.

"Host of Heaven," he gasped. Ranked waves walled him in, his breath loud between them.

Hoofbeats circled, flashing spray. Then there was a liquid thunder, as though some sea-beast was hauling a warship down by its anchor ropes.

"Host of Heaven," Durand swore and kicked with all his strength.

Something was rising before him, black with rot. Rushes hung. He saw a broad curve like the stern rail of some sunken ship, but, as the water streamed away, he understood: it was a massive sweep of horns and a broad brow of hair. A bovine head broke the surface before him, rotten and bulking greater than the whole carcass of a festival bull. The milky globes of its eyes shone like pale lanterns, while its nostrils disgorged torrents of bottom clay.

Durand clung to his raft. His stare took in the drumhead hollows of its muzzle and the gray rings of its nostrils.

And suddenly he thought of the Fey Gates. "The bull of the—"

"*—Bole?!*" the monster boomed. Now, the vast head soared, carried skyward by the eruption of a monstrous neck and shoulders from the mere. The brute's chest and vast belly followed, rivulets lashing in the coarse hair. The monster climbed atop the waves, now tall as a sanctuary bell.

"No bole, I," it said. Its milk-lamp eyes swiveled. "Noboll!" it tolled. "Lord King God of Silver Mere, am I!"

Durand fled like an animal in terror, striking out between the monster's black legs.

The thing twisted.

"Nobollord. Kinggod!" it thundered.

Head down, Durand swam, cursing himself and Creation. He was meant to be saving Deorwen, the duke, and Acconel—

or drowning in the attempt. Drowning ought to have been hazard enough.

But, even wild with terror, a man can only kick so far. He clawed the water while the giant stalked beside him. Soon, it was all he could do to lock his fingers onto the planks with the sword's old angle across his back.

The monster ducked near, his breath close and putrid. *"Noboll I . . ."*

"No b-bull," Durand managed.

When he risked a shaking look, the thing's head was swiveling, scanning the line of the horizon. It dripped fragments.

"Who are you to trespass here? What does this mean? Long have I waited the fall of these shore-priests. Long have they kept Heaven's Eye upon my cool waters. But now, my traitor children are burnt from their city. The last sons of my enemy are penned in their stone house. The old chains, they hang slack. Nearly, am I avenged. And now?" The monster stooped, its rotten head swinging low. "One worm splashes from my stolen shore with the blade of my ancient enemy round his neck. Do they make an offering?"

It snuffed air through its soft nostrils, and shook its great head. "Long was I king over the men of the shores—fat with blood." Its tongue slid like a curl of gray excrement, savoring some remembered pleasure. "The firstborn of man and beast they slid down to me. Cool bodies to comfort me in the dark. But now my traitor people cringe at my enemy's heels."

A great belch of indignation erupted from the rotten giant: a stink like foul egg. "Long now has mockery been my meat. 'Bull' these Sons of Atthi called me, and bull they send me, riddled with their darts of iron."

The thing blinked its lamp eyes, the bulk of its great head reeking and dripping putrefaction. "You wore their bull talisman. I smell its stink on your neck. I've had my fill of mockery."

It flashed teeth like a row of hog's ribs.

"Two thousand winters have I cringed in the slime with the whisker-fishes! Like some toothless elder, I've supped on watered blood from the sailors' flagons." The thing hammered the water with one knotted fist, and Durand rocked on his few planks.

If he could not reach the far shore, Deorwen would die. They all would. And so Durand sucked a breath through his nostrils, and snarled, "You must let me pass."

The monster cocked its putrid skull. "'Must'?" And then it was moving.

Durand snatched Gunderic's Sword of Judgment free, but the monster was swifter. An iron grip caught his shins, pulling down—the waves slammed shut beyond his fingertips. He thundered fathoms deep, the weight of the dark stamping air from his lungs.

He had a moment before drowning.

In the milk-light of the fiend's gaze, gray dunes rippled under the twitching ceiling of the waves. The monster leered with Durand in its fist; the great globes of its eyes pulsed.

"What did he tell you, the walking God?" said the monster.

Durand struggled. He remembered the Traveler—the strange encounter he'd had, the promises the Traveler had made. It had saved him from drowning.

In a cloud of rot, the great teeth were bare once more. The gelid fires of the monster's eyes flared again: midnight lightning that flickered over a forest of unwholesome shapes, far and wide: bloated corpses tethered by ankles and wrists. Soft men in sailor's garb. Blue maidens in billowing shifts. Knotted with black weed. Bulls dangling toward the waves.

Then the grip was gone, and Durand burst back into the air.

"You are not for me to steal from Creation. Not yet. Even now, the Eye is upon you. Powers above and below, they watch you.

"But you will not gloat long, I think." The thing bared teeth. "Men are greedy. Men are fools. Men are treacherous children—they hoard slights in their darkest hearts. Even now, the fools wrangling for the Great Seat prise at the long chains your Patriarchs set upon this realm. The bonds are slack, and soon I will have outlasted the spawn of my enemy. Two thousand bitter winters, mocked, forgotten."

The thing grunted.

"You are dangled under my nostrils, but I will not bite. I will not call the great Powers down on my head for you and that blade. But I will leave something with you as I have been left here. Something for your darkest heart.

"Do the wise women still play their Firstborn game? For every babe, a forefather from the First Dawning—and a doom to share across the gulf of ages." The monster flashed its rotten grin.

"For you it must be Bruna, Bruna of the Broadshoulders. Bruna Betrayer, Bruna Betrayed. Your soul reeks of treason." Durand grimaced. He had heard the name in the mouths of blind savants, Green Ladies, monsters, and mad abbots. A long-ago lover who betrayed and was betrayed.

The monster made a show of sniffing the air, before bending close—this was no giant now, but only a black calf stretched over a man's bones.

"And I scent the man who will turn on *you.*"

Durand blinked.

"You flinch, I see," said the Banished thing. "How should you be treated, traitor? And I see the hour and the hand. And he is known to you. This one who strikes you down; he has struck you before. Yes. Well you know him, this traitor to traitors."

The brute sneered, a twist of its half-bovine features that cut deep creases across its muzzle. "Betrayal is bitter, but it is the savor of the day. And soon you will drink long of it."

Durand's fist clenched around the grip of the old sword. He wondered how the brute would like the bite of steel.

The monster leaned close, almost daring him to strike. "The next to paddle in my mere will not be so fortunate. And you . . . when this kingdom falls, see me then and I will treat you to a proper welcome." With that, the thing slapped a scythe of water across Durand's face, and fell back into the waves—dark lightning diving deep.

DURAND LOOKED UP when coarse reeds brushed his knuckles. His legs settled to the bottom sand. Through panes of ice caught among the reeds, he dragged himself ashore and lay shuddering on the sand.

The dark hummocks of upturned boats indicated that he

had come up near a fishing village of some kind. For a moment, his eyes fell shut despite the urgency of his mission. His every muscle was as flaccid as the organs of a man's belly. Then a light blazed around him.

Soldiers in the liveries of Gireth's houses stood around him. "By the Powers," they said.

The Eye of Heaven had split the pale horizon. Light lanced into the foggy passageways of Durand's skull. He winced.

The picket soldiers dropped to their knees, touching their heads to the ground as though Durand were one of the Powers of Heaven.

"What're you doing, eh?" A sturdy man, bone white and gray-stubbled, had tramped up to the guards and now gave each a good boot—Durand took him for a captain.

The man turned his attention on Durand. "I'm not sure you're much of a spy, friend. Get up."

Durand climbed onto his knuckles.

"Now, what are you up to?" The grizzled captain knelt, looking hard into Durand's face. He had an old sword in his fist.

"I've come from the d-duke," said Durand.

The captain narrowed one green eye, lifting Durand's chin with the blade. "Right. Which one, eh? That's what I'm wondering."

Slowly, Durand reached for the Sword of Judgment.

"Careful," said the captain, but Durand didn't draw the blade. Gems winked in the man's squinting eyes where some long-ago smith had worked the Gireth bull into the cross guard.

Now the man winced, tired or disgusted. "It's awful bloody early. Their Lordships won't like to be wakened."

"Th-there's no time."

⊗ 23. The Relief of Acconel

While the others ran news of Durand's arrival across the camp, Durand followed the grumbling captain through a maze of chill shadows, guy ropes, and latrine pits to a blue and gold pavilion: the Baron of Swanskin Down's tent. It was striped like a child's toy. Dripping, Durand thought of the streets of Acconel and the days of choking smoke. "Here, boy," grunted the captain. "I'd wager they'll be here soon enough."

With that, the man left.

A page stood staring up at Durand.

Durand dripped. "I have come from Acconel."

"You are Durand of the Col," said the page.

Thinking that the boy must have been told, Durand managed a quick nod.

The page stared into Durand's eye—almost insolent. "You're the baron's son. The one who left after the Traveler's Night last year."

The boy looked ten years old. His hair was dark and roughly shorn. He wore a surcoat to match the baron's arms.

"You fought Duke Radomor at Tern Gyre," the boy continued. "And his Champion. You were with Sir Coensar at the River Glass and at Hesperand."

Only fatigue kept astonishment from Durand's face. Watching the boy, he waited for his frozen mind to supply some explanation, then the boy's serious expression reminded him: "The Col. The clerk's boy. I met you in the courtyard of my father's hall when you were throwing messages down that old well."

Durand still had a tiny dimple in his forehead where the boy's lead petition had struck him as he climbed the well stairs from his meeting with the Traveler. The boy had been just as inscrutable then.

"They say the duke named you Bull."

Durand laughed, a puff of air. He blinked slowly to find strength. "How do you come to be *here* of all places?"

"Your father. My father approached him. I am to be a

knight. The baron sent me as page to the hall of the Baron of Swanskin Down."

It was not possible. "Baron Hroc is making landless knights?"

"My aunt has some noble blood."

The clerk must have asked at just the right time; Durand couldn't grudge the boy a chance.

He took the page by the shoulder.

"I must see the baron."

The clerk's boy pulled open the flap of the pavilion. His eyes never left Durand.

"Your father is in camp," the boy added.

THE BARON OF Swanskin Down was a stout man with a silver brush of a mustache. At Durand's entrance, he climbed from his cot and scowled, wrapped in his bedclothes. "Lord o' Dooms," was all he said. Bald on top, the man was otherwise pelted in white curls from the tops of his feet to the ends of his ears.

Soon others made their appearance.

The Baron of Sallow Hythe slid into the pavilion looking like some villain out of a child's play from the arch of his brow to the end of his pointed beard. Bluff young Baron Honefells strode in smiling, and laughed out loud at Swanskin in his bedclothes. The baron of nearby Mereness, a small fellow with curling red hair, took a place by the tent wall.

As did Durand's father, Baron Hroc of Col.

Despite shudders, Durand managed to set out the situation, and give the gathered barons their orders.

Sallow Hythe spoke through steepled fingers. "With our numbers, an attack is unlikely to break the siege. We are no match for Radomor's strength. I had hoped to hear from Mornaway."

Swanskin grunted. "By rights, we should have had word from his bloody Highness. It should be his host putting Radomor back in his place."

Sallow Hythe raised an eyebrow. "Cousin, while the king bridles at his rebel brother's border, do you think he will send his battalions to us? Now that Prince Eodan has pulled

Windhover from Errest, Ragnal will not step one foot from his brother's border."

Durand smeared his eyes. Here was the Rooks' rumor confirmed. The kingdom was coming to pieces.

"Prince Eodan's pride will be our ruin," Swanskin grunted.

"While the royal brothers wrangle, we must consider sending an emissary to Radomor," said Sallow Hythe. "He might agree to terms. It is possible that for the right price we might ransom those trapped within the castle."

Now, a true cold shot through Durand. It was impossible.

Swanskin nodded. "Radomor's always been an honorable man, though sullen. I saw him ride on the Hallow Downs, battering back those bloody savages."

Before they'd even begun their haggling, every man, woman, and child in the castle would have died waiting.

"You do not know the man," said Durand.

The barons swiveled. "Sir," said Swanskin, "I served beside Sir Radomor in the King's Host. While he led the contingent of Yrlac, I led that of Gireth. I have known his noble father and seen him wedded to His Grace's daughter. He is—"

"They are all dead!" snarled Durand. "All those you mention. Alwen. Duke Ailnor, Radomor's father. Even his own son." Blood thundered in Durand's ears. He was going to wind up on his face.

Meanwhile, blotches had bloomed over Swanskin's cheeks. "Sir, by Heaven, you forget yourself!"

Durand shook his head, wavering where he stood. "The Radomor you knew is lost. I've seen him since Hallow Down. His own father knew. He and his pack of fiends have written their terms in blood. Silver will not buy him now." It was getting harder to stand.

Now, the smiling Baron of Honefells stepped forward, setting his hand on Durand's arm. "He's not a friend, then, eh?" The blond stubble on the man's big jaw twinkled as he grinned. He was hardly older than Durand. "The duke knew our numbers?"

Durand took a breath. "Aye, Your Lordship. He knew. Kieren knew. Lamoric. Before you could bargain them free, they'll all be dead. The order was 'come at once.'"

With a broad and shrugging smile, Honefells said, "That's settled then."

Swanskin grunted.

"Agreed," said the Sallow Hythe. "We try for the city."

Astonished, Durand happened to catch his father's glance: Baron Hroc, though closemouthed, scowled at these carryings-on. Baronies like Swanskin Down, Sallow Hythe, or Honefells dwarfed the Col. And the bear-like mountain baron, himself, seemed smaller here than on his own lands.

The Baron of Sallow Hythe rubbed his jaw. "Our force will require a day's march to reach the city—even with our pack train behind. If we strike camp and march within the hour, we could never reach the city before twilight."

"Marching up in broad daylight," said Honefells. "And arriving too late to fight."

"Yes." Sallow Hythe's expression was sly.

Honefells clapped broad hands. "So. You'd have us hold off, then. Is that it?"

Sallow Hythe's answer was a small tilt of his head.

"I suppose. If we set out at dusk," Honefells allowed, "we might reach the city at dawn, or before."

"What use is an army that's marched all night?" grumbled Swanskin.

Baron Honefells shrugged wide. "It won't be easy. There are seven leagues of cart tracks between here and the city. The ground is wet and the ruts will be knee deep if my Honefells is anything to go by."

Sallow Hythe smiled once more. "But we may achieve surprise."

"That we'll need for certain," said Honefells. "If Radomor guesses we're near, he'll dig in. And if our friends from Yrlac so much as foul the gateways, we'll be outside with no engines, no engineers, and no time to build."

Swanskin grimaced, raising his hands in exhaustion with the bantering debate of the younger men. "So be it, then. If we're to have any hope of shaking Yrlac loose, it will be at dawn: one day's time. I'll give the orders." He shook his head. "Bloody King Ragnal. Garelyn's in irons. Prince Eodan and his lands of Windhover have broken loose. Heaven knows what's become of Mornaway. The king should be here himself."

"Clearly, it does not seem so to His Highness," said Sallow Hythe. "In any case, we had better notify Duke Abravanal of our intentions."

Honefells nodded. "Aye, it'd be a shame to come bowling into Acconel with the garrison asleep in Gunderic's Tower."

Now, Swanskin snorted. "Where will we find another fool to swim the mere, you mean."

"—I'll go back," said Durand. He remembered the rambling threats of the fiend upon the mere. Another man would not get past it. And Durand was tired of these men.

Honefells put a big hand on Durand's shoulder. "I suppose, friend, we might *just* be able to find a more exhausted man. . . ."

"Send him," Swanskin grunted. He may have muttered something about fools.

Durand glanced at his father—who looked ready to snarl at Swanskin. "Lordships, if I'm to get past Radomor's men, I'll have to come in after nightfall. I'll put my head down for a few hours, and then be on my way. That should give me time enough."

Sallow Hythe spread his fingers. "He has made the crossing once. . . ."

Durand thought he saw his father move to say something.

DURAND WOKE LOOKING into his brother's face.

The moons of the last winter had left no mark upon it. Hathcyn was precisely the same man that had worried over Durand at the Col. Beyond him, a golden light bloomed against the west wall of the tent.

"They tell me it's time," said Hathcyn. "You're to cross as soon as you're ready."

Durand had spent the day on the straw floor of a borrowed tent, rather than seeking out his family—something more a collapse than a decision.

"Hathcyn," Durand said by way of greeting.

Hathcyn forced a gentle enthusiasm. "News of your exploits has reached us all the way up in the Col. I heard you even pulled Lamoric out of the Mount of Eagles: a perilous place to be hostage now that Ragnal is summoning his barons into—"

"I am wanted at the mere," Durand grunted. Someone must have given him a blanket. It seemed that every muscle in his body had been torn during the events of the day before.

"Father is outside," Hathcyn said.

Durand had already stepped out. The camp he'd found at dawn was gone now. His was the only tent surviving of a thousand others.

Durand's father stood with arms locked over his chest. Behind him, the Eye of Heaven gleamed low over a mere now more gold than silver.

"Durand," he said.

Durand nodded.

"You're at Acconel?"

Durand nearly laughed. "Aye."

"Mm. With Lamoric." This might have been disapproval.

"The heir now," Durand reminded him.

"Aye." His father nodded.

The two men stood in the warm brilliance, saying nothing.

"You're carrying messages for the duke?"

Durand looked his father in the eye. "Aye." The baron scratched his bearded neck, eyeing the ground between his son's boots.

"Your mother mentioned you—spent time on her knees praying over one thing and another since you left. She wouldn't know you were in Acconel now, of course."

"I must go back."

After this deep and thoughtful conversation, the baron nodded.

THEY RIGHTED ONE of the rowboats and shoved its nose onto the gilded flash of the mere. With a couple of nods, Durand was off, rowing out as his father and brother squinted from the bank. The Vairian's boy watched as well, the Eye of Heaven glowing in his face. Durand watched the three dwindle as he hauled the oars. And grunted at a pang of loneliness when, long past waving distance, he saw them turn from shore.

GUNDERIC'S TOWER STOOD like one pale tooth in the black sweep of the moonlit shore.

He'd heard the buggane, but the thing had never come near.

As Durand rowed nearer the ruined city, however, shapes bobbed in the waves all around him. Some resolved themselves into casks and boxes. Most, however, were the swollen forms of corpses urged into the bay by the flow of the Banderol. More than once, the tip of Durand's oars fingered some yielding bulk under the waves. If he glanced, a face might roll into sight before sinking away once more. He muttered charms.

Watching the city walls, he edged as near as he could to the harbor mouth without drawing the eye of Radomor's sentries. Finally, he could hear voices and see the glints of helmets in the moonlight. And so he put the oars overboard, laying them on the ripples and sloshing down into the cold himself—every gasp and splash sharp over the water. The empty boat skittered away like a nutshell.

For a few moments then, he clung to the oars, waiting for a next breath full of arrows and razor points, but nothing broke the stillness.

With a narrowed eye, Durand struck off, swimming into the pull of the Banderol. For a time, he swam hard with his head down. He blundered past a barrel and a corpse. Heaven knew how many of the things tumbled around him.

When he glanced up to check his bearings, he found that the tower had come no closer. His abandoned rowboat had scudded off like a bit of thistledown on the current, and the water was very cold.

There was nothing for it. Seeing the wall falling away from him as the current dragged, he set to work once more.

A body bumped past him. He felt his fingers snag in long hair. But he kept swimming.

Radomor's fools must hear him soon. He couldn't keep quiet.

Then he heard a splash—very close.

And he froze; his heartbeat shuddered out through the water. Gunderic's Tower was dark against the Heavens. He was glad he couldn't see the bodies. He pictured the buggane looking on.

It occurred to him that he might easily have imagined the sound.

A thrash shattered that thought. Durand twisted. It could have been a fish leaping, but Durand couldn't see the length of his arm. Whatever had made the sound would be on him before he knew what it was.

At the sound of yet another splash, Durand vowed that he would at least make a race of it, and lit out for Gunderic's Tower.

His fingertips jabbed a wet bulk like a bladder of lard. Before he could flinch, an icy hand had raked his ribs.

The waves erupted all around him as he swam. Empty faces thrust forward. Here were men he had seen in the streets, women, the children who played in the crossroads. Vagrant spirits had taken up each shape. And now, though every eye was like a bead of gray glass, every hand was reaching.

He did not get far. Dead hands curled in his collar and clamped his wrists. His mouth filled with water, but fists threatened to rip him apart before he could drown. Everywhere were white faces whose eyes bulged with blackness. They pulled him down. He thought of the garrison in the castle, waiting for word of an army. They must be ready.

Suddenly, the mere was full of light.

Every blue visage twitched toward the surface where an impossible daylight had touched the dark with crystal brilliance.

Overhead, the bow of a ship rocked on the glassy waves, light throwing blades of shadow down.

A man's voice tolled within the bones of Durand's skull, deep. "Go mockers! Leave what you have stolen. In the name of Warders, I command you. By the light of Heaven, I charge you: *Go!*"

At this last word, the revenants twitched as if they were about to rush away—then water seemed to catch them. Each body hung slack, abandoned.

Durand floated where they had left him, watching the rag-doll corpses adrift. The body of one child hung in a gray skirt that flared as if it were the cap of a mushroom. Her dangling legs looked as pale and soft as curdled milk.

Durand kicked for the surface.

The light had dimmed by the time he reached the air.

Strong arms pulled him from the mere. Tall men surrounded him in a pocket of sudden mist.

SOPPING WET, DURAND stumbled from a window into the Painted Hall, aided by calloused hands that smelled of incense and candle wax and dead man's balsam. The strangers hadn't uttered a word since the confrontation on the mere. And, though pale light shimmered in the links of the strangers' hauberks, not one of Radomor's sentries had spotted their climb from the boats.

In the Painted Hall, the crowd shrank.

Forty white knights had appeared from the darkness. They could only be the Holy Ghosts, the Septarim, the Knights of Ash. If half the rumors were true, the duke might find himself chained to an altar while the Holy Ghosts sharpened their knives.

The staring crowd parted as the duke tottered from his sanctuary beneath a mountain of bedclothes.

"What in the name of Heaven?"

At this, a giant knight stepped forward. Over a chest like a cask balanced on its back edge stretched the battlemented blazon of the Warders' Shield. Heavy-knuckled hands lifted his helm to uncover a face all knots and hollows under hair like gray wire. One eye stared down from this face of crags: blue as a child's sky.

Abravanal wavered in his tracks.

"Greetings, Lord of Gireth," the one-eyed giant said, his voice the rumble under Silvermere. And he bowed in a whisper of iron rings.

"Who are you?" breathed the duke.

"My brothers and I are newly come from the Court at Eldinor," he said evenly. "I am Conran, Marshal of House Loegern. Servant of the Warders. My brothers and I have come to aid your cause."

"I had begun to think the king would send no aid to Gireth," Abravanal murmured. They had sent no hostage to Ragnal's oathtaking.

The blue eye shivered like a blade's point. "Ragnal moves against his royal brother now: Prince Eodan has withdrawn his lands from Ragnal's rule, declaring himself sovereign in Windhover. Archers steal among his trees. The king summons his host to flush his rebel brother from his forest fastness, but the barons are slow to answer Ragnal now."

Abravanal closed his eyes. "The sons of Carlomund . . . Brother wars against brother."

"Neither will relent."

"But Ragnal sends you, his Knights of Ash."

"No, Your Grace. The king cast my brethren from his side. The court is a web of whispers; for the first time in all the rolling years since my order was founded, a king of Errest marches to war without his sworn guardians."

"Lord of Dooms," said Abravanal. "Whom must we thank for your coming?"

"Biedin, youngest of Carlomund's brood. The prince stole a moment as we rode from the court. He must march with his brother Ragnal; a whisper was all he could offer."

The old duke's fingers fluttered at his lips. "For that much we are grateful, Marshal Conran, for it is more than his brothers spared us."

"We have slept too long," rumbled the marshal. "Accident, fire, and war have thrown down high sanctuaries in Ferangore, Acconel, Beoran, Lawerin. Soon, only Eldinor by the Mount of Eagles will stand. I tell you power works to shake the Wards of the Ancient Patriarchs: to loose the bonds that tie crown, Banished, men, and land. On the mere we met an old buggane of the water, making free as in former days. And we have heard whispers of these dark twins who walk with the Leopard of Yrlac. Errest comes apart around us."

Abravanal glanced to his councilors: Lamoric, Kieren, Coensar. His lips met. Shivering half out of sight, Durand remembered Landast and Alwen and Adelind. There had even been a grandson now lost somewhere with Alwen. He wondered why the Septarim had chosen to act only now.

Wings flapped at the black windows.

"Your Grace," said Marshal Conran. "These twins work their sorcery even now. Radomor has been still too long." People around the hall raised the fist and fingers sign, looking to the arrow loops. "We will mount the battlements and watch from the high places."

Abravanal's voice, when he spoke, was hardly louder than a whisper. "Only a fool would refuse aid at such a time. Do as you see fit. I . . ." He swallowed. "I commend your courage in joining us at this dark hour."

Marshal Conran bowed deeply in another whisper of steel rings. And, with that, the one-eyed knight directed his men to the stairs.

Every soul watched the strange company file out—leaving Durand, dripping, alone at the head of the hall.

Someone gasped across the hall; he found Deorwen's face in the multitude. He could see the wet glint of her eyes.

"Host of Heaven!" This was Kieren the Fox, gaping around his red-silver mustaches. "Durand! Have you been there all along?"

Durand stirred himself from the shadows. The cold had him stiff as a palsied old man.

"Yes, Milord," he managed.

After the shock of the Septarim, the crowd was done with silent gawking. Now they chattered.

Lamoric took Durand by the arm. "When we saw nothing by nightfall, Coensar had me thinking you were done for. Is the army with you?"

"No, L-lordship." They'd be slogging south of the Bay of Acconel now, or just swinging north.

"*Oh, no . . .*" breathed Lamoric.

Coensar pressed: "Did you find them, boy? Is there an army at all?"

Durand waved a hand. "I—it's Sallow Hythe, Captain." He tried a smile. "The plan's to march on the city by night. They are coming."

Lamoric wheeled slowly as comprehension dawned. "Sallow Hythe . . . Him I knew from the Burrstones. That man never walks a straight path if he can find a crooked one."

"They were camped just where that messenger said they'd be," Durand said. "We must make ready. By dawn, they should be on top of us."

A broad grin was spreading on Duke Abravanal's face, and he seemed about to speak. Just then, a strange sound became audible. As they stood, bewildered, the sound grew louder until the monotonous syllables of a chant had risen up all around the hall. All the knights, Durand included, had hold of their swords.

Coensar narrowed his eyes. *"Another attack?"*

But Abravanal spoke then. "No. *Listen.* It's *priest*craft."

And the eyes of the crowd looked from the walls to each other. The chant sank deep roots through the stones of the old keep. It seemed that Durand could almost feel the brush of lips at his ears.

Abravanal was shaking his head.

"Father," said Lamoric. "What is in your mind?"

"That man. Conran. When I was a page in Eldinor—under old King Carondas before he set his crown aside. Before Bren, his brother, before Carlomund the son and now Ragnal. There was a marshal of the Septarim standing guard at the Hazelwood Throne, always there. I am sure he was called Conran. I remember he was *so* big." The old man was blinking, staring off into memory. "And that eye."

The old man smiled. "We must prepare the garrison or Sallow Hythe's plan will be straws in the furnace." His eyes flashed Durand's way. "And it would be a shame to waste two cold nights on the mere."

AT A NOD from the revitalized duke, men stole up the battlements, keeping lookout over the southern approaches to the city. Hauberks, gambesons, and blades were passed from hand to hand, and every tower whispered with the hiss of whetstones.

Before Durand could join in, Guthred, Berchard, Heremund, and Kieren had cornered him and were working him over with rugs and rough blankets, having stripped his soaking clothes.

"There's no time for all this," said Durand.

"Hells," grunted Guthred. "Dullard." And Durand was blinded by a hairy fistful of blanket.

"Hey, Badan, you bugger," said Berchard, "there's still a bed frame and at least one good trunk up in Abravanal's chamber. Lug 'em down and we'll have some heat." And somewhere beyond the woolen rasps, Badan was spitting oaths.

"He can work some of that out of him, busting up the furniture, I reckon."

"I'll be all right," Durand said.

"Shut up," said Guthred.

"Yes," said Kieren. "We're all glad to see you back."

"Just help me find my gear."

"Everyone will hear how you crossed the mere and brought back the army when all the lords here had given in."

"Mooncalf," said Guthred.

"You're cold as a Harskan's arse, boy," said Kieren. "And the man whose raft you borrowed? We lost him two hours after you pushed off."

"Stone dead—and I reckon he'll keep till midsummer before he starts to go off, poor bugger," said Berchard, pouring out something thick from a red pot. "And he wasn't making a habit of the crossing."

"Fool," said Guthred.

"I'll take Lamoric's old blade off you. And then it's by the fire with you—when we've got one," ordered Kieren.

"And shut up," said Guthred.

His four nurses nodded, the Fox peeling Durand's fingers off the Sword of Judgment.

"Lord o' Dooms," said Kieren, shaking his head.

DURAND SQUATTED BY the fireside as long as he could hold still. He felt like a bull in a bin full of darting mice the way the castle folk swarmed past him. Finally, he stole a corner from the scurrying mob to wrestle the weight of a gambeson and hauberk over his head. He blinked at the reek of it, but it felt good to have the gear on. The wait would soon be over: one way or the other, it would all be done before long.

As he hauled his surcoat over his head and then the heavy layers of mail and padding, he found someone giving him a hand. He turned to find Deorwen tugging his surcoat down and sliding his belt around his waist.

"Deorwen!" Durand said.

"That's better, I think," she muttered.

"Soon, this will be over."

The woman caught a fistful of his surcoat, looking up at him. For an instant, it seemed as if she didn't remember him. Then she blinked hard. "Durand."

When he peered close, her eyes darted. "You're still seeing them?" he said.

"It's hard to sleep." She seemed as pale as the things in the mere.

"Hells, Deorwen. Soon, I'll have you out of this place. I *found* the army. And they're coming for us now. They'll give Radomor a good shock, no matter how many sellswords he's bought. We may get ourselves free of this place by noon."

It was all muddled. He couldn't serve Lamoric and love Deorwen. But he couldn't let her die.

He squeezed her shoulder, but felt her start in his grip.

He thought of his hand. "I know it's cold—"

"What is that sound?" she said.

Across the Painted Hall, dozens shifted uneasily, looking round.

"Heaven knows, Deorwen. There've been engines, and prayers, and—" Durand began, but he faltered.

For there were whispers.

"I hear . . ." he said.

And he knew the sly sibilance. He'd heard the same whispers across a prince's table at Tern Gyre while the Rooks preened and grinned at him.

"You are tired," the whispers said. *"It has been a valiant stand. Who could fault you?"* Each hissing syllable chased the next round Durand's head, beating in circles like a thick plague of moths.

He saw others around the room catch at their hair; he pitched against the black wall.

"Come with us," said the whisperers. *"You have done so much. It is time to rest. No one could expect more. It is time, I think. Yes."*

Deorwen was staring back at him, the only one not clutching—or falling.

"Durand," she said. He saw her lips moving.

But the room around her was shuddering. Pale flames shivered at the lips of every soul in the long hall. Creation itself twitched before his eyes. And, while the whispers stormed, he thought, *That's what I'm seeing now. The world from the pale flame.*

Deorwen was catching him as he slid to the floor. She shoved at his mouth with her bare fingers—ramming his soul into his body. She might have been screaming.

He tried to mouth a word—

But another voice spoke with his, louder than he could imagine.

"*No.*"

The word shuddered through Creation, and the whispers shrank.

"By the Host of Heaven, by the King, Queen, and Warders." It was fearsome Conran on the rooftop, and each slow word drove the whispers back. "By the Champion, and the Maid of Spring, Errest is not yet fallen. And the Eye reigns unconquered."

Durand felt Deorwen's hands on his shoulders, pulling. He shoved himself from the floor, meaning to give her a word or two of comfort, but she was quickly on her feet. "Almora!" She was off for the girl.

They found the Patriarch of Acconel sprawled like a fallen eagle in the duke's sanctuary, overcome. Almora sat beside him with her dark eyes full of tears. "Don't worry," said Durand. He gave the little girl a squeeze. And, together, they saw the old Patriarch's eyes flicker open.

Durand smiled. Tonight, they'd scotched the Rooks. Tomorrow, they'd fix their master. After that, Durand's doom was his own to work out.

IN THE NARROW stone lane that was the inner yard, Durand found two hundred men in greasy gambesons and rust-red hauberks. Some were still making the Eye of Heaven.

Lamoric had the whole garrison of Acconel crowded there. On the walls above, archers crouched in the predawn twilight.

Above them all, the Knights of Ash stood like carved icons atop Gunderic's Tower, motionless except for the wind in their surcoats. Each man stood with his hands on the pommel of a bared sword. And their chant rolled on.

As Durand took in the scene, a wry smile—mirroring the expression dawning on his own lips—spread from face to face in the garrison. A few nodded his way. It was as though they had been waiting to share their joke with him, the Bull of their festival. He breathed deep and saw the wild edge of his own smile gleaming back at him in the teeth of two hundred men.

He climbed the battlements to join the lookouts.

As TWILIGHT GLOWED in the Heavens, they watched the misty curve of the bay from the battlements of Gunderic's Tower.

"They are coming," whispered Lamoric. Durand noticed something strange about the motion of the waves along the beach.

"Keep low . . ." Abravanal cautioned. "We can't be seen watching."

"If only it were a darker day," Kieren muttered. The Heavens were already blue and clear. "If they're seen, it's all useless."

"You've got to look close," one-eyed Berchard said, jabbing with his finger.

And Durand squinted out the nearest embrasure. Tiny horses pounded through the shallows, and miniature footmen stole along the bank above the shore. Battalion after glittering battalion marched five abreast through the surf.

"It's like a vision," Lamoric said. "After all this time."

The duke crouched close, a new blade on his hip. "Hells, I still cannot see."

"With the breaking of the waves and the sun on the mist, they are cursed hard to make out," said Lamoric. "That Sallow Hythe is a dangerous man."

The duke peered. "What makes you so certain it is he?"

"Who else among your barons is so sly?"

The duke nodded. "I cannot see old Swanskin daring a thing like this. Sallow Hythe likely has that big Honefells lad leading the way."

The old man glanced to Coensar. "All right, Captain. How many are there?"

"More than a thousand, Your Grace."

"—More like fifteen hundred," Lamoric declared, though such estimates were the baldest guesswork.

Now, the duke turned to his oldest counselor. "Sir Kieren, how does our garrison stand?"

"We have two hundred and sixty fighting men," said the Fox.

"What would you say Radomor has?"

"Four thousand, Your Grace," said Kieren. "At least."

SOON, THE EYE of Heaven broke over the mere, and Radomor's men were stirring in the mists and long shadows of the ruined city. One party of engineers had even set up flinging stones.

Under the anxious eyes of Abravanal's household knights, the Host of Gireth flashed and glinted in the waves. Durand could see Radomor's men stumbling through the long shadows here and there in the ruined streets. On the distant Harper's Gate, he saw helmets wink, turning.

Durand closed his eyes. "We'll never get an army close enough. There are thousands of eyes."

Lamoric quirked an eyebrow. "You remember that day on the battlements? The big stone and the archers all trying to shoot me the moment I put my head up?"

"Aye," Durand said.

"Coensar and I have got a little show planned that will turn poor Radomor's head. Ah. Coen found a little fellow who—Here's the man now!"

A muddy commoner climbed onto the parapet, crouching as low as he could manage.

"Master Torold," said Lamoric.

There was a white flash of teeth. "It's prepared, Lordship."

Lamoric nodded. "Master Torold's from Highshields. The mines."

"Tin, Lordship," said the man, bowing. "And I'm hardly my own 'master,' Lordship."

"He'd only been in the city since the Blood Moon. What did you say? In-laws are wool merchants?"

Under the mud, the man looked forty or fifty. "Aye, Lordship." He winked, all wrinkles and curls when he pulled his cap off. "Good to toil out under Heaven. Spent long enough grubbing underground."

"His wife and daughters are in the Painted Hall. Knights now."

Durand gave the man a slow nod.

"While I've had you on the mere, Sir Durand," said Lamoric, "I've put Master Torold to work on our north tower."

It made little sense. "Shoring up the walls, Lordship?"

"Master Torold and his volunteers have been digging. They've got the whole edifice balanced on a couple of props by now."

"It's about that bad." Torold nodded. "I think we've pulled all we can without the thing coming down on our heads. The kindling's heaped round the last few now, and we're ready for your order, Lordship."

The crouched nobles of the court peered southward. It seemed impossible that no one had shouted.

Still low, Lamoric drew the Sword of Judgment. "Bring it down, Master Torold. They'll be spotted anytime."

THE TWO HUNDRED in the yard watched smoke billow from a pit below the north tower, knowing that an army was waiting to leap upon them. In the stone bowl of the inner yard, they chanted prayers and old songs: "Dawn Thanksgiving," "The Young Princes," and "Praise to the Powers of Heaven."

For the last hour, the thing had burned while the men wrung the handles of their weapons. But the props held, and Torold paced. Durand crouched near Torold like a man peering down an oven.

"How long, Master Torold?"

"There's a thousand tons on a few charred spindles now. I'd have bet my life." He eyed Gunderic's Tower behind them. The man's wife and children huddled with the others inside. He'd bet more than his life.

Durand gripped the man's arm. "I know."

"Sir Durand!" A chain of whispers called him to the battlements where the noble lookouts still peered south.

He nodded up and left the onetime miner, squeezing through the grim soldiers to climb the open stair to the battlements. The impact of one of Radomor's missiles had him staggering against the stones, but he found Lamoric where the lord bent close to his captain.

"Radomor's sighted the barons," Coensar said evenly.

"Then . . . I can't be too late," Durand breathed.

Lamoric's lips were pale. "There are messengers riding from battalion to battalion. They must have seen something."

The army of Gireth was still strung out a thousand paces from the Banderol.

"Has he dug in?" asked Durand.

Coensar was shaking his head, when his eyes flickered to the beach. "Ah," he said, "Sallow Hythe's scouts have seen."

"It must be now," Durand said. If the stubborn northern tower didn't fall, Radomor would turn his whole force against the Host of Gireth.

And the beach seemed to shimmer, as though the mere had leapt the shore. Durand heard a dislocated rumble of hooves. Rank after rank vaulted from the shoreline, charging past the shells of upturned boats.

As Durand tried to gauge distances and imagine reactions, the castle yard behind him erupted in shouts. Durand saw what he took for a brawl at the north end. But it was Torold. The miner broke from the grip of the garrison. In his fists, he had a maul. It took only a heartbeat, but, in a few quick strides, he had plunged into the flames below the tower.

Durand stood—in plain sight of a thousand Yrlaci archers.

Arrows whistled by him; he faintly noticed startled curses from his comrades.

But by the mere, horsemen were outracing a ragged scythe of infantrymen. Shields and trappers in every color shouted their owners' name and line: men from the far corners of Gireth.

"Down, idiot," Coen said.

But then the north tower was falling—in the blazing depths, Torold had done his work. On the battlements, every man caught hold of the rock as the mighty tower tore free of the curtain walls and thundered into the outer yard. In a thousand years, there had never been such a sound on the shores of the Silvermere. Dust billowed with the shock; the world heaved under their feet.

Durand bared his teeth.

With his last glance, Durand saw knights sweep for the

Banderol bridges. Then, he and half the knights on the battlements had charged into the boiling cauldron of the yard.

Coensar bellowed into the dust, "Lap shields! Front ranks down!" As Radomor's battalion hit the breach, a hundred soldiers dropped to their knees, shields locked, and spears jutting into the dust. Radomor's men skidded down the rubble, shrieking glee and hatred—but falling on lances or rebounding from shields. Durand saw one green soldier pitched over the front rank on the blade of a lance. Crossbowmen snapped bolts past the ears of their comrades, and scores of green killers howled through the breach, off balance and dead before they knew what faced them. Coensar had planned it all. The men of Acconel roared and shook their lances like the jaws of a single monstrous animal.

Trapped in the rear, Durand pictured the scene beyond the blank walls. Radomor would be roaring to heave his divided army through the ruined streets. A wild mob had surged for the broken tower, but Radomor must fling the rest at the charging barons at the Banderol. It would be chaos—Durand only hoped it would be enough.

A scream called Durand's attention back to the narrow yard: an armored wedge of Yrlaci heroes bowled down the rubble, Acconel arrows glancing from the shields in their fists. As they struck the front rank of lancers, Yrlaci axemen surged through the attacking line, blades swiping heads from shoulders. High on the rubble, archers leapt into the gap, chopping further breaches in the line.

With a furious roar, Coensar spurred the garrison at their attackers. Durand leapt into the surge, swinging Ouen's blade and feeling blows and arrows bounce from his hauberk.

While Coensar stood bellowing and laying about with blade and flail, one great brute broke through—unseen in the wild press. As he flashed his axe round for Coen's neck, Durand reached—almost too far—and shot his blade through the fiend's bearded jaw.

In a hard minute's work, they'd mauled every man of the latest onslaught, and Coensar was roaring to bring fresh soldiers forward. They'd never hold long enough if they couldn't keep fresh blood in the front line.

Durand made to leap into one gap when Coen caught his

shoulder. "I need to know what's happening out there!" And, when Durand gaped, "Get up to the wall!"

Astonished—half-furious—Durand staggered, then left the fight.

"They're holding?" asked Kieren.

"For now," said Durand. From atop the wall, the din below rang like a hundred foundries.

Durand joined Lamoric, peering south at the Host of Gireth.

"They came through the Harper's Gate like swallows from a hayloft," said Kieren.

Now, the riders of Durand's homeland looked more like a boiling river as they rushed to strike before Radomor could draw his host together. Knights thundered after the banners of their commanders, bolting down the channels of the ruined streets.

Before Durand's eyes, the first conrois struck, tearing into confused knots of Radomor's army. Across two hundred paces of broken streets, the hosts locked together in a collision like a hundred tourney charges. Durand watched Yrlaci commanders urging their men forward. But, even shocked from their beds, there were too many soldiers in Yrlac green.

Abruptly, Lamoric started. "Hells."

"Lamoric?" the duke asked.

Lamoric's finger jutted down.

The greater part of Radomor's army was still swinging round to crash into the Host of Gireth. But Radomor's turn was heavily lopsided. Confusion or fear of the archers high in Acconel Castle left the flank below the castle's wall weak.

"And Sallow Hythe's seen it," said Lamoric.

From their vantage on the battlements, they could see a sudden flood of men—squadrons of flying lancers—rush against Yrlac's weak flank.

"Hells!" Lamoric swore, hands in his hair. "It is too much, too clear."

"Lamoric," said Kieren, "Sallow Hythe's pouncing on Radomor's weakness." Radomor's flank was indeed crumbling under the onslaught of Gireth's vanguard.

"No, he's taking Radomor's bait," said Lamoric. "I'm sure of it."

Before Kieren could argue, Abravanal had raised his hand. "Show me," he said.

Lamoric stepped up between the merlons, teetering over the streets. "There!" His arm struck like a snake.

"An alley between stone walls," said Abravanal. "He's herding our riders there." Radomor's retreat led to a channel between two stone ruins. Durand saw movement among the black and jagged ruins.

"Crossbowmen," said Abravanal. "Hundreds. Radomor's rushing our men straight into them. We will be destroyed."

The old man shook his head. "Radomor is the ablest commander of his generation. . . ."

Lamoric took a deep breath. "I'll be damned if I let him spring his bloody trap! How many horses did we save?"

THEY WERE GOING to ride out.

Lamoric would lead them. They couldn't talk him down. But Coensar and Durand would ride on either side. They pulled the last eighteen warhorses from the stables—Durand on black Pale—and mustered under the gate. No one knew whether they could break through the outer wall. Lamoric wore the iron slit of his helm as though it were his own expression.

Men were poised at the portcullis.

Coensar ducked close. "We are ready, Lord."

Lamoric's nod was crisp. Durand curled his toes in his boots, shifting his lance for balance. This was a good way to get killed. Beyond Lamoric, he watched Coensar seat his azure battle helm.

"Now," Lamoric said, and though it was no more than a murmur, two dozen soldiers from the castle heaved the portcullis high.

Eighteen knights charged out into the instant before five hundred heads turned. Durand saw the press at the fallen tower, but Lamoric spurred for the castle's main gate—abandoned in the chaos—and the conroi shot through into the cobbled market beyond the walls.

Durand's head spun in the eerie emptiness as he rode at Lamoric's side. Shattered masonry, ladders, and abandoned engines of war littered the market. Durand could barely keep pace as Lamoric flew over the dangerous ground. In moments, they saw the stone alley of Radomor's trap. The ruins were full of archers, and a shield wall was set to catch and hold the men of Gireth.

Lamoric lowered his lance, launching the whole conroi into a headlong charge at the back of this wall: two hundred men in iron. Durand caught a last breath as Badan took up a high shriek.

"Wait!" Coensar shouted, but the captain might as well have been snatching for a flying arrow's feathers. Lamoric's men were already on top of Radomor's line.

With only a heartbeat's warning, Lamoric's conroi hit the hundreds packed between the broken walls. Radomor's men had nowhere to run. Lances, hooves, and horsemen hammered bodily into the mob of soldiers. Sane horses threw their riders at the madness of it. Other beasts leapt, vaulting onto the cattle-pen crush between the walls.

Durand had an eye-corner flash of Lamoric flying into the ranks—unhorsed and plunging into the mob like an iron missile—just as Durand's own lance stamped home, the shock nearly wrenching him limb from limb.

Beyond Lamoric's flight, Coensar had leapt from the fight. His warhorse struck, but he sprang, like some boy acrobat, straight from his saddle and onto the jagged wall of the ruin above them.

As Pale pitched and bobbed under him, Durand made out Sir Coensar bounding among fifty bowmen. The devils would have foiled Lamoric's rescue, but now Coensar tightroped into that den of assassins as bows snapped, Keening flashed, and the archers were defenseless before the fatal captain.

But, down below, Lamoric was lost somewhere in the seething multitude. Big Pale managed to stay on his feet, buoyant as a barrel. Men fought with swords and teeth and the edges of their shields, screaming under lashing hooves and the press of braying soldiers. Durand wrought havoc with Pale and Ouen's big sword, trying to get to his master— who never surfaced in the press. Lamoric was dead or dying under the mob. A deafening blow clapped one of Durand's narrow eye-slits shut. He swatted the attacker down.

He couldn't get through.

Ahead, Badan flailed at the masses; Durand fought to see from his mangled helm.

"Badan, is he there?"

Frantic, Badan lashed at the crowd around him—Durand couldn't get by the fool. He hacked and kicked, pawing at his helm. Lamoric had to be in the throng somewhere.

"Badan! Do you see him? Badan, you whoreson!"

Lamoric was Durand's to watch. He had to see. "Out of my way, idiot!" he roared at Badan's back. Skipping toothless Badan against the wall, Durand plowed by, scarcely hearing the last crossbows clatter in the stone shells above him, or the bolts pegging hips to saddles and helms to heads.

Badan was screaming: "You son of a whore! You nearly killed me!" But Durand didn't care if he'd thrown the man onto a dozen swords.

Durand reversed Ouen's sword, clawing men aside as he drove Pale onto the heap of soldiers. Lamoric was down there somewhere, and Durand clawed men aside by hair, surcoat, and whatever else he could catch hold of. He heard Coensar. He fought to draw air through his smashed helm.

And rage carried him up in his stirrups, blade high. A hundred faces turned, and he wrenched the thing from the air. Again and again. There were eggshell *clops* and metal *clangs*. Durand's face was a clenched fist.

Then, for a moment only, he saw Lamoric's red and white surcoat at the bottom of it all.

In an instant, he reached through the chaos to pluck the boneless form from the street and fling his master over Pale's neck.

Durand was finished with the battle. This had been his mission: keeping Lamoric alive. And what had he done?

He spurred Pale for the gates, back on the market cobbles, bolting past the high walls and clear of Radomor's men.

Hoofbeats rang on the stones behind him: some of his comrades. When he might have turned, Pale was jumping something in the rubble. Durand fought to hold Lamoric as they landed. And the shock brought a gasp from the body over the saddlebow. Alive! Durand thought. He had done it. A wild grin knotted his face.

A hundred Acconel defenders met Pale as they crossed

the old market. They stopped the throng of Yrlac's men peeling away from the castle's face to catch Durand. Arrows from the castle's archers picked at the stalled battalion like crows on a wasteland corpse.

Free, Durand wrenched the smothering helm from his head. He had done it.

Or so he thought.

24. A Broken Victory

Durand drifted. He might have been a corpse at the bottom of some bog, dead a thousand winters. He did not know where he was. He had no memory of how he had come to be there. Creation had come adrift. There wasn't a trace left in his head.

Something hissed: a dry shrilling that swept the image of black water from his mind.

He tried to listen, but the sound whispered away. Then, after a time suspended in the distance, it swung closer: crisp and bright above the murk.

And it brought with it a sea of noise: men howling, people roaring orders, madness.

Durand fought to peel his eyes open. There was pain—big sick waves of it—and only one eye answered his command. But he caught sight of a brassy glitter swinging under a blackened ceiling. For a moment, Durand fixed his attention on the twinkling thing as it floated by on a blur of damselfly wings. It was gone before he could remember it: a little thing as plump as a pigeon. It sported a lion's head and a glint of gemstones.

"Pale didn't get hurt," said a little voice—so close lips brushed his ear. "I saw him. Some of those men brought oats. They didn't comb him. I wanted to, but he's not a horse for little girls.

"I don't know what happened to Star. But Pale came home." And Durand remembered: Almora. There were screams all around. She shouldn't be in this place.

Durand tried to remember what had happened to him: he

had a sense that it was very bad. He tried very hard to answer the little voice, to raise his head—

He heard only a hopeless bleat from his lips before the blackness thundered back in.

ANOTHER LIGHT DAWNED over the dark, and Durand heard voices swell. It seemed to him as though feet were landing round his ears. And the pain! Like he'd fallen from a tower into a barracks hallway—with his face nailed to the floor. The thought of even a single accidental kick from all the trampling feet sent a shot of nausea through his guts. There were shouts and groans all round him, but from somewhere much nearer came a familiar voice.

"Hurry, man!"

Only one eye would open. Durand was looking up from two men's ankles. The pair straddled a bench. It was Berchard sitting nose-to-nose with a rough-looking barber-surgeon. The room was full of howling, but old Berchard glanced down to smile.

"You're alive, are you?" The man's face was bloody, his beard appalling.

Durand managed a wet croak meant to be "Aye." He'd done something to his mouth.

"Here!" called Berchard. "He's alive after all!" The old campaigner tried to wave someone in. But the barber-surgeon yanked his bloody chin around; the surgeon was tugging thread through a ragged gash above the old knight's good eye.

Berchard scowled at the surgeon. "Are you sure this ain't dangerous? I mean, a fellow hears the evil's got to be drawn out before you stitch up. And you're—"

The surgeon clopped the old knight's mouth shut with a tug of his bit of thread: Berchard could have been a puppet.

Wincing and blinking, Berchard kept up his wave. "Here. Durand's come round!"

The knight tried a wink—full of blood and stitches—confessing, "One of Radomor's bowmen rang a bolt off the old dome. But I keep telling the girls that they love a good scar—and the bugger missed the good eye." The eye blinked up: "Ah, here they are. Looks like some folk've got a moment to gawp at you."

Just the twitch of muscles as Durand tried to grimace nearly put his lights out again: he'd done something ugly to his face.

When Durand blinked his good eye clear, he made out someone else nearby, crouching close: a face like his own under a mop of black curls.

"Hathcyn?" he said, the sound mostly spit and gurgles.

A pale grin flickered over the face of Durand's brother. "Oh, good. Good. You should try to drink."

The brim of a jug clicked against Durand's teeth, gushing bad wine. And every splutter as he choked shot skewers through his bones. It took Durand several heartbeats to wince his eyes back open.

But, when he looked up again, his brother's face was gone and his father's beard loomed above him. "Hells, boy. What made you take your fool helmet off?"

"Father?" Durand half expected his mother, the king, and half of Burrstone Walls to pop up next.

"You could have killed yourself," said Baron Hroc.

Durand forced his mind back into the fog, managing to croak a half truth like, "Couldn't see." But even saying that much hauled memories from the mist. He could feel the weight of a man—Lamoric—lying across his saddlebow. He thought he'd taken the man to safety, and now . . . He strained to look around though the pain was terrific. As he fought to keep breathing, he managed to croak something he meant to be, "His Lordship?"

Baron Hroc's eyes darted. "I'll fetch one of these leeches," he said, and disappeared.

Durand felt a wave of dread. "What's happened to—?"

But Hathcyn leaned close. "Lamoric's right here. You could reach out and touch him. He insisted on it. He got a good knock on the head, but he's suffered less than you, I think. After the fall, your good captain got him clear."

Durand sagged back, gasping. Memories were rising around him like ice from deep water: the siege, the charge out the gates, the ride across the market with Acconel's men all around.

"What've I done . . . to myself?" he managed.

"They were saying that you fell from your horse," Hathcyn explained. "Hit the market cobbles."

"'Fell'?" he grunted. How could he fall? It had nearly killed him—nearly killed the man he'd meant to be saving. It was hard to get air.

"It doesn't matter," said Hathcyn.

"—Aye," said Berchard. "Doesn't matter. We've knocked Rado's rebellion on the head. Routed the bugger! Hero of Hallow Down or not."

There was a groan from the floor off in Lamoric's direction; Hathcyn continued more quietly. "Sallow Hythe and Honefells ran over Radomor's weak side and hit his center hard enough to slaughter most of the duke's commanders. Father and I rode under young Honefells's banner. Men from the Col all around us."

"Just mauled 'em!" said Berchard. "Rolled 'em up and ran 'em down. Not moderate, exactly, but if they didn't have it coming, who did, eh? There are still fights swinging through the city. Coen made me come in." He waved his hand at the blood over his face. "Couldn't see out the good eye. Yes. Anyway."

Durand put himself to the effort of nodding, then mumbled something he meant to be "Radomor?"

Hathcyn shook his head. "Not yet. He was on the run. We saw men kill horses out from under him. He's a fiend with that sword of his, but I'm sure I saw him stabbed."

"I saw him shot," said Berchard. "His host jumped off him like fleas when we hit. Fear-mad buggers bolting into the Banderol, mail and all. Knights treed like cats. But we'll find Rado soon enough, I reckon. He'll be at the bottom of some heap or other, hatching maggots."

They were still dragging wounded men down the hall. Durand let his eyes—his eye—close on the chaos. Acconel was free, though he was sure they'd all be happier with mad Radomor's head tarred and spiked over the gate.

Even his good eye didn't want to open in a moment.

Scores of wounded men groaned all around on the rushes of the hall.

Hathcyn touched Durand's good shoulder. "We have them on the run; they say Abravanal will name your captain Champion to replace old Geridon—the one who died with Landast?—and your Lamoric has a good chance."

Berchard stood up, saying, "Yes. Well. It's been a fine day. And I must let you talk. There's work to be done in the streets."

Coensar had finally won his way back from Tern Gyre. Durand thought of the faraway castle over the sea where Coensar's journey had begun.

"How'd I fall?" Durand slurred.

Hathcyn nodded. "Someone caught you with a chained flail—your helmet."

Durand grimaced—a painful thing. But he couldn't quite make sense of it. He had been clear of the mêlée. Or nearly . . . He had a memory of hoofbeats. He had assumed that he was clear, not checking. Some rescuer he was.

His tongue moved over a row of broken teeth like knife edges. "Who?" he asked.

Hathcyn glanced around the room, finally saying, "With a whole battle churning round and knights bolting in a thousand directions?"

"Right," said Durand. He remembered Coensar leaping from his saddle to crash through the nest of archers. He remembered Badan—shoving the man—Badan's face, snarling and savage at being thrown off balance while fighting for his life.

It was becoming difficult to fix his mind on the subject.

"The leech put sssomething in the wine?" Durand mumbled.

"Poppy, morel. That sort of thing, I should expect."

Blackness rose.

WHEN NEXT DURAND came around, he was in the dark: Gunderic's Tower was silent—or nearly. Night air moved around him. He became conscious of whispers: dry sounds that scrabbled around his head. He peered at the gloom—

A black shape crouched upon the reeds beside him. Durand imagined the Rooks—with him pegged out and helpless. But it was not their whispers he heard. Lips brushed his sweating brow. A hand caressed his cheek.

"Surely, we don't deserve such pain."

Durand took a whole breath for the first time in hours and a stupid tear caught him by surprise.

"I had to see," said Deorwen. "Hells. But, Durand, I've been walking the streets." Her "streets" would be smoking wreckage, torn bodies, men wild with blood and fear. She shouldn't be out in it. "I found the place where she fell. The woman?"

"Wha—?"

"The dream. The woman in the ditch? Do you remember? With the soldiers coming? She was still there in the weeds, shining under the moon—and I brought the wise women down. You should have seen them." Wise women in a latrine ditch. "We set her on the bank, and the old women said the words.

"And now I think she's gone. We've sent her to her rest." She scrabbled at her head.

And Durand remembered the first of Deorwen's nightmares: the barefoot woman at the cook pot as the soldiers came, the gush of ditchwater from Deorwen's mouth. He reached for her, gripping her fingers in the reeds.

"We've found six more since," she said. "Following them to their dream's ending."

Searching for the dead in a burned city. She would be muck to her knees and soot to the top of her head. And what she must have seen. He wanted to tell her "Stop!"

"Soon we will all have peace," she said. "These dreams. They were calling to me." Finding the Lost of a ruined city. It would be a task greater than a war. "I'll walk wherever I must."

A new voice croaked. "Wha? Host of . . . Deorwen, you shouldn't be out there." The voice was Lamoric's. "Is . . . izit the middle of the night? What are you doing awake? I've told you, you need sleep. You'll worry yourself to the Gates of . . . Iz the middle of the night."

"You are awake, Milord," said Deorwen. Her fingers

slipped from Durand's, and, with a little hesitation, she stood. Durand smelled cold mud on her dress, it slid like a wet brush over his bare wrist as she crept to her husband's side.

Durand heard Lamoric mutter off into delirium.

IN THE MORNING, Durand woke to the whack and scream of surgeon's hatchets and the hiss of their cautery irons and began a day of straining to hear how the battle progressed. There were dozens of men—dead and dying—sprawled on the floor all around. Servants ran with ewers of water, blankets, and bandages. Nothing was over, that much was clear. After a lull in the night, there were too many armed men on the run.

From his spot on the floor, Durand could nearly catch the drift of conversations between Abravanal's officers at the head of the hall.

Beside him, Lamoric lay—not conscious since Deorwen's visit in the night—but Durand couldn't even turn his head to look at the man. He was comforted, however, by the sound of the man's steady breathing.

Lying there as so many other men ran, Durand groped at the fragments of his memory, trying to piece together what had happened during his charge for the castle gate. He had been sure that the enemy was far behind him—dismounted in the street. But he should at least have turned—or kept his bloody helm on his head. He might have seen whoever swung the blow; he might have avoided it. Now, he could only guess.

Shifting his hands, he found a dry, smooth, round *something* in each palm—like a stone. His fingers were caught. Threads tied them round each hard roundness. He turned his hands over and grimaced in confusion, but couldn't even manage a look at his own fists.

Then he glimpsed Heremund's bowlegs from the corner of his eye.

"Heremund!" The sound was more a croak than a shout; Heremund was already out of sight. "Hells."

Then Heremund bobbed back into view, upside down and grinning. "Good morning."

"Whadz—what's hap'ning?" asked Durand.

"Ah," said Heremund, and, with a conjurer's flourish, he snapped the threads and produced a pair of hen's eggs.

Durand, even with his jaw locked and full of broken teeth, managed to gape.

"Here, boy," said the skald, finding a basin and smashing the eggs. The reek seemed to leap down Durand's lungs, and the mass that flopped from the shells was as thick and gray as mucus.

"Hells, Her'munn . . ."

The skald smiled. "Better in these here eggs than in you, I reckon, eh?"

"Leechcraft . . ." Durand said, appalled. He tried to gesture with his broken head: "Lamoric?"

Heremund looked over at the sprawled heir of Acconel. "Still breathing. There was a little muddled shouting when Coen carried him in, but he's been out since: wise enough after such a rap on the skull. If he didn't have a good hard head, Abravanal would have talked him into a feather bed—not lying sprawled here on the reeds with the likes of you, eh?"

Durand swallowed. "Coen?"

"Mmm. He's still in the streets, fought like a hundred madmen, they say." Durand blinked hard, picturing the captain in the city. "Led the garrison out. All blood. Scourging the devils from Acconel."

"How do we fare out there?"

Just as Heremund was about to answer, a long, rattling sigh issued from the stranger sleeping at Durand's right hand. Heremund frowned. "Ah," he said, and took a moment to pull the blanket up over the man's eyes. "Well."

"Hells," said Durand.

"As to the world outside," Heremund said. "If you can't be bothered to mind what's going on around you . . ."

"Men are still running. Swanskin's cursing."

"Coensar led a squadron of Acconel men who rode over the Banderol an hour or two back and got their noses bloodied. Radomor's boys ain't done."

"Should be out there," Durand managed.

"Aye, right. You'd do our boys no end of good right now. We drag you out and you'd show 'em what becomes of brave men, eh?"

One of the physicians turned to Durand, peeling a dressing back: the poultice writhed with a gray mass of worms such as a man might find under some forest carcass. With a narrow expression, the graybeard physician gathered up the corrupt thing and Heremund's basin.

Heremund wrinkled his saddle-backed nose. "I'm not sure I truly understand leechcraft either. But they'll have the priests work those over before they toss 'em out," said Heremund.

"They're still fighting," Durand pressed. "That's what you're saying. . . ."

"And you've got more snapped bones than's good for a man. You should let it take what time it takes. The barbers'll have done some tugging when they dragged you in—matched the ends up, like—but I'll wager they ain't sure now with all the swelling. There are ways to force such things, but the buggers might leave you worse than you started."

"Fair enough." And it was. If a man couldn't roll over, he wouldn't be much use in a fight.

"I should let you rest," said Heremund. "Where you ain't purple, you're a nasty shade of green."

Durand reached with his good hand.

"Wait, Heremund. Get me closer to the head of the hall," Durand asked. "If I can't ride . . ." He took a quick breath, thinking as quick as he could manage. "Tell them, Lamoric. He should be up there."

Heremund raised one eyebrow. "He should be at the top of the hall. And you beside him still . . . Easier to hear up there. Aye. I'll see."

DURAND GOT HIS wish and was soon lugged to a spot near the dais steps: a painful process that he had cause to regret for some hours after the move. Still—laid on his face to save his shoulder—he was privy to the barons' talk of how many barrels of bacon had rolled in, how many carts were caught in what mud, and guesses at how many bolts of canvas the refugees would need for tents. Oh, it was worth the pain.

Soon, he would wish for boredom.

He could see only a foot or two of bare reeds—and the rise and fall of a new stranger's chest beside him. As the light bled from the evening hall, however, this new bedfellow gave out a fearsomely long sigh. Durand found himself listening, straining for the next breath. He called for help, but neither physician, leech, nor surgeon could bring the poor soul back.

As the medical men drew the dead man's cloak over his face—an act Durand could only see the edges of—a heavy stride rumbled down the Painted Hall. The shadow of several knights passed over Durand, followed by the crash of mail skirts as a troop of armored men knelt before the dais.

"Your Grace"—Durand knew Marshal Conran's rumble—"the carrion birds have returned to the city."

Durand heard a goblet clatter on the dais steps. The cup—winking jewels—bounced to a halt in the reeds beyond Durand's dead bedfellow.

"Honestly," the blond Baron of Honefells answered, "Brother Conran, friend, the crows will still be finding men and horses for—"

"—This is no vague omen! Something stepped from hiding as the Eye left the Heavens. It is on the move in the west, My Lords: a thing new to us. And black wings rage before it as the storm cloud swells before the thunderbolt."

"I'd say Radomor will not be found among the bodies. . . ." was Sallow Hythe's wry conclusion.

Old Swanskin grunted. "We were lucky to drive the fiend off. We must call our battalions together and mount a defense at the Fuller's Bridge."

As the barons rumbled assent, Durand felt something crackle among the reeds under his ear. The hall's contingent of vermin was likely on the prowl with so much fresh meat abroad, but they would have to wait for him.

Durand heard Conran rise to his feet. "No. It has crossed the Fuller's Bridge and moves among the ruins of the city." Durand could hear the Ash Knights drawing their blades. "Very near . . ."

The children should go into the sanctuary," said Abravanal. "Father Oredgar, mind them."

"Our friend Radomor is not infallible," Honefells said. "He played his game with Acconel, but could not break her. We took him unawares and snapped the prettiest snare his wit could fashion."

Durand heard a shy murmur: "Father, must I—?"

"Almora, join the pageboys with old Oredgar in the sanctuary, please."

The carpet of reeds under Durand's cheek came alive: earwigs, woodlice, and uncounted other crawling things erupted over Durand's wincing face.

"Hurry, Almora," said the duke. The girl's metal Power zipped through the sooty vaults. Then a great shock caused the little Power to jump. Somewhere a door—a portcullis—thundered against its frame.

A second slam was full of splinters and torn metal. Bodies crashed and slid. But Durand could see nothing. At the duke's dais, a few tardy blades whisked from their scabbards. The blond reeds on the floor at Durand's side silvered impossibly before his eyes.

"What've they done?" Abravanal rasped.

Something had entered the hall, Durand was certain. The mighty scrape of its passage shivered in Durand's broken bones.

"Come no farther!" thundered Conran the Marshal, but the dragging progress continued, the sound grating louder and louder.

A metal goblet clopped shut. And a clawed hand slapped the rushes a step from Durand, turning the gray reeds wet-black at the touch of its split nails. Durand saw copper wire glinting in knots of white bone, and mail swinging in sheets. Then the horror levered its bulk forward—as huge and dry and dead as a team of warhorses from a chieftain's tomb.

Durand undid a good day's mending as he twisted to see more, but if this horror had come to kill them all, it didn't matter. Jutting before a torso like whale's ruin, the thing's head swung: a knot of tusks and spidersilk. Across its eyes, an old helm had split, leaving an iron eye-slit like a blind-folding shackle. A serpent, a thicket of bones, the fiend dragged its bulk forward. Somehow, Durand knew it: in the line of its shoulders and the style of its ruined war gear, he saw Radomor's bloody Champion, transfigured.

It faced the duke and his officers.

"*Host of Heaven,*" Abravanal whispered.

The Septarim ringed the duke. "By the Lord of Dooms, come no farther!" Conran warned.

But Radomor's monstrous Champion subsided in its own time, a long tail of bone knobs and wire lashing across the rushes. Durand felt a panicked animal's yearning to get away. He heard the man beside him trying: heels dragging on the reeds, fingers clawing.

It was several heartbeats before Durand remembered that the man was meant to be dead.

"Stop!" roared Conran.

All around the Painted Hall, a scrabbling defied the Master, rising like whispers: all the dead men on the floor of the hall squirmed. Lungs wheezed in stiffened chests, hauling air through gray lips all around.

And, all at once, they spoke: "His Majesty, Ragnal, King of Old Errest, bidss you greetingsss, Abravanal, Duke of Gireth. Yourz izs the victory, yes-s-s. But you will not long s-savor it. His Majesty, Radomor, has sent riders to every baron, banner knight, and man-at-arms, summoning all to his host. This will be no meager army gathered in secret. No force stirred by whispers-s. His Majesty comes for you with all the liegemen due his royal blood. Gather whom you will to oppose sense and justice, you will not save your gray head, Duke of Gireth. These knights of the ashes will not preserve you." There was a faint chuckle among the dead voices. "There will soon be many more to sing in this grave chorus-s-s-s."

Durand tore his wounds to twist and see the gray faces speak.

And—as if in silent homage to this Champion—the gray dead sat up. The horror nodded low, spreading its great hands.

Then there was a snarl at Durand's ear: "Slave! Slave of Traitors. Stop!" Lamoric climbed to his feet. Now, he faced his enemy over Durand's back.

The Champion heaved, upsetting a table with an eerily fluid slither of its knobbed tail. Poised right over Durand's smashed shoulder, it faced Lamoric, larger than bulls. With Durand's one peering eye, he could see up through a vast, hollow basketry of bones in mail and silk and dusty coronets. A shrill whine issued from somewhere among the brittle arches.

Lamoric snarled on, panting. "Tell your master: tell him we've bested him once. He needn't trouble himself to march on Acconel. We'll come for him!"

The whistle in the Champion's bulk seemed to swell for an instant, then the monster dropped into a crooked bow that brought the spidersilk of its beard spilling down over Durand's clammy neck.

After an instant of this misery, the monster leapt up and swarmed from the hall, flying with the sudden agility of an eel in a stream. Its clawed hands smacked soot from the ceiling, and then it was gone.

Durand remembered the Rooks' words: Lamoric would be drawn out, undefended.

The Heir of Acconel collapsed.

25. Path of Ashes

When Lord Lamoric ordered his physicians to get him back in the saddle and his barons to prepare the host to march, the whole court of Acconel came alive around Durand's ears. Lamoric would make Radomor choke on his threats. They would chase the demon Champion back to its master. They would throw the Host of Gireth upon the would-be king before a single traitor could rally to the Leopard Banner of Yrlac. Boots tramped round Durand's head. War gear rattled and the officers bellowed.

Durand ground his teeth in frustration. He could do nothing more than listen—and squint at the ankles of the excited throng with his one good eye—for he lay among the blind, the dead, and the victims of the doctor's axes while trumpets called through the dark. The gathering roar of hundreds boiled in the courtyards beyond the arrow slits of Gunderic's Tower. It echoed in the great mouth of the courtyard stair. And Durand pressed his eyes shut, his thoughts knotting around memories of his last ride to the castle gate: Lamoric on the saddlebow, the breath of clean air when the helmet came free, Acconel men all around him. But, of the last moment, he could recall nothing. Who had swung the blow that knocked him flying? Who had broken his jaw and ribs and shoulder? But, even when dawn glowed in the arrow slits, no memory came.

With the army marshaled somewhere outside, Berchard and Hathcyn climbed back to the Painted Hall—Berchard with his eye glinting, Hathcyn with a hard gleam of teeth. Each man ducked close to say he'd be back before Durand knew he'd gone, then they were bowing and sprinting for the courtyard stair. Durand could do nothing but snarl at himself.

Finally, Lord Lamoric himself appeared at Durand's side in every stitch of his crimson war gear. It could have been their Red Knight days again. The army was ready. Every ox was creaking in its harness, hundreds of horses stood in their saddles.

"Lordship," Durand said.

Lamoric's hair bobbed in his eyes as he bent with a sheepish smile. "My head's still ringing," he confessed. "Tell no one. These leeches will have me back on the reeds."

"Hells," said Durand. He didn't like to see how badly Lamoric was hurt.

"You did well enough to get me free of the battle," said Lamoric. He mashed his eyes with one hand. "But I'd be happier if I could keep anything down."

"I should have been watching," Durand said, but Lamoric was already on his feet—not steady.

Lamoric's lip twisted. "Fear not!" he said. "I'll bring the devil's head back and pike it on the Fuller's Bridge." And a crowd of Acconel men roared from the courtyard stair. "To Yrlac!" And, in moments, Lamoric was gone. Their shouts echoed till the hall was silent.

Scarcely a fighting man remained.

Durand's broken ribs kept each breath short and panting. He fixed his will on slow, regular breaths in the silence. "Hells," he said.

IN THE DARKNESS of the hall-come-infirmary that night, Durand still lay sprawled on the reeds, trapped under his broken shoulder. Durand's father and brother would be marching west. His lord. His captain. He could imagine a thousand black dooms for the army, but there was nothing for him to do but wait.

They'd pulled a cloak over the nearest man to Durand— the dead man. The corpse's silhouette stood against the greater darkness of the distant walls as still as a mountain. Durand tried not to picture the poor wretch under the cloak, gray and stiff. His good eye followed the ridgeline of the man's silhouette as though it were the mountains above his father's hall.

Then the silhouette moved.

"God," said Durand.

The folds of the man's surcoat bulged. Under caked layers of wool and linen, something scrabbled, making wet sounds. With the Ash Knights in Yrlac and the Patriach among his people, Durand could only hope for rats; there was no one to ward off the darkness. "God," Durand repeated, and tried to move.

It was no use.

Something dropped in the putrid reeds by Durand's chin. It blundered against the wool at his throat, reeking enough to choke him. Another shape thrust against the surcoat of the dead man, before a rancid voice snapped Durand's attention back to the thing at his chin.

"*S-i-r D-u-r-a-nd.*" The voice sizzled from the darkness between the dead man and Durand. And something feathered past his eyelids.

The second creature won free, standing on the breast of the dead man where Durand could make out its shape: black wings scissored above spindly legs, scattering lice or maggots into Durand's face. "*You are not asleep?*" the new creature said.

The bird—a rook—hopped to Durand's smashed shoulder. Durand felt a stab of pain as though a spear had been jabbed through the length of him. For that instant, he was paralyzed by the rook's mortal touch. Then it tumbled onto the floor at Durand's back. "*So easy now the Knights of Ash have gone. We are more free to speak.*"

Durand shook with the memory of the thing's touch in his muscles. It peered at his eyes and ears.

"Sleep can be elusive."

"Perhaps he is plagued by dreams, brother."

"Like the dreams that called us to these misty north-lands?"

"Perhaps."

Durand wondered if he could get an arm free to make a snatch at one of the devils without tearing himself to pieces. Just the tension had him fighting for air. But he couldn't do so much as lift his chin from the floor. "To the Hells with you," he said.

"You are not the first to suggest such an outing." The beak razored across his ear, sending another flinch of agony through his lungs. *"But not before we play out our little game."*

Durand gulped air. "Lamoric will put an end to that soon enough."

"Ah yes, Lamoric's march. Such trouble to arrange. As a man of brawn and daylight, you would have no idea. Even with the Wards of your Ancient Patriarchs so threadbare and the high sanctuaries all a-tumble, it was no easy feat for our messenger to reach Lamoric here. Was he not splendid though, our emissary?"

Durand blinked at the miserable reek and snarled into the reeds: "Your master. He'll be well paid for your troubles. He's brought the Host of Gireth down on him. Our men will be in a bloody mood when they get hold of him." The creatures were still breathing close, and he gasped at the foul air.

A long skull tilted. *"But surely we can be forgiven our little threats. An invitation is no invitation unless one believes that it might be accepted."*

Durand grunted. "What?"

"Our messenger applied the goad," the bird sprang onto Durand's broken shoulder in a rain of crawling things. Its touch stopped his lungs, his heart—it threw lances of pain down every crack in his bones. The rotten beak caught at his ear. *"Now your master brings his army to us. We may, one hopes, be forgiven a moment's rudeness."*

Durand grunted, suffocating in the open air. He desperately wanted to get one of these devil birds into his fist. Through knotted jaws, he croaked, "You lie."

"Brother, how can he doubt us?" one bird lamented.

Broken teeth creaked in Durand's jaw.

The rook on his shoulder loomed in Durand's eye, blotting out the room. Vermin writhed audibly in its feathers. *"Everything is prepared, friend Durand. Fear not. The fires are lit. We have spared no pains."*

"Ah, brother! What a shame it would have been if Lamoric had stayed at home. So many dark hours wasted."

Durand grunted into the reeds. The spasm had lifted his knees from the floor. His fists and feet had curled into knots of bones. If the rook didn't release him, its devil's touch would crack his bones or choke the life from his chest. But his mind fought. What had these devils driven Lamoric into? What sorcery did they work in the dark hours? He pictured the army marching west, blind and deluded. Certain that they'd got Radomor running—that they were striking in time.

"Children's stories," he gasped. "You waste your breath."

"No, Sir Durand. For you, we would take great trouble and never count the cost. You have played such a mighty role in our past encounters," said the voice at Durand's ear. *"It is a shame."*

Blood thundered in his skull. He wondered how long he could keep breathing.

Then, with a flap, the first rook joined its brother on Durand's shoulder—the simple hop ramming a dozen more lances through Durand's bones. The spasm wrenched his creaking jaw from the reeds. He twisted while the devil peered down the blade of its beak into his eye. *"And this one will be missed, I think, brother. Here was Lamoric so long secure among the crowds of his followers with his formidable bodyguard at his side."*

"—And the Patriarch to pray for him, and the Knights of Ash all around."

"Who could touch such a man? How could an enemy strike at him?"

"Even if there were some turncoat among poor Lamoric's men—a traitor—waiting only a whisper from his true master, how could he dare to strike with so many loyal men pressed close?" The birds circled, claws and dagger beaks

darting around his eye and ears. He had only heartbeats more.

"*The frustration! The waiting, brother! Always, His Lordship was surrounded. Always, he was watched. The poor traitor would be sharpening his dagger, hoping only for the very first lonely moment in which to strike.*"

A beak slipped close. "*Riding into that solitary heartbeat when an army's back was turned? His poor master draped over a saddlebow?*"

"*Aye. Well, brother.*"

Both birds now trickled their words straight down into his ear, stepping from face to neck to shoulder.

"*Such a fleeting chance.*"

"*The very first!*"

Durand gasped, bent like a trussed deer. He saw the picture the two devils were painting: a man planted close to Lamoric waiting for his chance to strike their lord down. A man turned by fear or pride or silver, praying for an unguarded moment in which to strike Lamoric down and slip away. Such a man, undiscovered, would not wait long to move again.

One of the creatures flapped to catch its balance as Durand rocked on his belly. "*What will happen now, in the hurlyburly of a marching army?*"

A talon needled Durand's broken cheek. "*Where even the walls are canvas.*"

No one had spoken of an assassin—not a word. Lamoric was marching his army into some snare of these fiends' devising, and, all the while, a traitor had his knife poised at the man's throat. And here was Durand, pinned by his broken bones to the floor of the Painted Hall as they slid further into disaster.

One of the birds stepped too close to Durand's grasping hand. Despite the iron bands of suffocation and paralysis, Durand lashed out. And felt greasy feathers and cracking bones in his fist. Living things lashed around his fingers, and, for a dozen harried heartbeats, the thing thrashed its wings against its captor, shrieking its life out.

But he could breathe again.

The little corpse burst into stinking gobbets between

Durand's fingers. The surviving rook alighted on Durand's dead friend as the commotion drew running feet. The crowd trampled near.

Durand gasped against the ground, "I will come for you."

"Ha!" was the only answer, and the bird pinwheeled through shins and warding hands, off into the night.

Heremund was first. "Durand! What's going on? God!" He snorted at the reek. "Are you—"

Durand locked his slimy fist on Heremund's wrist. "Heremund. You said I ought to wait, that I shouldn't rush while the bones knit."

"And so you—"

"They must be warned. Called back. The time for waiting is over."

The skald wrenched his hand free of Durand's fist. "Hells."

AFTER AN HOUR'S wondering, a scowling Heremund appeared with Hagon, Kieren, and the Patriarch of Acconel himself. They set something in the reeds where Durand couldn't see.

"It's too much for these masters of physic," said Heremund, "but I've found a man."

Blind Hagon grinned down. Kieren's fox mustaches twitched in disapproval.

The fearsome Patriarch scowled at Durand. "You are a bloody fool, but ask and we will do what can be done."

"Who did they leave behind who could make the journey?" Durand said.

The Patriarch grunted, but gave the others a nod. And so, in a bright constellation of sliding broken bones, the three men rolled Durand onto a litter and lugged him from the castle.

AFTER A JOLTING age of delirium, Durand recognized a web of high, naked arches swinging above his bearers: the wreck of the high sanctuary. A slanted light poured through.

Knight, skald, Patriarch, and leech grunted along until they reached the head of the old nave where the three rolled Durand out once more—they might as well have dropped him over a harrow.

"Don't worry," said Hagon, "the hard part's over." He grinned at the others. "I always tell them that. It won't hurt a bit. Or me more than you, anyway. Eh?" Durand saw the blind man's teeth. "Don't worry, close your eyes and breathe. You'll have your wind back soon enough."

Durand grunted.

"Durand," said Sir Kieren. "This pigheadedness is going to kill you. There's an army riding at Lamoric's back. What's one more man in all that? If anything goes wrong there's no one but old men here."

"Unless one of them can catch the army and turn it back, I must go," Durand managed.

Hagon turned his face to Durand. "Now, you've been told there may be a price to pay for all this, have you?"

Durand didn't answer.

A smile flickered. "All right. I am no court master of physic, but I've worked two winters for every one you've been breathing—and there are too many folk too battered for any of the masters to attend you. So, you and I will work the Sunwheel through, dawn to dawn, friend Durand."

"A day . . ." Durand pictured the army tramping west, a step farther away with every heartbeat.

"Keep breathing. It's always this way with ribs—should be a year. As it is, you'll see men spell me, I think." The man had set a satchel at his side, and now his long fingers plucked pots from its depths, breaking seals and peeling back lids. "Some fine remedies here. Best I've had my hands on." There were herbs and organs and Heaven knew what else. "And your high sanctuary is the best place for this sort of work: holy ground, I hope. Even now."

"Don't stray far from the altar, leech," muttered the Patriarch. "The Wards of the Ancient Patriarchs are falling, one end of Errest to another. The Strangers march upon the Bourne of Jade. The Banished are restive in the shadows. Some dark hand is on the move. Soon, the trembling realm will be given over to the Banished and the fiends. The oaths of ten thousand lords will scatter like breath on a winter—"

"But here, yes? It's holy enough. So we'll see what we'll see," said Hagon. The blind man turned to Durand.

"Now, you're certain you want this? I'll make these three lug you back if you're not. I don't mind."

Durand blinked up at the pale empty Heavens beyond Oredgar, Kieren, Hagon, and the skald, feeling that the army was rushing away from him like a tide—thinking that Lamoric had a knife to his back and didn't know it. Some man in Lamoric's host had struck his lord down. "Hagon, if there's only you, I'm grateful."

"Fair spoken," said Hagon, "for a man with a battered head. So, begging Your Grace's pardon, I'll get started."

Patriarch Oredgar stood. The hem of his saffron robes was black with ashes. Knight and skald shook their heads. And Durand was left alone.

Hagon's pale features settled below his blank blue eyes. He lifted his long hands. "Sorry, friend, but I must know the lay of the land." And the strong fingers pressed deep—not pleasant. "Eye, cheek, nose, jaw, teeth, collar, ribs, ribs again." The hands lifted. "Now, you just try to get some wind in you. Hang on. Breathe."

Durand did nothing but try to get air in his lungs.

Hagon's hands worked over the scattered pots. Heremund left a fire, and Hagon sang. "Bone to bone, blood to blood, limb to limb," he chanted. He called upon the Host of Heaven. He warned the agents of decay. "As Heaven's Champion thrust his lance in the earth that he might not fall, so may these bones stand fast. As the Warders of the Bright Gates knotted iron coats of nails to fight at Farandell, so may these limbs lock and link and grow strong. May you worms of darkness drink deep of disappointment. Bone to bone, marrow to marrow . . ."

The Heavens rolled over Durand's head, Heaven's Eye lancing through high clouds. A squall tumbled in from the mere, washing Durand and the city in cold rain. He woke from crawling nightmares only to learn that the creeping sensations did not vanish when his eyes opened. Hagon's chant drifted through the Noontide Lauds, the Plea of Sunset, and the Last Twilight. The Heavens filled with stars, and the waning Sowing Moon glinted like a new-honed blade.

Blind Hagon chanted on, cursing and praying, binding and damning.

In the dark, battles shot through Durand's memory: the amazement on spattered faces, the dread of sudden wounds. He remembered Sir Waer on the cliffs of Tern Gyre; Sir Gol on his back in that Hellebore Road; Cerlac: a man like him at Bower Mead—all dead.

He could feel his mind coming adrift under the pressure of Hagon's leechcraft. For a time he was back on the cobblestones at the gates of Castle Acconel, blind with blood and astonishment.

Suddenly, Hagon's voice was a cheerful whisper. Durand lay on his back with the man looking down on him, ruddy with firelight. "All right," the leech said, "I'll just take a moment to tend the fire then. There's some of this is better hot, they say. It can't be long, mind you, but I understand these things, eh? No one can say I don't."

"What?" Durand winced in bafflement.

Hagon stepped away, and a bright garden scent filled Durand's nostrils—and there was Deorwen, her face swaying in the firelight just beyond his nose. The dark glitter of eyes searched his face. Almost, she touched him.

"Not so bad?" Durand tried.

"Your hair," she said. Then, her fingertips touched the bare scalp Durand hadn't noticed. The leeches must have sheared him to make their stitches.

"You're out again. At night," he said.

"I liked the curls."

"You are better?" Durand marveled up at the black shimmer of eyes, and she laughed—just a flash—before looking up where the moon hung.

"You're going to follow him," she said. "It doesn't occur to you that it might be madness?"

Durand wet his lips. "Have you slept? Does it let you sleep? Finding them?"

Again, the merest flicker of a smile. This one came nowhere near her eyes. "Do you remember that I spoke of my brother? I've found many of the others. But he is still there. One call rising as the other voices fade." Her eyes flickered toward Hagon's fire. "Twisting in darkness, Durand."

Durand tried to shake his head—there was pain. "Not dead."

She cast her glance west across the charred bones of the sanctuary. "He hangs in"—she made a grasping gesture with both hands—"a ribbed blackness. Bound there. They are cackling round him. He can neither fight nor flee." She took a quick breath. "That is the dream I have of my brother."

Durand's mouth was open before he spoke. "They're not all omens, Deorwen. Even these dreams of yours. These are grave days, but they're passing. No surprise he'd be in your mind. We'll do what we must. We'll set it right."

"These wise women . . ." She glanced from the firelight to a gaggle of women scarcely visible beyond the rubble. "They say that I'll do the most good here. That nothing can come of a wild journey to God knows. That a woman understands what must be borne and bears it, what can be mended and what must be suffered, what can be kept and what we must give up."

"We'll find Lord Moryn. Fix Radomor. The king, he'll come round." He gripped her hand hard. "When it's over, we'll have a chance to think and breathe."

Deorwen glanced back to Durand. With a twist, Durand made out the women watching from beyond the sanctuary flagstones. A few had shovels in their muddy hands.

Deorwen bent very near. "When this is over," she breathed, and she pressed a kiss hard against Durand's snapped teeth. All of this madness, and Durand wanted nothing more than this woman. He pictured a small hall somewhere where he could be master and she his wife. Her hands ran over his broken face, clutching and caressing.

A hot tear struck his neck.

She caught her breath.

And, in a moment, she was bidding Hagon good fortune.

IT GOT WORSE. There were times when he couldn't help but twist and arch against the ground—the pain as bad as the Rooks' grip. He'd drop from consciousness as though he'd never lived. He'd wake sweating or desperate. Hagon held him like a wrestler or wrote upon his skin or smeared his limbs with reeking fluids. Leechcraft was madness.

Past midnight, Durand became conscious of a new sound rising beyond Hagon's chanting: a hollow knock upon the flagstones of the sanctuary floor—and another. *Tock . . . tock. . . .* The stone's chill touched his heart, for he knew the slow rhythm: a staff's brass heel, closer and closer with each empty rap on the stones.

Hagon rocked and mumbled, seemingly as deaf as he was blind. But Durand flinched at the course of the man's muttering. "By the Traveler's whisper that cast a Power onto the roads and set Creation in the hands of the created, I set bone to bone and marrow to marrow!"

With this for a fanfare, a being stepped across the flagstones in a great swirl of chill air—a being huge as a gallows tree with a wide pilgrim's hat caught as high and dark as a black moon. A fist of bone and twine clutched a forked staff.

Durand ceased to breathe.

The giant loomed at Hagon's side—and high above—while Hagon mumbled on without a glance or shiver. Durand struggled, too shattered to move as, with a creak like a ship's rigging, the giant began to bend. The black moon of its hat swung low, blotting out sanctuary and Creation and the Heavens beyond. A breath like winter ditchwater flowed between the peg teeth in that void.

At the wink of one bright-penny eye hardly beyond Durand's nose, Durand tumbled from the world.

HIS NEXT VISITOR came as dawn's twilight first touched Heavens. Durand heard wings—feathered landings. A twist of his head brought him a look across the plain of moonlit rubble where thousands of dark birds tumbled from the air, hopping and twitching just beyond the broken walls.

At first, he thought of the Rooks and their minion birds, but these were small, jittering creatures. The chatter that rose from their tumbling clouds was incredible: clicks and trills and whistles like a whole forest poured into the streets. Starlings. Starlings like storm in the beacon tower. Like the flock that pitched Lamoric into the Maidensbier.

Durand cursed the morel and poppy in his skull. Something was looking in on him—on all of them. Something wanted to see what Hagon was doing in his circle of firelight.

"I THINK THAT'S done it," the man croaked. "The Sun-wheel right through."

Durand lay for several heartbeats on the cold stones with Dawn red on his eyelids, and he set the night's madness behind him. It was time to put Hagon's work to the test. Opening his eyes, he took a few thoughtful breaths, stretching the long moment before hope met whatever the truth must be.

He levered himself up.

"Right. You can move," said Hagon. The breeze played with the white thatch of the man's hair. "Slow."

Durand worked his shoulder, and, amid pops and winces, he rolled onto a pair of very numb feet; it had been days. He took a deep breath. He lifted his bad arm and worked the hand. He turned his head and flexed his jaw. It all took some gasps and hisses, but it would serve. He could move.

With a fierce grin, Durand took Hagon's shoulder. "Hagon, sir, I am grateful." He swung his arms, wincing and puffing when he had to. "Truly."

With a fierce nod that he regretted, Durand started toward the castle.

"Here!" said Hagon. "You'd leave a blind man behind in all this?"

26. A Leopard by the Tail

Gunderic's Tower seemed like a house of spirits, empty but for the groans of the sickest as Durand tramped back to collect his things. Heremund called him mad and wished him luck. Kieren could not leave the business of the struggling city. And among the sleeping bodies crowding the passageways, Durand could find no sign of Deorwen.

He pulled together his few belongings, found Pale tethered in the yard, and rode out, hoping that a lone rider—battered but determined—could overtake an army. His head was still spinning.

Finally, Durand rode up to the pitted tooth of marble that marked the border. Beyond, he could see the rolling country of Yrlac. Behind him were the hardscrabble Warrens—and scarcely a single soldier between his back and the Painted Hall. Unless Durand could catch and turn Lamoric, the Host of Gireth was lost—and every life in the dukedom with it.

Durand took a pull from a skin of drugged claret Hagon had given him and then urged Pale on, gritting his teeth at the big brute's jarring gait.

As Pale set foot in Yrlac, Creation shuddered. Durand clung tight as the big brute shied. A knock was rolling through the sky above and around them. Before his eyes, the Heavens curdled. "Hells," said Durand. Low clouds knotted, squeezing the light out of the world.

Durand gripped the big stallion and watched as this false twilight settled on the Yrlac.

"Get up," said Durand, and they rode on.

He took another long pull an hour later when great sheets of rain dropped from the sky. Every step had the big horse lurching to get his feet free of the rutted muck. Durand's bones wouldn't last long. Durand snarled, "Midnight at noon." And smeared water from his face, trying not to notice the tremor in his hand. "We'll pick up the pace."

He forced Pale south and east, splashing down sunken tracks. They skirted the looming wood where the duke had concealed his army and rode deeper into an Yrlac where loaded gibbets swung over every crossroads. Pale lashed his head. Each field and barn Durand passed was a charred wreck, and soot ran black in the roads.

In a bit of ditch-deep road, Durand caught sight of yet another creaking bunch of corpses, and hissed between his teeth, "Is this what the devil's left of Yrlac now?" Again, he remembered those few long days in Radomor's hall, and the impossible silence of the man's fury.

This load of black shapes dangled from the gnarled elbows of a bloated beech tree, its foot hidden by the curve of the deep track ahead. Durand had visions of steaming ruins from Mornaway to the mountains, league after league hissing in the rain. Pale stamped.

"He's burnt everything. These'll be his own plowmen he's

hanged. What a kingdom he would rule!" But a more calculating part of Durand's mind wondered just how Lamoric would feed his army. They couldn't march far on smoke and ashes, and there'd been no time to load weeks of salt pork.

He winced at the hideous remains up the track. Despite the twenty or thirty rainy paces between Durand and the dark shapes on the tree, he could see plenty of blood. As Durand made to spur on past the gibbet tree, Pale balked, half-turning in the deep track. His ears had shot toward the rigid shapes on the tree where now even Durand made out a strange scrabbling.

Stroking Pale's muscled neck, Durand got up in the stirrups to get a good look over the banks of the road at the beech's swollen foot. Low shapes slunk around the tree.

They were dogs. A whole pack of lean-looking brutes slavered below the stiff and dripping toes of the corpses. One big devil hopped against the fat tree, straining upward.

Durand didn't like the thought of bringing live prey through such a starveling pack. "We'd better let the buggers eat in peace," Durand muttered—and spurred Pale up the roadside back into the field.

But, as Pale wallowed up the bank, the dogs swiveled their long skulls in his direction, their lips writhing back in a collection of very human leers.

Just as Durand froze there above the road, another rider splashed into sight. Coming up the track in Durand's wake was a boy on a donkey. He wore a sopping blue hood.

Durand and the dogs spotted the stranger at the same instant. Every head swiveled, man and dog.

"Here!" Durand called. "This way!"

The pack was on the move, shooting down the track. Just as the first dog struck the donkey, Durand caught the wrist of the rider, hauling him out of the road.

With a twist that nearly sprung his ribs, Durand set the boy on Pale's back and rode for it.

The pack snarled around the still-kicking donkey, pulling out of sight in a hail of kicks and lean bodies.

THEY RODE AT a ground-covering canter as long as Durand could stand it. Pale bounded like a bear. Finally, somewhere on the high back of a trampled field, Durand found himself lolling over Pale's neck, rigid.

It hurt. He could hardly think or see.

Then the stranger's voice moved at the nape of Durand's neck. "Durand." But it was Deorwen, her breath warm on his neck.

"You must breathe," she said.

Durand flinched around. Suddenly, he felt every inch of the woman pressed against his back, his hips, his thighs. She'd thrown on a boy's surcoat, cloak, and tunic. Beads of rain stood on her cheeks. Her lips. What was she doing here?

In the rolling country ahead, he heard some tributary of the River Rushes burbling. And the sound gave him something to catch hold of. "There. Pale will need water."

And over the next rise, a shallow stream ran by the track, swollen with the rain.

Durand lowered himself from the saddle with as much speed as he could manage, then stood with his hands on his knees waiting for Creation to hold still.

Deorwen was moving around him, seeming nimble as a squirrel.

He reached out, catching her sleeve. "Why? Why are you here?"

"Who's left for fool's errands now?"

Her grin snatched Durand's breath. "You must go back."

"I've left Almora with the wise women. And I will learn what's become of my brother."

"You'll be killed." As Creation stopped spinning around him, Durand resolved to get a drink of cold water. He must think. Shining water ran over green reeds with a few flat stones to make a ford. He set his cupped hands into the mirror glint, and—just as the water touched his lips—

"Durand!" Deorwen caught him by the shoulders, pitching Durand into a splash of icy water.

The shock of the water on his half-broken bones was like falling flat off a high roof. Durand wallowed back out of the water.

"Lord of Dooms!" Durand spluttered.

Deorwen was pointing upstream. Through the glassy shimmer of clouds on the water, Durand picked out something pale: a long shape, and then another and another. He made out the fork of legs.

"*Hells,*" he said.

Deorwen sat on the bank with her knees up in the boy's long hose she was wearing. "Someone's tied them into the rushes along the streambed: bodies."

Durand watched open hands trail like swimming fish below the surface. "Hemlock's dear and dead men cheap."

Deorwen didn't shrink. "There was a woman in my brother's lands. Her man's family had a well behind their house, still they made her walk half a league to the village to draw water. Then their sow had a litter of piglets. She strangled them, one by one, and plopped the little things down the well. Moryn had to hang her."

Durand squinted from the gray corpses to the gray skies ahead. "You must go back," said Durand. "I must catch Lamoric. I must reach the River Rushes before the day's out." He couldn't carry Deorwen into this nightmare.

Deorwen stood very straight despite her sopping blue cloak, her hair running in strings. "We are five leagues from my husband's city, Sir Durand. Will you send me back on your Pale, here? Or shall I walk? You have ten leagues to cover by nightfall, I'd guess."

Durand blinked at a momentary vision of arriving too late—finding a scorched field of sprawled bodies. Banners trampled in the earth. "Madness." He could not leave Deorwen; he could not abandon Lamoric.

"I will not be wise." She had sat by her mother's side. She had tracked her fool of a husband. She had taken care of Almora and the laying of the Lost. "Not yet."

At that moment, Pale tossed his head, nodding a rolling eye. A low shape shuttled along the track behind them. "Lord of Dooms. They've trailed us," Durand said.

Deorwen followed his glance. Her mouth opened. "But they are dogs."

"It is too much. I cannot think. We must go on," said Durand.

He sprang aboard the warhorse, whisked Deorwen from the track, and together they crossed the ford of corpses.

SOUTH AND EAST, they pushed on, Pale jogging through narrow places that the wary army they followed had avoided to gain a pace or two every league. This was, in part, the country where Durand had ridden with Captain Gol and Duke Ailnor—very likely the last ride old Ailnor ever took. Now, as Durand clung to his saddlebow, he recognized very little. The people had been driven off, their storehouses burnt, and everything lost.

This would be the legacy of King Radomor if the devil won.

He ached over his decision to bring Deorwen. She'd been mad to ride into this mess on a donkey; a boy's costume would hardly have saved her. But he could think of no way to turn back and no safe place to set her down. She must come with him.

Behind him, Durand saw further signs of the silent pack on their trail. Once some great brute slouched atop a high ridge. Later, flowing forms loped across a scabbed hill's flank. Durand wanted to tell Deorwen that he would save her, even if it cost the army and the kingdom both. He wanted to carry her to the Dreaming Lands or the Shattered Isle beyond the Westering Sea. He wondered whether he could still work a sword.

And Deorwen clutched him tight. From time to time, her grip on his ribs had him gasping—though he worked hard not to let on. "Wolves will stalk an army," she said. "They saw it on Hallow Down. Like gulls after a fishing boat. Looking for scraps. The wise women speak of it."

The things on the hillsides leered. They kept pace through burnt gorse and torched field.

"Scraps is right, I'm sure," said Durand. "These will be strays. If they're used to butcher's bones, they'll be hungry now. The roads must be full of strays between mere and mountains these days: men and beasts." He tried a blithe smile. "The country'll be teeming with folk making their way to distant kin."

At that moment, he glanced up to find the first pack of curs *ahead* of them. The things curled round some lump on a nearby hill, a good stone's throw off the road.

"Lugging their tools to new towns," he continued. "Prince Eodan and the king growling at each other."

As they passed below, Durand made out the cocked angle of a limb where the brutes were working: a horse lay curled on its back. The dogs worried at its bowels. Saddle brass winked.

"Errest must be patient with strays for a good long while."

What might have been the torn shape of a rider—something in blue wool—sprawled nearby. It couldn't have been dogs.

"They might have found him that way," Deorwen tried. But, at her words, the whole hilltop pack raised its muzzles, all leering down on Pale and the two fools on the big stallion's back.

Durand set the spurs.

REAL DARKNESS SPREAD over the wasteland.

Durand rode, knotted around Pale's saddlebow while the pack closed in all around. Deorwen told him: "Breathe." And it was all he could do to manage it.

The brutes ranged down hollows and flowed over ridges in numbers far larger than ever prowled around one gallows tree. As Durand bullied Pale onward, he saw mastiffs with cinder muzzles; staghounds and boarhounds and butcher's dogs—some whip-lean, others as thick as bulls. Every one ran with a hitched gait, as if their bones had been joined by a loom-maker. Durand no longer doubted that these ghouls could snap up a mounted man if the mood took them. Deorwen pointed out packhorses, scraps of tack, and even an iron helm trampled in the road to prove it.

Deorwen clung to his back while, beyond the clouds, the Eye of Heaven failed.

"Do you hear that?" said Deorwen.

"Huh?" He peered around, hearing only the click and thud of paws on stone and roadway. "I hear nothing." The long line of the pack swept like great wings closing over them as the last light ebbed away. "Deorwen, King of Heaven. We must make our stand."

"The devils are whispering!" Deorwen pressed.

Durand blinked. And he heard it. Another sound hissing up like waves upon a shingle beach—a whisper that swelled into life, alive and scrabbling before the pack. "Like the Rooks," Durand said. It swelled around them.

"I can almost make it out," Deorwen said.

Durand spurred Pale into the blackness, sure that teeth would flash from the dark at any moment. Long shapes flickered beyond shocks of gorse and bracken as the dogs swarmed over every rise and bounded on every side.

Durand could stand no more. He thought of throwing himself down—stealing Deorwen a few extra heartbeats before Pale stepped in some hole—when Deorwen shouted out, pointing over the hillocks to a pale shape cut out of the darkness. "There! Durand! A bell tower! A sanctuary!"

And they charged through a place of walls and dark lanes for a high white tower. There was a gate. With the pack all around, they pelted through and rode for a black door in the tall sanctuary wall. Durand threw himself tumbling down. He flung his shoulder at the door, but the thing was standing wide—a trick of light—and he plunged through with Deorwen darting in behind him.

They were on holy ground in the house of Heaven's King and the road was behind them: safe!

But no sooner had he breathed relief than the first dogs shot through the door to bowl him backward into the sanctuary.

"Deorwen!"

In the dark, Durand struck some immense and hidden timber. The animals struck from every side, filling the dark with teeth and flashing pain while the sky gaped open above the sanctuary—the ruin.

Then the timber at Durand's back gave way.

In a heartbeat, a tower's weight of rafters, trusses, and beams plunged down on Durand's neck, battering him and the first curs senseless. He thought of Deorwen. Then, with a lethal flicker through the dark, a great solid shape plunged after the debris. Its impact—hard on one edge and a breath from Durand's fingers—rang a fierce pure note shuddering through Durand's skull.

The sound—the clang of a stout bronze bell—shot through the pack, knocking the devils sprawling, hoisting the things from their feet, and blasting their whispers into the high darkness.

Durand staggered, pitching over the broken timbers to roll in clenched rigidity. He wanted to find Deorwen, but he couldn't even say her name.

Someone crouched over him. "Breathe, Durand!"

He felt the warmth of her as her boy's cloak opened around them. Around the room, he saw that every icon had been toppled. A few white shapes stood headless.

"Oh, God. Try to breathe," said Deorwen. "Where is that flask of Hagon's?"

Durand tried to get his hands down underneath him—to fish for his blade.

But even as Deorwen's fingers darted over him for the leather bottle, Pale was already shrieking outside. The whisper of the devil dogs was pressing in once more.

"Radomor's men have defiled the shrine," said Deorwen. "I wonder if there's still a shrine standing in Yrlac. These will be the Wards of the Patriarchs, picked to thread." All to clear the way for the Rooks' midnight labors. "Durand, you must give me your sword."

Durand bared a few broken teeth in misery.

There was a clatter at the door. Black Pale stumbled in while the pack churned in deep circles around the yard, edging nearer and nearer as its courage built.

Now, the mad words of the whispered chorus were plain. *"Beyond the empty Hall of Heaven, Heaven's Queen rankled at the silence, her king gone to his Creation while she stayed behind. Nearly she relented, but one of her own people stole upon her from the outer darkness: the Hag, hungering now with the small souls, vanished away. 'Where have they gone, cousin?' simpered the Hag."*

"The *Book of Moons*," croaked Durand, astonished. It was a story from the beginning of the world: the Queen of Heaven betraying her King. It was hardly spoken of.

"In the mouth of dogs," said Deorwen.

One great mastiff stepped over the threshold, pausing to

leer up at the ruined walls. Its stink cut the air. Another dog slunk into the sanctuary, and another. They moved with the misjointed hitch of puppets.

" 'Where have they gone, cousin: the bright souls, the small ones?' " came the shivering whispers. " 'So dim is the darkness without them. So alone are we now. I would see them once more. Where have they gone?' " This was the Hag's part as she wheedled the secret of Creation from Heaven's lonely Queen as she pined for the Creator King who had gone to dwell in his Creation.

Deorwen plucked a rough cudgel of charred timber from the floor, squaring with the worst of the brutes. There was no way they could fight the things off—not with Durand on his back, not with so many.

His eyes found the bell and a few new words from the *Book of Moons* cast around its waist: . . . *come hale the new day.* He fought to force his thoughts in order.

The leering brutes poured their flat whispers rattling into his skull. Greenish light flickered in their eyes. " '*This dream of his. This Creation. It is a plaything that has taken him from us, your King, your Consort.*' " This was the Hag wheedling favors from the Queen of Heaven. " '*He has gone off with the small ones and left us to the darkness. Where have they gone, pray tell me, O Queen?*' " The Hag was hunting souls. She was bringing death and the Creator's treacherous Son of Morning to Creation.

"*And the Queen of Heaven knew jealousy. In that moment, she turned to the Hag, the Devourer, and revealed Creation.*

" '*And this is where he has taken them? Well, it will warm my heart to see them once more,*' said the Hag, and she smiled.*"

He would not let the dogs have them. To start, Durand plucked his old belt dagger free and—just as the devils made to leap—rang the pommel off the bronze letters.

The dogs flinched from the brazen note. And, although the creatures had moved only a few steps, Durand took hold of this slim chance. Devils didn't like sanctuary bells. Despite the wreckage of his ribs and shoulder, he surged onto his feet. Deorwen wouldn't die here with him on his back. Blinking back the flashes in his eyes, he wrenched the old bell right off the floor while one big cur leered up at him. Durand heaved the great bell straight into the pack.

By the time the bell had clanged and clattered through its wild carillon of bounding notes, the fiends had all lurched from the yard.

IN THAT DARK place, they clung to each other. Durand found space where he could crush the dark from his skull, pulling and tearing at Deorwen's tunic and leggings, pressing her to the floor of that ruined shrine.

He did not want to let her go. He did not want Creation to move another moment forward.

FAR TOO SOON, the whispers returned, and the two fled into the night, Pale dragging the bell from a bit of rope lashed to his saddle. The scrape of stones and the bounce of the clapper seemed to make enough sacred racket to keep the dogs off, though the fiends were forever on the move. Only Deorwen's murmurs kept Durand alive.

Somewhere in the black of night, he felt the chill of the River Rushes boil up in the darkness before them. He heard Deorwen trying to work out some way to keep the bell ringing with both of them asleep, but there was nothing to do but press on.

"We will come through this. We will smile at the thought of it. And when we reach the other side we will be together. Moryn too," she said.

"Doubtless," said Durand.

Down the Valley of the Rushes they dragged their bell through night and day until the holy scrawl round its waist was ground to smudges and the devil dogs were sniffing close. Where the valley wall shouldered them nearer the river, they saw the great town of Penseval spread on the far bank.

Durand focused his whole being on hanging on. When he wavered, the saddlebow creaked under his fingernails. If he fell, they were dead.

Deorwen murmured at his ear. "There is a famous well in Penseval: the Well of the Spring Maid. And ten sanctuaries. My father took us before she was ill. The baron's castle was red as a cockerel's blood. They say the city has seen two thousand winters." Before Durand's eyes, its towers lay in heaps. Pale plodded past a bridge to the great ruin that stood in the Rushes like a row of broken teeth. And Durand began to think he should climb down. The horse couldn't go much farther—he might walk farther with just one rider.

"Don't think of it," said Deorwen.

Somehow she had read his mind. "You're twitching like a sleeping dog. If you drop, I will not go another step."

Overhead, the clouds had dimmed from pewter to old lead—and darker. The dogs' whispers gabbled faintly under the scrape of the worn bell, and their lurching shapes were back on the move among the thornbushes and tall grasses along the river.

"You are a contrary little thing," Durand said.

For the first time in hours, Durand turned and looked into Deorwen's face. Even pale as ice, she dazzled his eyes.

She raised a hand to wipe something from his face.

"We are well matched," she answered.

And the whisper of the dog asserted itself. The things were now so near that Durand was sure they were playing games, filling the dark to watch the slow flight of their certain prey.

"A person could grow tired of hearing these verses," said Deorwen into the growing darkness, her voice hollow. "I'm surprised that the Queen of Heaven lets these devils ramble on. She cannot like to hear the old story told. Repeating the slip that looses the Hag on Creation. She must be livid. Incandescent. Though perhaps she suffers willingly. The shame of that old betrayal."

"Perhaps she's hard of hearing?" Durand said.

Deorwen laughed—just a puff of air at Durand's ear. "It might explain a thing or two. The King of Heaven, silent. And His dear Queen, deaf. What can we expect of our prayers?"

Durand did not answer. They were rounding a gloomy shoulder of land that pushed them nearer the current.

"Soon enough, poor Pale will falter and the bell will go silent," she said. "These fiends will keep up their whispers. Perhaps I will lead us into the river—we will float away like the lady of the Maidensbier." Drowning as sure as they were

)orn. "Past Ferangore to the sea. I do not regret leaving Ac-
:onel.

"My father's hall is on the sea," she whispered.

Durand's eyes stung. "Deorwen, I would give the world to
see you away from—"

Pale took another dragging step. Beyond the near shoulder of land, a valley opened: narrow, steep, and towering
fifty fathoms above the river road.

Three thousand wide-eyed soldiers glared down the blades
of glinting spears and swords and axes. Some crowded the
road. Hundreds more watched from the terraced walls. Durand
saw stone tombs high among the ranks and campfires, step after step of a high necropolis like some giant's amphitheater.

The nearest men seemed frozen: fifty or sixty soldiers
with their eyes wide and their fists creaking tight on their
crossbows.

Durand pried his crabbed hands from the saddlebow and
raised them for the mob, knowing how easy it was to knock
a crossbow's bolt through a man. And soon he heard hoofbeats. A horse pelted down the terraces, flashing through
alternating gloom and firelight until its cloaked rider could
bull his way through the lines. At the last, Durand spotted
Coensar's blazon of white terns on blue. The man's charger
was dancing.

"Sir Coensar," Durand croaked. It was like a dream. Impossible.

He mashed a stray tear from his eye, trying to remember
his errand. He had found the army. Deorwen was safe. He
blinked hard.

"I must speak with Lamoric."

Coensar, new Champion of Gireth, stared down—the gleam
of his eyes unreadable in the gloom. Beyond him, the fist and
fingers of the Eye of Heaven sign spread among the multitude encamped in the valley necropolis. They knew Durand's
voice—and likely remembered how they'd left him: broken in
the Painted Hall.

"Sir Durand," said Coensar. "You'd best come on."

EVEN COENSAR WAS silent as he led them up between the
ranked tombs. And, though there were three thousand soldiers

upon the steps of that terraced valley, Durand could hear the crackle of every campfire. Living faces stared from between the monuments as gray and still as the dead.

"Oh, no, no," breathed Deorwen from her hood. Durand saw men flinch from his glance as he fought to stay in the saddle. In their eyes he saw himself scarred, hunched, shaved, and blacker than cinders: a specter from Radomor's burnt wastes. But Durand had ridden uncounted leagues through dark and death and devils; he could not give himself time for vanity. He gripped the saddlebow, fixing his will on staying upright long enough to speak his piece to Lamoric.

As Coensar led them through a shadowy switchback corner, Durand felt Deorwen's whisper at his neck. "Do what you must, Durand. But I will not see Lamoric. Not now. I must find my brother." She hopped away, unintroduced in her boy's hood and surcoat. With a pointed look, she disappeared between two white tombs.

Durand nearly fell from the saddle.

Before Durand could curse or rein in, Coensar was speaking. "We are here."

Pale clopped out upon a gloomy terrace, and Durand faced a cadre of Ash Knights, for all the world like a ring of mortuary statues in their silvery mail and ashen surcoats. Beyond the wary circle, Durand made out Lamoric's pavilion slung like a market stall between the two mightiest mausoleums, and he swung himself down. The barons of Gireth shoved their way out of the pavilion, some with blades bare. One by one, they stared up in various shapes of horror. Durand tried to smear some of the soot from his sodden coat, but the hands he raised were black as a bear's paws.

As he glanced back, Lamoric followed his horrified barons, saying only, "Lord of Dooms . . ."

"Lordship." Durand settled onto one knee, grimacing at the waves of fatigue that threatened to toss him on his face.

"How have you done this?" said Lamoric. "How have you come to this place? I'd half took you for some messenger from the Otherworld. God." He stepped closer. Saffron circled the young man's eyes.

Durand teetered on his knee. "Lordship. Take the host out of Yrlac. You must—"

Lamoric raised a hand. "Sir Coensar, what's this man doing here?"

"Who could stop him?" Coensar murmured.

"It is a trap, Lordship." Durand mashed his eyes tight a moment. "The Rooks. Radomor. They have tried to kill you." The ride across the market cobbles flashed before Durand's mind's eye. "They are not finished."

Durand noted Berchard looking on with some bafflement, his eye still bristling with stitches. Badan glowered at the man's side, his thumbs were hooked in a chained flail he'd knotted in his belt. As waves of exhaustion beat at Durand, his eye fixed on the chain. Every knob and corner. A thing like it had smashed his face and thrown him down. He could feel each link in the bones of his face: lock and key. Was Badan Radomor's man? Durand could think of no more likely traitor.

He pressed on. "And the army. The host. This march is what Radomor wants."

"Sir Durand!" said Lamoric.

"We must pull the army back. They're laughing. Licking their—"

Lamoric snapped his hand up. A wind battered the hundreds of campfires against their coals, and Lord Lamoric clawed his hair from his face.

"Sir Durand, we cannot carry you. The land is laid waste. The men are shaken. Already, our horses are failing. And there are these dogs at our bloody heels." His eyes glittered as red as his surcoat in the firelight.

"It's death to carry on." He heard his voice echo from the tombs and down toward the river.

"Hells, man."

"We've put our head on the block."

"Durand!" Lamoric caught Durand by the surcoat. "Shut up. Conran's got us camped with the dead. Radomor's got the dukedom in cinders. And we've lost every man who's ducked behind a bush to yank his breeches down."

"Lordship—"

"Here you are, black as cinders, riding hunched over your saddle on a great black horse straight from the edge of your own grave. You're bloody lucky we didn't cut your throat or sick the Septarim on you. How in the Hells did you manage to break through the cursed dogs?"

Durand found he couldn't keep his balance.

In a wincing swoon, he fell from Lamoric's fist.

Face in the turf, Durand tried a crack-toothed grin. "A bell," he said. "Took a toll on the dogs."

He felt hands on his shoulders. "Get up, man."

He struggled, but he couldn't clear his head.

"Durand?" Lamoric demanded. Then he was shouting elsewhere. "Get this fool into the tent. They've burying grounds enough round Acconel. He could have saved himself a journey."

And then his tone caught a wilder edge, "Durand? Get Guthred! Where's Conran? Someone get Guthred!"

Durand let them find him a place to close his eyes.

DURAND WOKE IN a strange tent. The straw was damp. He heard voices outside. The nearest was old Guthred's.

"Don't doubt there's a dark hand back of all this. It don't take no lord to think it through, neither. Does it start with our Radomor? Five years back, someone slays the old king a-hunting in Prince Eodan's woods up there. But it's Ragnal that takes his father's throne, of course. Being eldest. But who'll trust either son after that? And then Ragnal can't keep a penny in his pouch. And there's war in the marches. And Ragnal hazards his crown for a mad loan, and then these hostages. And Radomor? He rides in the van of the king's host, but gets himself struck down. And these damned Rooks find him just as he falls and they start with their whispering just as his wife betrays him. Now, Eodan's pulling his Windhover from Errest and King Ragnal's marching to put him down. And the sanctuaries are falling, one after another. The Banished go abroad. And more and more sanctuaries fall, pulling the wards of them old Patriarchs with them. So there's no ties between king and land and the lands coming apart. That's what you'd do if you could stand to lie your three days under stone. If you wasn't fit to rule. If you didn't have a drop of royal blood. Ain't it? Now, get to work. I'll see if our sleeping prince is ready to take the air."

And Guthred poked his heavy nose in from a dawn both vague and wary with mist.

"Lads got to roll up this here tent," grunted Guthred. "Most of the army's down the road. You're with me in the baggage. We've got a cart for—"

Durand lurched to life, surging past the old shield-bearer only to find the army vanishing all around him: the valley was a cauldron of mist with tombs bobbing like fat in a stew. Backs and horse's backsides disappeared into the clouds. Already, the vanguard would be at the riverbank far below. There were only carts and carters left behind, maybe a man or two to ride rearguard. There was a cart waiting for him and Lamoric's damned tent. Turning in place, Durand cried aloud for a horse.

"You ain't gonna catch 'em!" called Guthred.

But Durand spotted a liver palfrey, neat and nimble. "I'll catch them, and I'll turn 'em back!" Durand snarled. And snatching the palfrey from its groom's hands, he plunged down the tomb valley and into the mist.

DURAND GOT NOWHERE. The track was narrow. With three thousand men, hundreds of horses, and scores of mules and oxen all wallowing down one riverbank track, Durand could not reach Lamoric. The slope climbing above the river was too steep to pass: all steep banks and rubble. An hour after beginning his chase, Durand was still trapped a bowshot from his master—and from any hope of turning the host back to Acconel.

Every step of the palfrey had him wincing. He rode, curled up like a fist around his bad ribs, and resolved to catch Lamoric the first time the army halted: food or water, he'd bolt up the column and get hold of the man. And the plan gave him a chance to breathe.

He would turn the army back. King Ragnal would summon his host against the upstart in Yrlac. And with the Kingdom safe, he might find a way to untie the knots in his heart. He would confess it all to Lamoric, and lay himself at the man's feet. He would run for the world's ending. She would call him mad. Whatever might happen, everything depended on getting them out of Yrlac.

He risked a painful twist to search for Deorwen—she would be somewhere among the staring masses marching east. But as Durand had wrestled his way forward, he had not caught sight of her blue cloak. He tried to remember the dreams that had led her east. Wherever she rode, she was safer with the host than she was alone with him on horseback. The dogs still ranged the valley. Men jumped at every noise, and even the outriders clung to the column.

This last fact had Durand scowling. With the scouts drawn back, the host was like a blind man groping with a stick: the whole army could see no farther than the tallest man; at any bend in the river, there could be ten thousand swords.

If Radomor chose to block the valley in a narrow pass, fifty men could bottle up a thousand. If he dropped on their backs as they crowded between the river and the valley wall, he'd cut them to pieces.

Again, Durand twisted in the saddle. All of this was just what Radomor would want: the host caught blind in a valley as narrow as a horse trough. It was more trap than an able commander would need. He scoured the ridgeline above them. A battalion could fall on their necks at any moment; they were blind and strung out for half a league. This was how Radomor would take them.

He would not wait for a convenient halt. Durand looked up and down the column: three thousand men strung in the narrowest chain. It could happen any moment, and every doom he could imagine would collapse on him.

With a pang of desperation, Durand spurred the palfrey straight into the mob ahead of him. He barged between the knees and hindquarters of ten ranks of cavalry—and got nowhere.

Frantic, he craned his neck—and spotted a way. He could see stones out beyond the riverbank. With a fierce grin, he spurred the little palfrey from the mashed track and straight into the shallow Rushes.

All along the army he rode, spray flying and hidden pits catching at the horse's legs. But, by luck and force of will, he brought the palfrey splashing to Lamoric's side.

Lamoric raised an arm against the spray. "Lord of Dooms! You might have killed that poor devil."

"*This* is Radomor's trap, Lordship," Durand panted. No one could stop, so the palfrey was still diving and splashing.

"Where's Guthred?" Lamoric glanced back down the long line of nodding men and beasts. "I thought we had a cart to haul you."

"Lordship, the army's going mad back there. These valley walls closing us in. Without our scouts and pickets riding, Duke Radomor can drop on us whenever he likes."

"Durand, I'll have you sent back in irons, dogs or no dogs. Bring the damned horse up here. You'll kill it."

Durand vaulted the bank, jostling in among Lamoric and his officers.

"I've tried to warn you. The Rooks. They came to me in the Painted Hall," said Durand.

"With your head full of poppy and morel and God knows, you're so sure, Durand?"

"Then forget the Rooks, Lordship, and only look at what's before you. We stand in the track the duke has made. That Champion was a goad to start us moving." He blinked hard. "Now, he has us blinded! Our necks stretched. How long till—"

Lamoric's barons hissed like snakes. Swanskin spluttered, "By Heaven, who is this man?"

They had an audience: knights in the next ranks were looking on—knights who likely had all the dread they needed with the dogs and the gibbets and the burnt acres all around them. But Durand had not ridden alone into Yrlac just to ease his countrymen into Radomor's trap.

"How long till the Rooks, the Champion, and Radomor's host come tearing down the valley? We'll be slaughtered, and the way to Gireth will be open behind us."

Sallow Hythe raised his bearded chin. "The traitor has missed his guess before."

Big Honefells flashed a row of white teeth. "We set off damned quick!"

"Indeed," said the Baron of Sallow Hythe. "We may yet find his snares half-strung, his pits half-dug. His men amazed."

Honefells waved one broad hand. "If he's set a trap to catch an army, we'll bring him a bloody thunderbolt. Eh, Sir Durand?"

Lamoric raised his hand, wanting no thin good humor. "The sooner we can force Duke Radomor to battle, the better."

"Lordship. This is just what the devils hope we'll believe. While your barons argue that Radomor's devices cannot be ready for us, the devil's already tied a blindfold on your host and burnt a dukedom." They had to turn back.

Lamoric glanced to Coensar and his officers, Sallow Hythe among them. Honefells didn't know where to rest his gaze. "We've discussed reconnaissance in force," said Lamoric.

"Fair enough, but . . ."

"They have not returned," said Lamoric. His officers now wore darker expressions.

"What do you—?"

"They rode, but there's been no sign."

Durand set his broken teeth together. "Hells," he said. "How many?"

"Three fighting conroi. Two score and eight. They rode out an hour ago," confessed Lamoric.

"Lord of Dooms, we are just where the devils want us!" Uphill he could see the top of the rise rippling against the leaden sky. He swung his arm across all of it. "His road, his valley, his plan." Was it too late?

Now, Lamoric paused a moment. "*That* we *could* change." There were glances among the officers.

"Why not take the high ground?" said Lamoric.

Through his mustaches, old Swanskin Down spluttered the obvious objection: "And be seen for five leagues in every direction, plain as day!"

"Aye," said Lamoric. "Seen for leagues, but we're marching up a path Radomor's rolled out for us. Every man here knows it. And these are his creatures we've got ranging around us on every side. By now, the whoreson knows just where we march and precisely our number."

Lamoric stared into Durand's face for several long heartbeats while the company plodded deeper into Radomor's duchy. "I will not turn tail. I will not let Radomor build his strength. Let him do his worst. A man might catch a tiger in his net, but does he know what to do once he's got it?"

"Radomor knows," said Durand.

"Enough! I have said my piece. We knew it would come to fighting. We knew what we faced in Radomor. Not every man will ride home. Now, stop trailing after me like some toy on a string. You will ride in my guard. Take your post by Sir Badan, I think our poor old Berchard's tired of the devil."

Durand managed a grim bow. If Lamoric meant to go on, Durand must follow. He could not abandon Deorwen. He could not abandon Lamoric. He must urge his countrymen back to safety or share their doom.

THEY CLIMBED, RIDING the broad spine of Radomor's dukedom, farther from escape and with Deorwen in tow. Dogs took three more men as bowels and modesty drove them from the line. The ride over the bare back of the high ground was rougher, but the men could breathe a little more deeply with the black walls drawn back and a few leagues of open country around. Honefells got some of his liegemen singing, but, despite the army's longer views, there wasn't an unclenched jaw in the armed line that teetered along the valley top.

Radomor would have foreseen all this: an army willing to march blind would have been too much to hope for. But Durand had no doubt that Radomor would have taken advantage of the chance if they'd given him much longer.

"Hey!"

Durand twisted—too fast for his aching ribs—and found Badan sneering at him. The man hauled his mail hood down in a rusty gesture that left his forehead bulging, bald as a dead man's backside. "*Much* better," he spat. "Your idea, this riding on the ridge." Their horses lurched up some farmer's berm. "The boys loved the climb, I'm sure. They all needed a good stiff scramble after the rain and the soot and the mud. And there's no road to worry about up here. Just lovely peasant berms and ditches. It's a wonder."

But Durand was looking at the old chain flail knotted round the whoreson's middle, and feeling the knobbed aches in his skull and bones as a man might finger a sharp knife's edge. "You carry a chained flail," he said.

Badan winced. "What of it, mooncalf?"

"You weren't happy in that alley back in Acconel. Were you . . . ?"

"What? That push of yours? Huh. Maybe someone will give you a good shove at the wrong time, eh? Teach *you* a lesson."

"Maybe," said Durand, "they will." Maybe they did. He could almost see the sneering whoreson in front of him, chasing him from the battle at Acconel, old flail rattling like a sack of nails. He could feel every leather strip round the grip of Ouen's sword.

Then there were shouts; somewhere alongside the column one of the devil dogs trotted a gully, orange and streaked as old iron. Durand hauled Ouen's blade from its scabbard, but, before he could spur his palfrey, crossbows were clanking and snapping death from every side.

As the column looked on, bolt after black bolt flickered through the bounding devil. "Hells," said Badan, "they've missed. Must have." And finally, the brute bobbed over the next rise. The barbs of razored iron might have been sticks and pebbles shied by plowmen's children.

Still, Lamoric drove them deeper and deeper into Yrlac.

While the officers spoke of strategy and the lay of the land toward Ferangore, Durand twisted with an agony beyond bones and bruises. They had to turn back. With Lamoric and his commanders all determined to march on, he could do nothing but keep his eyes open, and ride beside Badan at the back of Lamoric's guard.

Riding got no easier. Hagon's bottle was soon dry. Durand's winces merged into a long, drifting time when he might have been on the waves of the Broken Crown. Or tumbling in the cold grip of Silvermere.

He woke when a brittle weight snatched him from gray dreams like a stroke of lightning. Needle claws held him, his muscles twisting, and black wings battered his jaw. Durand could neither flinch nor fall to escape. He had a rook on each shoulder.

One dagger beak poured its long whisper into Durand's skull, *"At long last, the hour draws near when all dooms must be revealed."* The sound skittered round and round.

"King or carrion for our poor duke," said the other. Mag-

gots crawled over the feathers beyond Durand's nose, while his head crawled with the damned whispers. He hoped the duke and his creatures would soon be carrion.

Since Durand had dozed off, the army had become a thing of shadows and soft voices. Whatever the hour, the clouds and drizzle had nearly choked the daylight.

"How long have we waited, brother?"

"I would measure since the first whisper that called us north."

"The dream! Three moons before Radomor's battle upon the Hallow Down."

Durand had choked down enough of the Rooks and their games, but, twisting between pain and the confusion, there was little left to him but fury.

"A bare smile in darkness. Night after night."

"Have we told you, Sir Durand?"

Durand grimaced, snarling, "What are you talking—"

"A smiling man. Waiting. Locked in a stony night."

"We never spoke of it?"

"Swathed in webs. Cloaked in dust. He whispered. We could not quite hear."

As the cursed whispers scrambled round Durand's skull, he caught fleeting images of the two sorcerers, three hundred leagues south. Berchard had told stories of fallen priests, skulking among the tombs and desert places, drawn to murder and rebellion: the Rooks.

"How could we not come nearer?" said one.

"You're mad," snarled Durand. What devil would summon these fiends? Not Radomor. By their own words, they set out for the north when Radomor was still a hero, a married heir riding at the head of the Royal Host.

The gray sky pitched beyond the column of shadowed soldiers. He ached to breathe. In the grip of the damned claws, he could drown in the open air, with a thousand men around him.

"Impulsive, perhaps—and curiosity has long had the most fervent grip on our hearts. But hardly had we reached the northlands when we were greeted by the sounds of battle: the red flight of kites and the black of crows."

"The rightful king lying stricken on the field!"

"Happy doom after happy doom has befallen us."

As they bragged and prattled, the vault of Heaven flashed with the beating of Durand's heart. The sorcerers' grip held him like skewers. His lungs convulsed. "Devils," said Durand.

"And we have been faithful in our curiosity, plucking up each jolly bauble laid in our path. Rightful kings to play with! How could any man doubt such a providence?"

Durand snatched another half breath: "You will pay."

"Ah, Durand. Such surprises await you. You will never guess. Not for us, the life of the dull herd."

"To the Hells with you!" He could hardly prise his teeth apart to say it.

"Please," purred one Rook. *"We were speaking of dreams."*

"Where," said the other, *"is that little dreamer of yours, by the way? Is it possible that Lamoric's lady has been bundled up in the baggage train?"*

"No," said Durand. They had eyes everywhere. What had they seen?

The Rooks laughed. *"We are so happy you have come."*

"Off! Off! Get off him!" Someone was shouting—the voice familiar.

Both birds hopped into the air. And, with a gasp, Durand was free and nearly pitching from his saddle. As his head cleared, he heard the Rooks cackling into the low Heavens. He had to find Deorwen.

"Here, here. Easy, boy. They must've taken him for dead!" declared a rougher voice. And, in a clumsy whisper: *"You can't blame the devils. Look at the state of him."*

"Durand," said the first voice. And now Durand caught hold of the sounds. He saw Deorwen staring back at him from her blue hood. She had been there all along. A fat man in a red cap sat with her on the same pack mule.

". . . That's Sir Durand who fought with Lord Lamoric," Deorwen finished, drawing a veil over her accidental intimacy. Durand caught her eye for an instant under her boyish blue hood.

Durand heard the wooden thump and squeal of cartwheels and the gusty breath of oxen, and he understood that he'd drifted back from the head of the column to fetch up among the baggage. Badan would have watched him doze off and half an army would have passed him, sleeping. He didn't like the thought.

"Bastard. The Rooks," he mumbled. "Gloating."

Red-Cap put a hand to his mouth, trying another ham-fisted whisper. *"You're sure it's him? A fellow'd hardly know the poor devil! And he's nearly killed himself to get out here—I'm just saying—maybe a man's got to know when he's—"*

Just as Durand made ready to knock the cap off the man's head, a strange whisper sizzled to life. The sound came from everywhere and nowhere: familiar verses from the old *Book of Moons*.

At once, Durand flashed Ouen's blade into the gloom, though he saw nothing but carts and packhorses. Tall brown grass swept the horses' bellies.

"Here," spluttered Red-Cap. His face gleamed with sweat or grease. "There's no call for anger, Lordship! The lad! It was the lad! He was just curious. Saw we was passing you, like. And the crows, and—"

—The tall grass boiled, full of dogs.

The horses screamed out.

All around, the dogs tore through the column, leaping and snapping at men and beasts. Scores of the things. Pack upon pack. While Durand clung to his spinning palfrey with spurs and fists, men all around him leapt from carts to save themselves as their animals ran mad with fear.

Durand twisted in his saddle, catching a fistful of ear and bridle to hold Deorwen's mule; the fool beast made to bite him.

All across the eerie darkness, he saw snatches of flying blood—and soldiers staggering into wild-eyed knots, their weapons aimed at the grass. The baggage train was tearing itself to pieces. Carts tumbled at the heels of wild oxen.

As quickly as they'd come, the dogs were flowing off through the tall grass like pike under the skin of a pond. Somewhere, an ox bellowed on and on. Anyone pulled from the cavalcade was dead. The brutes had waited for the first stretch of tall grass.

With a glance that nearly left him flat with relief, Durand

saw that Deorwen had survived—though her companion was missing. He loosed the twisting mule. And shouts nearby summoned his attention.

A few paces away, her red-capped comrade had turned up: he had caught one of the brutes. Durand gave Deorwen a glance, then jumped down into the marveling circle around the body of a ruddy mastiff. The thing lay spitted on the end of an old boar spear in Red-Cap's fists, motionless but for a mass of flies.

This was how close the things had come to Deorwen.

The wind ran over the high grass as the circle of men muttered charms against evil and held their hands in the Eye of Heaven or tight on the hafts of their weapons. The fields were still alive beyond the column, but they had one of the creatures before them.

Deorwen spoke. "Hadn't you better give him some room, Braca?"

"No, here. Look, boy!" Even Durand flinched as red-capped Braca abruptly hoisted the dog from the turf, scattering flies and worse over the onlookers. His old spear could have been a pitchfork.

Durand and the ring of common soldiers gaped: the stiff shape could have been dead a month. Durand felt the faintest trace of the dogs' whisper—as though over leagues of grassland.

Someone rode close; the jingle of tack turned a few heads from the carcass. Lamoric and his officers rode down the flanks from the column's head: Conran, Coensar, Sallow Hythe, and the rest, ready to drive off the dogs or assess the disaster. Now, they found the circle around the dead creature.

As Lamoric dropped from his saddle, the soldiers made way—Lady Deorwen retreating a step faster than the soldier crowd. A bow neatly hid her face. And there, Braca stood alone before the mighty, autumn tufts of stubble on the greasy bladder of his face.

"Lord of Dooms . . ." murmured Lamoric, coming closer. Braca flinched a dyspeptic grin. The red mastiff's limbs stood stiffly. "Now, we'll have a look at the bastard. Here—" He reached to take Braca's spear.

"A moment, Lordship," Coen said. In a smooth gesture, he drove old Keening through hide and gristle and into the turf below. Piercing the thing, again, provoked a nasty reek, but Coensar only muttered and gave the blade a good twist. Durand heard the earth grate under Keening's point, though there was never a twitch from the carcass. The thing's reddish hair fluttered in the wind.

Coensar bent, marveling. He looked to Braca. "You're sure you saw—?"

As Coen's knee touched the turf, the faded whisper in Durand's skull returned with the force of a thunderbolt. In a flash of teeth, the carcass twisted. And only a sudden blow from Durand knocked his captain from the thing's reach.

Staggering, Durand made to sweep his own blade down on the thing, but Conran the Marshal had stepped into the circle.

"Ah!" The giant knight stood over the fiend-dog, with his solitary eye flashing, and the point of his sword through the monster's neck. Now, the thing writhed. Though it might ignore Keening, it could not pretend to sleep with the marshal's blade in its gullet.

"Days now, I have waited for you," Conran rumbled.

Each baron had found his sword, and the blades ringed the marshal as though the men were ready to dance the Turning of the Year.

The dog snarled; Durand's head shuddered with the *Book of Moons*: "*She looked upon the waste her delay had caused. She saw the pain brought by the Hag and Son of Morning: death, hunger, want, jealousy. She looked and her Tears fell upon Creation.*" Its tongue flapped and curled.

But the marshal held the monster. His knuckles bulged as thick as ankle bones. "See what your games have cost you now, vile one! By the King of Heaven! By the Warders' shields. By the Champion's lance! By the Traveler's crooked staff!"

Now, the dog shrieked—a whistle. It kicked and beat the ground. But Conran only leaned on his great blade, pouring out invocations until the very clouds curdled over the heads of the army.

The Heavens changed. Men gaped at the churning cloud.

They tottered in circles as flickers of yellow light slipped through the gray ceiling to fall upon marshal and monster.

For a league or more across the fields, the giant knight's voice rolled. *"Creeping thief!"* he roared. *"You are helpless!"* His free hand shot into the sky. *"Under the glance of Heaven, you are destroyed!"*

At his word, the Eye flashed down upon the ancient knight and crooked dog. Beyond Yrlac it must be noon, for the Eye blazed, kindling Conran's blade. And the rotten creature split. From its hide, a shadow burst into the sky, towering in an instant higher than a stand of oaks over the army.

The men shrank against the earth, among the roots of the stinking cloud, breathing foul air that frayed the soul. But the darkness could not endure the Eye of Heaven. The long blade of the Eye turned through the heart of it, and soon the shadow faded and was gone. Durand peered out across the high ridge, where there was nothing but breeze and empty air between the host and Heaven.

But the clouds were knotting overhead, and Conran slid his blade from the carcass as the gloom returned.

"Hmph. The Tears," the great man muttered.

Lamoric and a hundred others looked into the crags of Conran's face. "I don't—"

"The Tears of Heaven's Queen." The giant took a moment to wipe the length of his blade in a pinch of his cloak. "A man might find it all in the *Book of Moons,* but I will tell it. The King of Heaven wrought Creation, dreamed it, made it turn in the Heavens. Only late did the Queen join her King here in his Creation. As he left, she revealed Creation to the Hag. And she mourned the grief her act and absence wrought among us: the death and fear the Son of Morning and the Hag brought.

"One such creature runs the land for every tear she shed when, finally, she joined us here—and understood what she had done." He brushed a spatter from the hanging sleeves of his mantle.

"It's the story the devils whisper," said Durand.

The man raised one snarled eyebrow, fixing Durand with a glance. "Aye. Some can hear a few words. Sour old devils they are, traveling like foul breath on the wind. Feeble things."

Now, Lamoric gaped. *"Feeble?"* he said.

"They would not allow my brothers close enough to know them. Wary, slinking things they are and loath to act. What power is in them, they have stolen—a drop of the divine for each—and they fear to lose it. A glance from Heaven's Eye is more than they can bear. Without such borrowed carcasses as these, they could not act upon Creation at all.

"I've not heard of their being met in such numbers before this day. Not in Errest the Old. Not in the Atthias at all." The man squinted westward toward the heart of Radomor's dukedom. "Our rebel's black-cloaked friends will have bound or bribed them to this little rebellion of theirs."

Durand was not alone in feeling a shiver at this.

Conran looked round him, the glass-pale eye glittering in his stony face as he noted the wary ring of blades around him and the empty carcass. He smiled. "It will not bite. Not now."

Lamoric raised his hands. "Put up those swords, gentlemen," he breathed. "We will trust the marshal, I think."

Old Swanskin scowled, slipping his sword back into its scabbard. "Who are you?"

"Brother Conran, Baron."

"But what are you? You Septarim. Why've you come?" the baron pressed.

"Some force is picking at the Wards of the Ancient Patriarchs, freeing every devil to walk the land." The giant cocked an eyebrow. "You would rather we left, Baron?"

Swanskin snorted, though from him it seemed a note of reconciliation. "Lord of Dooms. I won't count the teeth in a gift horse's jaw." He looked back over the column. "Aye. I'm more worried by the pack train. There'll be more tears shed when the men mark how little bacon these dogs have left us. They're none of them blind."

Broken carts and torn oxen were scattered for a bowshot in every direction.

"The choice was men or meat, Baron. My brothers cannot be everywhere."

Lamoric peered over the carnage. "I am content with the marshal's choice."

Durand scrubbed his aching shoulder and wondered why

Radomor would bother with the pack train. The sleeping dog might have beheaded Lamoric's army, but the baggage meant only that the army would be hungry if it managed to survive another week or so. Whatever Radomor planned, the dogs and gibbets and charred fields chilled the marrow of every man. Was it fear alone that Radomor intended? While he might believe it of the Rooks, he knew that Radomor was too pragmatic to bother with such petty victories. What was he planning?

Durand found Deorwen's brown eyes in the uneasy crowd and wished more than anything that she had stayed with the wise women in Acconel.

HOW MANY AND how far? These were the questions on Durand's mind as he rode the ridge through soaking drizzle. Radomor's army was still abroad. Durand had found Pale among the bags, and felt strong again with the thickset black bounding along under him. They had slain one dog, and Radomor's army was out there in the rain somewhere: the teeth of the trap.

It was an hour later that the vanguard of Lamoric's watchful army rode into an area of churned earth. And Durand was out of the saddle before Coensar called a halt. They'd stumbled into a broad, bowl-shaped basin above the Rushes. Durand stalked out among great, matted swathes of grass and thistle. Berchard and a few of the others from Lamoric's group were ordered to follow while Marshal Conran sent a ring of his pale knights to take up positions facing the fields and valley.

Each flattened rectangle conjured battalions in Durand's mind's eye, sellswords and renegades all hunkered low on the ridge. Durand turned to the valley side only to find a sheltered slope rolling straight down to the river track, perfect for a sudden downhill charge. This was where Radomor's host had slipped close, sharpening its blades in wait for Lamoric's slender column to snake below. The thought touched him like cold fingers. He could taste their sweat in the air. This was the spot where Radomor would have destroyed Gireth. But a shift in Lamoric's tactics had dislodged Radomor's army, and now they were on the move again somewhere beyond the veils of rain—not quite omnipotent, it seemed.

Berchard grunted.

"Could have been a city camped here," Durand murmured; he could see signs that a great many tents had been pitched in the basin. There were fire pits. "Hard to guess how many." But a good count would be the closest he had come to clapping eyes on the enemy. They were not infinite.

Badan picked across the place, a sour look on his face. "Keep your eye out for dogs, mooncalf. While you're sniffing."

Berchard laughed. "Fear not, brave Badan. We've got our Holy Ghosts to watch over us."

Durand glanced at the backs of the still knights as he limped over the rumpled ground. "Holy Ghosts." Old Sir Agryn from back in the Red Knight days had nearly joined their number—except that a woman had drawn him away. Durand wondered what they could really do. And what the Rooks had planned for them.

Berchard's beard split in a wide smile. "Servants of the king since the High Kingdom they are—and the bravest of knights to a man." He glanced at their pale and silent circle, then pitched his voice for only his comrades to hear. "I drank with a charcoal burner from near the Knights' House at Loegern one rainy night. We sat in his moldy hut while the old oaks dripped, he told a story about climbing the great curl of a beech limb near the Loegern walls—as a boy, you understand. And seeing a squadron of these Holy Ghosts stretched out on long slabs, pale and dead in every stitch of their war gear. And, being a boy, he couldn't resist slipping down among them. So, there he was, stealing along the white aisles of them, prodding cold flesh and fondling buckle-brass and iron ring, says he, when a great blade of ruddy light swung into the place: the old Eye of Heaven had sunk low enough to slide through the west windows, and the dead lads were up. *Rising from their slabs!*"

"Berchard . . ." said Durand.

Berchard was making a vow, hand raised. "It's the truth as I was told it. The man was called Kausi. We shared his hut and my wine. Up on the Red Winding." He peered at the ring of pale knights. "When the knights started up, our little Kausi Charcoal legged it."

"I wonder what the Rooks have fixed for them."

Durand had already limped by tent sites enough for a thousand men. He peered through the murk, guessing that there were as many more matted patches ahead. That was one question answered: Radomor was outnumbered by a thousand men. Now, Durand wondered where they had gone.

"Well, I've heard some tales about these Ghosts that would—Uh. Yes."

Berchard stopped, straightening suddenly. "And I suppose these campfires will tell us when the devils left camp. Maybe."

Durand glanced up at this sudden change of direction to find that Lamoric's officers had joined the examination while the halted column looked on—the stony Marshal Conran among them.

"Aye," said Durand. He stooped painfully by the nearest fire pit, sliding his hand deep into the wet ash and feeling heat tingle in his finger bones. "This morning. They're still near." He pictured the hideous Champion and could almost feel the Rooks prowling in the shadows of the tents. They would be somewhere within a few leagues.

When he looked up, he found Lamoric staring down. Conran and Coensar stood at his side.

"Is this what's left of Radomor's trap?" Lamoric asked. He looked hard in Durand's eye. "I think it is. I think he had his dogs. He had his lovely ambush just as you said. But, Durand, we have slipped both."

Durand climbed to his feet, not sure what to believe. "Perhaps, Lordship."

The young lord turned from his commanders to gaze down the neat slope that ran to the dark curl of the Rushes. "I wonder what the battle would have been called. Radomor has left no fields to name it by."

Durand opened his mouth, but it was Conran who answered. "By my reckoning, they will name it Ferangore." His glinting eye did not bother with the valley or the trap. He fixed his gaze on the western horizon.

"Hells," said Durand. He had seen and done dark things in Ferangore, but one man's private dread was nothing compared to what an army would face. A half day west, Ferangore stood behind high earthworks, ranked walls, and a moat of rivers that would hold them for seven moons.

"If Radomor shuts his gates against us," said Coensar, "we'll be hard-pressed to open them without engines or supplies." It was time to go. They would turn back.

"No," said Lamoric. A light seemed to dawn in his features even as Durand peered up from the mud and rain. "I read a different doom in these signs. *Here* we have Radomor's trap, abandoned. He meant to catch us here—pinning our column against the Rushes, charging from the heights and raining missiles down—but he's left it behind and flown for his walls. Radomor doesn't like the look of us—not without his tricks and traps." He flashed his teeth. "I say Radomor's lost his appetite."

Durand became conscious of the great cavalcade of men, splattered and exhausted, but gathered like a tournament crowd, every one of three thousand watching. Radomor's camp was Lamoric's stage.

"We will feed our Radomor what he's so hungry to escape. These fires were burning this morning. If we set out now, we will catch him before he makes the walls of Ferangore."

Durand saw hard grins spread among the multitude of splattered soldiers. And Lamoric stood taller, spreading his arms. "Men of Gireth, we have flushed Duke Radomor from his hiding place and now we will ride him down! His rebellion ends today!"

With force enough to wobble Durand and Berchard where they stood, three thousand soldiers roared.

Durand scanned the vague region where the rain obscured the more distant hills, and wondered if Radomor could hear them. Part of him hoped the whoreson could.

FROM THAT SPECIAL misery of riding with half-broken bones, Durand watched the gloom twist thicker around the column as they lurched deeper into Radomor's ruin. Carrion birds tumbled through the rainy dark, and the dogs played at the limits of vision. But, all along the men flashed wolf's grins, for they stumbled over wrecked carts and helmets left in the clay by their enemy. Could he truly be on the run? It seemed so.

Though the signs were fresher with each hour, every man knew they had little time left. Somewhere in the rain, the ramparts of Ferangore were perilously near.

From the back of his high-stepping gray, Lamoric spat curses into the rain. "Where are the devils? We must overtake them before they reach Ferangore."

"We'll *smell* the city in a heartbeat," muttered Coensar. "We'll come up against the army or the walls soon enough. It can't be long." As Durand looked on, the man pulled his hood over his face.

"Hells," said Lamoric. But there was nothing the man could do. Ox carts and footmen could go no faster. "They'll have bolted every door in Ferangore, and we'll be caught under his walls, half-provisioned with our backs to a wasteland. It is no good."

Lamoric turned to Marshal Conran. "And surely," he said, "it is plain folly for Radomor to seek the throne after all of this."

"Lordship?" said Conran, his bristling brows climbing.

"Should he best us here. Should he rally all the dukes to his cause. Should he ride through Eldinor to the sanctuary itself. All of these shoulds. How can he face the rite? His lands are steeped in the blood of the blameless. He has turned these necromancers loose upon the land. How can he lie his three days under stone and join the kings of Errest the Old?"

"Some men do not know their own hearts, Lordship," rumbled Conran. "But there exists another possibility: the wards are breaking. One after another, they fall. A moment may yet come when a devil can take the throne. But I fear that it is a game that risks the prize. For the realm may not endure defenseless. It was no whim that pushed the Ancient Patriarchs to set their wards upon Errest the Old."

"I had half thought of letting the fool have his coronation," said Lamoric. "Now, I see we'd best not risk it."

"When my brothers and I rode to Silvermere, the denizens of the byways prattled of the Banished. Pale figures moved beyond the borders of the Still Kingdom. Riders from the mists of Hesperand. Green hags teeming in the millponds. A worm in Heronleas. A giant of the Halls of Silence prophesying the doom of men in the tongue of priests."

"Hells," said Lamoric.

After flinching at Conran's mention of Hesperand, Durand searched the gloom for the devices of the enemy. He peered into the torn clay of their enemy's path, and shot long looks at every hill and ditch they passed in the dark.

With the wrist of one long gauntlet, Sallow Hythe smeared a bit of muck from his brow. "Lordship, if this is a race we *must* lose, we might rest the men. This is a killing pace. There may yet be storehouses beyond this wasted path. If a siege must come, we must prepare."

"Radomor will have burnt everything within leagues of the bloody city," declared Lamoric. But for the sodden wasteland grasses, they'd seen nothing green in Yrlac. "We must catch him before he can reach the city, or we will pay with blood. I will not let cowardice or despair give Radomor a chance to rally!"

"If we must besiege Ferangore," Sallow Hythe reasoned, "the few barrels of bacon we are dragging behind us will do us little good, Lordship."

Lamoric twisted to retaliate, but stopped. Some inspiration dawned in his face. "Then let us be rid of them!" said Lamoric.

The older, wiser men around Lamoric leaned in their saddles for a good look at their lord. The animals tramped up spray.

"What nonsense is this?" spluttered old Swanskin.

Lamoric wiped mud and spray from his face. "If our barrels are too few, then leave them! The dogs can *have* our pack train. We will run the devil down. I say, every man who does not wish to stay with the dogs should march with the army. Every knight will put his palfrey into common hands. And the rest can run!" His grin was fierce. "We will catch him yet!"

Despite Deorwen and the Rooks and all, Durand grinned at this.

WILD-EYED COMMONERS CLUNG to the last palfreys and carthorses as the company spurred itself away from the howls of their own oxen and the Queen's savage Tears swept down on the poor devils.

The host rode in a storm of flying mud. They blinked at it. They felt it in their teeth. And they could see little but blinding mist and clay.

On their left hand, the valley slope dropped away, leaving a steep precipice, and the wild host of Gireth careered along the brink, hooves tearing clods from the cliff's edge to fall from sight into the Rushes.

Durand couldn't breathe for agony. Big Pale bounded by a set of huge crescent gouges in the edge where some beast in Radomor's Host had plunged from the bank only moments before. Just as Durand flashed by, something jarred Durand's hip, and Pale's hooves chopped sickeningly at the brink.

"Just keeping you awake, Moonface!" shouted Badan. The man rode close at Durand's side, his flail jangling from his fist as he barged through.

Nearly, Durand caught hold of the fool.

But then, the whole track plunged from the high ridge and Durand could do nothing more than hold tight while he bowled down into the valley with three thousand others, all on the verge of tumbling. Before them, the Valley of the Rushes opened like a cavern of clear air under the cloud. And, on the broad floor of that valley, struggled a sprawling darkness. This was Radomor's army. Durand saw flags and limp banners bobbing above the mob as it fought to cross a long stone bridge.

"We have them!" shouted Lamoric.

Beyond it, Durand saw green ramparts rising: moments beyond the bridge, the city of Ferangore mounted into the clouds.

"Come on, lads!" howled Lamoric. "They're caught and can't turn! To the bridge!"

The whole of the army set its spurs, surging down the valley wall like all the charges of all the tournaments in the Atthias together. Badan's flail shrilled near Durand's ear, while Durand hauled his own blade into the thundering air.

They could have been a wave falling. As Durand and the first lancers swept down, they leapt the carts and slaughtered mules left to foul their hooves. They crashed down on the bridge, flinging the last rearguard aside. Durand gaped in joy and wonder; Radomor's rebellion would end in moments.

But then, just as Durand and Lamoric and every man he knew exploded onto the bridge, a second thunder roared up far louder than the storm of their hooves.

Pale skidded.

Durand felt great blocks sliding in the bowels of the bridge. While Lamoric and half his barons looked about in horror, columns of water exploded above the bridge all around them.

Durand glimpsed huge stone rollers bounding out over the waves, launched by the sliding weight of the span.

Someone was screaming: "Miners!" The whole bridge had been transformed into one enormous pitfall.

Durand saw Lamoric, Coensar, Berchard—all within an arm's reach and all a moment from a dragging oblivion of water and stone and iron mail. The bridge was collapsing into the Rushes.

Then, impossibly, the stone caught—it held.

While men and beasts gaped, wide-eyed, the thunder rolled out under the low sky. Foam closed over the great blocks that had fallen beneath the span. And the bridge hung naked, swaying like a thing of ropes.

It was impossible.

Radomor's host stood with their cheers caught in their gullets, and both armies held as still as painted figures.

Above the eerie stillness, Durand heard voices—chanting.

Hardly daring to turn his head, he spotted Conran's Holy Ghosts. Each pale knight stood stiff as a forked branch, head back and palms up. Some stood in their stirrups; others swayed in their saddles. The sound of their chanting seemed to twist the air around the bridge into something like thick glass. It boiled with warmth and cedar oil.

In the face of this miracle, no man dared move—until Lamoric shifted. Across the bridge, Durand finally caught sight of their enemy: Radomor of Yrlac sat a tall warhorse, his bald head bare—he'd snatched off helm and mail hood to gaze at the hanging bridge. This was no fool's gaping, but an inward look that Durand could not read.

On the bridge, Lamoric stood a dozen paces from his foe— this man who has slain his sister, his brother, his nephew. And countless friends. With a call to charge, the Host of Gireth could crash down on Radomor's force. They could win.

If the bridge held long enough to let them over.

Coensar caught his lord's arm. "This can't last: any moment, the bridge'll fall as it should have done. Radomor's been waiting. The mad flight, the axemen, it's all been a game. We won't get an army over. If the bridge falls, Radomor has us." With a nervous glance at Holy Ghosts and Heaven, he finished, "Miracles or no, you must turn back."

Lamoric met Radomor's stare. Durand half expected the force of Radomor's attention to stir the air like a storm.

But a man could feel the strain in the Septarim's chanting. And the scent on the shivering air had twisted from cedar and sweetness to something scorched like incense. Debris sifted into the Rushes.

"Lordship," said Coensar. "We retreat or we put our heads on the block. Forward or back. It must be now."

Lamoric closed his eyes. "Give the order," he said. "Back us off."

Radomor watched them go, holding his army like some monstrous huntsman with a pack beyond counting.

With Lamoric's vanguard safe on the far bank, everyone made ready to retreat from Radomor's glare. Just then, Coensar caught Durand by the surcoat for it seemed that the Septarim had not moved. The lot of them were frozen where they had first begun their chanting while the wavering air above the bridge darkened like honey over a fire.

Everyone else was safe when Coensar stepped back on the bridge. "Come on," he said. "Let's get them off!"

Durand slung himself from the saddle—feeling the deck of the old bridge give under his limping steps. But knights from the vanguard and common men all round skittered out, catching hold of bridles to lead the wild-eyed horses of the Holy Ghosts from the crumbling span.

Radomor watched in silence.

And, for a moment, bent Durand was the last on the

leck—but for the marshal himself. Durand tottered out to he man. The scalded air stung his eyes and the stones revolved under his soles, but he took hold of the great man's bridle and led the giant toward the far bank. The strange man's rigid face could have been the axle around which the Eye of Heaven turned, but the bridge dropped away stone by stone as they left it.

When Conran's horse left the bridge, the marshal's head sank with an ox's loose sigh and the last cobbles thundered into the water.

Across the river, Radomor and his two thousand men turned from their foes and resumed their retreat. The ranked earthworks of Ferangore loomed through the fog. A man could just make out the stained dagger of the sanctuary spire above the coiled walls. Just then, Durand could not imagine that men could build such a mountain.

"Now we must prise them out of their shell," Lamoric said. He eyed the feeble glow of the sinking Eye of Heaven. "And we have neither time nor means to do it. . . ."

NIGHT DESCENDED AS Lamoric drove them to a sprawling ford a few hours back up the Rushes. In the coal-sack blackness, the exhausted army blundered through the icy spring flood and its invisible stones, knowing that some splashes meant that men were tumbling off into the black torrent to pass lifeless below the ramparts of Ferangore—or to lie pinned to the bottom by the weight of armor. It was pointless to reach or hope.

The Holy Ghosts seemed to walk under a moonlight that touched them alone, and, in the depths of the night, the watery glow of their backs was the only light bobbing in a black Creation. The bleary soldiers marveled.

The traps were finished now. That much seemed clear to Durand on that blind night of weary agony. Neither army had a trick left worth playing. Lamoric was simply going to throw his force at Radomor's and hope that courage and numbers could break the devil's walls. Radomor would sit grimly in his city, waiting for the men of Gireth to starve.

Somewhere in that great shifting column, invisible between the Holy Ghosts, Deorwen would be riding. He could

not search for the girl. His only hope to find her would be to
call out: to call out for his master's wife hiding in a hostile
land. And he could not. So he set his broken face against
Pale's neck and prayed she had not been among those to fall
in the black Rushes.

27. The Empty Storm

With the return of light, Ferangore appeared from the
gloom like a monstrous thunderhead. The city's ramparts mounted where the River Rushes and Bercelet roared
together as the mighty Branche. And, somewhere beyond the
thickest walls were Radomor, his Rooks, his Champion, and
an unknowable throng of sellswords, liegemen, and rebels
from across the kingdom, sharpening their blades.

Below the lowest rampart, the Host of Gireth stood in long
dark ranks, shivering only a bowshot from the city while
Creation stood as still as a sickroom.

Durand peered up from the back of Lamoric's guard, big
Pale shivering like a drawn bow. The beast was mad. Durand
could make out the needle of Ferangore's black spire high
above them all—while his breath whistled at the iron face
of his helm. Around him, the barons wrangled over the last
plans, but Durand only wondered where Deorwen had gone.

Lamoric was throwing everyone at the city, leaving not a
soul behind. Where could Deorwen go?

Risking a painful twist in his saddle, he searched the ranks
through the slits of his helm. Lamoric's footmen stood at the
front of the formation, dark, drenched, and facing the city
with their knuckles shining white against the spears and axes
in their fists. She could not be among them, surely.

The barons finished their conference and scattered to play
captain to the men of their own lands.

Durand swallowed against the straps of his mail hood and
stared up. Over the dented helmets of the infantry, he could
see the first rampart, steep, gray-green, silent, and topped with
stone battlements.

This would be worse than Acconel. Bloodier for the men

of Gireth. They would be breaking walls, not holding them.
It would be murder.

Deorwen could easily have been swept up. No one was to
be left back.

He prayed that she'd found some spot in the rear—
perhaps behind that red-capped fool with his boar spear:
Braca. A man that size could, at least, stop an arrow or two
for her. She was no fool.

Durand twisted once more—only to find Deorwen peering up at him from the back of a dun pony. Her chin hardly
came to his belt.

"Host Below!" rasped Durand. Lamoric was only a few
paces away.

"There is nowhere to hide," she replied evenly. She
clutched Braca's spear: the thing seemed heavy as a fence
post. Her face was pale.

"You can't be here," said Durand.

"I have had enough cowering. Where will I be safer than
caught up in Lamoric's guard?"

"Have you ever met your husband? Safety has not been
among the man's priorities."

A few horses forward, Coensar twisted for a look at the
source of this chatter.

Durand gave the man a nod.

Coensar only blinked and stuffed the azure helm down
over his head.

"Deorwen, this is more than courage. They'll fill the sky
with arrows. They'll fight like devils for every step. You
think blue wool and linen will turn a blade?"

"I must either be with those men about to storm the wall,
or with the mounted men back here. If it makes no difference where I stand, I'll stand where I choose and not where
I'm driven."

Lamoric rode out before the army on his brother's tall gray,
drawing every commander's eye.

"Don't worry," whispered Deorwen. "I'm not mad. I'm no
tiltyard hero to face an army on my own."

The hours of darkness had allowed battalion-large raiding
parties to scour the countryside for timber and provisions.
Though there had been little enough to find, rough siege

ladders jutted from the ranks of infantry. Breath boiled in the chill.

"I can ride, I've hunted a thousand leagues, slipping branches," she said. "I'll make them work to take me." Durand wondered whether he had time to haul her from the line.

But Lamoric stood in his stirrups, hauling his blade from its scabbard. The entire host leaned toward Ferangore.

"Durand," said Deorwen. He didn't want to argue. He would watch her as best he could. It was madness, but there was no time.

"Durand!" she pressed.

She was looking down; the sopping grass under their feet moved.

Then, with a shriek from the horses, the plain came alive—worms and rats, mice and wood lice. All the vermin of a city spilled down the ramparts of Ferangore, spreading like wine over a bare floor, sliding over the hooves of the horses.

Lamoric fought to control his big gray.

Then, with every man eyeing his boots, a call rose from the heights above them. The blackened spire of the high sanctuary seemed to twitch as the army's glance found it— black to bone gray—and every man realized that the old tower was neither stained nor scorched: it was the roosting place of every carrion bird for a thousand leagues. An infinite maelstrom rose over the city—beyond the flocks at Acconel, beyond anything seen in Errest the Old in all its two thousand winters: a high and rising storm of carrion birds to empty forests beyond counting.

All across the front, Conran's Ash Knights threw their arms wide, braying out prayers that once more filled Creation with a boiling cedar wind. The storm broke over Lamoric's lines, diving in waves like a plowman's scythe.

But flocks split above the army like waves against stone as the Holy Ghosts roared the wrath of Powers.

"Lord of Dooms!" shouted Lamoric. He wrenched his helm from his head, snapping every eye back to the fight. "Enough! It's past time. Let us drive this fiend from his lair!"

With the wind snapping in his mantle, Lamoric stabbed his blade high over the army and—with a headsman's downward slash—unleashed the howl of three thousand voices. Gireth's infantry charged, ladders bobbing like straws on a flood tide. A storm to answer the storm of crows. Durand fought to hold Pale back. The ranks of horsemen all around him clutched at their reins as that tide of foot soldiers rushed out.

Coensar shouted, "Hold!" For heartbeats, the vulnerable army sprinted at an empty rampart.

Then, with the whole rushing throng under the battlements, Radomor's archers stepped into every embrasure over their heads, hundreds strong—snapping lethal arrows down with strong bows of yew and sinew. Soldiers curled around sudden arrowheads, their ladders crashing to the turf.

The men in Lamoric's guard hissed and swore.

Finally, ladders slapped the bank, blackening the green earthwork with swarming men. Arrows flickered up and down. Gaffs threw ladders back. Axes split helms.

Pale danced in Durand's fists.

"Hold!" shouted Coensar.

At the crest of the rampart, knotted duels rose, struggling over the crowd. The two armies seemed ready to lift each other above the city with the force of the struggle.

Finally, the stalemate broke and the foot soldiers of Gireth poured over that lowest rampart into the streets beyond. Horns brayed. And the army of Gireth vanished over the ridge.

Durand looked from side to side. For an instant, the cavalry were alone on the plain. Some men made the Creator's fist and fingers as best they could in the iron bags of their gauntlets. Durand glanced at Deorwen, her eyes shut. Then, with a return of all the cacophony of battle, the lower gate of Ferangore flew wide. Every knight surged forward.

As THEY TORE their way inside, Durand clung to Lamoric's flank, hacking his master's way through the ebbing throng of the enemy, and hoping to tear a broad enough wake for Deorwen to follow, riding sidelong into enemies. But after a few minutes of savagery, the men of Yrlac showed their heels, leaving the street empty.

Durand watched Coensar give chase—and found himself at Lamoric's side in an abandoned street between one rampart and the next. This was all there was: one street, one step on the way up Ferangore. Shops stood on either side.

Pale and Lamoric's big gray nipped and kicked at each other. The street was as noisy as a horse market. And every storefront along the road was crowded with men and beasts taking cover.

"What is this?" Lamoric wondered. Storefronts stood empty, and above their rooftops you could see the top of the next tier and the empty parapets atop it. "Can it be that we've beaten him?"

Durand had been kicked and punched and horse-bitten, with his breath coming in gasps and blood spinning from the tip of his sword. At a glance, he could see a dozen men writhing out their last breaths. Comrades hauled some into shelter.

"Radomor beaten? I would like that," said Durand, and earned a glance from Lamoric. He had to switch Pale around to get Deorwen under cover.

"Right enough," Lamoric began, smiling, "but it's—"

A torrent of black wings dropped from the storm above the rooftops, bullying every man against his horse's neck. Some of the creatures bounced to a landing among the dead and dying, while the rest tumbled and brayed for mad heart-beats over the street and then vaulted back into the storm.

On the heels of the devil birds came the first arrows and stones from above the rooftops. Stones clattered into the street. Almost as soon as this weird rain had begun, a bolt smacked from the brow of Durand's helm.

"They're pulling themselves together. We'll be safer under these shops," Durand said. Riders up and down the street were pulling their horses out of the road; the archers above couldn't see past the roofs right below them. Durand set his spurs and Pale bulled Deorwen and Lamoric's animals under cover of a potter's shop.

"Tie the horses here, Lordship?" Durand squinted past the crowds and up a littered road, fouled with the gory wreckage of the route. "Whatever comes next, there's no room for wild charges." He watched Deorwen hop down beyond the horses. "Radomor should have pulled these things down. A roof makes a better shield than a man could carry on his shoulder."

"It's not like him," Lamoric muttered and slipped from the saddle, watching for Coensar. Durand dropped painfully into the roadway.

A few paces away, a raven peered into a man's eye and rasped, *"Ha!"*

And Deorwen began muttering. "Queen of Heaven," she said, plain as day. "What is this place?"

But Coensar was already charging back through the mobs and wreckage, trailing Sallow Hythe and bluff Honefells. As the pack of them barged under the narrow cover with Durand and the others, Coensar dropped from the saddle. "Lordship, they've fled—a full rout—through the gates and up into the next bloody tier. Swanskin's trying to force the gates."

"We've treed the devils," said Honefells. The stubble on his chin glittered like a dusting of glass in the blood gleaming there.

"I'd never have guessed he'd give us the first rampart so easily," Lamoric said.

"They're marshaling upstairs. They may like their chances better with us bottled up in this—" Coensar gave a sharp glance Deorwen's way. Rather than keeping out of the way, she had begun tottering in small circles—that threatened to take her out under the eyes of Radomor's bowmen.

"What is wrong with the boy?" said Coen.

"Here," said Durand, and he dared a step out of cover to play shepherd. "Under cover." But Deorwen was murmuring, "No, no, no."

"What're you thinking?" he whispered, but as he brought Deorwen in, Durand caught sight of something on the rampart above the street: a hooked black smear between one building and the next.

Lamoric was speaking, "If I could have saved the boys this, I would. It's more than *any*one should see."

Durand picked out black smears both on the wall above them and on the inner face of the rampart they'd already conquered. The outlines of what might have been strange symbols seemed to shift in the shadows between the shops high and low.

Honefells grinned and wiped some blood from his chin. "The lad'll be fine. It's not every day a boy rides against a walled city. And on a pony! When other pages squint through their fingers at the crash of a good tiltyard bout, he's won his first battle. At this rate we'll have Radomor drawn and quartered by noon. Maybe he'll give in—save a few of his men."

"Lordships," said Durand. "What do you make of these markings on the ramparts? I swear, they're nearly moving."

"Friend," said Honefells. "You have a morbid turn of mind. I—"

"No," said Coensar. "What do you see?" The captain—the Champion of Gireth—closed his eyes, then tried to follow the direction of Durand's gaze.

But, just then, the whole city moved: a jolt in the roadbed shook crows from a score of corpses.

Around Durand, blades flashed up. And every man scanned the roadway.

"Those were boots," purred Sallow Hythe. The sound came from beyond the streets. "Men on the march."

"Aye," said Coensar.

"Sounds like bloody battalions," said Honefells.

They could see nothing but sky between the buildings across the road—across the killing ground. But Durand thought the shop's upper floors would make a better vantage point. "Here," said Durand and put his good shoulder through the latched door and led the others up into a dark third-story bedchamber that seemed to look out over the plain.

As each man reached the unglazed windows, he stuck there like a fly in honey. Durand was last, or nearly. Crows and rooks and ravens sailed past. But, between two buildings leaning across the road, he could see down over the city wall. An army swarmed over the wasted acres beyond the battlements. They had come down from the north, fording the Bercelet, as the men of Gireth had forded the Rushes from the south, and now they trooped in to block the only escape from Ferangore. There was no way out.

"It is six to one, at least." Honefells scarcely breathed the words in the stolen bedroom.

"Where have they come from?" Coensar murmured.

Through the screen of burgher's roofs, they saw hundreds of knights in mail—more men than Durand had seen at any tournament—perhaps more than two thousand men in the saddle. Beyond them marched nine thousand foot.

Sallow Hythe set his long fingers on his face, his tone was marveling. "There are not so many men fit to bear arms in all of Yrlac. And no man could hire so many. There is not coin enough in the whole kingdom. Where has he found them?"

Durand stepped into the window, closing his fingers over the raw wood of its mullions.

At the front, the men wore the even green of Yrlac. Toward the rear, however, the battalions lost their uniformity, breaking into the party-colored confusion of any host among the Sons of Atthi.

There were so many.

Then, in the midst of it all, Durand saw a broad banner he recognized: at the head of Radomor's new army floated blue and yellow diamonds. Durand remembered the bewildering pattern—he knew it from fights at Red Winding and High Ashes and Tern Gyre.

"The diamonds . . ." he said.

Faces darkened, squinting. A voice breathed, "Host of Heaven . . ."

Then, Durand heard Deorwen speak. "It's Mornaway," she said. One by one, the men turned to face her, the blue hood of her cloak now down about her shoulders.

"Moryn of Mornaway rides under those colors," said Durand. He remembered the Rooks taunting him about "friends and enemies" back on a boat on the Bay of Eldinor. Here was Deorwen's lost brother, found at last in the worst of places.

Lamoric came adrift from the window and the war. "How have you come here, Deorwen? Now, at this, of all moments?"

"Lord Moryn would not do this," said Sallow Hythe. "He is his father's son." Durand remembered old Duke Severin, Moryn's father. The venerable Duke of Mornaway had lived seventy winters without a broken word, and Moryn would be no different.

"Moryn did not come to the Mount of Eagles," said Durand.

In a dead tone of impossibility, Honefells murmured the only conclusion, "Mornaway has turned against the king."

Deorwen was still. The little room had a sturdy bed. The walls were primrose yellow.

"What are you doing here?" said Lamoric. "I don't understand." He looked at his wife as though he had never seen her before. "We must get you out of this place. We will throw ourselves on Radomor's mercy. He would not kill you with the rest of us."

Deorwen took a step, setting a hand on her husband's face.

And Durand looked away, dizzy.

He saw gray slices of the rampart stone between the shops and houses. He had seen these before, but now, with height and distance, what had seemed like smears became the tall letters of a barbed script that ran in chains behind the buildings, all very easy to see for a man who didn't care much about the army beyond. The brushstrokes circled the whole ring of Ferangore's walls, above and below that seemed uncannily like an audience of taloned shadows circling them round.

Something creaked on the stairs.

As the whole room twitched around, Conran ducked through the low doorway. "They've marked out this city in heart's blood," he rumbled. "Carrion crows snatch at the gasps of the dying. The streets drink our lifeblood. Only now in all the years since the *Cradle* landed. Only with the old wards in tatters could this be done! Radomor has brought the Hells into Errest."

"No," said Lamoric.

"We are upon his altar and the fires are lit, My Lord."

Lamoric looked to Deorwen. She had set her hand upon one bedpost, standing straight but small. There would be no parlay with a man who would turn his city into a shrine of devils. No mercy for any.

Sallow Hythe stepped from the shadows. "Lordship, there remains one avenue of escape." He was neither stroking his narrow beard nor tenting his long fingers, not now.

"What chance do you see?" pressed Lamoric. "What chance has you swallowing and avoiding my eye? Speak its name."

"Your wife. She is Mornaway's daughter." He glanced, for an instant, to Deorwen.

Lamoric's face was chalk, but Sallow Hythe was no coward. He pressed on.

"I am not proud to have conceived the notion; however, it must be said, a bargain might yet be struck. We have his daughter. The old man could refuse us nothing."

Lamoric looked from the baron to his wife. "We would hold her hostage? I would send my herald. Sir Durand, perhaps? He would tell Duke Severin: Free us from this snare, or His Lordship, Lamoric of Gireth, will kill your daughter? My lady wife?"

Sallow Hythe bowed another fraction.

Lamoric stepped closer to the baron, moving closer with each word. "Durand could carry her ear as proof that she was with us. Or we might dangle her from the battlements as Durand made his announcement." He turned from the man. "We are *not* beaten. We have come through Acconel. Before this ends, it will be Radomor who feeds the crows!"

He turned on Sallow Hythe. "And Deorwen is not here. Do you hear? Not with such talk already on your lips. I will kill the man who speaks of her, do you understand? We will roast bloody Radomor on his own bloody altar and be done with the devil once and for all!"

28. The Tiers of Ferangore

Lamoric charged into the street, howling, "To the upper gate! To the upper gate! With our bare hands, we'll take them!" And the army rose from its thousand resting places, charging up the street.

The fiercest men of Gireth surged forward with great axes flashing over their heads—though torrents of scalding water and great stones shuddered down from the battlements. The street seethed, and Lamoric's liegemen staggered for footing

on the flesh and bones of their fallen comrades. The lords of
Gireth roared commands, and storms of Gireth's arrows
lashed the teeth of the upper battlements, rebounding over
the crowd, splintering against stone, or catching in the flesh
of Yrlac's men.

All the while, the Septarim prayed even as arrows struck
them down and the shadowy glyphs writhed upon the walls,
bearing eager witness.

Behind the scrambling men of the vanguard, Durand staggered at Lamoric's side, trying to keep up as pain snatched
his breath away. He carried a great shield he'd stolen from a
dead man and the thing now kept Lord Lamoric safe from
the hail of arrows—Lamoric cared little for his own safety as
he watched the upper gate stand invulnerable while Coensar
ranged about the narrow battlefield throwing men into the
fight like a madman. The street between those upper and
lower ramparts was like a canal. And they threw wave after
wave into the same slaughter.

"You can't break iron bands with axemen, Durand," Lamoric howled in the midst of the maelstrom, his voice loud
under the arrow-studded shield. Radomor's bowmen nailed
helms to living skulls. "I'm a fool. I drove us in here. I rushed
and roared and spurred us every step from Acconel. And I
should have heard you when—"

A feathered creature checked its flight in both men's faces,
the snap of its feathers spraying live flecks in their eyes.
"Devils!" Lamoric spat. He struggled for air, smearing his
face with both hands as birds tumbled in rapture everywhere.
"We're caught, and we're not going to tear free. Mornaway
should be on our backs already. It's all—" Lamoric railed
and the men in the back ranks turned—catching their master's despair.

Before another head could turn, Durand took Lamoric by
the coat and threw him back into the shadow of a blacksmith's
shop. "What does any of that matter now? You reckon Radomor will stop? He'll come whether we fight or lie down, Lordship. *We* cannot stop. *You* cannot."

He had the man by the collar and, for an instant, Lamoric
looked like a green pageboy, gulping at the reeking air.

"Right," he said. "God, let me go." The man shook the clouds from his skull. "So where is Mornaway? Why don't I answer that before I run shrieking through the streets, eh?"

Suddenly, Lamoric was on the move once more, pushing past Durand, nearly shoving his way out of the shelter. "Where's our bloody lookouts? There!"

Across the road, one-eyed Berchard clung, tucked up an alley under a bit of roof where he could look down over the lower battlement. The Rooks' sooty glyphs bent and stretched up the wall like slow black flames reaching for his backside.

"Berchard! Berchard? Are the devils still down there?"

The man twisted a fraction—careful, lest some archer skewer a precious haunch or shoulder. "Aye, they are, Lordship! Great mute ranks. Battalions numbering in the thousands. A good deal of praying."

"Prayer? What Powers would answer them? They refuse every call to parlay. My wife's people! The devils are bent on slaughter. What are they waiting for?" Lamoric demanded.

"Can't say, Lordship. Moryn himself ain't out there; could be they're waiting on him."

Lamoric spat a curse. "And there's the mystery. Where is the man?"

Berchard knuckled his bad eye. "I see the old duke plain enough. Poor man's like a rake the way the armor swings from his bones. But there's no sign of the son."

And Durand began to wonder. The man had never seen the Mount of Eagles. And there were Deorwen's dreams of the man trapped. . . . What had happened to Lord Moryn?

"They're all in the saddle down there, whatever they're up to," said Berchard.

Lamoric smeared palms over his features. "I cannot fathom this: it *can't* be the old Duke of Mornaway. Durand, you know my wife. We've both seen what Moryn's like. Could the man who raised them turn traitor? Could old Severin—"

"Lordship!" Berchard called their attention back to the rampart as a hundred dull-throated trumpets moaned. "This'll be it!" The old campaigner scrambled to curl tighter under his corner of eaves. The trumpets bleated.

"Damn me. I must see!" said Lamoric, and he bolted for Berchard's spot, Durand chasing him with the big shield bouncing over their heads.

In a jostling instant, all three men crammed the sheltered corner to look down on their new enemy. Upon the fallow apron below the walls, old Severin of Mornaway's commanders held their swords high, calling their vast army to a stillness as tight as a bowstring. There were so many; more than Durand had ever seen in one glance. Helmets and blades glinted like waves on a solemn ocean. And Berchard's little hidey-hole was where they would strike first.

Durand glanced up and down the wall. Wherever a rooftop gave shelter from Radomor's archers in the upper city, a paltry knot of Lamoric's archers fitted arrows to their bowstrings, muttering charms. Here and there, swordsmen, knights, and plowmen-soldiers spit in their hands, making ready. But there weren't nearly enough, not by thousands. And the tide of Mornaway's ocean would carry every man before it.

"I had best not tell you what I'm thinking," Lamoric breathed. "You'll have me by the collar again."

"Not this time," said Durand. But as Durand spoke, he happened to glance into Lamoric's face—where he saw a strange glow. A hundred shimmering sparks glittered in Lamoric's wide eyes. "That devil!" he said.

Durand twisted in time to see torches tumbling down over the street behind them, bouncing upon thatched roofs. A blaze was already crawling in the thatch of the blacksmith's shop.

"Hells," said Lamoric. "With all the burning in this dukedom, he ought to be out of torches! It'll be a furnace. And I've got Coensar rushing from gate to gate, trying to hold both doors to the oven. We must break out."

A hiss from Berchard snapped their attention back to the field below the wall: the blades of Mornaway flashed down in a blaze of mirrored fire. And the Host of Mornaway advanced.

"*Durand,*" said Lamoric. "*Get to my wife.* Watch over her. *God.* I've never been much good to her, she won't die for my damned foolishness here."

Above them, the flames leapt over themselves, already sealing the street under a vault of fire.

"Lordship—" Durand protested.

But Lamoric caught him by the back of his neck. "*I won't have her held ransom by my own men!* I won't have her dead. Who can I trust if not you? Save her if you can. Swear it!" And, when Durand could only gape at his lord: "Go! Durand, go! I have business at the gates!"

Lamoric snatched Durand's shield and leapt into the alley, darting uphill.

Berchard's eye was on Durand's face—with more grim scrutiny than a man could endure.

"By Heaven, Lord," he called, "I swear it." And, half in horror, he threw himself from Berchard and lurched into the street.

Who can I trust if not you? He flinched from the bloody words.

Once more in the street, Durand threw himself into motion. Beasts and cinders, birds and soldiers, churned in the narrow channel, but he fought toward the potter's shop where he'd last seen the girl. Tall men stood along the battlements, sweeping attackers down with huge blows of their axes or swords. The fire at their backs snatched arrows away like straw in a furnace.

"Deorwen!" he shouted.

The Rooks' sigils slithered in the parching heat like a crowd pressing in and rubbing its paws. The army was set to tumble down the Hells already aflame.

"Deorwen?" he called.

"She's here!" It was Coensar who answered as he pitched through the chaos of beasts and cinders. "Durand, where's His Lordship?"

Durand could hardly meet his captain's eyes. "He'll be at the upper gates," Durand said. Smoke boiled, and horses charged in circles, vaulting over one another and leaping at the walls. "He's sent me for Deorwen."

Coensar cursed. "That potter's shop. Here!"

In a few moments, they made the shop, Durand catching hold of the door frame and spotting a crowd of priests, pages, cooks, and grooms—all wavering between the crushing violence of the horses and the heat of the mounting fire. Deorwen stared back at him, frantic and only half-disguised.

"I'm to watch you," Durand said.

"I've been a child," she said. "How did I ever think to find poor Moryn?"

Durand had almost forgotten.

Abruptly, Deorwen's eyes widened. "Where's my husband?"

"He's gone to the upper gate," said Durand.

She touched her face. "And he's sent his shield-bearer to me?"

Before Durand could answer, another pack of mad horses bolted through, buffeting him against the storefront—and against Deorwen. For an instant, he balanced between agony and—he wanted to hold her; he wanted to carry her from this burning world. But he pushed himself back. The effort of will nearly shut his eyes. Coensar was looking on; Durand could only guess at what that gallant captain saw. Lamoric deserved better than a faithless servant groping his wife.

As Durand rallied his muddled thoughts, a soldier barged in among the muleteers and camp followers cowering all around. "Bastard cowards! Every man with ballocks and backbone to the walls!"

It was Badan.

"On the walls, they're butchering men on your account," he said, throwing boys and old men into the cauldron of fire and wild horses. "Find what you can and mount the bloody rampart or I'll gut you sure as ever will Mornaway or Yrlac!"

Old men and boys scrambled as Badan darted back and forth, barking and snapping. Suddenly, the fool was snarling at Deorwen's arm. "Come on you! You'll fight or I'll—"

Though Coensar moved to stop the man, Durand was quicker—in an instant, he'd sent the whoreson sprawling. "Get your bloody hand off!"

Badan swarmed up with bare steel already in his fist. "I've had a bellyful of your shoving, mooncalf! Host of Hell, I have!" And there was Durand squared off with the whoreson, a crowd on one side and the churning street on the other. And Deorwen looking on.

In pain and fury, Durand snarled, shoving the point of his

sword flashing at Badan. "You've had your own back for that push, haven't you? Your bit of petty vengeance! There's Lamoric sprawled on the stones! Me, half torn to pieces!" His broken teeth, his hitched shoulder, his battered face.

Though Badan ought to have been distracted, he found a moment to peer closely at the supposed stranger Durand was shielding. And, in an instant, his baffled anger had hitched itself into a leer. "Oh!" His gaze darted over hidden curves, spotting the dark eyes of Lamoric's lady looking back at him. "I see now, I think. Who've you got under your wing, Sir Durand, eh?"

The answering flash of Durand's blade sent Badan skittering back across the burning storefront, dancing clear.

Durand ignored shouts and reaching hands, stalking Badan through the flying cinders. "The damned city might have fallen for your vengeance. Your pride nearly put Radomor in Gunderic's Tower!"

He swatted Badan's shield, two-handed, once and twice. "Did the Rooks give you silver? Or did you do their work without fee?"

Coensar shouted; he had Deorwen by the arm. But, fighting at the limit of his strength, Durand could not answer. Every switch of Ouen's old sword was nearly enough to tear the thing from Durand's grip. The blade struck rust and sparks from sword and shield and iron mail as he battered Badan back.

Then, at the door of the potter's shop, the fool slipped. His bald skull cracked from the door frame and Durand made to finish him.

But as Durand lunged over the threshold, the fire had finished its work among the upper floors of the shop. And, somewhere in the heart of the old building, a great beam gave way in the heat. In a crashing instant, the weight of four floors thundered down, the blaze shuddering through the wide door, filling Durand's throat, the street—and searing the faces of the crowd.

As Durand tottered, eyes stung, the black shape of Badan bulled from the wrecked door. Durand swished Ouen's sword high, hoping only to—

But suddenly Coensar landed on Durand's shoulders.

Upon the burning doorstep, the master swordsman grappled with Durand like a child, saving Badan for the moment, and leaving Durand to stagger free, facing both men. Deorwen looked on. "What do you mean by—?"

"Durand," Coensar reasoned, "you cannot kill a—"

"This thing is no peer! What liegeman seeks to slay his lord? What do I owe him?"

Scarcely clear of the fire, Badan capsized.

"He's thrown his master in the street before his own citadel." Durand hoisted the point of the sword up, angling toward the wretched traitor. "What pain does the devil not deserve?"

Hands caught hold of Badan, pulling him free of the inferno's verges. The man's head lolled and Coensar grimaced in the chaos of the street. All the while, Deorwen was watching.

The fierce captain squeezed his eyes tight. "God, boy. The fool did none of those things!"

Durand wavered, his glance flickering to the dome of Badan's lolling head.

"What?"

The captain covered his face. The childish gesture shot through Durand like ice and premonition. "He's not the man!"

Durand shook his head. "What do you—?"

"Host of Heaven, you fool boy!" the captain shouted over the firestorm. "There was nothing else. . . . Half a thousand men I've fought." The words had him twisting. "Then, Radomor's fiends took Geridon." The Champion. "Not since I was a boy had such a chance fallen within my grasp. Not in a lifetime. And I was the hero of the hour, remember, scattering that nest of archers above the city! Freeing our last hope from Radomor's bloody trap. There were smiles on a hundred hard faces looking my way, and I was *Champion*, near as damnit. But when I wheeled about, there you were: you had our Lamoric slung over your saddlebow and you were riding. Snatching him from death. Hells, you were on bloody Geridon's own horse, Durand!"

The point of Durand's sword touched the mud; the thing might have been leagues from Durand's hand for all he felt it. He could scarcely see the mad street around him. "*No.*"

But the fires flashed in Coensar's eyes. "Look close, Durand." Durand saw gray hair, bruises: an old man. "A duke cannot cast his champion out, lame or broken. Not with honor. How many other chances would I have before it's too late?"

A chained flail was twisted in Coensar's belt, the spines of its urchin head matching the marks in Durand's bones as neatly as the teeth of a key. It had always been there.

Over the man's shoulder, Deorwen wavered, her eyes wide with God knew what. The street burned. Wild horses crushed men or carried them into the ranks of the enemy. Axes clopped in helms on the ramparts and every man would be dead before the Eye could burn another hour. Durand found the captain's soot black face. Badan hung between a muleteer and a priest, an arm over each shoulder. The blackened cloaks of the whole lot struggled as if to fly.

In the Heavens, Radomor's sanctuary spire stood like a blade in the maelstrom's heart. Durand pictured the Rooks laughing in the empty sanctuary while the storm of wings and the fire churned round and round.

He pictured the ribbed darkness of its vaults high above the madhouse city.

And his mouth opened. The image brought back a memory; a memory of Deorwen's dream. Here was Deorwen watching him. And before his eyes was the ribbed darkness she'd seen. Cackling. Where would the devil Rooks be but in the high sanctuary, defiled? What had they said in the muddy Gulf of Eldinor when he'd been half-dead on the deck of a stranger's ship and they had croaked down from the masthead? "Hostages." They had laughed—hostages who made enemies of friends and friends of enemies. Now, here was Mornaway, playing friend to the devils. "How else could they have brought old Duke Severin to their side?"

For an instant and without meaning to, he met Deorwen's eyes.

"I will end it," Durand rasped, and, without one word more, he lurched from girl and frozen men.

There was rope among the horses. Some must have belonged to engineers. He found a grappling iron and he pitched down the burning street, his eyes on high gaps between the rooftops—past the gawking shadows of the Rooks' dark sigils where Radomor's men walked the battlements. Wild horses darted round him.

Finally, Durand staggered between two burning houses. He'd seen an empty parapet. Radomor's fools would all be at the gate.

Deorwen nearly skidded past him and the alley.

He seized the woman's arm. "Go back." There was hardly room for two people to stand in the narrow alley. Around him, the plaster walls were as hot as fresh loaves. She was too close. His bent back had them standing nearly eye to eye.

"It's the sanctuary, isn't it?" she said. Smoke boiled around them.

"No." But he wasn't sure what question he was answering. Deorwen could not be in his mind. Not now.

"He's there. And you're going for him."

Durand gulped a breath of air and mashed his eyes shut. "You must stay. Stay with bloody Coensar." He turned from the girl and swung the grapnel slithering to the battlements. The first ten feet were a high slope, the rest was an old wall. He stamped one boot on the bank and started to walk himself up the line. He breathed in gulps. To end all this, he would pull the city down with his hands.

She called from behind him. "Durand, you can't—"

"Leave me." His back and shoulder twisted as they took his weight.

"No," she said. But Durand was gone.

Hand-over-hand, he climbed the mud slope and then started on the stone wall atop it. The Rooks' devil figures pressed shadow faces against the stone, but they smeared and eddied at the touch of Durand's boots, erupting into flies. The nearby fires licked his coat of mail. But he reached, wrestling with the parapet's overhang and, finally, heaved himself through an embrasure with pounding blood ready to burst from his skull.

Coensar and Lamoric and the whole world were below him now. The city was above. He could concentrate on Moryn and the Rooks.

Only as he spilled onto the parapet and his shaking hands

and knees did he notice Deorwen: nose to soot-blackened nose with him. She'd slithered up behind him. "By God, how did—" he began, but an inexplicable terror flashed over her face.

He twisted, and a crossbow's bolt hacked at his mailed arm. The thing could have struck Deorwen. Only a few paces down the battlement, a sentry stood, his crossbow clattering as he scrabbled for a mace at his belt.

And the man fell with Durand's grappling iron in his jaw. Durand followed the iron hook in the next heartbeat, mashing the man's mouth shut and whipping a dagger across his throat.

Deorwen was gasping. But even before Durand could roll away, some bit of the mad darkness overhead seemed to tumble free. It swooped to dart between Durand's wrists and snatch at the dying soldier's lips. A raven, the thing flapped in just as the poor devil breathed his death rattle, then it was away.

"Hells! It's taken his last breath." Durand rocked onto his haunches. His hands were greasy with blood, shaking. Coen, Badan, Deorwen—feeding this damned soldier to the crows. He could stand nothing else.

"Durand," Deorwen said. "Durand! There isn't time."

But Durand could only shake his head; her voice was too much.

"There are others on the wall." She touched him. "Please."

And Durand fought his thoughts into order. He forced himself to give the battlements a good look. Fires in the streets below the parapet threw high shadows. But faces glowed here and there where sentries peered down into the inferno—one no more than a dozen paces away, a few more beyond that.

Deorwen was looking up into Durand's face, and Durand understood that he must have been staring. "Durand, we cannot stay here. Wipe off your hands. I didn't scale a building to die on the first landing. We must leave this place. They'll find us."

They covered an open stretch of gleaming cobbles before the first building. Durand could hear Radomor's men roaring over the ramparts, sprinting with messages, and fighting at the gates. In this poorer quarter of the city, there were even a few poor fools still cowering at their windows.

As they lurched onward, Durand struggled to get command of the spinning through his aching head. He'd been a fool not to understand how hungry Coensar must be. He'd been a fool to stay so near the wife of his lord and master. That was enough. Now, he would break Radomor's hold over the Duke of Mornaway and end the fight if he could.

Below the second rampart, Ferangore was a single street. Above, the city began to sprawl. Without Deorwen leading, Durand might have blundered anywhere. But, as it was, she led him ducking through gutters and alleys till they came up against the third rampart.

And, in an instant he knew that although he had been to Ferangore, he had never really paid attention to the third rampart. Now, it loomed above his broken head and shoulder like a storm cloud. The earthwork at the base stood as high as a castle mount, while the curtain wall atop the bank soared like the walls of Acconel.

Deorwen had the grapnel in her hands. "Durand, can you throw so high?"

Durand thought of the men dying in the city behind them. Carrion birds zipped above the wall and rooftops overhead as he opened and closed his fists. "Hells."

"God," said Deorwen. "And I think that's shouting." Durand heard the howls of alarm. "They'll have found our friend. There's no place to hide here. We'll have to find another way onward," said Deorwen. Already he could hear the boots in the alleys behind them. "Durand! We will find another way. There will be a longer rope or a drain or a doorway or just—"

But Durand had seen something as he stared at the rooftops and the sky. Some of the crooked rooftops stood very near the wall.

"No," Durand said. "Follow me."

With a bound into the street, he found the tenement door and was groping his way up narrow stairs and passageways, even as the aged building shifted and creaked under his feet. He barged through door after door, sometimes startling whole dens of wide-eyed children in dark and musty cells. Higher and higher.

Deorwen whispered after him: "Are you all right?"

The thin walls thrummed like a drum skin at the touch of rough voices outside. Durand heaved himself to the stair's creaking end and a last meager room. The racket of horsemen rang from the street below the tenement.

Durand found neither smoke hole nor rear windows. The room was hardly broad enough for two people to stand. He heard shouts.

"They're right outside," Deorwen said. "It's up or nothing."

"'Up or nothing,'" Durand repeated, seeing no way up. But, as he made to turn in the narrow space, his aching shoulder brushed what he had taken for another patch of scabbed plaster—and outdoor air spilled into the room. He'd blundered into a hairy curtain of wool.

"They've draped a window!" said Deorwen.

Durand tore the thing away, but found only a construction of pine boards thrust out above the alley. A sad twist of wire held a dry spray of pennyroyal above a hole in the floor.

"A privy," said Deorwen, close. "We are trapped." The tenement was already shaking to the din of new boots on its rickety stair.

"Not yet." Durand ducked into the creaking perch, his shoulder powdering the flowers. Walls and ceiling were nothing but dry pine. With a quick crash, Durand was looking at the eaves of the tenement, only a few feet away.

"Here," he said.

He took big handfuls of thatch in his fists and, despite the protests of every bone, hauled himself up. In moments, Deorwen was crawling on the black straw beside him.

Even on the very peak of the roof, the battlements stood five fathoms over their heads. He unlimbered the grapnel and, tottering on the rotten straw, managed a fierce throw that caught the battlements at the very limit of his reach.

There were soldiers shouting in the pennyroyal room.

Durand caught Deorwen up and jumped into a crushing pendulum swing that slammed his elbows into the masonry.

But he climbed, strangling with Deorwen's arms around his neck.

ATOP THE WALL, the bulk of the upper city loomed. Here were the empty mansions of the sensible rich and the abandoned halls of the craft guilds. Durand took it all in with a weaving glance. The heart of Ferangore stretched from the battlements behind them to the final rampart, a sixty-acre jumble. Above it was the last tier. Durand could see the citadel and sanctuary spire, bone gray without its cloak of ravens.

"One last hurdle and we'll be up with the Rooks and their sanctuary," he said, and Deorwen touched his cheek. "Now we must be moving," he muttered—and hauled himself into motion once more.

There were soldiers between the rich men's walls. Once, a horse's clatter drove the pair into a vaulted doorway. Next, watchmen's shouts had them skirt a square of open flagstones. In the end, they ran a zigzagged league to cover a stone's throw of the city. Finally, though, Durand pitched into a broad, cobbled street. Above him towered the last and most fearsome of the ramparts: the wall of the citadel upon which stood Radomor's keep and the high sanctuary.

"In a thousand years, our host could not have climbed so high," Durand murmured.

All the walls below were toys beside the one that guarded the citadel. Under the churning crows, this gray wall soared twenty fathoms from the street to its rude crown of timber hoardings. Durand imagined standing in those wooden galleries with the whole city small below one's feet.

He felt the rope in his hands, hairy, rough, and useless.

"It is too much," Deorwen murmured.

Even on Durand's best day, the climb would have been impossible. The wall stood easily twice the height of the tallest mansion in the streets below. "I'd do better trying to hook the moon."

A creak from the hoardings hinted at the presence of sentries in the high dark—an arrow from that height could end the climb in an instant. Durand and Deorwen slipped through the black door of a nearby building.

As bent, trying to catch his breath, he realized that he and Deorwen had stepped into the front room of a proper inn with long wooden benches and a flagstone floor—and that it was all very familiar. "Hells," he said. "I've been in this place." The smell of the dining hall took him back half a year—back to an evening when dust had sifted from the ceiling at the street-side windows as he'd peered through shutters up at Alwen's tower. "With Radomor and the Rooks and that bloody Gol Lazaridge." He opened and closed his hands, thinking that there'd still be blood in the creases. He had killed Gol just as he'd killed the soldier on the wall down below: with a knife across the gullet. "This is where we waited for poor Alwen to play her tune. They took Radomor upstairs to witness. The stairs will be back there." He waved at the gloom.

"I don't—" murmured Deorwen.

"She played to call her lover."

"Oh."

"Aldoin of Warrendel . . ." Durand began. But he stopped, remembering: Aldoin had known a way into the keep.

"Durand, you make little sense. I—"

"He was swimming for the great hall, Deorwen. Aldoin waited for Alwen to play from her tower window—and then he found some way. There were cisterns. Something under the city. A well." Though he'd heard it all from the Rooks' crooked mouths, the story had been true enough to drown Warrendel under Radomor's keep.

He could almost hear the murderous duke creaking on the floorboards upstairs, almost feel the brooding man about to charge down. The place swelled with memory.

"Aldoin had a house," Durand gulped. "A bawdy house. Or so Heremund said. Once. The Maiden and the Mother at the door, I think it was."

Deorwen spoke into the empty room. "Durand, we've just passed such a place."

And Durand caught her arms, ignoring her flinch of pain. He wanted very much to get out of Radomor's inn. "Can you remember where?"

They pelted back into the smoke once more while the sanctuary spire peered down over the shoulders.

HER PATH TOOK them very near Radomor's main gate—and so near the fifty mailed soldiers on guard that the garlic on their breath stung Durand's nostrils as he panted by the stone Queen of Heaven at Aldoin's doorway.

The doors on the other side of the Queen's hip were locked and studded with iron. The house was strong. A quick glance showed no ground-floor windows in the stone walls that a man could slip through. And Durand could think of nothing but to try his remaining strength against the doors. A running start might do it.

Deorwen raised her hand. "Wait!"

"There's no time."

But Deorwen was right. At Radomor's gate, some of the guards were hopping off their backsides. There were hooves clattering closer up some other road, and the men were jumping to the windlasses to haul the gate high.

Every man was distracted.

As that providential rider swung through the gates, Durand lurched into the street—free to be seen by any fool who glanced—and bowled into the doors with all the weight of man, mail, and madness.

The doors cracked and Durand reeled. Instead of walls and floors and furnishings, he pitched into a house of broken beams, landing in a deafening clatter of debris where the ceiling was open to the carrion birds wheeling above.

Behind him, Deorwen pushed the broken doors shut—or as nearly as she could.

"What happened here?" Deorwen gasped.

Durand crushed his face with both hands. Stone walls and gloom had conspired to make him forget. "The Rooks. A fire. Radomor set the place ablaze when Aldoin swam. Quickly!"

"He couldn't swim back. . . ." He could see the thought trembling in her eyes.

"There must be a cellar door or a wellhead here somewhere." Durand scrambled off among broken beams and scorched walls. Joist ends stood like blades from the walls ringing the place.

But Deorwen had slipped through to an interior courtyard,

knowing better what a nobleman's town house should be. "It would have been here, I think." She heaved back a knot of joist or rafter to reveal a narrow ring of broken limestone. "Here," she said. As Durand ducked close, sure enough, he felt the chill of dank air curling up from that dark throat.

Once more, voices reached them. As he made to pull one timber loose, swaggering talk flickered over the ruin. The jingle of mail coats and harsh laughter told him that an armed patrol was nearby. Remembering the half-broken doors, Durand ripped the black throat of the well open.

"How deep?" Deorwen said.

Durand shook his head. He was already shucking off his iron coat; the thing was so loud, like a rain of coins. Boots scuffed in the street just beyond the broken door. He dared not even whisper.

Deorwen peered around the broken courtyard. "We will have to tie the—"

But Durand caught her close, breathing his words into her ear. "Deorwen, when the battle's done, you'll look for a wise woman." She struggled, but he crushed her tight. "Make your way to your father's people." He didn't want to tell her that the swim was madness—to face the duke alone was madness. He was leaping into death. "Please. I swore to Lamoric."

"Here. What's this?" said a voice—just outside.

Deorwen pushed him back, just far enough to see: nose to nose. In her eyes, Durand read a thousand moods.

But the door was opening. "Hide," Durand said, and threw himself into the dark.

IF HE'D HAVE landed straight, he'd have snapped both legs. As it was, he tumbled backward in the long, black plunge before he slapped the water. Every splash echoed through leagues of dark vaults, and the light of the smoky world above fell in one dancing circle upon the black water. Beyond this, a man could see only rumors of low arches hunkered over squat columns of stone.

Durand had just begun to stand when Deorwen flashed through the light. He broke her fall with a slap of open hands. Agony was like lightning. "God." But he gripped her hard, and felt her muscles against him. She was mad. She was a fool. They would both die and no one would know where or why.

"They'll have heard us," she spluttered, her lips against his jaw.

Right overhead, the well hung like a moon in the dark ceiling. Their fall had taken them through a massive stone vault and now they waded in a cistern that had hollowed the hilltop. A man looking down might spot them.

"Come on," she said, shrugging to strip off her woolen outer layers until she stood in nothing more than a boy's linen shirt and breeches. "We must get away from the well. I don't know what they'll think up there. Which way?"

Durand took his eyes from the girl, peered up at their patch of sky, and did his best to guess. In a moment, the wellhead rang with shouts.

COLD WATER IS a crushing thing that twists the muscles tight and squeezes the marrow in a grip of creaking pain. As Durand sloshed out of the light, he picked out fanciful creatures snaking around the capitals of each stout column. Fiends leered and plowmen danced.

He pushed on into a gloom without shape.

"*This* is where Aldoin came," breathed Deorwen, her voice all shivers in the dark.

"He'll have been the last man to walk this way, I'd guess."

There was a moment's breathing hesitation. "I wonder: Did Alwen know where her man went when she called for him?"

"I wouldn't think so," Durand said. He hardly needed to think. "Imagine what would have happened if he'd told her." If Alwen had known, she would never have summoned him to drag himself through. "He'll have kept his trap shut."

The frigid grip of the water worked higher round Durand's chest and soon he was swimming awkwardly and fighting to breathe. He heard skitterings among the bright and hollow sounds of water, but could see nothing.

Finally, his paddling fingers struck a stone wall—blank, without seam or flaw. For an instant, he shut his eyes.

Deorwen sloshed up at his side, scrabbling in vain for purchase. "How did he get on from here?" she asked.

"God knows." Durand felt her foot flutter against his numb shin.

"Are you sure you're up to this. I can hear you breathing—"

"There'll be some kind of pipe," Durand said. "There must be something."

With an awkward kick, he pushed off along the wall, scrabbling at the clammy stone until his fingers juddered over something under the surface like a lip of pottery.

"Here!" he gasped, groping around an empty ring.

"It is the right way," said Deorwen. "Gods. I think. I see the wellhead behind us. We might have come anywhere. I don't know how much longer I can keep swimming."

Durand felt a rim of pottery—a curve above and below—and he thought that the tunnel the two arcs described might be broad enough to let him pass. Just.

"An opening. Big enough, I think. We go under," Durand breathed. And with luck they would come up in the keep's well. "Yes?"

"Under. Yes. Queen of Heaven!"

Durand closed his eyes, steeling himself for the duck into the frigid black.

"Don't think, 'How many conduits must run from this place?'" said Deorwen.

Durand reached out. He wanted to only touch her, to know that she was more than a voice in the dark. Or so he thought. At the touch of her skin, he could do nothing but crush his cold lips to her cheek, her brow, the gasp of her lips.

When he shoved himself clear, he gulped deep and dove below, a traitor to the end.

HE KICKED THROUGH a space tighter than barrel hoops. He pulled at black joints where sections met, his damned shoulders lodging and forcing him to twist.

In these frigid confines, he closed his mind. There wasn't space to turn back. He already felt the ache of drowning in his lungs. But he clawed onward. And yard after yard, he came upon nothing but more of the narrow conduit.

Dark thoughts shivered up like bubbles: if this Aldoin swam like a water rat, Durand would drown. If Aldoin had been slim as an otter, Durand would drown. An omission as simple as either of these from the story would leave him jammed in a clay pot coffin with Deorwen behind him—and she unable to turn back. He remembered the bodies tied in the Rushes under the twining crystal of their river tombs. He squeezed his eyes shut against a sudden ache for air.

Yard by yard, he struggled on until his heart thundered and he clenched his face against the prying force of the water's black fingers. Bubbles burst between his teeth.

It was then he struck a wall—and couldn't turn. In a flash, he pictured himself, a fool swimming up some long-blocked conduit the builders had forsaken. And he scrabbled at the wall mindlessly until his splayed fingers fell into a void. It was no wall, but a sudden bend in the tunnel.

He'd spent nearly every instant of his air in panic. Now, he lashed, twisting fit to burst his lungs and snap his bad ribs. Ouen's sword clanked and rang. Rising up, he clawed upward: a race between what was left of his will—

—And he tore clear air from the black skin of the water.

His own gasps and splashes clattered back in his ears; the racket would be heard by any fool for leagues. Every breath was like a kick in his sides. The great veins of his neck leapt against his jawbone while he gulped and shook. Fathoms above him, a faint disk of gray ceiling hung like another moon.

When the shuddering elation of clear air let him free, he clung along the wall so that the water might settle while he waited for Deorwen to break the surface.

And he waited in that well, shaking.

He waited so long that the sloshing water grew still as midnight glass—as still as a pond after a drowning, shivering only with the beat of Durand's heart.

A legion of cold images flooded his mind's eye: Deorwen trapped, Deorwen thrashing and dying, Deorwen silent in the black—all down below his bare feet, beyond reach. "Hells." He couldn't go back for her. He imagined the cost of meeting her in that narrow pipe.

But then, hands and a hard head collided with his beating

legs, and Deorwen burst into the air, gasping and splashing. There was hardly room for both the swimmers and their elbows. But Durand beamed liked the war was won and caught the girl in a bear's fierce grip, spluttering, "Uh! Thank Heaven."

Deorwen laughed, or gasped. "You'll drown us!" she said, shuddering through the length of her body. "Is it the right place?"

Durand looked up. How could he know? "It must be."

"Swimming under Radomor's stronghold. Gods. Quiet."

"Aye. Right."

"Now, how did Aldoin get himself up? I see neither rungs nor rope. Are there handholds?" she asked, but it was not a well with tidy stairs or a neat ladder.

"We'll have to think," Durand growled. He could not imagine having swum so far only to drown like a child in a well. "Hells."

The shaft was three feet across and lined with neat courses of masonry that gave no purchase. The crushing chill had them like a torturer's vise.

Deorwen gave a scoffing laugh. "We'll freeze and drown here while they roast and choke below."

"No," said Durand.

He slapped his hands against the opposite walls, trying to hoist himself up. Pain lanced through his back; he could never climb that way. "No good."

"Your legs. Try with your legs."

Stirring around in their frigid cauldron, Durand set his feet against one wall and again drove his back into the opposite. "Right," he grunted. "Maybe." It was the only way.

Braced between the walls, he lifted himself. "I remember," said Deorwen. "I used to climb the chamber doorway. I could get near to the lintel."

It was a child's game, meant to be played by agile children for a few feet up a doorpost. Now, there were four or five clammy fathoms over Durand's aching head.

He tried to think of something to say to Deorwen, but nothing came and thinking was a dangerous pastime for him just then. He had no desire to remember who had smashed his teeth, broken his shoulder, scarred his face. With gritted teeth, he walked his wet boots up one wall, twisting his shoulders up the other. It was easier than thinking.

"Go on," said Deorwen.

"There'll be rope," Durand grunted.

His shirt slid up his back as he twisted his shoulders higher. His sword belt tangled round his shoulder. He slid an inch for every inch he gained. "You have it," Deorwen called. "You must be near." But Durand found that it helped if he held his breath. Soon, the drops tumbling from his breeches had far to fall. His legs burned.

"You must be there. You must be."

And Durand cracked his head on something hard—his heart shivered.

"What was that?" Deorwen's voice demanded from the depths.

Durand twisted his neck and reached up, scrabbling at a barrier of hard corners that stretched from wall to wall across the well mouth. The castle had dropped the grille over the well. It was a siege; this was a way in. They'd dropped the same grille that had drowned Aldoin.

"Durand?" Deorwen's voice echoed around him.

He shoved and the grate clanked against its fittings, barred tight. His boots slid like wet bladders. And the flinch of catching himself snatched his breath away.

"Durand?"

"A moment," he managed.

The only light above came from around the well chamber's door—the faintest thread. But he could see large holes and, when he crammed himself as near to the bars as he could, the well's windlass. Somewhere there would be a bar or latch to pin the thing down.

Deorwen pressed him: "What is it?"

"The grille," said Durand. "Barred."

And Deorwen's answer was slow in coming. "Queen of Heaven," she breathed, finally. He could feel her eyes on the dark tangle of him struggling under the bars.

Aldoin had died when these bars dropped. There had been no way out for him: a young man in good health. What did Durand have that Aldoin lacked? The man had been fit enough to swim the pipe and cistern. No one could snap iron bars. Durand scrambled for advantages. They'd left the rope in Aldoin's burnt house. They'd left the hook with it.

Abruptly, Durand realized that he did have one thing Aldoin had lacked all those moons ago: the damned sword knotted round his neck. Not waiting an instant, he fed the clattering thing up through the grating, feeling with its steel tip across the irregular grille beyond his sight, hunting for hinges and bars while his back slipped and his hams burned.

But it worked. Twisting with his fingertips, he felt the blade catch against a sliding bit of bent iron. With a gasp of air, he scrabbled and jabbed, trying to slide the bolt one way or the other at the very edge of his reach and strength. Finally, it jerked free.

IN COMPARISON, PULLING Deorwen up was simplicity.

As he held the shivering girl to his chest, she looked up past his chin. "I'll tell you one thing that's certain: Those harlots of Heremund's never swam up that thing. I don't care what the fool skalds say."

DRIPPING AND HALF-NAKED, Durand set his ear to the well room's door, wincing at memories of the keep beyond it. He would rather have been anywhere else in Creation. "It is a crooked path to the sanctuary," he muttered. Memories of the hot silence of the hall shouldered back into his thoughts. He remembered Radomor squatting on his father's throne and Alwen locked in her tower. All of it waited beyond the door.

But he forced himself to turn the handle—and stepped into a passage echoing with voices. Not too far away, a bench scraped on stone. There were still men in the duke's hall. He had hoped the place might have been abandoned.

"Follow me," Durand whispered and led Deorwen swiftly through the darkness of the keep, putting distance between them and the dark hall. He thought of the puddles left behind them as slams and drags echoed from upstairs.

"Most of Radomor's army must be in the streets, but someone is on the move in this place," Deorwen concluded. Durand kept his blade in his fist, knowing that any corner could hide a guard or God knew what.

They dripped and hobbled and shivered down into the depths of the keep until—after wet ages—Durand found the slender passage between the foundation stones to the tiny sally port. There had been a man on the little door the last time Durand had come this way: a small man who'd tried to extort a few pennies from the new boy trying to slip away. But now the dank passage was empty, and when he glanced at his hands, the blood was gone. "I killed a man here," he said.

"Open it," was Deorwen's answer.

THE INTRUDERS SLIPPED into a cold alley under a ceiling of carrion birds. They stole between keep and curtain wall, taking only a moment to reach the keep's ancient shoulder for a glimpse of their goal. The high sanctuary of Ferangore soared gray from the pavement to spires now lost among the wings that tumbled through high windows and choked the Heavens. The West Portal of the edifice—two doors like standing warships—stood flanked by rows of lofty kings and Powers in stone.

Durand cared little for the artistry of the ancient place; he thought only of distances: fifty paces of open courtyard stood between him and the building, right at the heart of the enemy's citadel.

"We are here," said Deorwen. "Now, if we can only—"

Durand fixed his aim on the portals between their old kings. Whatever the commotion inside the keep, outside, the entrance to Radomor's fortress was still. Durand set off running.

Twenty paces into his breakneck charge, however, there was a strangled yelp at Durand's heels—Deorwen had followed him. She pointed up at the dark mouth of the covered stair of the keep's entrance.

"I don't—" Durand began, but stopped when he heard a rumble pouring from the mouth of the keep stair. Deorwen had heard it first, but Durand knew the sound as well as any in Creation: armored men thundered down those stairs.

The two invaders stood in the midst of an open yard. For a moment, Durand was sure that he had killed them both, then he saw the narrowest of bolt-holes: among the feet of the

anctuary's portal kings were shadows. "Run," said Durand,
ven as the hinges of the keep door began to squawk.

In a headlong rush fit to break bones, they pelted toward
anctuary. Durand knew the door was swinging wide behind
hem. He dove, throwing Deorwen, and the two tumbled into
a heap at the royal feet a pace from the great portal's steps.
Durand fought not to howl like an animal at the bruises left
by the cobblestones.

"Very still, Durand," said Deorwen. "And breathe."

And she was wise, for the armored men came marching
and only the merest film of shadow covered the intruders.
The path of the soldiers took them within paces of the sanctuary. But as they came, Durand realized that these were not
merely a few laggard men marching late to the battle. Between the two files of grim soldiers, he saw the green wings
of a lord's mantle gaping as wide as if he might climb into
the flocks above the city. Here walked Radomor of Yrlac
himself.

In an openmouthed moment, Durand saw that he might
end the siege with one flash of steel. Through the whole long
assault on the citadel, he'd kept his sword. Radomor's boys
would be flat-footed at finding an armed enemy in the heart
of the citadel. But there were so many guards. And any movement must draw the eyes of more men than he could hope to
stop. His eyes twitched to Deorwen, imagining what would
become of the girl.

So he watched, shivering as coldhearted as any of the
carved things on the flank of the sanctuary porch, numbering the bodyguard, feeling Deorwen's fist on his arm as she
read his strangled thoughts.

Radomor marched near, then, just as he would have passed,
a voice croaked from the sanctuary steps, hardly a pace from
the long gray portal kings.

"Highness!" it called, and like a flash of claws, every blade
was bare among Radomor's guard.

Radomor, himself, did not turn more than his bald head.
"Do not seek to check me in this, sorcerer." His eyes glittered like black glass in a furnace.

"Oh, Your Highness, never! It is only that I am surprised
to see you venture forth," continued what was clearly one of

the simpering Rooks. Durand heard the devil's black sleeve swish upon the steps, the fiend bowed so low. "There is little need."

Radomor's guards had not sheathed their swords.

"There is every need," Radomor rumbled. "This boy Lamoric championed Ragnal's cause before every lord of Errest the Old. Now, Acconel is burned and I am driven even from its ruins."

"But he must die in any case," the Rook reasoned. "The boy is caught in a snare of your devising; his death can hardly be prevented."

As Durand shivered by the sanctuary step, a thick reek seemed to flow around him. The guardsmen winced and swallowed while the birds stormed round.

"There are times when death does not suffice," said Radomor. "I must end this with my own hand. You know little of kingship if you imagine I can do less."

"Yours is the blood of kings, Highness. My brother and I, we are but servants. It is only that, had we realized what you intended, we might have made your Champion available to you. But we are caught up in our little explorations just now. Harvest time, as it were. It is all a bit of a jumble, Highness," he added confidingly.

"Play your games if you must, but I grow weary of the reek. I do not need those old bones to watch over me." The man's head sank the smallest fraction. "I will do as I must with or without him in attendance. I am not a child."

"No, Highness." Again, the Rook's sleeves slapped the sanctuary steps. "We will await news of your triumph."

Durand watched as the Duke of Yrlac turned from his sorcerer and stalked toward the battle—and Lamoric. He tried to convince himself that there had been nothing he could do.

A sniff and chuckle hissed from the sanctuary's porch, and the sorcerer's soft footfalls retreated into the great nave.

Durand twitched up from the pavement. And, with Radomor's men still jingling for the gates, two intruders in clinging linens slipped into the reeking sanctuary of Ferangore.

BEYOND THE MIGHTY portals, the sanctuary gaped like a gutted mountain choked with carrion birds. Columns dripped

ке the ribs of some putrid leviathan. Every surface seethed
ith worms. Durand could scarcely breathe, and gales of
ack wings spun through the light of the sanctuary's greasy
andles.

"A ribbed darkness," Deorwen said under feathered din
id again at Durand's side. "The resting place of Radomor's
eople back to the dawn of ages—some interred here sailed
ith Saerden Voyager." Stone tombs crowded the pillars. "If
e heaps these atrocities upon his ancient kin, what will he
ave done to my poor brother?" she wondered.

"There," Durand said. "That is where they'll be." He would
ot play guessing games about the depravities of the Rooks
ith Deorwen; they would soon learn more than either of
nem could stomach.

"There are so many here. Lost. So very many. Hundreds.
housands. The air is thick with them. These devil birds."

Durand turned to her and found eyes spinning. "Deor-
ven!" There was no time.

"Every mouth is full of howling. So much despair. Du-
and, I cannot think. Hopelessness to the ceiling. To the sky!
t is too much. I cannot see." Almost, she fell, but Durand
aught her shoulders.

At the very moment Deorwen fell, a scrap of laughter is-
ued from the putrid warren of one side arcade. And Durand
vas trapped, feeling as though he'd been left alone without
varning.

Deorwen seemed beyond reason, overwhelmed by the
ecromancers' stinking hell. Filth smeared every inch of the
loor under Durand's feet. Birds wheeled.

"I can feel them all—every snatched breath. Their dreams,
aprooted. Devils!"

Durand pressed his hand over the girl's mouth. Whatever
ner wise woman's sight revealed to her, she could not see him.

"For the world, I would not drag you farther, but I cannot
eave you here," Durand said, and tugged Deorwen down the
aisle. He raced through a hundred desecrations: relics
smeared with feces, Powers hung by their heels, choked with
ags, or robbed of their heads. Still, he pressed on, barefoot,
ill he spotted the bent shape of their quarry flapping round
a distant pillar, vanishing down.

Durand pulled Deorwen into a loping run—he would n[ot]
lose his man—and found a twist of stairs curling into th[e]
sanctuary's bowels. He had no doubt that he must fin[d]
Moryn with these fiends, and this had been the Rook's dest[i-]
nation. Though Durand could see the putrid air standing be[-]
fore him as thick as a stagnant pool, he forced himself t[o]
duck low and descended.

The birds from above now spun through a crypt tha[t]
stretched like a sunken forest, choked to its horizons wit[h]
mounds that glistened abhorrently. The birds lit upon thes[e]
wet heaps in a frenzy.

Durand's Rook capered around one such pile to make hi[s]
way toward the rotten head of the crypt and out of sight.

"What have they done?" Deorwen said. *"What is this?"*

"Shh," Durand said. "I am here." And lifted his slende[r]
blade between them and the madness.

Oily stalks crowded every niche in the walls and ever[y]
sarcophagus on the floor. Durand's bare toes slithered, and
when the knuckles of his sword hand glanced across some[-]
thing bulbous in the muck, he found a skull grinning back a[t]
him. Someone had packed the thing's eyes with red muck[.]
And white-edged knots of bloody symbols had been cut i[n]
the raw bone.

Before Durand could shudder back, a crow lit upon th[e]
thing. The bird seemed to whisper in the skull's ear—it[s]
stony beak dabbling—then the creature flashed back into th[e]
dark. Durand thought of the raven who'd landed on the dy[-]
ing sentry back on that first parapet. Here was the errand o[f]
every crow and kite in the city, flying from the mouths of th[e]
dead to this cavern of hollow, painted bones.

"Lost," breathed Deorwen. "And bound here. Poo[r]
Moryn!"

"Please," said Durand. Again he covered her mouth with
a shaking hand while her eyes started. "They will not have
done this to your brother. A hostage must live." He hoped i[t]
was so.

He might have said more, but now he heard the Rooks[']
voices.

"Brother," called the nearest. "It is as you suggested."

From somewhere at the head of the crypt, a voice an[-]

vered, "His Highness cannot resist." Durand could hear the
et clicks of vigorous work with a knife. "He is a slave to
ppearances."

"There are many eyes upon a king."

Durand gestured to Deorwen that she should stay where
ne stood—resting against a pillar—and stole toward the
oices, silently closing the gap like some back-alley mur-
erer as the nearest Rook pressed on.

"The common man must see strength if he's to believe it.
.adomor is not a complete fool."

"Eyes. Many eyes . . ." The wet clicks continued.

As Durand limped closer, the nearer Rook came in sight,
tanding, his fingertips playing over one mound of skulls as
e chatted below the altar's ruin.

Durand reached the flank of the last squat pillar, wincing
s the wet floor popped and sucked at his toes, unable to
eep memories of the paralyzing touch of the fiends from
iis mind. What would become of Deorwen if they caught
iim? They had pulled the life's breath from helpless men be-
ore his eyes, but Durand had no choice. He must find Moryn.

"The preparations are complete?"

Durand leaned from his hiding place and spied the second
Rook perched on the flank of the greatest bone heap in all
he dark sanctuary. It mounted up beyond the ceiling to the
uptured sanctuary floor. With a slender knife, the perching
Rook worked upon one wet skull. A last flick of the blade's
ip finished his work and he held the bone—eye to eye.
"What shall we do with them all? An army? Radomor's poor
Champion? What can we not do, brother?"

"Perhaps our Whisperer will tell us soon. We have come
so far at his behest. He must greet us before long."

Durand scowled at this. He wondered who could have
summoned such creatures into Errest.

Meanwhile, the carver fished two fingers of ruddy clay
from a pot and smeared blobs into the eyes and nose of the
skull before him. "There. What do you think?" he said. He
had to swat away one of the storming crows. "Bold things!"

"The life's breath bound in death. It is a pretty vessel,
brother. But His Highness rides to battle, naked but for a coat
of iron."

"Yes, yes. You nag like our poor mother. I will only be moment, and what would we do without these pretty vessels eh? I can scarcely keep up." The sorcerer finished briskly flipping the skull, nicking his finger, and letting a fat drop tumble inside.

"An embarrassment of riches sealed in heart's blood. We have been greedy."

The carver answered his brother with a splattered grin and a wet kiss on the skull's yellow teeth. "The purest madness."

"Madness. Yes, I begin to wonder, my brother. Now, on to His Highness."

And the two nodded into motion. Before Durand could flinch, the carver had snatched a gulp from a bloody ewer while the second Rook popped the plug from one wet skull. Out from the hideous container poured a sudden swarm of flies. They boiled into the air, flapping the heavy wings of the Rooks' cloaks and flickering through Durand's hiding place to force him back into the shadows. It was all he could do not to bolt, but he steeled himself, thinking that the Rooks were not his business: he must only find Moryn—lost somewhere in the acres of this reeking hell—and escape this place of death and flies and crows.

But no sooner had the necromancers filled the dark than they were pursing their lips and sucking down the bizarre swarm. And the flitting things spun in. In swirling eddies and ropy clouds, they darted down the necromancers' throats until the chests of the two men had swelled like balloons and the crypt was empty of the darting things. And the two men grinned and drooled like boys eating berries.

Is this what had become of so many dead men?

"Ugh! Too many," croaked the carver Rook—a few flies escaped his lips.

"Let us begin," was his brother's grunt.

Now that they had decanted the raw material of their trade, the pair raised their spattered hands. "Life to life we bind you," they said. "Heart to heart and marrow to marrow." Now, the viscous swarms spooled from their mouths once more, but weaving and climbing, not wild. "Blood to his blood, bone to his bone, we knot and join you. Your life to his life!" They spat to clear their lips.

Durand's glance followed the swirling flies and shadows up the crypt's old pillars and up the mountain of skulls until they churned through the ruptured vaults and into the sanctuary above.

And as Durand looked into the choked and lofty dark, he saw a white figure suspended among the shrieking crows high above. "Oh, no. It cannot be him," breathed Durand. The Rooks had stretched a man across the great east window of the sanctuary—binding him pillar to pillar, strung up like some desecrated icon from thongs knotted at his wrists. The insect things were marching upon him. Marching up the thongs. And Durand knew the face when it looked down, though a long winter had passed since he had seen it last upon the fields at Red Winding and Tern Gyre. When the gaunt and ravaged face looked down, Durand knew the eyes that found him: this was the Lord of Mornaway.

"Her brother," Durand said.

The Rooks had wrapped Mornaway in their hooked script and now Durand could see the shadow-things teeming up the knotted tethers and spidering over every figure among the maze of sigils on the man's jutting bones. It could not be good.

Had Durand only looked up, he might have plucked Mornaway and fled without setting foot in the crypt. Now, they were deep in the rotten place without reason. His head pounded. He turned to catch Deorwen's arm.

And found her already on her feet and stepping from her hiding place. She had seen what the Rooks had done to her brother and, already, the Rooks had noticed her.

"What is this?" said a Rook.

"By Heaven, it cannot be! Lady Deorwen?"

Whatever Deorwen had intended for that moment, Durand threw himself in the way. He would rush the devils, his sword swinging, and see what evil they could work in bloody pieces.

As Durand lurched from the shadows, the nearest Rook laughed. And, with a deft sweep of his hanging sleeves, the fiend summoned the whole storm of the carrion flock battering down through the broken ceiling. They packed the air in Durand's path, crashing through the riven sanctuary and striking Durand like a herd of stallions that bowled him backward over mounded skulls.

He tumbled and righted himself with a clank of his big sword some two dozen paces from the grinning Rooks. It felt like he'd just fallen from his damned horse again. And, as Durand spat maggots and feathers, the fiends took up courtly postures, half bowing in mockery of Durand's lady.

"Sons of whores," Durand snarled.

"Marvelous!" said the carver Rook.

"Her brother. Her lover? And the lady herself. Oh yes!" said the other.

"Were we quite finished with our little bit of magic before we were interrupted, by the way, brother?"

"I think," began the carver, "that we were very—"

As Durand steeled himself to rush the devils once again, a hollow *thunk* and a shout sounded above their heads. An arrow jutted from Moryn's naked ribs. There was even a drop of blood. The gleaming point stood as though the shot had come from the wall or the perfect panes of the window. There was neither space nor place to have shot from.

"I had been ready to say 'very nearly' but it seems that we were quite finished, brother."

"And thus, Ladyship, we see the merit of sorcery for all that it is decried by skalds and priests!" said the second Rook, peering up.

"Monsters," said Deorwen.

"His Highness would have been little pleased by that unkind dart," said the carver.

Durand saw Deorwen's posture shift—as though she would launch herself on one or other of the Rooks. And, once again, he charged to save her from herself and the fiends.

This time, the Rooks' blast caught Durand like a broken dam. His feet left the floor and he tumbled amid wings and claws, kicking in space until he crashed down, not in the crypt, but sprawling in the sanctuary nave. His blade skidded and clanged, and he felt his knees smacked near to breaking.

"Enough of this, I think," chattered a Rook. "Come now."

As he fought to breathe, Durand heard slithering where the great gulf lay in the nave. He set his hand on the great block of some old tomb, struggling to his feet and daring the flocking crows to steal a glimpse through the gap. Shapes moved upon the sliding heap of skulls: the Rooks were climbing—while above, Moryn jerked at his bonds, tied and living still.

Durand gritted his teeth and tottered on through the churning birds. Deorwen was mad and half-blind and down with the fiends.

"Hurry," nagged one Rook to his brother. He had to shout against the storming feathers.

"Has it ever helped to rush me?"

Durand found his sword once again, wrenching the blade from the slime. Creation spun with the devil birds and he could scarcely see.

Between one flock and the next, Durand saw that the two sorcerers had plucked up skulls; their arms were full. Moryn kicked against his bonds, having seen this before. "Carefully," said the tidier Rook. And while the birds shot past, the Rooks raised the skulls to their lips like oyster shells, tipping treacle-shadows down their throats.

Durand fought forward like a sailor in a gale.

He heard the sorcerers' voices as soul after soul slid past their teeth and they bloated with the effort, their skins shining like drowned men's. "We must begin," croaked the carver. Their necks ballooned with dead men, bulging at the blades of their jaws. "Too many. Too much." Their chests swelled their robes. "Before it is too late!" And with a spasm like vomiting, both men poured out thick souls. Shadows splashed into blowfly droplets; they flew high under the vaults. And the birds flew.

Durand batted at the hell before his eyes. Could he but reach the devils, a single thrust might have burst them like bladders, but the rising storm of black feathers threw him on his hip and flipped him on his shoulder. The birds moved with new purpose. As the sorcerers conjured, the flocks shot across the nave like pouncing fiends. Under Durand's hand, a tomb jerked into motion, caught in a mass of claws; and across the sanctuary slabs shrieked under the mauling of the lunatic birds; long stones swung high or slid like shearing blades. The birds stormed, tearing up webs and winding sheets to pluck the dead from their resting places. Under Durand's knee, a basalt lid pitched up.

In the depths of this wild storm, Durand knew they were finished. He was caught; it was too late for Moryn. He could only hope that Deorwen had the sense to fly while the devils had their minds elsewhere.

Talons snatched up corpse after dry corpse, sweeping them from their niches and spinning the flying fragments toward the Rooks.

A pitching Durand fought the birds and caught glimpses of the Rooks heaving like stricken drunkards in the grip of their spell. He saw corruption flop from their mouths, bursting into flies and maggots. He saw the dead's dry limbs spinning around the men, caught up by the crows and ravens in a frenzy that saw bones weaving in the air.

In the midst of it all, a figure took shape. At first, Durand perceived a tall man, stooped in a flapping coat of mail: a sad and half-familiar form. But soon the hail of long bones tangled in the space about it—clattering. Copper wire spun in black beaks, knotting bone to bone. Durand watched as birds and bones plucked up and dismembered that sad man, spinning his limbs and ribs and a multitude of rags until the lonely, wracked figure was torn and lost within a greater frame more massive than a team of oxen. Limbs woven of a hundred limbs bore the monstrous weight. A tail of a thousand bones lashed out the brute's pain. The helm of the stricken man burst around great tusks and swung over a beard of cobwebs— until, finally, the stooped figure had become the Champion of the Painted Hall: a hundred tombs upturned in a storm that left a monster.

With a silence like an ebbing sea, the carrion birds alighted. And now, in their breathing stillness, the Champion seethed, rocking like an anchored ship as its iron mask turned—turned toward Durand. And Durand knew the terror of the mouse in the den of a tiger.

Once more, the Rooks took up courtly postures, now poised comfortably behind their creation. "This is marvelous indeed," said one. "A fitting doom. We stand on the cusp of destroying the truculent Host of Gireth. And you, Sir

Durand, Bull of Gireth, are here at the last to face us. And the Champion of Yrlac."

The storm had left Durand alive with a blade in his fist. An army was dying in the streets; Moryn must be freed. To reach the Rooks, he would have to cover sixty feet. And pass the Champion. Durand resolved to let the devils bait him. Let them gloat and threaten. While they talked, he would ravel up the distance to their throats, step by step.

It was as he moved the first careful inch that he spotted motion beyond the Rooks: a pale shape darted behind one of the pillars near Lord Moryn. Deorwen had left the crypt. Durand staggered the next step not knowing whether to curse or sob.

"It seems a shame to end it, but we must move on," said a Rook.

"Yes, brother. And, in time, this whole struggle will seem little more than the fanfare that announced the arrival of King Ragnal."

"My brother has a poet's soul," explained one of the stinking necromancers while the rhapsodizing Rook favored his brother with a sly smile. "It is possible, you know. There have been so many."

Durand fought not to let a glance or look from him betray Deorwen's movements. He wondered whether she had recovered her reason; the crows and their cargo of souls had nearly finished her. But now, somewhere, she had found a knife. Durand tottered nearer, limbering Ouen's sword. It took a great effort of will to fix his gaze only on the sorcerers. The Champion creaked as tight as some engine of war, ready to obliterate him.

The nearest Rook raised an eyebrow at Durand's stealthy progress. "But there has been preamble enough, I think. Doom cannot be delayed. A hero must face his end—and in its proper time." The sorcerer glanced at his monster. "Let that time be now, Champion." The little man stabbed a finger at Durand.

Durand's breath stopped.

But nothing happened. He was not torn like a child in a bullring. The monster did not swarm over him. It did not move. Instead, thin words hissed from the ruin of its helm. *"Free us-s-s-s."*

The hiss was still in the air when Durand leapt for the sorcerers. Both Rooks sprang back. One of the creatures shielded his bald skull, but—in the instant before Durand could bring his blade down—the other snatched at the air: a crabbed gesture that jerked the Champion to life.

The thing's bony fist lashed out like the slap of a catapult's arm. And Durand was torn from the ground. Yards away, he smacked a pillar hard enough to smack sparks into the darkness. He struck and fell to lie, winded, at the pillar's foot.

While he gulped, a Rook was speaking. "Do not tarry when we call, Your Grace. . . ." For the first time in Durand's hearing, there was anger in the Rook's voice.

Who would the Rooks call "Your Grace"? He thought of the tall, sad figure at the heart of the monster.

"Free me," breathed the dead giant.

"These sad entreaties ill-suit your dignity, Your Grace. You are ours. You have been ours since your deathbed. Ours as your bastard 'grandson' has been. Now, I direct you to recall the particular nature of your bonds; it seems to have slipped your mind. Recall that what pains are inflicted upon you must also be shared by the child. You are joined in this."

The mountain of bones writhed against the floor.

"Poor mite," said the second sorcerer.

"For the sake of the child, Duke Ailnor, accept your doom."

And, even gasping for air on the brink of annihilation, Durand remembered tall Duke Ailnor of Yrlac: the sober lord he had met at the Well of Noontide among gray guardians, the son of kings who would hear no talk of rebellion, the old man who had commanded Durand to flee from the hill at Fetch Hollow. Who must have died in the hours thereafter—shortly after his grandson.

Durand twisted, trying to fill his lungs once more before the Rooks blotted him from Creation. He spotted the sorcerers just in time to see one of the two men twitch his fingers in the air. That was all: a twitch. But the howl that rose from the old bones as the sorcerer squeezed his taloned little hand stung the dark and sent the thing that had been Ailnor lashing fit to fly to apart.

The Rook danced at a just-prudent distance and called over his victim's howl: "If you had done as we asked, we might have stopped with you alone. But you were obstinate and your obstinacy has inspired this twist of poetry: treacherous father and bastard son bound forever."

A shrill wheeze wailed over the sanctuary: "*A babe in arms,*" the monster said.

"And usurper, Your Grace. There was our master, stricken by betrayal—and you sought to raise his wife's bastard above him."

A second note shot through the old man's spectral howl: a piping cry that shimmered through the darkness, sounding for all the world like the wail of a child down some forsaken well.

Durand could not stand to think. Deorwen was climbing with the knife in her teeth, working her way up a carved pillar to her brother's bonds.

Durand was hearing Alwen's baby. It could only be that child. He remembered the cry from a tower room and a locked door in Radomor's keep. Now, that same voice was somehow trapped in the sorcerers' abomination.

"You have been ours since you breathed your death rattle over my brother's tongue," one Rook was saying. "Save the child pain. It is time."

With his grandchild's wail still in the air, Ailnor turned to Durand.

And Durand caught up his sword. Only Moryn mattered. Only Deorwen and her knife; she could still save Gireth, so long as the Rooks didn't look up and behind them. He would have to dance awhile to hold their attention. With a little luck, he might live long enough to see Moryn free and Deorwen running.

The Champion sprang, and before Durand could step, the monster had snatched him from his feet and thrown him crashing into an explosion of heaped skulls. Black souls boiled free, flashing in visions of night and darkness as they leapt past his eyelids and fled for their vile masters.

"Uh! Watch what you do, fool!" groaned a Rook.

Durand was pleased to cause the devils some indigestion. But the Champion crashed down among the rolling bones and a blow sent him sailing once more, his temple brushing the crisscrossed ribs of the aisle vault. He landed at the crushing end of the creature's throw with bone heaps bursting around him. He heard the Rooks curse, and his sword rebounding from the flagstones, rippling like a ribbon in the air.

This time, the Champion swarmed over him. Lashing with its clattering tail. Spinning him with its talons, the raging monster tossed and smashed him like millstones. And all the while, souls spun through the air, blinding him, choking him. Durand saw Moryn hanging beyond the Rooks. He saw Deorwen—so small and pale—high upon the pillar's flank. Mad. He saw the great shadow of the Champion now prowling near, shivering with darkness. Coming slow. Weeping. Raging.

Durand hoped the Rooks were choking on the stray souls he'd scattered. He hoped Deorwen had got her knife on Moryn's bonds.

His fingers slipped round the grip of his sword, and he began the long climb to his feet before the prowling horror—at least he would try to meet death standing. But the thing that had been Ailnor rushed in with a sound like a thunder of dry scrolls—

And stopped a breath from Durand's chin.

Durand wavered where he stood with his gorge rising, and peeled his eyelids open.

"Champion?" called one of the sorcerers. "What is this now? Finish him." There was a gulping sound from the man, a belch—choking, Durand prayed. "Do you know how many pots you have upset? Kill him, by God. Now!"

Wings of shadow were folding up around Durand. He couldn't tell whether they were the Rooks' doing, or artifacts of the battering his skull had taken. He looked up at the Champion.

The monstrous thing loomed over him like a wall of bones. Its stench filled his throat, but he could see the iron band of the thing's eyes. "Ailnor," he said. Maybe it was because he was on the verge of death himself, but Durand could only think of the old man, still there and as trapped as Durand and Moryn or any of them. "Ailnor. Moryn must be freed. His father holds the Host of Gireth to the flame of your son's armies. If we are destroyed, the kingdom will fall. It will all be like this hell. Rot and madness. From the mountains to the sea."

Shadows slithered over the Champion like black flames, like Ouen's sending. Teetering on the edge of death, Durand understood what he saw: here was soul upon soul bound to these dead bones, all stinging to drive the monster on. An eddy in the dark flame drew Durand's eyes to an unusual shape within woven bones. Beyond the cobweb banners and rusted finery, he saw a tiny bundle swaddled tight in rags. Right at the heart of it all. The great distorted head of the Champion swiveled, staring down upon Durand.

"Please," said Durand.

Somewhere one of the Rooks spluttered in frustration. "Oh, how tedious!" The sorcerer reeled into view, literally bulging with the load of souls Durand's throes had scattered. The sorcerer's hand leapt up, and the soul-fires blazed upon the Champion's bones, standing like the hackles of a mad dog.

But Ailnor scarcely moved.

Durand's eyes darted between the swaddled shape at the heart of the monster, and the iron mask that bound Ailnor's dead face. He remembered finding a bit of bone at the heart of Ouen's sending, but this wrapped shape was no fragment of some man's shin.

The necromancer's bloated face soured, and his fingers curled. The baby's sob whistled out on the air, and Durand saw the swaddled bundle twist. The soul-shadows blazed now, standing a yard from the monster, sending spines of ice through the slime upon the floor.

Durand closed his eyes, setting the brittle points of his teeth together.

But Ailnor spoke: *"Not for blood. Not for one child only."*

The bearing of the old duke transformed the monstrous shape, the frame of bones rising despite the blaze of souls on its kindling limbs. Durand saw the blood of kings in the distorted figure. And the slot of the ruined visor stared level into Durand's eyes. The monster's arms began to open, the baby screamed in the midst of the black flame. Bones popped like firewood in an agony beyond endurance.

Meanwhile, the swollen sorcerers struggled with their creation, flies darting loose with every grunt. Durand wondered how many dead men one sorcerer could contain. He wondered how many had been bound up in the spell that gave life to the Champion.

Durand looked up at the old duke's mask. He saw the swaddled child. And he drove his sword home.

IN THE HIGH passes beyond Durand's native hall, there were winter days when whole white mountainsides might slump from their stark heights to fill Creation with ice and thunder. At the touch of some traveler's staff, a whole village might vanish but for fragments to be found in the moons of springtide.

The touch of Durand's blade was like such a traveler's staff.

In the moment when his point found the Champion's swaddled heart, the whole of Creation came down.

Souls beyond number burst from their bonds while the bones of dry generations flew like a hundred storms of arrows, rattling from the ceilings of the old sanctuary.

The hellish explosion threw Durand flat and battered him into some dead man's tomb. As he scrambled in that stone socket, dark shapes raked the air over his head. He heard screams fit to stiffen the blood. And then the place was silent.

Deorwen had been out there.

He burst from his grizzly shelter into a soft rain of feathers. Every candle was out. Every heap of bones, upturned.

He found the broken shape of the old duke at the heart of the destruction. The withered form of the old man clutched the broken bundle to his hollow chest. Both figures were as dead as the winter moons should have left them and—Durand hoped—gone to the Gates of Heaven.

Something moved beyond the gray wreck of the old man. Still weak, Durand stole through drifted feathers to find a splayed shape of blue-gray flesh. As he approached the broken thing, he slowly made out its shape: here were cocked arms, here bent legs. Between these features, however, Durand found flesh, both white and blue. One of the Rooks had been blown open to his belt and laid bare to his ribs and chine. Small bones crunched under Durand's feet. Already, worms teemed upon the carcass.

He left the thing and called, "Deorwen?" stalking over crackling bones to the space beyond the high altar where Moryn had been hung.

A cool wind thick with pitch and timber stirred the feathered wreckage. Durand imagined the girl thrown from the pillar and crashing down. But the first motion he saw was a small dark bird.

"You are not one of ours," wheezed a voice.

Durand rounded a pillar to find the second Rook sprawled upon his back and torn as though a pack of dogs had caught him, his fingers chalk white against the blue loops of his bowels. The bird bounced near his pale skull. It was a starling, jittering and iridescent.

The sorcerer seemed not to see Durand at all.

"How long have you been among our flocks, looking on, eh?" The Rook spoke to the bird. "Are you one from our Whisperer? To see how we progressed?" The starling hopped, its brown eyes flickering like flint chips, as the Rook reached vaguely toward it with one bloody hand. "We'd been expecting . . . we'd expected to hear more. We had come so far—" A fit interrupted the sorcerer. His dark eyes rolled and his tongue scrabbled at his lips.

Already, pale worms were crawling over him. Thick clots teemed. "Ah well," he said, and the trailing wheeze of his final breath spluttered out as the first of the worms went in.

Durand made the Eye of Heaven and shook his head.

A few moments later, he found Moryn in a heap beyond the altar. The impossible arrow still jutted from the man's bare shoulder, but Durand ducked close enough to see that the man's lungs still labored. There was no sign of Deorwen. Through the shattered east window above, Durand could hear the clangor of the fight in the streets. He smelled the fires. Men were dying every heartbeat, and he'd found Moryn.

He turned back into the darkness, shouting, "Deorwen!" desperate.

His voice rang down the length of a silent sanctuary where black feathers still sifted down. The place needed priests—Patriarchs. Legions of Holy Ghosts. And somewhere in the midst of it all was Deorwen, unable to answer him. Durand could hardly breathe with the dread of losing her.

"Deorwen?"

He hunted frantically among the columns on either side of the altar, and then his glance fell upon the chasm in the sanctuary floor only a few paces farther on.

"Hells," Durand said, and hurried over crackling bones to the stairs. He left Moryn and the clash of the battle behind.

At first, the stairs were blocked; Durand had to heave the lids of a dozen tombs aside to scramble down. Finally, he reached the putrid dark. Without even the sickly candlelight, he could only feel his way between the pillars by memory.

He prayed. He named every Power in Heaven, begging that he not be parted from Deorwen. That she was somewhere in the dark, safe. That he would not lose her.

It was all so silent as he hunted through the blackness that the sound of the battle seemed to follow him—a nagging whisper haunting him as he fumbled deeper through that charnel ruin. But he could not leave her even as he felt the time rushing away from him.

Finally, on a third or fourth passage through the dark pit, he heard the whispered edge of faint breathing. The sound caught him like the touch of lightning. "Deorwen?" he called, and he clawed his way to a place under the high altar. Skin and linen glowed against black feathers, and Durand skidded to the woman's side on his knees.

"They're dead," he said. "The Rooks. And the Champion. Moryn—your brother—he's alive. Deorwen?"

He couldn't hear the breathing. "Aw, no. No, no."

He searched the girl for obvious wounds. He lifted the girl's head, looking down on her eyelids, but it did no good.

He bent close enough to kiss her, even as smeared with death as he was. He had to feel her breath; he had to know. He had seen plenty of men knocked from consciousness, and knew that it might mean anything.

"Host of Heaven, don't take her from me. Let her be with me." He was not sure she was breathing.

"Deorwen? I am begging," he whispered.

The girl's eyes fluttered open. "Uh."

"Deorwen? Oh, God." With a grip that had killed a dozen men, he squeezed her for being alive. And the touch of her stirring in his arms overwhelmed every oath he'd taken, pitching him into great, deep, gulping kisses that forgot everything in Creation but the girl and the feel of her living body in his hands and the traitor's joy in his racing blood.

FINALLY, DEORWEN HAD to convince him to let her go. "They are gone," she said. "The Lost. The birds."

"Yes." That much, at least, was true.

When he crashed into the stables, sweating and shaking with strain, he found a bony gray nag that kicked for the ceiling at the death-house stink suddenly in her stall. But Durand couldn't carry Deorwen and her brother both, and he gave the horse no choice.

"And now the ramparts again," murmured Deorwen. Durand lifted her—light as a rabbit—behind his saddle and hauled her gaunt brother over the horse's withers.

"Your father must see his son," said Durand, and he spurred the horse into the courtyard. The last man who'd passed this way was Radomor himself, but Durand was almost drunk with elation.

As the citadel gates swung into sight, Deorwen caught hold of Durand's tunic. "What do you mean to do?" She was waking up as he drove for mighty grates of oak and iron and stone turrets higher than the walls. "They'll never open!"

But Durand's blood sang. He kicked the gray to greater speed. And saw the gatekeepers boggle at a rider coming *from* the citadel. He pictured himself stained and hunched and black and scarred—all in rags and storming from the sorcerers' citadel. A few shards of teeth glinting, the flash of eyes. "Durand!" Deorwen demanded, but Durand only gritted his broken teeth and hoped the whoresons would think "devil" or "messenger" and get out of his way.

The men scrambled as the stolen gray sparked the cobbles and they careened for the portcullis. But the gates flew wide, and as they plunged into the empty alleys beyond, Durand thanked his creator.

They stormed another gate that same way, and then the smoke was thick in the streets and they were bearing down on the ramparts where Gireth and Yrlac fought for the wall.

He swung the gray toward what should have been a mighty gatehouse, shut fast against an army and packed with soldiers. What he found, however, was a gate that gaped wide—like the mouth of a forge packed with the black shapes of Radomor's men. The Duke of Yrlac had thrown the doors open and leapt into his own blazing trap.

Durand blinked at the smoke as the nag danced. Only in these fires would they find Severin of Mornaway. Somehow he must crash through the rear of Radomor's army and win through to Mornaway's lines. His heart hammered. He pictured a wild leap. The horse driving. Hundreds of men, startled—maybe. He tightened his grip and squared the skittish gray, ready to spur for the gates.

But caught him.

"Durand! What are you thinking?" she demanded. "I think you've done enough plotting for one day. Get down."

Durand boggled, pointing through the gates. "Your father's through there. If he sees his son, all of this is finished."

"That's Radomor's army you're waving at. Get down, damn you." She caught his sleeve and, leaping down herself, hauled him staggering from the saddle.

"That's not the way," said Deorwen.

Durand blinked and pulled Moryn from the gray's withers while the man groaned his agony. "Damn me," Moryn said and tried to get his feet under him. "I know you from somewhere." He turned the great baffled hollows of his eyes upon Durand's face. "What is this nightmare? What is my sister—?"

But there was no time to chat, not twenty paces from an army where any of half a thousand men might glance and wonder at the strange trio in ragged linens.

"Brother," said Deorwen. "Durand must carry you. Our father's spilling half the blood of Gireth for your sake. We must finish it."

"God. The fool," Moryn said. "Damn him."

But Deorwen didn't wait to listen. She shot for the battlements—darting near the throng in the gates and scampering the steps for a look over the top.

"Durand. Get me to my father," said Moryn. And Durand followed, lifting and dragging Moryn past the backs of an army. His eyes pulsed with stars. Finally, he joined Deorwen in an embrasure where they could peer into the blazing oven of the street below. Durand's eyes were drawn to the battle at the gatehouse. A few dozen paces down the parapet, he could stand on the gatehouse, right on the heads of two armies. "Lamoric's men will see us up there."

"There are soldiers between—" Deorwen began, but Durand was off.

He heaved the Lord of Mornaway across his hitched shoulders, and staggered down the parapet. "Are you mad?" Moryn grunted. But Durand could not even grunt for fear of collapsing, and every instant down below was snatching lives away while they could stop it all. Durand rushed up against one of Yrlac's men, bowling the devil tumbling into the fires. A second soldier fell the same way—no one expected to meet an enemy on the wall. "What will this achieve?" Moryn demanded.

"Duke Severin must know you're free or there's been no point prying you from the sanctuary. I left friends in those fires."

Thousands surged in the press at the gates. Durand strained in the smoke. Pain was breaking him down. He must catch someone's eye soon—without getting himself shot in the process. As he peered down and staggered nearer to the fight, he spotted the dark hair of a man in red and white and a sword sparking in the firelight. The glimpse touched him like a tongue of lightning. Here was Lamoric himself. The man seemed hard-pressed by some champion of the enemy. Durand wanted to leap the distance. He had to stop the battle.

"Durand, no!" said Deorwen, but Durand was already shouting. With luck, he might be able to heave the man down onto friendly hands. He couldn't be sure where Gireth ended and Yrlac began. "I have him! Lord Moryn is free!" ignoring a gasp from Moryn to wrestle the man above the parapet. *"By the King of Heaven, I have Moryn!"* But not a soul looked up from the deadly work in the street.

On the gatehouse itself, however, men heard him. In an

instant, three dozen of Radomor's wolves had spun in a flash of eyes and blades and teeth.

"Hells," said Durand.

As Durand ran, half the gatehouse poured down on his heels. He blundered past a fallen guardsman and flinched under flights of Gireth arrows, catching Deorwen's hand and pulling her into motion. He had to get her free.

A soldier appeared in their way, swinging a heavy spear, and all Durand could do was leap from the walk up to the high merlons of the parapet, hauling Deorwen in long strides over fire and empty space with a premonition of arrowheads pricking at his back. And he knew he was running *away* from every chance of turning the fight.

Worse yet, he could not run fast enough with a man on his neck. They would have Deorwen in an instant. He could feel the blades of a dozen soldiers swinging nearer. Twenty more soldiers vaulted the steps ahead.

"There," grunted Moryn. "The banner!"

Through flames and shadow, Durand glimpsed the men of Mornaway hunkered in solemn lines, Mornaway's blue diamonds flapping in the furnace—out of reach. And after days and hours of fighting, Durand stopped. Despite a hundred wild victories, the string of improbabilities was at its end.

Then he felt a tug from Deorwen's hand.

They had only heartbeats.

She looked him squarely in the eyes, and Durand let Moryn's feet to the ground. "It's better," said Moryn.

And the three leapt into the flames, vanishing from the battlements just as the charging men of Yrlac crashed together behind them.

THERE WAS A flying moment of flame and distant screams.

Then Durand's heel struck some joist or truss high in a burning building. He managed a wild running step before the impetus of his fall pitched him into a breakneck somersault. Curtains of flame swung up around him and beams snapped at the touch of his hands.

When the plunge met its crushing end, Durand was left to gulp at the bottom of an inferno. He blinked up into the rippling complexity of flame where timbers twisted like the wicks of candles.

In another instant, he would have died. But a tug at his hand brought him to his senses. Deorwen. And, if she was alive, he could not lie down. He heaved with the last of his strength, feeling the heat peel away as he pulled them all into the street.

And straight into kettle-helms and the backs of armored men. This was the army of Mornaway, and every soldier twitched back from Durand as if he were a fiend who'd burst from the earth.

"Get me up," said Moryn. "By Heaven, get me on my feet."

Durand wrenched Moryn upright. Something devilish had happened to the man's shoulder, but he stepped among the soldiers. Horror and bewilderment warred in the men's expressions. Durand struggled to wedge himself between Deorwen and the uneasy mob. None of this was safe. "This is Lord *Moryn*," he said. He could see the pack of baffled soldiers cocking weapons. He caught one man's tunic. "Let us—" and a gauntlet knocked spikes through his jaw.

Durand tore the man down, snatching a mace from the fool's hand before he fell. The mob erupted. With a grunt, Durand had Moryn's weight on his good shoulder and the mace was flying. It skipped from helmet and shoulder, cracking collarbones and crumpling helmets. He used its spikes like claws to climb. He drove, bulling men and boys aside with Deorwen lost behind him as he bludgeoned anyone who wouldn't move. *"Moryn! Moryn!"* he screamed, fighting against the thrashing undertow as he hauled the heir of Mornaway into the mass of his kinsmen. Flesh and bone slid under his soles.

He would maul every knight of Mornaway if it would get him to their bloody duke.

Finally, a flash of blue diamonds rippled above the heaving line: the duke's standard. Durand had almost reached the man. He swatted one man down and found himself staring into the grief and despair of old Duke Severin of Mornaway himself. The frail duke sent an unthinking blow whistling from his tears, but Durand parried, roaring *Moryn*'s name loud enough to open the duke's eyes. At first, revulsion wavered over old Mornaway's hollow features. Durand couldn't know what the man thought or saw.

"Father!" said Moryn and tore himself free from Durand to stand, gaunt and bloody, before his father. Apprehension dawned on the old man's ravaged face, and in that instant among those grim soldiers, every bond that held Mornaway's host in Ferangore flew apart.

RADOMOR WAS NO fool: he knew that a reluctant ally needed watching. And so, to lend his borrowed host teeth and backbone, the Duke of Yrlac had set fierce squadrons of his own men in the van and rearguard of Mornaway's host. Now, the men of Mornaway unleashed their rage and shame on these startled men, and blood flew.

Durand launched himself like a thing of teeth and talons. He couldn't think, or he would stop or die. Against the gates, the battle was slaughtering Gireth, and so Durand tore into Radomor's men like a true savage, armored in rags. He opened a path with cruelty, smashing throats and hammering joints and faces. He stole shields where he could, fighting under one man's colors and then the next as wood and leather split before the driving battalion. He hardly recognized the attempts of knights to yield. He swung from agony, sure the time was slipping from them.

From the battlements, a man might have seen the shape of the fighting, but in the midst of it, there was nothing but smoke and the press of screaming faces. There was a thumb in his eye and a blade slick against his ribs. But somewhere ahead, Berchard and Guthred and Lamoric and all of the Knights of the Painted Hall were at the heart of the mauling. Durand could do nothing but claw onward.

Finally, they tore through the last of Radomor's vanguard and the battle seemed to fly apart. Startled and overwhelmed, the mercenaries under Radomor's leopard blazon scattered before the gateway. And soon, all that remained of the army of Yrlac was a bloody ring of Radomor's fiercest liegemen hunkered under in the very teeth of the gates.

And the sound of one last scuffle.

Durand tottered out alone between the armies. By some

unspoken signal, the combined hosts of Gireth and Mornaway had stopped. The ground was slick under Durand's bare feet and the fires snapped among the rooftops. Before him, the faces of Yrlac's last knights shone with sweat and soot and blood—and from beyond their ring, Durand heard the clang and stamp of the last duel in that tortured city.

He saw the men he knew, exhausted among the soldiers of Gireth: Guthred, Berchard, even Coensar. All of his comrades; all of the men he'd fought with—all but one.

Through the screen of surcoats and armored limbs, he saw two figures circling under the gates. He saw snatches of Gireth's crimson and Yrlac's green. Here were Lamoric and Radomor, fighting on.

"God," Durand said. Nothing was finished; Lamoric was still trapped with the monster, Radomor.

Durand shook the cobwebs from his skull and threw himself upon the heavy ring of Radomor's last knights. He swung his stolen mace, beating shields and shoulders.

But they sent him staggering back. And not one man of Lamoric's host joined his attack.

Durand saw glimpses of Lamoric. The young lord leapt and scrambled as the hunched duke lashed with his blade, his beard jutting round a purple scowl.

Durand looked into the faces of Lamoric's army. Their eyes glittered. Weapons hung in slack fingers. He gaped in astonishment, in fury. Someone was saying, "Durand." But Durand would not hear, and he launched himself once more at the barricade of Radomor's soldiers.

Beyond reach, he saw Lamoric's shield twitch and spin like a curl of parchment under the mighty strokes of Radomor's blade. The powerful duke threw himself into every attack, sometimes spinning and leaping like a fairground tumbler, carving every hope of attack and escape from Lamoric's world. Durand threw men aside.

After a hundred narrow escapes, Lamoric staggered, his sword wavering high just as the circle broke under Durand's fists.

Durand saw Radomor lunge inches beyond his fingers—only an instant too late.

And in that instant, the duke shot a straight and sudden

blow through Lamoric of Gireth. The broad point punched through mail and surcoat to stand in the fabric between Lamoric's shoulders right before Durand's eyes and had Lamoric's own blade wavering over their heads.

Creation had stopped and the blade hung there, glittering in the flames.

Durand had been too late only by heartbeats. He'd climbed the city, he'd swum its wells, he'd fought the devils in its churches, but he'd been too late—too late by moments.

Hands caught at Durand's tunic. There were blows. But he thought only of Deorwen in his arms and how he'd stopped to hold her while the army burned in the street and the man who'd brought him from starvation fought for his life. Durand had prayed to have her, and now Lamoric was dead.

Back in the street, Radomor crouched with both fists still on the skewering blade. Lamoric's sword wobbled over his head, trembling to the last beats of his heart. Lamoric could have seen no friend.

But as he tottered there on Radomor's blade with his last strength giving way, a final spark of resolve caught light in him. Before Durand could blink, the man's slack fingers clamped tight on his sword, and in a single mighty spasm, the blade flashed down.

Radomor was without defense. What could he do with his sword trapped?

Blood sprang from the steel, and the Duke of Yrlac pitched. The two lords were falling together. A piggish eye widened in astonishment, seeing God knew what. Lamoric swung the gleaming edge a second time, but it did not matter. Radomor of Yrlac and Lamoric of Gireth fell to the bloody street.

Now, RADOMOR'S MEN relented. Durand was freed to skid to Lamoric's side and to throw the duke's still-heaving corpse from his master's body.

"Lamoric! Lamoric!"

For an instant, the young lord's eyes only drifted darkly, but then they snapped around, and the man managed a tight smile. *"Durand!"* he marveled, grunting the name.

"Aye, Lordship. God. I tried to reach you. Moryn is free. Deorwen lives. This war is finished. I—"

"—You saw. You saw. You must have!"

Durand wrestled with the man's surcoat, thinking that he should shut up and do something.

"You saw?" Lamoric gasped, trying to catch Durand's wrists.

"I did," Durand admitted. He probed the gash in the iron mail.

"I could have had him that first day."

Bright blood welled from the wound, filling the folds of his surcoat. Radomor's blade had caught one of the vessels in the man's guts. Durand pressed his hands into the mess.

"I could have had him," Lamoric repeated, wincing.

Durand pressed, doubling over. "I'm certain."

"While the cities stood. And all—" he winced. "And all the banners were flying."

The hopeless gush came warm over Durand's wrists, and Durand shut his eyes. He wondered how much death a man could stand.

He felt Lamoric's hand bat at his jaw. Then the man's bloody gauntlet dropped. His face was white and still as wax and his breath rattled out into the empty air above Ferangore, safe now from Rooks and ravens.

There was not a sound in that city of armies but the crackling of fires.

🪢 29. Homecoming

Among the prisoners, the barons of Gireth could find no greater lord than a red-haired youth called Leovere of Penseval to offer the surrender of Radomor's followers. Penseval had fought in the last knot of Radomor's liegemen, standing in the ring that had kept Durand from Lamoric's side.

Before the man could stammer submission, Durand pushed into the mob and joined the silent men already gathering the dead—keeping far from those who knew him as the smoke of the day gave way to the chill darkness of the night. He had no wish to think or speak. And he could not see Deorwen. Not then.

The gruesome drudgery of the work pushed Durand beyond thought and pain and exhaustion. Through the evening, he dragged cold, slack men beyond the walls. And, in the darkness thereafter, he fumbled at the rigid absurdity of stiffened limbs.

Durand spoke to no one. Men found barrows and stretchers, but mostly they carted the dead by ankles and armpits, shuffling without words through gates and into the dark.

Badan had died. Durand learned that as he dragged another armored man through the gates. Shuffling backward past a scrap of torchlight, he saw a gleam of bald forehead and lank red hair hanging behind. Durand wasn't sure which of them felt more numb as he brought the body to lie among the others.

For much of that night, he was scarcely more than hands and eyes.

AT DAWN, A hundred carts waited in the clay below the city gates. It seemed that the dead were not to be left behind, and so Mornaway's men had ransacked a hundred leagues and pillaged every farmer's cart. Durand and the rest of the mute laborers had simply turned to the task of sliding their chill comrades high between cart rails.

And when Durand could find no more bodies waiting on the field, he climbed aboard the cart where he'd laid his last corpse—thankfully, there was room on the bench beside the driver. Rain fell and the carts labored away from Ferangore in a column that seemed to straggle leagues along the River Rushes. Oblivion snatched at Durand as he rocked beside the driver. The horse's head nodded under the jumbled tomb of the lurching cart before them.

AS THE KNIGHTS of Ash intoned the Eventide, the column curled into a broad basin by the Rushes. Durand's driver slipped down without a word and freed his horse to crop the sparse valley. Already, men had kindled fires against the grass some distance from the gray muddle of carts.

Durand watched men settle around those fires—feeling no great longing to join them as the darkness settled quick and cold and dim expanses stretched on every side. Mornaway's men trundled barrels from their supply wagons and the serving men had pots and tents ready. The camp looked like an island of color and firelight in the gloom.

Where Durand stood, peeping like a stranger at a window, he could see the long shadows thrown by the men at the fires. And a familiar movement in the dark where trenches and potholes brimmed with the living shadows of the Lost. The things shivered to life all around, opening like midnight flowers into Creation and swimming over the turf to sniff for blood and life. It had Durand thinking of the dead behind him.

And so, Durand flinched when a voice called his name. But this was not some utterance from the Otherworld. Not far down the row of charnal carts, Deorwen hurried from the firelight; she had slipped from her family. She looked no taller than a child as she struggled through the wet grass.

"Where've you been?"

Durand avoided her touch. "Here." He couldn't stand to have her so close, and now she hugged herself tight—cold and alone only a step away. He held his ground.

"My father, he has been walking," she said. "All these leagues since Ferangore. He's cropped his hair with a dagger's blade and will wear neither shoes nor mantle. 'Not a man of Gireth is to lie under the sod of Yrlac,' he has said. And now we must cart the bodies. There is ice in the ruts until noon and he has seen more than sixty winters, Durand."

Durand only nodded, a coward among the shadows.

But Deorwen stepped close and cornered him against the cart. "I won't ask why you've hidden yourself here with the dead any more than I'll ask my father why he works so hard to join them in the ground. I will not do these things, but neither will I pretend that you are a thousand leagues from me. Not now."

What another heartbeat might have brought, Durand would never know, for another figure had left the firelight and come marching toward them, calling out. Durand thought he heard the girl's name.

But she grabbed his cloak. "Durand. Lamoric is gone. My father is mad with the shame of his treasons. Please."

But before she could say more, their new guest called out loud and clear: "Deorwen!" The fellow had come close enough now that Durand could see the hitched way the man walked and how he clutched a long cloak at his throat with one hand. "Deorwen? By Heaven, where are you, sister?" Here was Moryn, walking despite his wounds.

"Moryn! What are you doing?" said Deorwen.

The man winced. Even in the gloom, Durand could see the man's eyes shining with fever. "I realized you'd gone, sister. Walked off. This is no safe place." Around him, the shadows were climbing the carts. "An armed camp at any time. And this."

While Moryn had the girl's attention, Durand stepped free, agreeing, "Aye. And the fires will be warmer than here, I'm sure. And hot food before long. His Lordship looks as though he'll need a shoulder to get back. This is no place for any of us."

And instead of offering his help, Durand left the girl standing there with her brother. She couldn't follow, not with Moryn lame and feverish. Not her.

Durand hobbled through the death-carts toward an empty sweep of river. Here and there, he saw old Conran's Holy Ghosts standing vigil, looking lonely as candles in their clean white gear.

Lamoric had deserved a better liegeman: one who could leave his master's wife alone and keep the oaths he'd spoken. But, instead, Lamoric had been left with Durand Col who couldn't master his heart, who delayed with lives waiting in fire and siege.

As he put the high walls of the carts behind him, he noticed the sky. Last Twilight glowed above a black valley, and the clouds were strange. They soared like a milky ceiling of ice—a remote, giant's Heaven. And amid these strange clouds, Durand perceived great movements: folds that crossed the Heavens, curling into mighty eddies, distinct in their pearl edges and as clear and colossal. They hung in the distant north, two enormous curls, each like an upturned mountain.

And Durand had nearly stumbled into Conran. "The king makes war and we, his servants, are far from him." The man's voice was scarcely human; a cartload of dead men could have breathed on Durand's neck. Now, the ancient giant's single eye held the light of those northern clouds and did not turn as Durand stopped.

In that valley at that moment, the king seemed very far away. "His brother," Durand recalled: Prince Eodan of Windhover. Lord of the wood where their father, Carondas, had died.

"Eodan is nearly the king's match in pride." The man's voice was like the creak of an oak. "He declares his lands free of his brother's rule, free of Errest the Old. And here we are."

Durand peered at the hanging mountains. They might have been stone or glass, they were so clear before his eyes—north, over the forests of Windhover. Durand's answer was little more than a whisper. "What could you do if you were there with so few men to turn a great battle?"

"Our king sent my brethren and I from his side. He clutches fools and flatterers close and wages war upon his brother where his royal father died."

At this, a light flashed—a light flickering beyond the clouds. But this was not a thing of the skies alone.

This was nearer at hand; Creation itself twitched.

And in the shocked moment afterward, Durand heard something on the move over Yrlac: a breeze careered through the land like the ghost of horses, sweeping down the Rushes to batter the light of a hundred fires against the valley floor.

"Another high sanctuary!" hissed giant Conran. "By the sea." And there was a strange scent of salt air on the wind. Salt and fire. "It can only be Evensands. And now there is only the king's high sanctuary in the heart of Eldinor." Tendons leapt in the man's neck. All around, it seemed that the shadows bulged. "And here," he said, "look what watches. Soon they will be free."

Where Durand had not noticed a tangle of blackthorns near the bank, now he saw crabbed figures with needle claws. The Lost moved in the long grass. And on the crest of

the far valley, a figure as tall as a sanctuary tower slippe
back into hiding.

"The Banished wait while we run in our circles," sai
Conran. "The wards are breaking, strand by strand. The kin
wages war within his realm. Ferangore and Acconel are i
ruins. The Septarim scattered. The high sanctuaries hav
fallen. And Errest has not been so bare to the night in twent
centuries. These things do not come singly or by chance
Someone plays a dreadful game in Errest the Old, and eve
the least part of it is dark to us."

As Conran spoke, the Banished spirits settled back int
the gloom. "But Radomor is dead . . ." Durand breathed.

Conran's glinting eye was on the move lest fiends pou
from some unobserved quarter of the horizon. His men hel
their blades against the dark.

"Aye, Durand Col. And his sorcerers with him. But ou
king fights in Windhover while his barons cower behin
their walls. And here we stand.

"In the fastness of the shadows a hand is moving, an
none but the Silent King can know from whence our doon
will fall!"

WHILE THE PORTENTS roiled in the northern skies, the
column lurched for Acconel. Time and again, Creation
flinched and Durand caught glimpses of shadowy watchers
along the roadway, of giants on the ridgelines, of spirits in
the trees. Until, quite suddenly, Durand's driver called out,
"Whoa!"

Durand knew the damp odor of the River Banderol in the
weeds. They had crossed the bourn of Gireth, their column
had halted, and now a stout rider jounced between the roadside and the riverbank breathlessly puffing, "His Grace stands
before the Fuller's Bridge and waits upon Abravanal of
Gireth. His Grace stands before the Fuller's Bridge and waits
upon Abravanal of Gireth. His Grace stands before—"

This breathless knight was Berchard of the One Eye and
jolted to a stop at Durand's side—before his horse could
pitch him in the river.

"Durand?" Teeth flashed in the man's beard. "That's

nough, I think. The rest will get the message. I'll be damned
' I get myself washed into the mere to tell them.

"Here. Listen to that." The sound of hammers hung upon
ae air, and there was green sawdust on the breeze. "They're
wful quick to rebuild."

Durand thought of Conran's portents. "Conran's not so
ure we've won anything yet."

"I'm not sure I like the look of the Heavens either. And
've seen a thing or two in my day." He jostled his mount
longside Durand's bench. He scrubbed his puckered eye. "I
ver tell you about this damned thing?"

"What will Abravanal do?" Durand muttered.

"Abravanal? I'm waiting for old Severin. Every knight in
is retinue has black-barred his colors. Should be a show.
Ie's up there, a duke in linens! Muck to his hams. Not a
loak between him and the wind and the rain. And I must
ay, he doesn't seem himself—though I suppose I don't
now the fellow so well that I can be sure. In any case, as
was saying, we were pulling thieves from the bushes down
n Aubairn. These whoresons, they were hiding in the Fey
Wood, playing on the infamy of the place. You could always
lame a missing caravan on the Lost or the Banished and
vho'd know different? That was the dullards' bright idea."

Durand blinked. Somewhere beyond the carts ahead, the
nead of the column must be in the Tenter's Field yard be-
ore the Fuller's Bridge. Before his mind's eye, Durand saw
he ancient Duke of Gireth walking through a city of soot
and sawdust, his heir a girl-child of six winters.

"We were trailing one pack of fools who reckoned nobody'd notice that some flitting forest pisky was crashing
through the woods on eight warhorses and sleeping round
a campfire every night—when every trace of the whoresons
just up and disappeared.

"We should have known better than to go poking around.
But we started. And we ran across this old woman.

"Some of us had these arbalests—the *really* heavy crossbows." He tapped a fresh scar on his forehead. "Bigger than
the bow that bit me. And this old woman blundered out in
front of us. And I must've touched the trigger. And it was *so*

quick. *Snap!* and the bolt was gone—like a wasp for th
crone's gray head. I just stared. I'm no crack shot with a cross
bow, and I hadn't taken aim. It could've gone anywhere. Bu
she flopped on her backside, and the bolt clattered off half
league through the trees."

"Berchard . . ." Durand raised his hand. All around ancien
Acconel, the sound of hammers and axes died away. One ma
somewhere in the vast ruin persisted, and a man could hea
the sharp *chop, chop, chop.*

But Berchard pressed on. "Aye. Abravanal will be comin,
soon, I'm sure. But, back in the woods, there she was: thi
old woman in the track. And the quiet. And I'm thinking
here's somebody's grandma. And I bent down over her to
see if—maybe, God help me—the bolt had just grazed her
But she's lying like a sack of corn and there's this blood
great hole where her eye ought to have been.

"I was just about sick, her white hair floating all round thi
bloody slop."

"Berchard . . ."

"I'm nearly there, boy. You see, the old hag gave a sort o
twitch. All I could think was: 'Ugh! And there's nothing fo
it but to finish her. And what a day I'm having.' When, from
nowhere, the old bat's hand snaps out, adder quick. And
whack! she's got hold of my *eye!* Same one as I'd shot out of
her head! And I could feel her knobbed old fingers curling in
there as though my flesh and bones were made of clay. No
pain. Just these fingers moving, and a sound like scooping
up sand."

There was no one speaking for a league in any direction
and no sound but the river and Berchard as he leaned close.
"And she *spoke* to me. 'I'll have what I'm owed,' she said.
And I couldn't move with her hand. And my mates were too
stunned to move. Just as well, though, probably.

"That's what I reckon happened to the other bunch, by the
way. Think on it: I put her eye out. Imagine if I'd come for
her with a blade! I would hate to think if I'd whacked a bolt
through her heart.

"Funny thing is, though, I still see a thing or two sometimes with the other eye. Mostly trees and branches. Dark
paths winding through the Fey Wood down there. Some-

mes a cellar full of crocks and skulls. Sometimes other
ings. But I can't complain. She was owed. And settling
cores is a tricky thing."

A hollow fanfare moaned from somewhere downriver past
arts and the naked dead.

"Ah here. That'll be old Abravanal coming out, poor dev-
l. They sent riders ahead to hint, maybe. Poor Deorwen, she
nd some of the other women cleaned the boy up. He could
e sleeping." He sniffed and looked up at the cart's load.
This cold is God's mercy."

Here was the gray homecoming of Durand's lord. Durand
ad ridden and rowed and marched and killed and betrayed
n the man's service. He wasn't waiting.

"Here, where are you going?" Berchard demanded. Du-
and swung himself down from the bench while Berchard
gave clumsy chase on horseback.

Durand heard the clack of hooves upon the Fuller's
Bridge. All around Durand, men wiped their caps and hoods
from their heads—and he pushed forward until, finally, he
stood in the first circle of that solemn crowd where Abravanal and Severin faced one another.

On the bridge, Abravanal sat a pale horse, bent and fragile
under the heaps of his regalia. His guard included Kieren
Arbourhall and—Durand noted with a flinch—Durand's
father, hunched on a sturdy warhorse.

Severin of Mornaway tottered out before them all and
bowed low at the muddy bridgehead. "Abravanal," he quavered, "Duke of Gireth, I, your cousin, Severin, Duke of
Mornaway, bring you greetings."

Abravanal's flat blue eyes did not blink.

". . . Your Grace. I . . . I am come from Ferangore in the
land of your enemy. Your host has fought a great battle. Between the Rushes and the Bercelet where Radomor the
Usurper set himself against your host with devices mundane
and supernatural, but . . . But the courage of your liegemen.
He could not resist.

"Victory is yours."

Abravanal was as still as the stones of the Fuller's Bridge
as water churned around the piers below and the wind sighed
over the Warrens.

Severin knelt. "But this is not the end. What would I no give if it were? The Barons of Errest have looked on from their strongholds while Gireth sent its sons against our common enemy, friendless and alone. Cowards watched an weighed the best course while your liegemen spent thei blood. Of all these craven lords, I . . . I am worst! In terror o losing my own son, I have stood against your house with the enemy of our realm. To the shame of my line, I have at tended the slaughter of your liegemen and sacrificed you flesh to save my own. And now—immortal infamy beyond forgiveness or remedy!—your son is among those lost be fore the gates of the enemy. Bravest of the bravest race Brightest of the Sons of Atthi, he fell alone, slaying the en emy of our kingdom with his last breath.

"My crime is beyond forgiveness," said Severin and the thin old man lowered himself into the ruts and puddles while Abravanal stared down with his flat blue eyes.

Finally, Abravanal spoke into the silence: "I will take you at your word," he said. "You have said that you would give much, and I know what I would have of you." Durand felt his neck prickle in the airless moment as Abravanal breathed The man blinked his pale eyes. "With your own bargain, you will repay me. Your son for mine. And you, Severin of Mornaway, I will hold for his murder.

"Bind them! I will not have them wander free while my son is bound in death. Creation will not suffer them to see another dawn!"

DURAND CAME LATE to the shocked feast that followed, mounting the entry stair through silent ranks of servants. No man could wish to feast at such a time. But the Powers must be thanked, even with the world at its end and the victory so costly. And a man of Lamoric's retinue could not escape without offending his master's memory.

As Durand stepped into Abravanal's Painted Hall, he found a room as deep in madness as Radomor's hall in Ferangore. He had entered at the bottom of the feasting hall, and, though hundreds sat at the long tables inside, not one man uttered a word. Every face was grim, every eye in motion. And, at the hall's distant head, Duke Abravanal sat in dull finery, his

arons arrayed on each hand, everyone sitting in the wary glit-
er of his hauberk, a sharp blade at his hip.

One thing explained the unease of that place: like beasts
before some dark altar, Severin and his son lay chained in
ags before Abravanal's high table while five-score knights
f Mornaway sat among the guests.

Gunderic's ancient Sword of Justice gleamed upon the
loth before Abravanal's seat.

Durand shook his head. Had he torn Moryn from the
Rooks, had he freed Mornaway from Radomor's trap, only
o watch them battle here? Near the entry arch, Berchard had
aved a place and Durand stole to it. Heremund Skald took
im by the shoulder as he sat. The little man ducked close to
whisper, "Seems little call for players this afternoon." Du-
and's answering glance should have killed the skald like
Berchard's basilisk, but the fool merely shrugged his apolo-
gies.

On the benches, the long rows of Mornaway's troops sat
with their mouths shut tight. Not one had so much as an elbow on the table. And no wonder. There, under their very
noses, lay their liege lord shackled to the floor, and there was
his heir. And the men of Gireth were armed.

Heremund was looking too. "The Patriarch has his beard
n knots over the signs in the north. He's standing like a
sailor with the deck awash, waiting for the end. The old spir-
ts stirring. The wards of the Ancient Patriarchs parting—
everywhere there are stories of things unseen in ages now
abroad. Errest is as deep with monsters as the sea, and if the
last ward passes, we shall all meet our dooms. But I'm not
sure we'll live so long. Oh, and I'm pleased to see that you've
not got yourself killed, by the by."

"The lad did his best," muttered Berchard. "He really
did."

At Abravanal's right hand, a seat stood empty: for Lamoric or Landast or both. At the duke's left was little Almora.
Already, the girl had found Deorwen. Almora sat with her
chin scarcely over the table, chatting with wide eyes. Deorwen's eyes darted from the little girl to her own father, her
own brother. Durand wondered what the child was saying.

The feast should begin; they needed a priest to start it.

"Abravanal spent every instant staring from Gunderic' Tower," said Heremund. "Watching, with the child playing round him like a robin. Kieren has been Lord of Gireth in his master's absence; and your father, its marshal. I suppose, together they—"

Just then, every head turned to the entry stair and Oredga the Patriarch stalked into the room. The tall priest scowled disapproving of the gathering. Grease and soot streaked his beard. And he wore no fine vestments. But still, he stalked to the top of the hall and stood by the high table. "Peers of Errest. Lords, ladies. Serving men. Sons and Daughters of Atthi. Praised be the Silent King of Heaven and the dread Powers of his Host," he said into the silence.

"A great victory has been won. And we are wise to render the Powers their due thanks." The tall priest swiveled his sea-eagle's fierce gaze over the tables, and men of both dukedoms mumbled gratitude.

For a moment, he closed those piercing eyes and clamped his mouth tight shut, then he began as Durand had heard him begin before: "The Westering Sea is broad, Saerdan's *Cradle* sailed many days, and the Sons of Atthi knew thirst. Some despaired of reaching the far havens, turning back for the sunset, though the brave pressed on as days and weeks crept by upon the empty ocean and the last crumbs were gobbled down and the hairy dregs drunk up. But I will go farther. Madness crept among those aboard that ship. The weak slept to their deaths, and poor bleeding wretches died staring at the Heavens."

He raised a woolly eyebrow and scanned the crowded hall once more.

"I think of that packed ship now—alone upon the broad back of the ocean," he said. "Of the hold, empty. The barrels, dry, and the bleeding gums, the weeping sores. And the secret doubts of every man who knew he'd sailed his family onto the empty deeps beyond hope of return. For that is what Saerdan's story means; do not be deceived!"

Oredgar looked over the room as if daring some fool to deny it.

"But then! There came a last day upon that still-empty

deep when the Voyager sounded the fathomless sea—beyond
hope of land and with shaking hand, he heaved his leadline
out and—at the very last fathom with the last wisps of line in
his fingertips—he felt the tap of the bottom far below. A
touch he could scarcely feel. The horizon was as bare as a
ring of steel, but the sea was *not* fathomless. And he hauled
that line back as if he were reeling in the far shore and that
old lead came back to him stuffed with mud—with silt,
sweet with the taste of rivers. At the darkest. At the last cast."

The Patriarch turned to Abravanal, to Severin, to the assembled peers, and he thrust his bearded chin high.

"I stand before you as cities lie in ashes. The king wages
war. Sanctuaries fall. And I think of Saerdan's final heave of
the lead—plunging through the darkness, reaching down,
down for the very bed of the sea when all was lost.

"Now, when you have done here, there is a mighty funeral
beginning. For this, I think, we shall mark the night in procession. There may yet be holy ground enough at the old
sanctuary."

With that, Oredgar left the denizens of the Painted Hall in
fierce and shamefaced silence.

HOW LONG THEY sat in that dark hall, Durand could not
say. But after an age served in grim celebration, a runner
slipped through the crowd to Kieren, like a bird winging in
through a sickroom window. And, in moments, Abravanal
was on his feet and stalking from the hall with his robes flapping behind him.

Durand got up to follow and found that he was not alone
as barons, lords, and fighting men joined. And the crowd became a baffled procession groping through the narrow
spaces of the castle and pouring out into the twilit marketplace where the duke hesitated. Alone, the old man gaped at
a vision that spread before them in the gloom: thousands of
men and women had climbed the ruined citadel. Their silent
multitude now gathered round the ruins of a high sanctuary
whose broken walls stood in an island of rushlight and
torches.

They blundered after Abravanal like nursemaids on a

sleepwalker's heels as the old man staggered through the charred city, until soon the towering blades of the sanctuary's walls pitched near and their makeshift procession was among the mute crowd. People cast their eyes down and parted to let the procession through to the eerie place in the midst of the gathering. It seemed to Durand that Oredgar had rebuilt his sanctuary with a press of living men in place of dead stone. Above, the purple Heavens gaped with twilight. But on the tiles at their feet lay every man who'd been carted from Ferangore, blue-pale and as still as eternity. Slack skin shone with oil, and the air was thick with balsam and ginger.

The Patriarch of Acconel spread his arms at the head of the candlelit multitude. "Join as we sing the Last Twilight and walk the hours of darkness as they did in the days of the High Kingdom. For now, our land is laid bare to the Otherworld, the Banished groan at their ancient fetters, and the Lost spin above our heads. But we shall not despair. And neither shall we sleep, for the prayers of the priests and Knights of Ash suffice no longer, and we must take the burden in our own hands. Those who lie in this place faced death and disaster for our sakes and we must do likewise now. The wise women have prepared them and now we must wait the dawn to send them onward. Over this last night, we must keep vigil. We shall not sleep so that our brothers may rest untroubled until their passage through the Bright Gates of far Heaven."

"Dawn," Abravanal said. "One night is not enough to bid him good-bye! My son!" And Durand wondered if the old man knew how Lamoric had fought for just such a sob—for anyone to think him worth it. Abravanal doubled over and Kieren, nearest, rushed to his elbow. But the old man reared up.

"It will be here!" he said, turning to the crowd. Facing them all, wild-eyed. "We will build a gibbet here where all can see what becomes of traitors! Of traitors and killers all! They shall not see the dawn. They shall not see it!" Men took hold of the old man, though Kieren gave a quick and reluctant nod to the duke's mad orders: they would build a scaffold in the funeral's midst.

———————

AND SO DURAND joined the heaving circle around the wrecked sanctuary while a gang of workmen hammered and sawed for the duke, and Durand cursed the madness of it all. Great songs rose among the masses, their arcane harmonies curling in the high darkness while the labor of marching took place in the rutted earth below. People caught each other's elbows and watched for the children and the old.

As he jostled in the throng, Durand found himself stealing glances through piers and broken windows of the sanctuary where the dead lay like ivory men in the candlelight. The duke sat crumpled at the head of his son, while Almora, with her ink-brush hair, nestled against Deorwen's chest—the little thing was not sleeping, but Durand thanked Heaven that Deorwen could be there with the girl's father half-mad. And then he saw Deorwen's eyes searching the darkness where he marched, hidden, and he wondered what comfort there was for her in all this chaos.

Her father and brother were marching among the mourners—barefoot and stained, dragging their chains like souls already deep in some Hell.

"I should grab them and fly this city of madmen," Durand muttered. He'd pulled Moryn from a mountaintop with the Rooks ranged against him and three armies fighting in the streets. "And here, there's half an army that would lend me aid." But, that night, such a clumsy stroke must mean war. Abravanal's men were bound with ancient oaths and they too had suffered for Mornaway's sin. Worse, after what Durand had seen at the Fuller's Bridge, he doubted that Severin would submit to any attempt at rescuing him. In his own way, the old man was more stiff-necked than his bloody son.

Durand looked into the Heavens—only to be reminded of greater disasters. Great glacial landscapes of cloud swung low over the duchies of the north like the face of a falling moon.

And he circled through the dark beneath the ominous Heavens, making wide swinging pass after wide swinging pass. Near the candlelit mouth of the sanctuary, his course brought him near the scaffold where delegations of Abravanal's trusted lords slipped through the sanctuary in ones and twos to plead. They scowled and muttered at the scaffold. But Abravanal was unmoved.

He saw Coensar the Champion standing watch in the sanctuary. Turn after turn, Durand watched the man: his gray hair, the slim blade of Keening—but the glint of an *inward* gaze. This was not the captain, alert. This was a man trapped and thinking, his eyes fixed. It would have been so much tidier if one or the other of them had died. There had been a wealth of chances for bad luck in the last weeks—Durand felt a wry tug of irony as he stumbled through the gloom—and Coensar had certainly done his best. Now though, Durand haunted the city Coensar meant to command, an untidy reminder.

A glance into the dark beyond the marching circle revealed that there were indeed creeping things half-visible among the scorched acres just as Oredgar had warned: long-limbed creatures with slack bellies, shadows with vulpine gazes. At the limits of sight, Durand thought he saw something as tall as an oak, watching.

But the song climbed higher around Durand, and he pictured Coensar on the day they broke the siege, striding among the rafters as he cleared that nest of bowmen above the fight. He conjured up the heartbeats before the betrayal. It had all happened very quickly. There Coensar had been, standing above the fighting like a ship's master on a pitching deck. Alone, he had thwarted an ambush that should have slain their army, commanding the battle he was winning. But then he must have spotted Durand—the shield-bearer he had trained to knighthood—charging off with Lamoric on his saddlebow and Coensar's chance was lost, the whole of his future bundled up on another man's horse.

But when Coensar swung his ugly peasant's ball of tines, Durand had been trying to save their blasted liege lord! But now . . . if Kieren was cunning, Coensar was the hero, the Champion. Men would follow him no matter how Abravanal faltered. They could rebuild the dukedom on his shoulders.

Durand rubbed at his knotted cheek—and glanced up to spot the Baron of Swanskin Down. The man picked Durand's face from the crowd in a glum instant. He passed Sallow Hythe and the others, each man ignoring Durand except, perhaps, for a flicker of his eyes.

Durand shook his head, bewildered. "Has Coen told them?" The turf seethed with secret watchers. And, out against the dark, the giant figure still looked on. It leaned upon a crook. Why should the Champion of Gireth stain his own colors? There should be no reason for these men to look his way, unless something had forced Coen's hand and they were puzzling over what to do with the man who knew Coensar's secret.

With so many of his thoughts unsettled, Durand had been keeping clear of Berchard. Now, he wondered if it wasn't time to ask the man a question.

Finding Berchard was the work of a moment, and in a few heartbeats, he had pulled the stocky knight out into the dark. "Berchard," he said, "when did you know?"

The startled man gulped. "Hells, boy. I thought one of the Strangers had—"

"When did you know what our captain had done?"

The knight's eye rolled. "Do you *see* them? It's thick with spirits, man." A taloned hand spread near the man's ankle. "Ah. You must see the devils. Fighting men and leeches often do—it's death that opens the eyes."

"I've good reason, Berchard." If the barons knew, they had choices to make about what to do with their heroes. Could they trust the secret to a man like Durand? "I think I've a right, haven't I?"

With a grunt, Berchard squinted up into Durand's face. "I came upon an empty village once upon a time—on the River Tresses up near the Blackroot Mountains. Just a few hovels on the bank with gardens plowed back into the wood, and I'd been walking days, coming up from Sallow Hythe, if I remember, and night was coming on. And the last thing I wanted to do was sleep under a thornbush. Did I say it was raining?"

Durand seized the man. There were things in the gloom prowling nearer, low and catlike. "By Heaven, man! It's a plain enough question."

Berchard stopped cold. There was no joking in his face, and, when Durand freed him, the man continued almost as if he were reading the words from the *Book of Moons*. "—Pelting down," he said. "And I looked through the whole place, thumping on the doors and pushing my way into the little wooden sanctuary they had. But there wasn't a soul to be found.

"And then it struck me that there was grass standing pretty high in the street. And I thought: there'd been sheep on the meadow and pigs in the forest, but there was precious little moving in the town. So I shoved my way through the door of the first old hovel—and the reek I met!

"You hear stories of whole villages where some fever carries off every living soul—"

"Aye."

"—And no one's left to bury the dead. But this was only an ox. Dead, tied, and sinking into its own filth behind barred doors. Maybe been there for a moon or two. Every hovel was the same. I found a dog who'd strangled himself on a stout lime lead. And dead stock barred or fenced in. But not a man.

"I didn't know what had befallen the poor devils, but I was ready to take my leave. So I started back toward the well-head where I'd tied my horse—when I saw it.

"It could have been someone's washing: just a patch of red homespun matting the tall grass. But it was a body; hardly anything left of her. Brown as roots and yellow as old crockery. No sign of why. And I picked out another patch of cloth, and another—a path leading back behind one of the hovels. Body after body lying in the bindweed, thistle, and cabbages. Not a stain, nor sign of murder.

"Now, standing over the yard in back of the house was this dung heap. And the bodies made a path to the thing. First women, then little children—sprawled and horrible. Little kirtles. Bonnets. Finally, hard against the dung heap, five or six men, armed with hoes and forks.

"So there I am back of some hovel with bodies strewn like stiff mats in the grass all round. It's still raining. An open grave fanned round this dung heap and me in the middle— when I hear it—*Sssss!* Like eggs on a hot pan. I leap, and the dung heap is shifting, big clods rolling. Something alive is uncurling in that warm reek. And I knew that I was just in time. And so I got my good eye shut and ran like a child, tramping on more than one empty suit of clothes on the way I'll tell you—cracking them bones."

"Just in time for what?" prompted Durand.

"I'd seen a wet glint of scales. But I'm no fool, and I've lived when others have died beside me. I'd heard tales down the Gray Road of a serpent born of a dung heap. Born of a cockerel's egg, choked with poison. And a glance that'll kill a man, certain, if he sees it. They call him the basilisk.

"It'll have been one of the little lads who stumbled on it. And the others will have come to see what their friend had done, or if he was teasing them. And then the mothers, and then the husbands mad and armed with what they could find. All dead. And any one of them would have been fine if they'd just left bad enough alone. If they'd just decided that they didn't need to know what had happened. Or if they'd just turned their backs. But that's never the way."

"From the day Coen struck me down. You've known since the very day."

Berchard shook his head. "You see?"

"You were there in the Painted Hall." When Durand lay torn to pieces, his face smashed like a jug. They'd known before Badan and Ferangore. Before Durand could think or stop himself, he'd knocked the old knight sprawling and was striding over him. "Who else? Who else knew?"

You could see the cords in Berchard's neck, straining under his beard. If the barons knew, they might be plotting anything, even now.

"Everyone," said Berchard. "Lamoric. Your brother got it out of me. Heremund . . . Our Badan might've been the only—"

"I'll speak to the barons," Durand snarled. He wouldn't run. Two-score faces turned his way as he left his friend lying in the rubble and pushed into the procession. All the hours upon the floor in the Painted Hall, all the days in Yrlac, and they had known.

His face was burning when he broke free of the crowd and stalked toward the gaggle of barons where they colluded by the scaffold—if he'd had a sword, God knew what he might have done. As it was, he set his hand on Sallow Hythe's shoulder and spun the man round.

"We must speak," he said. Sallow Hythe turned slightly, letting candlelight fall on Durand's face—his brow clouded a moment. "You could be no one but Durand Col," he said, and Durand remembered that he still bore scars and that his head remained bare from the surgeons' razors.

"Here," said the elegant baron. "I suppose we must deal with every issue when it comes to us. There is a chamber or two remaining in this old shell. At the foot of the tower." The barons ushered Durand to a low door where the masonry survived. As he stepped over the threshold, the door rattled shut behind him.

Durand's father lifted a torch. And Durand stood alone with his father and the barons of Gireth just as he had been on the far shores of the mere ages before. Even Kieren was there.

"He has no business dragging us anywhere against our will," Swanskin grunted. The gruff old man paced the room, peering about himself as though he expected the ceiling to come down.

Sallow Hythe merely closed his eyes. "We will forgive the lapse, I think. For the conversation is one that must be had." They had the look of men choosing an uncomfortable course, and were bracing themselves to follow through.

"We have heard a story," said Sallow Hythe, kneading his temples. "It seems that our Champion has allowed ambition to tempt him into dishonor. And that you were the principal victim of his . . . error in judgment."

Durand's father stood across the room, saying nothing.

"We are further led to believe," continued Sallow Hythe, "that Coensar intends to allow you to decide what becomes of him. It is my belief that Coensar is unable to accord his recent actions with his beliefs concerning his own character."

"Is that what bothers him?"

"Did we need more trouble at this moment? You have asked. You are granted as clear an explanation as may be. Lamoric is gone and half the peers of Gireth are lost with him. The city has been laid waste, and manors for leagues around have been sacked by the raiding parties of Yrlac's army. But have you seen how the people rally? How they gathered here? Even before we returned, they were rebuilding.

"I imagine that self-absorption is to be expected of a man in your position, but you must have noticed the work gangs—they are not paid laborers." He raised his hands toward the city beyond the vaults of the chamber ceiling. "It is good will. The undaunted spirit of a land uncowed by the indifference of its faraway king and the brutality of its enemies. When you see the masses marching in their circles. When you hear the mallets and axes in the streets, you hear their defiance.

"I do not wish to debase this spirit with too much calculation, but morale can be squandered if close account is not taken of it."

Young Honefells interrupted, his blue eyes rolling at his elder's elaborate diction. "Host Above, Sallow Hythe."

But Swanskin preempted an argument with a rumble from the dark. "It is simple, boy. There's not the coin for this work. Whether we war with Mornaway or no, we'll be sweeping the treasury floor for the last penny long before we've so much as renewed the walls. All the silver in Abravanal's lands will be gone in a thousand hire-swords' purses. Is it not so, Kieren?"

Kieren nodded low. "Abravanal is scarcely able to put food in the mouths of those who have volunteered."

And so Sallow Hythe spread his long-fingered hands. "His Grace cannot afford justice. Not for you. Our heroes cannot be rapists or thieves or oathbreakers or traitors, for we cannot afford to dishearten their admirers. Not just now, anyway. Not while they are needed."

"I have not asked," said Durand.

"How many men would desert us if we poisoned the tales of brave Sir Coensar, the Champion of Ancient Gireth, and his holding the rampart for his young lord? Perhaps they would decide that he'd let Lamoric die—or killed him. The duke and his son might both have been made fools of by this mercenary captain. However it came to pass, we would lose some, that much is sure. It might be a third of all our laborers."

His face was grim as he paused. "It is more than one man is worth."

Durand's gaze traveled over eyes of flint and winter blue, his father's included. And for the first time, Durand wondered if these men meant to kill him.

"Why does the duke not say these things with his own

tongue?" he murmured, conscious of being a large man in a small space.

Swanskin's broad nostrils flared. "Because you are little better than a common soldier! Because he thought four barons might suffice to serve as messengers! We've no time to bandy bloody words with children! There is a host beyond these doors with its lord trussed and ready for the chopping block!" His shout was a physical blow, and Durand felt a stab of panic.

But then he looked closer at the great men, and saw them shifting in their boots like guilty children. "But that's not the reason; His Grace does not know."

"No," said Honefells. The bluff young lord gave a grudging, slanted smile. "You're no fool, Durand. Outrage is the best cloak for a lie, and Abravanal has not come himself, because he does not know. We know. His son has died. Both sons. That is enough for him. He is not party to this. Don't think ill of the old man."

Swanskin frowned. "But, one way or another, the tale must die. We must be satisfied." Durand knew what he should say. He should let Coen's treason stand. He thought of his nights with Deorwen. Of the things Coensar knew—or guessed—and did not say. "Long ago, Coensar told me that I need let no blow go unanswered. . . ."

"You see," said Swanskin. "A young man's blood is quick and this injustice will work like a sliver. How if there is some other sleight? How can there not be? How long will he hold his tongue while Coensar lives in fame? We must be finished here. How long have we got till dawn? Is there an hour?"

At this, Baron Hroc swelled like a bear. "Are you pushed for time? Why then have we been standing here gabbling with the boy? If he can say neither 'yes' nor 'no,' why'd we let him speak at all? The time to slit his throat was when he stepped through that door!"

"You mistake Swanskin's meaning," Sallow Hythe began.

Hroc's eyebrows shot up. "Oh! So you think I can't hear what's spoken plain before me, do you? The boy's been mad and a fool, but he's bled rivers for you bastards and he's never given any man alive cause to doubt his word."

As his father rose to defend him, all Durand could think

of was Lamoric. And the man's wife. He'd put a man off a cliff. He'd stolen through the dark of his master's house. He couldn't think.

But Swanskin was speaking. "Then, if we're to trust his word, we must hear it!"

Durand seized the door handle and propelled himself outside, hoping for space and air to think and reason.

Instead, he blundered smack into a scene from the end of the world.

A thousand bodies were stirring upon the sanctuary floor. Gleaming with sacred oils, they struggled and, finally, climbed to their knees, their winding sheets hanging from their bare limbs. Durand saw Abravanal on his feet, not knowing which way to turn. Deorwen clutched the awestricken child to her breast. And the crowd, at a standstill now, moaned like the sea—five thousand gaping faces. Over all their heads, the sky was churning, the hanging mountain twisting apart, wrenched into spines like the points of a crown. Row upon row, the dead turned with their eyes on the northern sky and their arms wide—each man summoned to prayer by the war in the Heavens.

At Durand's back, the barons stumbled from the sanctuary chamber, almost forgotten. While, at the very same instant, Marshal Conran reeled through the broken portals of the sanctuary, hardly a step from Durand. His enormous hands caught Durand's shoulders as if he were a child.

"The king," he breathed. His eye stared so wide that Durand wasn't sure he even knew there were dead men praying around him. "He is alone. He lashes at the trees. Gnarled branches. Unhorsed! *But there is someone in that forest with him!*" An impossible gust of wooded air boiled up around the towering knight: the smell of sopping acres under naked trees. His hands were ice and twisting tighter and tighter. Durand saw something moving in that broad, blue eye. In a moment, the big man would snap Durand's shoulders.

"Conran!" Durand tried to wrench free. Beyond the sanctuary, the crowd had ceased their singing. Creation was still under the spinning vault of Heaven.

"Oh! Oh, Heaven help us!" And Abravanal was careering through the sanctuary, the Sword of Judgment clutched to his bony chest, as huge in his arms as a grown man's weapon in the hands of a child. Coensar trailed the man, not sure whether to leave Deorwen and the child. "They rebel!" Abravanal shouted. "Our fallen sons! First Twilight is upon us . . ." He cast his searching gaze over the praying figures all around him. "It is the traitors! The traitors live!" he cried, now pelting down the nave, weaving closer. "They will not suffer it! It is a clear sign."

Now, the old man caught Durand's sleeve, and, for a moment, Durand was torn between madmen. "Your Grace, no!"

"The dawn is theirs and they will not suffer these devils to share it!" said Abravanal. He shouted, eyes starting from his skull, "Bring the butchers out! Bring—"

—But the duke and his son had already stepped from the crowd. "Duke Abravanal, we are here." Severin's face was still, though his skeletal frame trembled in its rags despite the support of his heir.

"Good. Good!" The old man clutched at Durand's tunic, and he seemed to recognize him. Tears shone on his face. "You were at his side. *You* must do this." He pushed the great blade upon Durand. "My boy would not take my father's Sword of Judgment. You must take it now."

"Your Grace—" Durand had the huge sword in his fists.

"No." The old man shook his head. "It is justice. It is their debt and freely they pay it." Durand saw two fools too mad to flee even with an army at their backs. And the old man hauled on Durand's sleeve, tugging him to the scaffold and up with the men of Mornaway. Abravanal jerked the scabbard from the ancient blade and flung the thing aside. This would be no hanging.

And there Durand stood, with the twilit Heavens spinning like a platter, five thousand shocked faces staring with the Banished beyond. Gunderic's old blade took both hands to wield; even to lift it was a struggle. He saw the dead mouthing words: mouthing some sort of prayer.

And he saw Almora staring up from the midst of the madness, clutched in Deorwen's arms. She was a brave thing, but now she was screaming so that she hardly breathed. And Deorwen—she was caught between the little girl and her brother on the scaffold, and her lover with the blade that would kill him.

In the Atthias, there is no block for the highborn: not when a sword is used, for a fine blade was no woodcutter's axe to risk in a knotted stump. "I will be first," said Severin. "It must be me."

"It is not just," said Abravanal. "I am living." And *his* son was dead: the unassailable reason of madness. And an anonymous soldier pulled the old man aside, leaving Moryn of Mornaway to step out on the fresh planks. The man scanned the crowd for an instant, taking in the Heavens and the ruins and the multitudes. He must have seen men among the crowd, hands on their blades.

Moryn's dark eyes flashed and he thrust his chin high. "I do this by my will! Let no man of mine seek to thwart my purpose. Let none seek to avenge me."

Durand saw Deorwen looking up as he heaved the enormous blade back. And when he turned back to his work, he saw Moryn staring into his eyes. Finally, the Lord of Mornaway gave the smallest fraction of a nod, taking his death from mad Abravanal. Consenting.

And there was Durand with the killing blade poised over his shoulder, the only sound Almora's screaming.

"No!" said a voice into Durand's daft silence. "It is too much!"

And it was not one of the men upon the platform.

Durand shared a tight-jawed look with Moryn before Coensar took the stairs. "Do not stop," Abravanal was saying. But Durand would not move now for worlds.

The captain limped the last step. "Your Grace, it mustn't be this way. What will be left if every traitor dies? The kingdom is falling." He stepped across the platform with his hands open.

"It is justice," the duke said.

"Have you seen Almora?"

The duke blinked across the sanctuary. Almora's dark eyes stared from streams of tears, clutching Deorwen.

"Who's held her with her sister gone?" said Coensar. "Who does she cling to now? And you would slay the woman's

brother, Your Grace? Her father? When her husband's ye
unburied? Could you trust her with your daughter after? Yo
will not do this, because you are a better man than Radomo
He would sneer at us all if he saw this."

As Coensar spoke, a sound pricked at Durand's ears,
whisper rising like the rustle of leaves before a storm. Al
around the sanctuary, the dead were still praying, faster an
faster, the tongues clicking and popping in their mouths lik
locusts in a field. Marshal Conran reeled among the rows o
dead men. "His Highness comes up on a clearing!" shoute
Conran and fell to the ground below the scaffold.

Durand leapt down, letting Gunderic's sword clatter.

Conran shook his head. "The branches give way and h
stumbles out into a place thick with rank grasses. He's calling out to the shadows: 'Do what you have come to do! Work
your master's will upon me.' And they come."

Durand looked into the dizzy eye. He could smell the forest in the midst of that burned city, and the sticky whispers
of the dead became the rush of leaves in the high branches
of Windhover as the giant twisted against the tiles. "They
come . . . there are so many." And in Conran's eye, Durand
could see the twilit sky full of branches, the shadows of
armed men, and the gleam of naked blades. The king had
fallen, crawling.

And the dead of Gireth stood, tipping their faces Heavenward. And Durand saw the forest explode with horses.

"Lancers!" gasped Conran. "A conroi or more."

Durand saw men torn from their feet. He could hear crash
and scream. Knights thundered down upon the assassins,
blades bare. And a gale of small birds stormed around them.

"He . . . he is free!" Conran breathed.

Durand saw the trees wheeling once more. Irridescent birds.
Was Ragnal saved or fleeing once more? Then a figure—a
long streak of shadow—and a gauntlet reaching. And there
was a smiling face. A thin and dog-tired smile.

"It is the prince. Prince Biedin has brought his brother
from the edge of death!"

The scent of those distant trees flooded the city by the
mere. A feverish ocean of leaves and growing things under
the Sowing Moon broke over the ruins. Conran spread his

ands upon the sanctuary steps, rising as, all around the
sanctuary, the fallen sank to the tiles, and the looming of gla-
ciers and mists churning overhead withdrew, stilled once
more.

WITH ONE BELEAGUERED twist of his head, Durand saw
Deorwen, Almora, Coensar, Abravanal, mourners in their
thousands, and he could not catch hold of it all—it was like
catching an ocean in his hands. And so he stumbled away,
pitching through the awestruck crowd and out into the twilight and the ruins. He wove between broke-toothed facades
beyond which he glimpsed tangles of charred timber like a
thousand-acre puzzle box; a touch might bring the black city
down in a cloud.

A wet voice chuckled, huge and warm at his neck. "You
are welcome now," it spluttered. The rotten breath boiled
around him, and he spun, reaching for a blade that he did not
carry. But the monstrous ancient of the mere was not in the
street with Durand. The voice addered between the broken
walls. "You have left old Gunderic's blade, Bull of their festival." It chuckled as Durand stumbled faster.

"Nearly, our kingdoms are returned to us. We have heard
the marching step. Temple after temple, falling. Moon after
moon. Nearer and tramping nearer. But now, that sandal
hangs. It hangs over us, but not falling. Not falling—and that
island temple stands by the house of eagles, the vilest brightest temple. That ring by which all chains are gathered, it
binds us still!"

No matter what the thing said about its bonds, Durand
heard it free in the streets with him. Its sigh shuddered and it
dragged its monstrous hooves or feet or talons through the
rubble not far away. And so Durand scrambled away, hoping
that some sanctuary or shrine stood intact in all the broken
lanes and he could shut its door on the monster.

"But you, Blood of Bruna," the brute said. "Bruna betrayed. Bruna betrayer. Dupe and deceiver who crawls my
stolen kingdom. Was I prophet enough for thee?"

Durand plunged into an ally. They read his fortune, every
mad thing in Creation, and they saw that betrayal there.
And Coensar. Some small part of his mind wondered at the

darkness of the old story of Bruna, a lover among the First-born of Creation's Dawning. A friend had betrayed him—or he'd betrayed that friend. And he'd taken his people to war. The first of men, maybe. Was this his doom?

But he heard the brute, scraping the high walls on his heels. And its footfalls shaking soot from the sky.

Ahead, Durand heard something *knock*. He pictured a great door swinging, and a chain across it. "Wait!" he called.

"Long was I king over the men of these shores! The first-born of man and beast they slid down to me. Cool bodies to comfort me in the dark. 'Bull' you Sons of Atthi called me, and bull you sent me full of iron darts. But you, at least, will mock no longer. Bull of their battles! You who have borne the pains I promised!"

With the thing's breath in his nostrils, Durand burst into the open street once more—there was no swinging door. He saw only the ruined Gates of Sunset and the scorched idol of the Silent King of Heaven, lying like a charred invalid among the empty tents of refugees. How they had fought there! Durand remembered the glorious route, the flight for Gunderic's Tower, the moment at the castle gates.

He turned and saw the monster stepping from the alley like a man crawling from a barrel—its lamp eyes wide, its great bull's skull streaming putrefaction. Its hog-rib teeth caught the twilight.

But, as Durand gave ground, he heard the chain still swinging: *tock . . . tock*. And his mind followed the sound, wondering with a dying man's dispassion just what he was hearing. The monster stood, the rotten king of this shore. And Durand blundered against the stone King in Silence—just a brush of fingertips.

HE WAS ELSEWHERE.

Tock.

He knew the sound now as a staff's clear rap on stone. But he was no longer where he had been. The touch of his fingertips upon that idol had taken him away from the city and the streets and now he stood in a forest track under a towering elm. And the Traveler loomed above him, its limbs hung with the rags of the roadside, its frame the bones of the dead in ditches. This was the giant he had seen beyond the sanctuary, looking on. The brim of the giant's pilgrim hat cut a swelling circle from the Heavens as the Power creaked low, the knotted cords of its beard swinging below its jaw.

"Once more, you've come to crossroads."

Durand shook his head, scrabbling once at his stubbled scalp. It had been a long time since the well at Col where he'd met this thing before. He had been a child, it seemed to him now. But he remembered the questions he had asked down by the water—and the Power's promises. "There were many promises," he rasped. And, nearly, a frayed laugh escaped him.

The Traveler rumbled: "So it has ever been."

Durand struggled to remember their last conversation; it seemed so long ago—though a man could scarcely forget his chats with gods. "A place, I wanted, when mine was gone. And, I think, success. That seemed far from me then." Though how much farther now? "And, though I asked about 'family' I wondered what woman would ever want a pauper-thug on the road." He stood with his hitched shoulder and the marks of Coensar's ambition plain on his face. There was more pain than he liked to admit. "What became of all that, then?"

Solemnly, the Power straightened against the sky. "It has come to pass."

Durand looked high into the Traveler's distant eyes—one penny bright, the other black. And he clenched his tiny fists. "This is no light matter to me."

"Did you not triumph at Red Winding and Tern Gyre? Were you not Bull of Acconel's festival? Did you not bring victory at Acconel and Ferangore and twice swim a mere to save a city?"

"You cannot mean what you say."

"You craved a place. A share of glory." The Power's string-knotted palms brushed dry whispers from his forked staff. "And a beauty . . ."

"Power, your promises weigh less than your brother's silence."

There was a dry rushing sound as the Traveler drew breath. "I am not perverse in this. The balance is ancient and we are, all of us, bound by it. Hosts Above; Hosts Below. A push above allows a pull below. Though I might set you upon the throne of dukedoms, the Powers of darkness would throw you down. The straight word is twisted."

"And so I have groveled for crooked whispers. I ask you, what have your whispers gained me? If I have had my share of fortune, thorned and meager though they have been, what is left to me? What would you have me do now?"

"I stand at the crossroads," said the Power. "Most hear but the tap of my stick. But much has turned about you."

Durand groped at his eyes, despairing. "I . . . I cannot fathom what you say. You have come to gloat and torment—"

Like all the seas together, the giant roared. With his staff, he struck the vault of Heaven a blow that flashed from horizon to horizon. And Durand knew that he had dared much in the face of such power.

"The Host may do as it might, but I will answer this. What will become of me? What must I do? The questions, the answers, they echo from heart to heart through the ages. Forever unchanging."

In mountains leagues away, the ice gave way and plunged headlong down high vales. The Power shook the earth with his staff's heel, and Durand crushed his face against the mud. "How can a man live and not wonder?"

Durand heard the ship's-rigging creak of the great frame bending once more. "The answers *do not change,* O child of my brother's dreaming. Glory, love. All of these." The smell of roots and stones and cold-water ditches brimmed the horizons as Durand sprawled on the earth. "Each and all shall be your own!"

And, with a rush of a forest's weight of leaves, every sound of the titan vanished from that place. "And will I find only the same fruitless harvest?" was Durand's whisper. But there was no sign of the Traveler when Durand found the courage to raise his eyes.

DEORWEN'S VOICE SUMMONED him once more into Creation. A familiar note reached the forest track: her call, it seemed to him, carried the echoes of stone walls where the

reeze was full of tentcloth and guylines. There was even the
rill of morning robins.

"Durand?" she whispered.

And he smiled up into a human face in a human place,
hard by a capsized idol.

"Where have you been?" she asked.

He blinked up at her. And, finally, saw the marks of exhaustion and fear upon her face. Her doe brown eyes glinted.

"Your father," Durand managed, "does he live?" And Deorwen blinked back tears, knuckling them from her cheeks.

"He does. Abravanal is like his people. Swords and stone
walls did not keep sorrow from his door. There is nothing to
do with such anguish. Nothing but rail or collapse and he has
relented now. My father has made promises: his host, should
there be war. And the free use of his roads and rivers, if
there's peace and trade. All till the death of Moryn's heir. It
is what he meant to offer from the beginning."

Almost, Durand reached for her—laughed for relief with
her. But the black she wore was widow's black. And a wife's
headcloth covering her hair. On that stone floor, Lamoric
would still be waiting. Durand pried himself from the street,
and when Deorwen touched his battered jaw, he stepped
back. "Almora will be missing you," he said.

DURAND MET A procession already gathering at the sanctuary ruin. Again, the crowd had found its voice, and it was a
singing multitude that lifted each dead man to its shoulders
and began the solemn march for the fields beyond the Gates
of Sunset.

And so Durand simply fell in line, taking his place under
the bier of one dead man. Soot-blackened plowmen bawled
hymns all around him while their pale burdens rode like
idols above the throng. Somewhere, Badan rode strangers'
shoulders. Men Durand had known since childhood or
marched with down the Valley of the Rushes rocked over
their heads, and he fought to keep his eyes closed, breathing
the oiled air and hearing the cry of the waking gulls from the
harbor.

Shadows led them from the sanctuary ruin past the Gates
of Sunset to the rutted fields where dark holes had been

opened in the earth. The fallen would lie between their cit
and the Duchy of Yrlac, standing watch as they had in life.

Through it all, Abravanal marched at the head of his peo
ple. In one night, he must have been broken and mended
dozen times. But his duty thrust him before the masses, and h
walked now with Almora at his side and the great Sword o
Judgment on Coen's shoulder as they came to the gravesides

Conran and his brother prayed. The Patriarch sung to the
Eye. And though the Sowing Moon hung huge and ghostly
over the mere, the Eye of Heaven split the horizon as they
laid the dead into the bosom of the earth. Five thousand head
turned and five thousand voices together sang the Dawn
Thanksgiving to the clear Heavens and its Silent King. They
had seen the storm part. Somewhere in the forest of Wind
hover, the crown was safe for a time. They had heard Con
ran's vision. And though they could not know why the last
sanctuary still stood, they knew peace when it came to them

Durand stayed as serving men and lords filled the graves.
He watched faces disappear and long shapes vanish in the
rising earth. And he stayed after the last word was sung and
the chill had sent all but a few to their beds.

Heremund tapped him gamely on the arm. "I tried to give
you some warning. I could see it coming in Coen's eyes, but
you couldn't hear. Maybe there wasn't anything you could
have done. And then we thought it might hurt you—hearing
what he'd done—and you needed to heal. Maybe you were
off to the Gates. And after, well, Coensar has been a good
man. The lads couldn't turn on a friend."

Durand stared over the mounded earth, and finally the
skald ducked his eyes and trudged away. Durand had meant
to find words, but none came.

At last, only he and the duke's few men remained. Abravanal let his hand settle on Durand's arm. He seemed very
small, and very old. Almora had been bundled over Kieren's
shoulder and the Fox wavered between concern for his duke
and his onetime shield-bearer. "His Grace wants a word," he
said.

And Durand looked.

The duke took his hand from Durand's arm. "Durand Col.
I know what you tried to do for my son. I know how many

imes his life was owed you. You were his guardian, though
he would not be guarded." But Durand was thinking that the
man might not have died at all if Durand had not lingered
with his wife. "I know what you suffered for him." Durand
blinked. "No other man living could have stolen Severin's
boy from Radomor's citadel. I saw you standing here—
brooding over these graves. You have the look of a man bidding good-bye. But I would not have you depart."

The old man saw in him the grief of a loyal servant. Durand felt like a liar. He could not have said what he felt.
Shame, perhaps. Perhaps other things.

But Abravanal looked into the clouds of Durand's eyes,
and hope seemed to glow through the wreck of the old man's
life like the Eye of Heaven through the empty windows of
the high sanctuary. Durand wondered what the old man
thought he saw.

"I have a daughter still," he said. "She is the last of my
blood. All that survives of my wife. My fathers. As you
served my son, Durand, I plead with you: serve my daughter.
She will have his wife to stand by her. I think that must be.
But the Powers will not have another child of mine. Not
while I live." The old man cast his eyes down, confessing, "I
could not endure it."

But Durand could not answer. He imagined years in Gunderic's Tower with Deorwen always near. No escaping, but
never touching. And, after a space of heartbeats, the duke
nodded and walked from the graves with his daughter—
leaving Durand entirely alone.

Or so he thought.

A shadow slipped over him. And he saw a figure against
the Eye of Heaven. A blade glinted in the man's fist.

"Who are you?" Durand challenged, wincing into the glare.

Durand could see the man's shoulders rising with deep
breaths, his blood pounding. And the slender blade winked,
turning in the stranger's hand. And Durand guessed whom
he faced.

"Coen."

For the space of two slow heartbeats, the figure was still.
Then he stepped from the light. And, without a further word,
stalked for the gates with a blue mantle swirling in his wake.

And Durand realized that everything must stay as it was—that his decision had always been made. He was no stronger than Berchard or Heremund. He could no more turn on Coensar than any of the others. And so, he would return to the court of Abravanal and stand guard over the duke's last child. He would watch beside Coensar and it would all go on as it was that day, but he would, at least, make good on his promises.

And he would have the prophecy of the Traveler.

Eyes around that city of ruins and green wood were raised at the sound of Durand's laughter.

TOR

Voted

#1 Science Fiction Publisher
20 Years in a Row

by the *Locus* Readers' Poll

Please join us at the website below
for more information about this
author and other science fiction,
fantasy, and horror selections, and to
sign up for our monthly newsletter!